A Sliver of Redemption

by David Dalglish

BOOKS BY DAVID DALGLISH

THE HALF-ORC SERIES

The Weight of Blood
The Cost of Betrayal
The Death of Promises
The Shadows of Grace
A Sliver of Redemption

THE WORLD OF DEZREL

A Dance of Cloaks
Guardian of the Mountain

A Sliver of Redemption

1

The images flickering through the portal were scattered at best, but Thulos watched them intently. Sometimes words passed through, accompanying the dilution of color. His fingers brushed the smoky substance, touching something like glass.

Forgive me, Tess, I was wrong. Close the damn thing!

The words stabbed a sliver of doubt into the war god's chest. The portal, closed? Not while his soldiers still fought among the virgin lands, not when he was so close to entering the long lost realm of Celestia. He thought he could see the goddess through the portal, standing with her arms wide and her hair flowing in a torrent of wind. Behind her, two shapes huddled together, and a third lay prone in the corner.

No, said the wraith-voice from the portal. *You've earned this.*

His generals and advisors kneeled around him on the lower steps of the massive pyramid. Regardless of which direction they looked upon it, the swirling vortex looked flat, like a painting. The sky was dull and red, as if the millions of slaughtered lives had saturated the heavens as well as the soil.

Thulos put a giant hand on the hilt of his sword and pressed harder against the portal with the other. Normally when entering a new world, his most powerful mages emerged first and combined their might to open a pathway. This one, however, had opened of its own accord, and the few messengers that traveled back assured him only two necromancers held open the gate.

Thulos's soldiers had passed through, with significant strain upon the two, but Thulos himself could not yet pass. The portal resisted, still far too weak. But now...

"Stand back," Thulos told his men, his eyes peering at the woman, her face obscured as if she were underneath starlit water. "The time is now."

The ground beneath them cracked. Wind howled into the portal. The glassy substance against his hand weakened, then broke. His arm pushed through. Without a moment of hesitation he followed within, passing from his world to one he had conquered untold centuries before.

Even for a god, the travel from world to world took its toll. Thulos closed his eyes, focused his breath, and then reopened them. Every muscle in his body coiled ready for action. He kept his hand on his sword as he surveyed what appeared to be a throne room, and was bewildered by what he saw. At the door, two identical men gazed at him with open-mouthed horror. In the corner by the door lay a black-robed man, his hands above his head, his face thin and bony. His maniacal laugh flooded the sudden silence. And then Thulos saw the goddess.

"Celestia," he said, drawing his sword.

The woman stared up at him with pure black eyes, her arms clutching her worn red dress that at one point must have been beautiful. Her long black hair settled against her back as the wind died. A tiny smile curled a side of her mouth, even as tears ran down her cheeks.

"That's my mother's name," she said, and the smile vanished. She turned toward the two at the door, their gray skin and odd ears vaguely familiar to him. "Go now, before he kills you."

"Your name?" Thulos said as he breathed in the foreign air. Even its taste was familiar. The presence of two of his brethren throbbed in his head—his other god-pieces. Karak and Ashhur were near, and they both had their eyes upon him, whether in fear or elation he did not know.

"Tessanna," she said, though she did not turn to look at him. She remained staring at the giant doors. All the while, the fool in the corner laughed.

"Praise be," Thulos heard the man shout. "Praise be, my glorious Karak, we have won!"

Thulos flinched at the name, as if an arrow had poked through his heavy, elaborate armor. Four players here in this game, and he did not know upon which side they stood on. It was time he knew.

"I am Thulos, god of war," he said. He did not need to shout, for his deep voice boomed in the quiet. "I command the bloody fist. I lead the Warseekers from star to star. Those who kneel may live in servitude. All others die."

The larger man at the door drew a pair of swords.

"And I'm Harruq Tun," he shouted. "Consider me your welcome."

Thulos shook his head. Centuries upon centuries later he had returned to a world he had once destroyed, and now some pathetic runt of a man wanted to challenge his rule? There were more pressing matters to attend to. He needed to find Celestia, as well as hunt down his two renegade brothers and make them answer for their cowardice. He did not have time for this. Where were his soldiers? Ulamn, leader of his invasion troops, where was he?

"Be gone, fool," Thulos told Harruq. "I will grant you death another time."

"Foolish, yes," the frail-bodied one beside Harruq said in a raspy, ruined voice. Thulos recognized him as the one who had begged for the portal to be closed. "But not so great a fool as you. Look behind you, supposed deity, and see your folly."

Thulos sensed no trick, so he glanced behind. The portal, the lifeline to his many worlds and near limitless troops, had faded away, like clouds broken by a warm summer breeze. His way out was gone. He was trapped on the world of Dezrel.

"Your name?" the war god demanded, pointing his sword. His arm shook with rage.

"Qurrah," the man said, and then a bitter smile creased his face. "Qurrah Tun."

Brothers, thought Thulos. So be it. He would kill them both.

He let his muscles relax, let his perfect reflexes and skill take over.

"Step aside," he told the image of the goddess. "I will have words with you when this matter is done."

Tessanna shivered and walked to the wall. The laughing man in the corner sat up, bracing his body against the stone so he might watch. Thulos shifted his sword into both hands, surveying his opponents. He was a full head's length taller than the warrior, and certainly stronger. The other had to be a caster of some sort, for he wore black robes like the man in the corner. He wondered if they were the necromancers that had borne the portal's burden.

He leapt, and with grim satisfaction saw their eyes widen in shock at his speed. He swung his sword in a single wide arc, unafraid of any counter. The one called Harruq crossed his swords and blocked. The swords connected in an ear-splitting crack. Magic sparked about them, and then Harruq flew backward, through the doors and down the stone steps. Qurrah remained, a spell on his lips, but Thulos was faster. He slammed the butt of his sword into Qurrah's belly ending the spell. His blade whipped around, edge aimed for the man's throat.

"*No!*"

The scream rolled over him, staying his hand. Qurrah fled in the brief respite. Thulos glared back at Tessanna, who lay crumpled on the floor, her face streaked with tears.

"I told him to run, and now he runs," she said. "Oh mother, why have you abandoned me?"

Thulos shook his head, feeling cruel anger burning within him. He would teach her who was master, who was leader, who was god. He stepped through the doors, and all his anger vanished as he witnessed a battle beyond anything he had ever witnessed. His soldiers, his winged war demons, flew in broken formations in the sky above a great city, fighting men in white robes and golden armor. He recognized them at once, the troops of his long lost brother, Ashhur. His own troops were far more numerous, but the flow of battle appeared uncertain.

The conflict was not limited to the sky alone. From the castle he saw a long, wide road, much of it covered with fallen bodies. Armored soldiers fought through file after file of mindless undead. They were taking heavy casualties, but their progress appeared more certain than that of those in the sky.

When Thulos looked back at the two troublesome brothers, he saw a body beside them, blood running down the steps from a gash in its throat.

"Ulamn," Thulos said, his anger rising. Ulamn had been his greatest general, overseeing the conquering of over twenty worlds. Now he lay dead, and by the way Harruq smirked, he had little doubt who had been the cause.

"He promised—what was it?— to crush my bones to pebbles and peel my flesh?" Harruq asked.

"Something like that," Qurrah said between coughs.

Thulos said not a word; he was too busy absorbing the details of the war. He counted the waves of undead that fought in the streets. He took in the number of demons and angels that warred in the sky. He knew his soldiers' worth, and in the passing of just a few seconds, he sensed the ability of the angels. The men who marched against him were only mortal, even if well-trained and adequately equipped. Thulos knew when he joined the fray, his troops would win, with a few undead and the vast bulk of the demons remaining. He smiled.

"Let you two be honored as the first of my sacred kills upon your land," he said, saluting with his sword. Harruq saluted back, a nervous grin on his face.

Three angels swerved low toward them, carrying passengers. Before Thulos could attack, the passengers extended their arms, and a massive barrage of fire, ice, and rock exploded forth. The war-god crossed his arms and grunted. The fire and ice did little, and the rocks, boulders half his size, shattered, leaving a few scrapes across his armor. The angels released their passengers at the foot of the stairs and joined the battle in the sky. A tall wizard with yellow robes and a small red beard bounded up the stairs as Thulos pushed away the chunks of rock that blocked his way.

"Please tell me that's not who I think it is," the yellow-robed man said.

At first Thulos thought the wizard spoke of him, but then noticed the hateful glance thrown at the smaller of the two brothers. He made a note of it, then looked to the two women, magic dangling from their fingertips. One was an elf, certainly beautiful, with long auburn hair, walnut eyes, a flowing green dress. The other appeared a twin of Tessanna, the second image of the goddess he had seen within moments of setting foot upon the world. This one had a healthy glow about her skin, and she wore a dress similar to the elf's.

"In everything, I see Celestia's hand," Thulos said to them. "Will she herself not come and face me?"

"You'll have to settle for us," the wizard said, tipping his hat. "My name's Tarlak. Meet my Eschaton."

As one they unleashed a barrage of spells, a swirling mix of fire and sheer magical power. Thulos batted the spells aside with his sword, knowing its enchantments, enhanced by the strongest spellcrafters of various worlds, could protect and endure. Harruq rushed up the steps, weapons ready. Thulos saw him between the powerful light of the spells, stepped to one side, and slammed his sword down in greeting. Their blades connected, and once more the mortal flew back.

He gave them no reprieve. Brushing aside their darts of ice and flame like they were wasps, he charged. His shoulder slammed the man named Tarlak in the face, plowing him several feet backward. With his sword he lashed out at the one who mirrored the goddess. It connected, but it did not cut skin, the woman somehow protected by strong magic. The force of the blow continued, however, and she cried out in pain as she rolled down the steps, several of her ribs most likely broken.

The elf slammed her hands together, trying a different tactic to defeat him. He felt the ground rumble beneath his feet, then crack and sink. She was trying to destroy his footing, as if the others could take advantage. Thulos shifted his feet, stepped twice, and backhanded her.

"Aurelia!" he heard Harruq shout.

Several lances of ice flew from her fingers as she stumbled back, the spells shattering against his breastplate like they were fragile glass. He paused a moment, knowing his skirmish was insignificant compared with the larger battle. He raised his sword, letting his demons take power and courage from his very presence.

"I am here!" he shouted, his voice carrying for miles. "Victory is at hand, my brethren!"

The angels in the sky reacted just as fiercely as the demons. The chaos above had formed into two solid armies, and those in white dived to the ground, shredding undead and calling out commands. Thulos could not hear them, but their meaning was clear. They were shouting retreat to the soldiers in the streets.

"This is our chance," the goddess mirror said as she pushed herself to her knees and stared at him. "Without his army. Without all his strength. Without Karak at his side. We must kill him."

Thulos admired her determination, but she was just a child. He dodged another ball of fire from Aurelia, smacked away a spear of magic from Tarlak, and closed the distance between him and the girl with blackest eyes. His hand closed around her throat, the tip of his sword hovering before her chest.

"Your name?" he demanded. "If you are indeed not the goddess."

"Mira," she said, still unafraid.

"Well Mira," Thulos said, even as the others surrounded him. "Give word to your goddess. This world is lost. I will do as I did a thousand years before. If she will not face me, then everything—*everything*—will burn."

He threw her away like a discarded doll. She crumpled on the hard ground and did not move.

Harruq lunged, his swords stabbing for openings in Thulos's armor. At the same time, Qurrah lashed with a whip wreathed in flame. As the leather wrapped around the war-god's neck he blocked one sword stab with his vambrace. The other he parried with his sword, looped his blade around, and thrust deep through the armor covering Harruq's chest. This time it was Aurelia who screamed at the sight, and Thulos noted their connection. They loved each other, and in her grief, the elf would be dangerous. He had to deal with her next.

Of course, there was still the matter of the whip burning into the stone-tough flesh of his neck. He grabbed it with his hand and yanked, sending Qurrah tumbling back down the stairs. The whip released its grip and snaked back to its master like a living thing.

The smoke from the whip blurred Thulos's vision, and in that momentary distraction he saw sets of white wings come flying in. He crouched down and held up his sword, preparing for an attack. None came. The angels swooped down and yanked his opponents into the air without ever slowing. Thulos sheathed his sword, frowning. Other than wounding the burly warrior, he was yet to score a solid blow, and even he might survive. Only Mira remained, still limp upon the ground.

"They flee!" he shouted to his troops. "Kill the slow! Kill the weak! Let blood rain upon the city, and our victory grow ever greater!"

An angel landed beside Mira, blood seeping from a wound above his right eye. He glanced at Thulos and tensed, waiting for the war-god to lash out and kill him.

"Go," Thulos said. "She has a message to deliver."

The angel took Mira into his arms, spread his wings, and fled. Thulos rubbed his neck, disappointment creeping through him. He held little doubt he had faced the greatest heroes this world had to offer, and all they could do was singe his neck and batter his armor. He consoled himself with the fact that the last of his brothers were here, and with their deaths, he could once again ascend to the heavens, reclaiming the power and glory that were his right.

His demons circled in groups, crashing into angels that lingered behind or exposing any openings in their retreat. Every time the battle was quick, bloody, and resulted in the death of either angel or demon. Thulos nodded in appreciation. At least Ashhur had trained and strengthened his army well. It had been years since his demons had fought worthy foes.

His eyes drifted to the fight in the streets. The undead surged forward, no longer oppressed by the human army. Only a few remained, and while they should have been quickly overrun, they were not. Thulos narrowed his eyes, and at the sight of glowing weapons and shining armor, he recognized the warriors of his brother, Ashhur.

"Still up to your old tricks," Thulos muttered. "I never understood your love affair with paladins."

He drew his sword and marched toward them, thinking he might have a bit of fun with his brother's champions. They were a beauty to behold, the two of them, especially against their most sworn enemy, the undead. One wielded a giant sword, shimmering as if made of a thick beam of holy light. The other had a hammer and a massive shield that shone brighter than the sun itself. Together, sword and shield, they held firm. Unsure of who commanded the undead, Thulos did not bother to part them, instead cutting a path through the rotting bodies.

The paladin with the sword noticed his approach.

"Uh, Jerico?" he shouted.

"Yeah, Lathaar?" Jerico shouted back.

"Time to go."

Thulos watched Jerico risk a glance, no doubt seeing him as a towering Goliath of muscle, sword, and armor. The paladins stepped back, cut down the nearest undead, and turned to run. Thulos swore. He was used to people fleeing his presence, but even the champions of Ashhur? Would they hide, denying him the glory of combat and their own honor in death?

"Face me," Thulos shouted, but his challenge went unmet. Furious, Thulos turned back to the castle. Under normal circumstances he would have given chase, but too much was going on that he didn't understand. Most damning, his portal to his home world was shut. He felt certain the woman named Tessanna was the reason. He couldn't let her slip away while he chased after a routed army in a selfish desire for combat.

He climbed the steps three at a time, pushed aside the wooden doors to the throne room, and looked about. Tessanna sat by the closed portal, absently running her fingers along the painted wall where it had been. Meanwhile, the laughing man in the corner had finally risen, and he greeted him at the door with a long bow.

"Mighty Thulos," the man said, his eyes to the ground. "I am your most humble servant."

"Rise, stranger," Thulos said. "And tell me your name."

"I am Velixar," the man said, standing erect. Thulos wondered for a moment as he saw the man's eyes glow a deep crimson, his facial features slowly shifting and changing. With a wave of his hand, Thulos banished the illusion. He saw Velixar's true face and understood.

"Nothing but a lich," Thulos said. "I have met your kind before. An annoyance at best. What is it you offer me in your servitude?"

"I am the one who opened the portal," Velixar said as his shifting face returned. "I am the mouth of Karak, his greatest prophet."

"Then you are worthy," Thulos said. He drew his sword and saluted, for he would bow to no man. "Consider yourself an honored member of my guard. If you hear the voice of Karak, then I have much to discuss with you."

His eyes hardened.

"Especially over the matter of his cowardice and departure."

"Matters he is eager to discuss as well," Velixar assured him.

Thulos sheathed his sword and turned to Tessanna, who appeared oblivious to his presence. Behind him, he heard one of his war demons land, ready with word of greeting and report of casualties. He held up a hand, silencing him, his eyes never leaving the strange woman. He walked over, spun her around, and flung her against the wall.

"How dare you close the portal!" he said, grabbing her hair and forcing her to look at him. To his surprise, she showed no fear, only anguish and sorrow.

"I am barren," she said, her voice strangely void of all emotion. "I have no power. Mother has forsaken me for doing what even she cannot forgive."

"You lie," Thulos said. "Open it now, or I will cut your head from your neck."

Tessanna smiled at him as tears ran down her face.

"Do it," she said. "Strand yourself here. You have none who can return you home. This world is not like the others you've conquered. Mother protected it from you, protected it even from me. Even Velixar can't open the way."

She gasped when he tightened his grip and glared death.

"Mother?" Thulos said, a look of distaste crossing over him. He dropped her, repulsed by her tears. How one as her could possess such powerful magic was beyond him.

"My lord," the war demon at the door said. "We request orders. Ashhur's army retreats west beyond the walls. Do we give chase?"

Thulos tore his eyes from Tessanna and turned to his soldier.

"No," he said. "We are out of supplies and reinforcements. Every action we take must be careful and controlled. Until I know this world and the dangers it offers, we solidify our position here. Besides..." He turned to Velixar. "I have much to discuss."

Velixar smiled, while in a corner of the room, Tessanna curled into a ball and sobbed.

2

Qurrah sat alone in a small tent, his hands probing the damp earth as his mind looped an endless replay of the past few weeks. He was supposed to have been a father, their child a gift given to Tessanna and him by Karak, god of everything wretched and dark. Then the birth, and the revealing of the lie. He shuddered, wanting to remember nothing of that long night, the blood, the sweat, and the still, still shell that was his daughter. Teralyn, his beloved had named the corpse...

"Qurrah?"

He glanced up, wiping away his tears. There were no torches or campfires nearby for light, but both the orcish and elvish blood in his veins granted him excellent vision in the darkness. When he saw the sleek figure sliding into his tent, her beautiful green dress rippling in the moonlight, he knew his tears would be seen by Aurelia's keen elven eyes. He said nothing, though he had much he wished to say. He knew so little of her. She was his brother's wife and, in a distant time, a friend. Now she was a stranger, wounded and tired.

"Harruq will be fine," she said, breaking the silence as she crossed her legs and sat across from him. Outside the tent, the angels guarding him shuffled, their weapons clacking against their armor.

"He has certainly endured far worse before," Qurrah said.

"You could say that," Aurelia said, and Qurrah felt a stab in his gut. How many of his brother's scars bore his name, scrawled with whip and dark magic? The elf saw the brief flash of pain in his eyes and quickly apologized.

"He told me what happened," she said, tucking errant strands of hair behind her ear. Her eyes refused to meet his. "Of what you wanted, and what he did. You have a good brother, Qurrah."

"And you a good husband."

Aurelia smiled again, a weak smile.

"Why is Tessanna not with you?" she asked.

Qurrah opened his mouth, a lie on his tongue. He closed it, and another lie replaced it in his heart. He brushed both away, and spoke freely to the woman he had so deeply hurt.

"Tessanna gave birth to a stillborn," he said. "It broke me. I never could have anticipated such pain. And as I held that small, lifeless form, I knew a shred of what I had done to you. Guilt is a funny thing, Aurelia. I had never felt it before, and when it came upon me, I was a wretched child lost in confusion and self-pity. I waited in Veldaren for my brother, for I wanted him to kill me. Dying was preferable to living with the guilt I felt. Tessanna figured as much, and was furious at my cowardice."

He felt more tears growing in his exhausted eyes. The gods damn it all, he was tired of crying, and tired of hiding it every time he did. He let his tears fall and his lower lip quiver.

"I saw no other way, Aurelia. You have to understand. I thought it would do him good, that maybe he could cut my throat, and the blood would cover some of the pain you two felt. But he didn't. He forgave me. For all of it. I didn't need blood or penance, he just...let it go."

He fell silent. Aurelia huddled her knees to her chest and pressed her shaking fist to her mouth. She stared at him, taking in every movement he made, every twitch of his eyes, every sad, whispered word.

"Harruq said he forgave you," she said. "Did I ever say the same?"

Qurrah shrugged and stared her in the eye.

"Years ago, when you two married, I told my brother I was proud of him, and that he'd found an excellent bride. I meant those words. I still do. Please, Aullienna was..."

"Don't," Aurelia said. She stood, her shoulders stooped and her head bowed by the low fabric of the tent. "Just...don't. Not tonight, not while my husband lies bleeding and bedridden with fever."

She stepped outside, whispered something to the angel guard, and then glanced to Qurrah, who did not look back.

"The others want you executed," she said. "I'm not sure Harruq can stop them."

"Will you stop them?" Qurrah asked. The quiet stretched out longer and longer.

"Good night, Qurrah," she said, slipping away.

It was the answer he deserved, he knew.

Thulos looked upon the city from the castle doors, his skin cold marble in the bright moonlight. Velixar stood beside him, quiet and attentive. Thulos had summoned him to listen, and so he would.

"I cannot hear my brothers," Thulos said, his eyes watching the land beyond the walls where the distant army of Ashhur camped. "Either of them. But you say you hear Karak's voice, and so I speak to you, in hopes that through you he may speak to me."

The wind blew. Velixar heard Karak whisper for him to hold his silence. In time, Thulos resumed.

"I will tell you much, mortal, so that you may understand what it is I came for, and why it is I seek your lord. I need you to understand, to ensure Karak hears the truth."

Thulos gestured to the stars above.

"Every one of them holds a single world filled with life. Celestia was the first to create such a place, and I was among the other gods, jealous of her beautiful creation. So we scattered, with the blessing of He Who Judges. We were all mirrors of his glory, but Celestia seemed special, elevated somehow. We created similar lands, for we only sought Celestia's splendor, not knowing how to create it on our own. When she created man, we did the same. But hers were the first, ours just shallow, imperfect imitations."

Thulos drifted off, his mind in times far beyond their own. Velixar waited, glad for the chance to absorb what he'd heard. Karak had whispered to him of other worlds, but never had he heard of their creation, nor mention of He Who Judges. Did gods themselves also have gods?

"I created men, much as Celestia did," Thulos continued several minutes later. "I armed them with weapons, and I opened a door to her world and let them through. My pets killed every shred of life. It was petty jealousy, nothing more, and I have forever carried the shame of that single, human moment. As punishment I was banished to my own world. Celestia created elves to heal the destruction, and in turn, the others of my kind copied her creation. She hoped the elves' docile nature would allow her to rest, and in this she was correct."

"You created man, and shaped worlds, yet here you stand before me in flesh and blood?" Velixar dared ask. "Why did you not wave your hand and dismiss those you fought today, and with a word split their very beings to water and dust?"

"Wave my hand?" Thulos said, a hint of anger giving life to his words. "Deny combat to a foe, however unworthy? What do skill and strength matter, what do *I* matter, if I render all need of such things pointless?"

He dismissed Velixar with a shrug of his head.

"You are too ignorant to understand. You crave only victory, not the battle itself. Karak has certainly fallen far if you are his wisest pupil."

Velixar accepted the stinging rebuke, knowing he should have stilled his tongue. The minutes crawled as again Thulos seemed to dig deep into a memory spanning thousands of years, searching for words to attach to moments that shaped entire worlds.

"Besides," Thulos said at last. "I can no longer do so. I am not a proper god, not as I once was. Neither is Karak or Ashhur."

"How is that possible?"

"I came to Him," Thulos said. "Told Him what I would do. The men of my world were ruthless, vile, and ignorant. I hovered outside it, peering in, and I felt that was the flaw. With His blessing, I shattered myself. Once we were Kaurthulos, all one, but afterward we were Ashhur and Karak, Kirm and Ra, Thulos and Verae, gods of Justice, Mercy, War, Order, Death, Life..."

He shook his head.

"I left the outside. I left all my power, and to the mortal world I fell. In time, I saw my error. The world was no better. Now my creations were divided, battling over worship of my various incarnations, putting one virtue higher than another, as if Justice were at war with Order, or Life in eternal conflict with Mercy. As Thulos, I was everywhere, for I was War. As my power grew, I slew my brothers, prism refractions of my own being. Each time, I felt myself returning to wholeness. But then Karak and Ashhur fled here, to the world they once helped destroy. Tell me, Velixar, what happened here, after my brothers denied me my right to ascend, to look from the outside once more and wield all of my divine power?"

"Karak and Ashhur created man, and then through man, waged war against each other," Velixar said. "Celestia imprisoned both, and so my master has called out to you. He wishes to be freed from his cage, to campaign at your side."

Thulos chuckled, the deep sound frightful in the night.

"I'm not sure that is possible. I wish to be whole. This conquest across the stars, it is merely preparation. We were told of a time when He Who Judges would view our creations, preserving for eternity those he deemed good, and casting into fire forever those he considered ill-wrought and vile. I seek to gather the power of all the stars, all the worlds, and all the gods, and in a loud voice declare to Him that *all* is good, and that I accept no judge. I do not need Karak as an ally. I need him to return to me, so we may be whole once more."

"You ask his death," Velixar said, his heart surrounded by the creeping feeling of betrayal.

"I ask his atonement," Thulos said. "Does a stream die when it joins a river?"

Velixar listened for Karak's answer, but none came to his ears. Thulos waited, saw he would be given no answer, and then swore in a language Velixar knew nothing off. A massive fist slammed into the stone of the castle. Cracks ran in all directions.

"How do I free them from their prison?" Thulos asked.

"Celestia must be defeated," Velixar said. "She gains her strength from the health of this world. Burn its trees, poison its rivers, and kill off her elves. We will find a way."

"Pray to your god you are right," Thulos said, trudging back into the castle. "And pray you both understand the inevitable future that awaits you."

3

The army traveled during the day, the angels flying above them, forced to slow to accommodate the collective earthbound troops from Mordan and Neldar. Antonil Copernus, their king, rode among them, but his voice was a hollow lie as he encouraged them on, insisting victory was not yet lost.

When night came, they held their tribunal.

Qurrah stepped into the light of the fire, flanked by two angels. Ahaesarus, leader of the angels, sat directly opposite him. Judarius, his greatest fighter, was on his right. Azariah, his high priest, sat to his left. The three looked upon him with strangely passive faces. The rest of the tribunal was filled with members of the Eschaton—what was left of it. Lathaar and Jerico on one side of the fire, Harruq and Aurelia on the other. Tarlak hovered as far from Qurrah as he could, his arms crossed and his hat pulled low.

"King Antonil has assured us he will abide by our decision in this matter," Ahaesarus said, nodding toward Qurrah. "But before we start, I must ask you as well, Qurrah Tun: do you yourself agree to honor the decision we make here, even if it results in your death?"

As the angelic voice ceased, Qurrah felt the silence swarm around him, bound tight by the many glares of hatred, pain, and sorrow aimed his way. He glanced from face to face, remembering how he had hurt them. Jerico, his helmet by his side, rubbed his face as if aware Qurrah's eyes lingered on the scar that ran from his ear to his cheek. The angels? They were there only because he had helped release Thulos's demons. Aurelia hugged her bandaged husband, who sat propped against a few logs of wood, his outgoing demeanor uncharacteristically subdued. Their drowned daughter haunted their waking eyes. At last Qurrah looked to Tarlak, whose sister he had cut open from ear to ear and bled out upon cold, wet grass.

"I will accept and honor it," Qurrah said. It felt akin to suicide.

Ahaesarus nodded at the words. He crossed his arms and addressed the gathering.

"This is not a court of man," he said. "No, this is a court unlike any before. We come to judge the worth of a life. Let there be no lies. We know of his crimes, as do you all. That is not in question. It is punishment we seek here, nothing more, nothing less."

"Punishment?" Tarlak said, spitting as he did. "How many thousands are dead because of him? You want to discuss punishment? Fire, rope, or blade: those should be our choices."

Azariah sadly shook his head.

"Is that what you believe, Tarlak Eschaton?" he asked. Tarlak waved a dismissive hand, not committing to any deeper meaning than that.

"You can't do this," Harruq started to say, but Aurelia shushed him. Qurrah saw her whisper something in his ear. His brother clearly did not approve, but he kept his mouth shut, fuming silently.

"You hear Tarlak's accusations," Ahaesarus said to Qurrah. "And you stand so accused. Will you respond?"

Qurrah looked to their faces, looked to their hurt, and every hollow argument died in his throat. What could he say to them? *I killed your daughter by accident. I scarred your flesh in humor. I killed your friends for power. I doomed this world in a desperate attempt to escape.*

"I deserve death," Qurrah said at last. "Let that be my response."

"No!" Harruq shouted. His whole body doubled over, the wound in his chest ripping open in spite of all the care. He pounded a fist into the dirt, still struggling to talk.

"I forgave him," he said between gasps of pain. "That must mean something!"

"Indeed," Azariah said, speaking for the first time. "What of that, Qurrah?"

Qurrah shrugged..

"It was offered, and I accepted. What other choice did I have?"

Azariah stood to his full height and glanced around the fire, his eyes settling on the two paladins.

"What choice did he have?" he asked them.

"Rejection of grace," Jerico said. "We do it every day."

Lathaar glanced up, as if realizing what Azariah was preparing to do. He opened his mouth to argue, realized the hypocrisy of such an action, and then closed it.

"I have just one question," Azariah said, crossing his arms over his chest. His voice rose in strength. Tarlak froze with dread while Harruq's face sparkled with kindled hope.

"I offer grace to you, mortal. Not the grace of man, but the grace of Ashhur. Will you accept it?"

Qurrah could not believe his ears. He didn't want to believe them. He had killed children, innocents, and mutilated life to meet his desires. Forgiven?

"And if I reject it?" Qurrah asked.

Ahaesarus drew his sword. No words were spoken. All watched. All waited. It seemed ridiculous to Qurrah. A court where the accused chose their guilt, a court where the crime mattered not, and all punishments were death.

"Then I..."

He stopped. He didn't just feel like he was getting away with murder; he *was* getting away with murder. To look upon the faces of all those he'd hurt and slide away unscathed, unchanged, how dare he? He had always thought himself stronger than that, better than that. Never before had he belittled his sin. How many times had he insisted his brother acknowledge the weight of their deeds? How many times had he laughed in the face of guilt, and smirked at the wails of sorrow?

He fell to his knees. He would not lie.

"I do not think I can," Qurrah said.

Tarlak breathed out a sigh. The paladins sadly shook their heads. Aurelia closed her eyes and fought away tears.

"No!" Harruq shouted. "No, no, you damn fool. Don't you dare!"

Ahaesarus raised the sword, its edge gleaming in the moonlight. Harruq lunged, not caring for the pain or the blood that ran down his shirt. He clutched his brother in his arms, a fragile sack of bone and wearied flesh. Tears ran down his face.

"I finally have you back," Harruq said. "You won't leave me now. Don't you dare, Qurrah! Stay with me, here. Stay and fight, gods be damned; can't you endure even that?"

Qurrah's tears fell, and he felt like he had the previous day, ready and waiting for his brother's executioner song, only to be granted love instead. He wept, he clutched his brother, and he wondered how so many years and deaths had come between them.

"How?" he whispered. "How could you still...?...still...By the gods, Harruq, don't you know what I've done? To you? To everyone?"

Harruq faced Ahaesarus, and he glared at the naked sword he held.

"My crimes are no different than his," he said. "Whatever punishment Qurrah receives, I demand the same."

"He's not the same as you," Tarlak said. "Stop being an idiot and realize that."

"You never asked," Harruq said, turning to him. "You never pried. But I killed the children at Woodhaven. My name—the Forest Butcher—I earned it in blood. I still bear the weight. Yet you have fought with me, nearly died with me. Would you banish me now?"

His voice lowered as Tarlak shook with rage.

"This is not about you," Tarlak said.

"But it is," Qurrah said. He faced off with Tarlak, their eyes locked on one another. "He stands at your side. He has murdered children. You call him friend. But he struck me first, nearly killed me for accusations that were baseless and false. And then you came to me, murder in your hearts, and then threw the blame yet again on me and my lover?"

"You killed without remorse!"

"As do you! How many have died by your fire and flame? Would you have shed a tear for my death? Tessanna's? How do we judge life, Tarlak? Or do we use your scale, where friends are everything, enemies are nothing, and all is forgiven once we adopt the Eschaton name?"

"Enough!" Azariah shouted. He stepped between them, and there was no hiding his displeasure. "You each accuse the other of murder, and yet how would you solve it? By more murder? You accuse them of death, but how do you see the solution? More death?"

"It might atone for what they've done," Tarlak said.

"Death atones for nothing!" Azariah insisted. "Let all men reap what they have sown in eternity, but would you wish any man—*any* man—that fate because of your own hurt? Your own hatred? Who here has the right to condemn a man to fire for eternity? The only judge of a man's soul is himself!"

Qurrah pulled Harruq close, his face pained by the blood spilling across his chest from the open wound. He purposefully put his back to Azariah, not wanting to see his glare. His anger faded, and with tired eyes he made his appeal.

"Don't do this," he whispered to his brother. "Don't die for me. You've already given me more than I deserve. Let my life end here. Let all their wounds close. The angel is wrong. My death will help. My death will let them heal."

"Never again," Harruq said, clutching Qurrah's hands tightly in his own. His face paled, and he stood with strength that still stunned him. "You're my brother. I won't lose you. Not again. Together, Qurrah. Always and forever. Tell them. Live."

"For you, brother," Qurrah said, "I will try."

He looked to the angel priest, whose face had remained steady as stone throughout the ordeal.

"You were given a wonderful gift, Qurrah Tun," Azariah said. A quick nod from Ahaesarus and he continued. "You did not ask for grace, but it was given anyway, and you accepted it over death. Such is the state of all men, no different from you. And now we play this game, as if the crimes mattered, as if we live by the limits of man instead of the limits of Ashhur. Who will you be, Qurrah? What life shall you have?"

Qurrah felt a mixture of shame, embarrassment, and relief as he spoke his words.

"If Ashhur's grace is as good as my brother's, then I accept it."

"Then consider yourself forgiven," Azariah said. Ahaesarus sheathed his sword. It was as if a bolt of lightning struck the campfire. The paladins stood and murmured to each other, seeing a sight they had seen so many times back at the Citadel, while Aurelia went to her husband, pulling him away so she could tend to his wounds. Tarlak, furious beyond control, stormed away. Azariah saw him and hurried after.

"You're fools and weaklings," Tarlak said as he heard the angel's approach. "He deserves death and you know it."

"Who said what he deserved held any sway?" Azariah asked. Tarlak glared at him, remembering his sister Delysia's smiling face. He turned to leave, but Azariah grabbed his shoulder and pulled him close, so their eyes were inches away.

"Listen well to me, Tarlak Eschaton," Azariah said. "Ashhur has said again and again that all who seek forgiveness, no matter what their sin, will find it. If grace has limits, then it is a sad, useless thing. Back there wept the greatest test this world has ever seen. If his desire for salvation is true, if his taste of grace lasts and Ashhur accepts him into his paradise, then who are you to argue?"

"After everything, he just falls to his knees, and that's it?" Tarlak asked, grabbing Azariah's wrist and matching him gaze for gaze. "And what of us?"

"As I said, it is your test. How much do you believe what you say you believe? That golden mountain that hangs above your chest, does it mean anything anymore?"

Tarlak pushed him away, feeling a tantrum building in his heart but not wishing to give in. He knew Azariah spoke truth, but to see such an egregious example, to see Qurrah Tun not only forgiven, but treated as brother, as equal, as friend, after everything he had done...

"Only human," Tarlak said, shaking his head as he walked away. "May Ashhur forgive me for that, but I'm only human. Leave grace for those better than I."

Azariah sighed, watching him go.

"There are few better than you," the angel said to the empty night. "But perhaps that is your burden."

He turned and rejoined the others by the fire.

Harruq grunted as Aurelia slid next to him underneath their blanket.

"Careful, I'm fragile," he muttered as she softly ran her fingers over his freshly bandaged chest.

"One of these days you'll learn your stupidity gets you hurt," she said.

"And that's when you'll leave me," he said, sighing heavily and leaning his head back. She poked a finger into his hip and glared a feline glare. The playfulness was forced, however, and she curled up against him as gently as she could.

"It's Qurrah, isn't it?" he asked as she nuzzled her face into his neck.

"Just seeing him," she said. "It brings back too many memories."

"Some were good," Harruq said. "The early days, when we first joined the Eschaton."

She smiled. "Those were good days, weren't they? You were still a goofy, scared half-orc. I thought you would die every time I grabbed your hand and kissed your cheek."

"Slain by beauty, isn't that what happens to beasts like me?" he asked.

She didn't answer, instead letting the quiet night envelop them. High above, a thin line of clouds blotted out the moon. Harruq watched, waiting for the light to return.

"He killed our daughter," Aurelia said, so quiet, so timid.

"I know," Harruq said.

"He's hurt you."

"I know."

The light of the moon returned.

"How do I let go of that?" she asked.

Harruq shrugged, the motion spiking pain along his ribs. "He's my brother. I love him more than I hate him."

Aurelia nestled closer in, wrapping an arm across his shoulders and burying her face, like an animal seeking refuge.

"But what else can he be to me?" she asked. "Not a brother. Not kin. Just a monster."

Harruq closed his eyes, remembering those words long, long ago.

You're an orc, aren't you?

He had nearly cleaved the boy in two, his blade slicing down from shoulder to chest.

"I was a monster, too," Harruq whispered.

They said no more, and after several hours, they found sleep.

◆

They kept Qurrah isolated from the rest of the troops. Many were unaware of his involvement, but his black robes and pallid demeanor signified him as different. Accusations of traitor, necromancer, and demon-worshiper filtered through the human soldiers until nearly all were aware of Qurrah's relevance to Neldar's destruction. When not carried in the air by an angel, he trudged along at the back of the army, with Harruq, sometimes Aurelia, as his only guard.

"They will never forgive me," Qurrah said after another long, exhausting day putting Veldaren farther and farther behind them. "I think one night I'll wake up to a rope around my neck."

"Hard to blame them," Harruq said, carefully watching Qurrah's movements for signs of exhaustion. He hadn't eaten well in days, and his weak lungs worried him.

"I don't," Qurrah said, stumbling over a sudden burrow in the dirt. Harruq instinctively reached to help him, but Qurrah waved him away.

"How could I blame them?" he continued. "I started this war. How many are from Neldar? How many watched their loved ones die while my undead chanted my name like I was some glorious conqueror? How many...?"

He couldn't go on, and for that Harruq was glad. Qurrah looked over at him, a rare moment of humility drenched him like reams of wet cloth.

"I always claimed we were superior," he said. "I was full of shit, wasn't I?"

At this Harruq laughed, hoping to dismiss the pall them.

"We were young, powerful, and poor," he said. "Of course we were full of shit."

Qurrah motioned to the angels flying overhead.

"They say I need no penance. No punishments. To even suggest it ruffles their feathers. But I must do something, for my whole heart aches for it. What should I do? How do I make it even? What does one man do to erase a debt owed to thousands?"

Harruq tried to think of his own moment of humility, knelt before Qurrah's army, weeping open tears as he begged for forgiveness.

"You do what you can," he said at last. "Perhaps you'll never make it even. But I don't think that's the point."

Qurrah smiled at him.

"It seems you've supplanted me as the older brother," he said.

"Bah. Hardly a job I want."

Up ahead, a soft chant rose through the groups of soldiers. They had started singing a song of home, and for each voice that took up the song two more were inspired to join. The deep, rumbling longing reached the two, and in its sound Qurrah halted his march.

"Leave me," he said, silencing his brother with a glare when he tried to object. "I must wait here. Bad blood lingers, and if I do not deal with it now, I may never have the courage."

"Who?" Harruq asked, glancing back at the marching army.

"It doesn't matter," Qurrah said. "Will you go?"

The larger half-orc glanced at the angels to see if they'd noticed their pause. So far, it seemed they had not.

"Will you return to us?" Harruq finally asked.

"If I have breath within me still," Qurrah said.

The promise wasn't very comforting.

⋈

The land beyond the capital, that which was not smooth and often tilled, was filled with hills, and beneath the carpet of grass the soil was rocky and difficult to dig. Trees clustered in random assortments of five or six, growing tall and surrounded by walls of bushes. It was in the shadow of one of these clusters that Qurrah waited, until day was gone and only the moon shone down upon him. His feet were thankful for the break, but his mind was not. The constant motion had given him little time to think, but now alone, his mind wandered down dark paths.

He nearly fled. It occurred to him his transformation may have been nothing more than a survival technique, a burning desire for life that held little regard for grace and forgiveness. Guilt was a foreign thing to him, and the temptation to cast it away was strong. He clutched the image of Harruq's daughter in his mind, using it to push away the weakness that tore into his flesh.

You killed her! Tessanna had shrieked as she clawed at his arms and chest, back when her attuned mind had sensed Aullienna's death. He let that memory slash away any growing sense of importance or infallibility. He had done wrong. There was no other way to view his morbid life. He had done wrong.

"Decide to run away and hide?" a voice asked from within the copse of trees. Qurrah turned, not at all surprised.

"Not run," Qurrah said. "Just waiting."

Tarlak stepped through the bushes, ignoring the brambles that stuck to his robe.

"For me?" Tarlak asked. "I'm flattered."

"I knew you would come, but I am still not sure the exact reason. Perhaps that alone shows how much I have hurt you. Why, Tarlak? Why are you here?"

The wizard hurled his hat to the ground between the two.

"How did she die?" he asked. "Answer me truthfully, half-orc. How did you and your witch kill her?"

Qurrah felt a flare of anger at hearing his beloved Tessanna called such a name.

"You want the truth?" he said. "Tessanna held her by her hair as I cut her throat. She did not scream, and her pain was short."

"Why?" Tarlak asked, tears in his eyes. "What did she do to you? What did *I* do to you?"

"Nothing," Qurrah said. "But so much blood was on Tessanna's hands, and I had none on my own."

He ran his fingers along the twin scars underneath his eyes.

"I cried tears of blood after her death," Qurrah said. "Out of all I've done, that was when I felt myself beyond salvation. And I will not lie to you, Tarlak. I did so willingly."

"Beyond salvation," Tarlak said, his clenched fists shaking. "Perhaps you were right, Qurrah. Maybe even gods have limits. Shall we test them? Will Karak and Ashhur fight over which must take you? Maybe you'll just fade away, eternally unwanted."

"Will you murder me?" Qurrah asked.

"Sounds good."

Tarlak hurled a ball of flame from each palm. Qurrah dropped to the ground, letting them sail past, consuming the trees. The half-orc labored to one knee, and before the red-orange glow of the fire, he appeared the demon Tarlak knew him to be. Lightning struck from the sky, beckoned by Tarlak's spell. Qurrah summoned a magical shield, but a portion of the attack broke through, jolting his muscles and flooding him with pain.

Anger and survival raged in his chest. He hurled a clump of grass, igniting it in a muffled explosion of darkness that sucked in all light and sound. Behind the wall of black Qurrah surrounded his body with purple fire that only blazed and did not consume. When the inky darkness dissipated, Tarlak was ready, a giant boulder ripped from the ground floating before him. He hurled it with his mind's eye. Qurrah let it crash into him, and like a statue, he did not move. The purple fire roared, cracking and twisting the chunk of earth and shoving it aside.

Flashing a dire grin, he outstretched his hands, letting the fire lash out, burning Tarlak's robes and searing the flesh of his arms and legs.

Tarlak stumbled away, summoning up protections against fire. The next wave that washed over him produced only smoke. Tarlak glared through watery eyes, doing his best to ignore the horrible pain of his blackened flesh. Qurrah's whip lashed the ground, uncurled from its hiding place about his arm.

"Just like in Veldaren," Qurrah hissed as he struck. Tarlak's spell died in mid-cast, the delicate hand motions required to cast it disrupted by the cord wrapped around his wrist. Desperate, he snapped his fingers. A massive burst of light shone in all directions, as if his fingers were the epicenter of a thousand suns plunged together. Qurrah back, his mind aching from the horrific brightness.

"Just like the King's Forest," Tarlak said, unleashing a blast of pure, raw magical energy. It struck like a beam, hitting Qurrah's outstretched palms as he channeled a shield. He felt his willpower cracking. Tarlak was riding a frenzy of hurt and anger, the emotions giving him strength Qurrah could not hope to match, not in his weakened state. Karak's strength had left him, but if he reached deep within, where that dark well waited...

"No," Qurrah said. He released his shield and let the spell hit. He felt his arms and legs stretch back, the bones strained to the edge of their breaking points. A hundred fists pummeled his chest. He flew back, rolling across the ground like a limp doll. Coughing blood, he sagged to his knees and glared at Tarlak, who stood with magic surrounding his hands.

"I won't do this," Qurrah said between coughs. "If you want Delysia back, then kill me. Watch her spring unharmed from my corpse, all your hurt and anguish made a forgotten memory. But I will not be pushed back into the monster you need me to be. As I am now, Tarlak, you will have to kill me. Not as I was."

Qurrah sat on his knees and waited for the deathblow. And waited.

"Tarlak," said Aurelia, stepping out from the burning trees, the fire parting for her like subjects before their queen. "Must it be this way?"

Tarlak glanced between the two, all the while channeling the power for his spell. The fire crackled in his ears, and he knew he could bathe Qurrah in it, burn his flesh and bones down to ash—ash he could scatter with another spell so only the wind knew where his remnants came to rest. He wanted to. So badly, he wanted to.

But Qurrah had invoked his sister's name.

"What would Delysia say to this?" Aurelia said, walking over and gently pushing his hands down to his sides. The fire faded. "You know this is wrong."

"How can it be wrong?" Tarlak asked, the tears returning. "He slit her throat. My sister. My little baby sister, he..."

Like Qurrah, he fell to his knees, his battle rush fading, overcome by sorrow and grief he had held out against for so long while they fled and fought the demon army. Now he had nothing. Nothing.

"What has he left me?" Tarlak asked the elf, who kissed away his tears and tried to smile.

"You have me," she said. "You have my husband. Your friends, the paladins. All around, men revere you as great and wise and humorous. Will you not fight for that? Will you sacrifice it all?"

"I can," he said. "I will. But I'm so numb. So tired of being numb."

He let her hold him. Tears fell, and he was numb no longer. Qurrah turned away, feeling unworthy of such grief. He doubted he had Tarlak's forgiveness, but the hatred was gone. He let them be, and, tired and cold, he returned to the many fires of the army's camp.

4

Her song floated along moonlight waves, drifting in and out of covering clouds. The entire city was one of ghosts, lifeless beings in armor without joy or happiness, only dire, ordered control. Her song punctured the quiet, lacking words but not a story. It rose high, and then lilted, a strong hum that drifted between whisper and heart-wrenching sob. Love lost, love found, brothers and sisters gone to the grave while mothers and fathers struggled on. Velixar heard, and was afraid.

He wandered through the castle, letting the song pull him closer, his chest aflame in a way he had not felt in ages. Through tattered halls and empty courts he traveled, until in a lone tower he found Tessanna, singing through a window to the starlit sky. Head bowed, he waited, letting the woman sing her course, his eyes closed as if in prayer. The respect wrapped around Tessanna like a warm blanket, and in its embrace she slowly quieted, humming only a few more aching notes before drifting away.

"That was beautiful," Velixar said, his voice ugly and deep in the sudden silence.

"I didn't think you were capable of hearing beauty," she said, her gaze distant.

"I am still a man, and still clinging to life," Velixar said, sitting on his knees at the top of the stairs. There was hardly room for the two of them, unless Velixar crowded close, and he would not dare such a bold gesture, not yet. He followed her gaze, knowing she looked after the long distant army of Ashhur. At one time her powerful mind easily could have passed the miles and looked right into the tent of her lover...if indeed she still did love Qurrah Tun. But her magic had left her. The goddess no longer shone down on her beloved daughter.

"We will march after them soon," he said, after waiting to ensure Tessanna had nothing she wished to say. "Thulos wanted to study maps and consult his most trusted before moving out. He's like a man with a game, wanting to know where every piece is and how it plays upon the board."

"What do I care?" she asked.

"Because you care for the one we chase," Velixar said. "Because you care for he that betrayed and abandoned you."

"He would rather die than live at my side," she said. "How can I care for one so weak?"

"Because we are all weak, in our own way," Velixar said. He put his hand on hers. She did not flinch in spite of how cold his flesh was and how strong his bony fingers clutched her.

"Weak?" she said. "Is that what we are?"

Her voice was shallow and distant. No emotion, not even sadness, dared rear its head.

"Love continues on," Velixar said. "Even after weakness, after lies, after anger and betrayal. It is not a weak thing, but it is weakness to bow before it and let it rule."

"I do not fear pain," she said. Tears ran down her cheeks. She put her other hand on top of his. "And I am used to hurt. But this was not that. So much worse, Velixar. I hurt so much worse, more than I ever thought possible. I am a mirror, twice broken, now abandoned. What hope do I have?"

Velixar laughed, and was pleased with how her eyes finally stole to his, a shred of passion flushing her cheeks.

"Hope?" he asked. "Forget hope. You are strong, stronger than even the god that walks among us. Anything you want, you can have. All you need to do is take it. You are a goddess among these mortals, and I smile at the mere presence of your divinity."

And indeed he was smiling, and stroking her face with his hand, wiping away tears with a smooth, pale thumb. He felt a heat building, and it thrilled him.

"I am not blind to your desires," she said, and it seemed her eyes sunk deeper into her face. "You are a corpse pretending at life, but perhaps Karak left that tiny piece of you working. Is that why you harass me here?"

"Dear child," Velixar said, not at all upset. "Do you think that is the kind of love I feel for you? Qurrah, perhaps, desired nothing more, but in you I have seen such beauty and strength."

He rose from his knees and sat beside her. He was death enveloping her, and with a small gasp she let his arms slide around her. Her heart quickened, and she felt her breath sticking in her throat.

"What will it be like?" she dared ask.

In answer, he kissed her.

She felt fierce, horrifying passion pour into her like a well underneath floodwaters. She felt his singular obsession, his devotion to his god overwhelming even his lust and fear. Images of his hundreds of years of life flashed before her closed eyes. His tongue flitted across hers, and she sensed the very essence of death tingling its way up and down her spine. More and more poured in, his life, his death, his *unlife*, all of it in random, startling detail. As his hand brushed her breast, she knew the amazing respect he held for her, as well as the tiny inkling of fear. All of him, she knew all of him, and then she saw what neither wished her to see.

She saw a bag, its contents moving slowly against the limits.

She felt her hatred roar to life like an unleashed demon, and at the sudden rage his own hatred spilled forth, no longer hidden behind his glowing eyes. He hated her as much as he desired her, all for her power, the power of a goddess. Her whole body trembling, she clutched her elbows and backed to the very edge of the window.

"Get away," she said, her voice colder than the blood in his veins. "Go now, or I will fall."

"I felt your desire," he said, pulling his hood back over his face.

"And I felt yours," she said. "Compared to Qurrah's inferno, you're nothing but a firefly."

He moved again, and she scooted further back, her whole body hanging precariously above the castle walls. Velixar turned and left, but before he did, he offered one last piece of advice.

"Careful of your heart," he said. "The whole world is ending. Do not let it end you as well."

And then he was gone, and her sobs that came after were far greater than any she sang of in her song.

❖

Thulos was looking over maps when Velixar joined him in the throne room. The maps lay scattered across the floor, and the war god stalked among them, staring, analyzing, memorizing.

"You have walked these lands for centuries," Thulos said at his appearance. "Stay. My demons know very little, for Ulamn led them on a mad chase without the reconnaissance he should have done."

He pointed to the northern plains stretching above Veldaren.

"I've been told orcs have run rampant here," he said. "Is this true?"

"The Mug Tribe has been pillaging all throughout the plains," Velixar said, leaning down at the map and pointing. His finger traced a path around the King's Forest to the northwest, and a castle drawn against the edge of the Vile Wedge.

"That is the Green Castle, and Lord Sully rules there. He should be bearing the brunt of the attack by the orcs, who by now must be pouring across the Bone Ditch and into the Hillock."

"And there?" Thulos asked, pointing to the north-east. At the edge of the Helforn Forest was another castle, not far from the Crestwall Mountains that lined the eastern coast.

"Felwood," said Velixar. "Ruled by Lord Gandrem. Unless Lord Sully has already fallen, they might pose a threat. Their cavalry is much revered among the Neldaren people."

"It is a wonder they did not retake this city while Ulamn went on his merry chase," Thulos muttered. Velixar chuckled.

"We marched at the start of winter, and I'm sure the orcs have kept them on the defensive. Besides, who would believe such a tale, a city conquered by men with wings? If they are massing an army, it is because now they truly understand their danger."

Thulos nodded. He paced for a bit, then pointed to a different map, this one showing the lands south of Veldaren.

"And what of here?" he asked. "This...Angelport...what might we expect there?"

Angelport was far to the south-east, its lords ruling the area known as the Ramere, bordered between the Erze and Quellan Forests.

"The trip will put us many weeks off the path west," Velixar said.

Thulos raised an eyebrow. "I asked a question, and I expect an answer."

Karak's prophet chuckled.

"So be it. Angelport is full of sellswords and men with more blood than honor. Nearly every ship that sails along the coast is owned or captained by a man with some sort of allegiance to the lords there."

Thulos nodded and seemed pleased. He folded his wings about him and sat on the throne.

"With my portal closed, I cannot conquer as I would any other world," he said. "My demons are now valuable beyond measure, and every one I lose will never be replaced, not until Celestia is dead and my brothers freed. I need men, human soldiers to fight and bleed for me. If the Green Castle is busy fighting our orc allies, then leave them be. Felwood is our only true threat, so that is where we shall go. They will swear their swords to me, turning a danger into a boon. From there we will go to Angelport. Have every demon ransack Veldaren inch by inch before we leave. Those who will not bow for honor or glory will succumb to gold instead. Besides, from Angelport I can send several men west. You've insisted the nation of Ker is loyal to Karak. I want to see if that loyalty still holds true."

"I will relay your orders," Velixar said. After a moment's hesitance, he bowed. Thulos's eyes narrowed at the gesture.

"You are just one of my many soldiers," he said. "I do not need your worship, nor do I expect it. I am the same as your god, yet greater, more whole. You will come to see that in time."

"Perhaps," Velixar said. "Many things change, in time."

❖

Tessanna searched the castle for clothes, a singular focus taking over her mind. Her thin red outfit no longer served her purpose. She cast it aside and put on a plain brown dress, the cloth rough against her skin. Not caring if it matched, she found a shirt and put it over her shoulders. She would not bare her skin for taunting enticement. All her life, she had flaunted the curves of her hips, the swell of her breasts, and the long, shining exoticness of her hair. No more. She didn't need that power anymore. Even swords needed sheathed once in awhile, and her beauty was no different.

Thulos's army had remained disturbingly quiet during its occupation, but when the order came to march, they took to it with a shocking intensity. Angry voices shouted across the city, armor clanked and banged incessantly, and not a soldier remained idle. Into that chaos Tessanna stepped out, no longer the princess with the power of the goddess. She looked like a tired, strained woman, too much of the world on her shoulders. She tried not to admit it, but she was eager for Velixar to see her, to see his reaction. Much as it might burn her, she wanted to be dismissed, no longer desirable to him.

"So the butterfly returns to the cocoon?" Velixar asked.

Tessanna startled and took a step back toward the castle door, surprised by how close his voice was. At one time she would have sensed his presence, but her magic had faded, and she felt blind and unaware.

His hands grabbed her arms, and she winced at the pain. His grip was iron.

"Qurrah will be so disappointed to see you like this," he said, his eyes flaring wide.

"I don't care what he thinks," she said.

Velixar laughed, and the sound, so dismissive, so superior, tightened the muscles in her stomach.

"Is that so?" he asked. "Then who is this charade for?"

"I felt your anger," she said, trying to pull away. He grabbed harder, bruising her arm. She stopped her struggle. If she kept going, kept fighting, she knew what would happen.

"I know how much you hate me," she said, her voice quieter. "I felt that too."

"I have much to hate," Velixar said. He pressed his body against hers. So cold, she thought. He's so cold, yet on fire.

"Your lover abandoned us," the man in black continued. "Just as his brother did years before. The dark paladins, my friends, have lost most of their rank. You closed the portal I spent centuries plotting and killing to open, and now you turn me away, as if afraid."

"I am not afraid," she said.

"Yet you tremble."

He gestured to the war demons that hurried about, not paying the slightest attention to them.

"Right here," he said, pressing her tighter against him. "What would you do, Tessanna? How twisted is your desire? Forget intimacy or beauty. You had your chance for that last night. But what about your lust? What about your perversions?"

He pressed his cheek against hers, his lips brushing against her left ear. Now her whole body trembled.

"Struggle," he whispered.

She pulled against his hands, but they held tight, latching her against him. Her legs twisted, she pushed back, but it was all false, and Velixar knew it. He let go of one of her wrists, instead wrapping his hand around her throat, his fingers pressing against the sides of her neck so that she felt the pressure but did not suffer any difficulty in breathing. He wanted her to breath. He needed to know.

"Scream," he whispered.

She did. For him to leave. Him to get away.

The glow in his eyes deepened. He smiled.

"Get on your knees," he commanded.

She did.

By now the war demons had noticed this commotion, but conflicted between curiosity and their orders, they chose their orders. Through the corner of their eyes they watched as they packed provisions and hurried to and fro, but none said a word, and none would interfere.

Velixar reached around and one by one undid the braids of her hair. He released her other wrist, and with his free hand covered her mouth with his palm, an icy gag to prevent any more screams. He felt her exhalations from her nose against his skin. It was warm. Strong. He leaned down and pressed his forehead to hers.

"I know what it is you need," he said, his deep voice barely audible. "What you want. Qurrah's gone now, but you still need it. You want it. Control. Order. It is everything I am, you wretched little whore. Right here. Right now. In front of all of them."

Tessanna looked up at him, tears in her eyes. All her anger and resolve from the night before seemed to have belonged to a different person.

"Say it," he ordered.

"I will," she said.

"I know you will," Velixar said. Her tilted her head to one side and gently rubbed her cheek with his thumb. "Say my name."

"Please..."

"Say it, or take off your dress."

Her tears ran down her cheeks. When they touched his thumb, they filled with frost and stopped.

"Master."

He kissed her forehead.

"Never forget it," he said, and the words felt like a death sentence.

"I won't," she said, her whole body shivering. Clutching her arms, she glared at the man she knew she had every reason to hate.

And then knelt on one knee and asked what her master wished.

Qurrah moaned in his sleep, his arms thrashing about in a desperate attempt to wake himself, but the dream would not let him. It had a power to it, magical in its source. He was surrounded by shadow, and within he saw hungry and beautiful creatures. The sound that filled his ears was their famished wailing. Beneath his feet was barren rock, stretching out until it merged with the shadows to become nothingness.

Before him two red eyes peered out from the shadows, followed by a grin, followed by the rest of the ever-changing face. Velixar laughed, the laugh of the victorious.

"I have her now," he told Qurrah, who sat on his knees in a helpless stupor. "I have twisted her desires against her. I have turned her hate into love, for with you, the two emotions were always so closely intertwined."

"You lie," Qurrah heard himself say.

Again that maddening laugh.

"I have told you time and time again," Velixar said, his grin growing. "I never lie."

The dream ended, abrupt as it was horrible. The half-orc sat up in his tent, sweat covering his body. He wiped his face, and was not surprised to find tears there.

"The gods damn you, Velixar," he said, clutching his head in his hands. "Even the Abyss is too little, too late for your kind."

A fleeting idea of returning to Veldaren and hunting him down burned through his veins. In the end, he let it die. Suicide would not win Tessanna back, and more importantly, he wasn't sure if he even wanted her. Whatever she represented, it wasn't anything pure. But he didn't want her with Velixar, that much he knew.

No one deserved that fate.

Especially someone he loved.

"Damn it all to the Abyss," he said, leaning back and covering his eyes with his forearm. Someone he loved, he'd thought. So he still did. One question answered, a million more made anew. Questions that should have waited until the dawn, but he knew would keep him awake, gnawing like tiny insects within his brain.

Damn it all, indeed.

They marched out, Tessanna at Velixar's side, looking like his beautiful bride in a silver dress and with thin strands of gold decorating her hair. She didn't feel like a princess. All around them shuffled rows and rows of undead. Among their ranks were many angels and demons, their golden skin pale and dead, their wings limp and featherless. She tried her best not to look at them.

High above, Thulos's troops flew in perfect triangular formations. In their center, tied by twenty ropes and carried by the demons, hung the throne of Veldaren. Like a conquering king, Thulos sat on its cushions and looked out across the land that was his.

They traveled until nightfall. The two might have shared a tent, but the cold of night meant nothing to Velixar, nor did sleep. He left her huddled under several blankets, seeking prayer with his dark god. When he left, Tessanna finally allowed herself to think freely.

She'd been terrified he would try to take her, although she was not sure how that would work, or if it could. She remembered that moment in the tower, and decided she did not want to know. She wrapped her blankets tighter and thought of Qurrah. She had called him master before, but she'd known he loved her, would do anything for her. In caring hands such as those, she could freely offer her body and soul, and do all that those loving hands demanded. But Velixar?

She shivered. He would have taken her, then and there, while Thulos's army watched. There was a time she might have been able to resist, but stripped of her power, she felt helpless, worthless, a pathetic girl sobbing in a dark tent. The lunacy in Velixar's eyes terrified her. Normally he was detached from his emotions, a calm puppet-master moving the strings as he desired. No longer. The world was ending, and his safeguards were crumbling. The man wanted victory, and all its fruits.

"I'm sorry, Qurrah," she whispered. Part of her cried out in pain against such an apology, declaring him undeserving. She ignored it. She didn't need that hurt anymore. At first, she had planned to go along with Velixar's game. It certainly wouldn't have been the first time she'd played along with a man who thought himself tougher, stronger. But no, this was different. Every shred of her soul had shrieked against those eyes as they had stared into her, ordering her to kneel. Yet she had anyway.

"What's happening to me, Qurrah?" she asked, feeling comforted by his imagined presence. That presence she could talk to, be herself without fear. Just like it had been when they were together. Before Aullienna. Before Velixar. Before Karak had smashed his fist into their lives and destroyed everything.

Aullienna. And her stillborn daughter, Teralyn. Gone. Gone.

Her rage exploded. She felt nothing but loathing and contempt for the miserable sack of bones. Velixar had killed those she loved, and never could she forget the blasphemy that had stirred within the small buried bag. Teralyn, brought back in a horrid state of undeath, the pathetic offering of a death god incapable of creating life.

She stared at the tent flap, pretending Qurrah sat on the other side, listening. In fact, she could almost see his shadow, his form hunched with his chin resting on his knuckles, hanging on every word.

"Your sorrow was as great as my rage," she whispered, her entire body shaking. "Wasn't it, my love?"

The shadow paused, then slowly nodded. Tears ran down her face.

"I understand," she said, clutching the blankets to her chest and burying her face. Even his pale shadow was suddenly too much. She drowned her sobs with her pillows as fleeting touches of Qurrah washed over her. His guilt. His shame. His sorrow. They had crushed him, and she had never known. She had always offered herself and expected it to be enough. But what was she to Teralyn? What was she to the years he spent with his brother? She was but a tourniquet halting the bleeding. She was no healing salve.

She looked back up at the shadow, saw its own hunched form convulsing with sobs.

"What was it they offered you?" she asked. "What was it your brother gave you that I could not?"

She didn't know, but she wanted to. So desperately she wanted to know what had saved her beloved Qurrah, for broken, alone, and miserable, she would gladly take the tiniest sliver of that same redemption.

The shadow stood. Its hand reached out, pushing against the tent flap. She crawled nearer on her hands and knees. Gently, she put her hand against the tent. It was cold and rough, but for the briefest moment, she sensed warmth. The shadow vanished. Exhausted, she returned to her blankets and wrapped herself within them, but before she did, she yanked the gold lace from her hair and tossed it to the ground. With that small bit of peace, she closed her eyes and slept.

Hundreds of miles away, Qurrah knelt inside his tent, his hand pressed against the flap. Tears soaked his face and neck.

"Tessanna," he whispered.

5

It seemed bizarre to him, but the night was no longer safe for Deathmask. Back in the chaotic city of Veldaren, he had been a master among assassins, feared for his ability to outwit, out-stealth, and outfight any challengers to his guild's revered position. But in Karak's newly conquered city of Mordeina, it was the daylight he wrapped himself in.

Veliana sat beside him as the two peered out the small second story window. Her short red hair fell past her face, hiding the long scar that had taken her right eye. The home's occupants lay unconscious on the far side of the room, no worse for wear other than the large bumps growing on the back of their heads.

"Karak's dogs will catch on eventually," Veliana said, twirling a dagger in her hand, her dexterous fingers handling it with ease. "And even if they don't, we're shaving a cow with a cat claw."

Deathmask pulled a gray cloth over his face and tied a stiff knot behind his head. The only features remaining visible were his mismatched eyes, one black, one red, and his long dark hair falling far past his shoulders. They both wore dark gray cloaks, once a symbol for their guild. But that was then, before the fall of Veldaren, before Karak's conquering of Mordeina. Now they had each other, and no one else.

"We have to do something," Deathmask said, dipping his hand into a small pouch tied at his waist. "There is no life for us here. No work. No honor. Let us die repaying those that took away everything."

He scooped out a tiny bit of ash and sprinkled it over his face. The magic of the mask took hold, grabbing the ash and spreading it out like a hazy shield. He was a phantom, an ill omen, and he would have the priests and paladins of Karak fear his visage before they died.

"They travel in larger groups with each passing day," Deathmask said as he resealed the pouch. "If we kill enough priests, their patrols will weaken. Perhaps then we can stir the revolt that is aching to erupt."

"They always have the ," Veliana said. She nodded toward a group of seven men marching down the street. They wore the official armor of the Mordan guard, but instead of polished gold breastplates and red tunics, they wore the white skull of a lion over their gray steel. Within days of capture, all the armor pieces had been painstakingly stripped of their golden sheen, dulling them down, removing all traces of former glory and leadership.

Now there was only Melorak, puppet of the dark god.

"The Lionsguard were recruited from Mordeina," Deathmask insisted. "Once they realize no one holds their chains, they should break free."

"Are you so sure?" Veliana asked, glancing at him with a mischievous smile on her face.

"Mostly," Deathmask said, grinning back.

"Leave one alive for me then," she said, drawing her other dagger. "We'll see just how fanatical their faith is."

The streets still bustled with plenty of activity. It was that general chaos they needed to carry out their attacks. They waited until they saw a patrol marching through the center of the street, four Lionsguard and two priests of Karak.

"Take out the guards," Deathmask said, rubbing his hands together. "The priests are mine."

"Do it fast," Veliana said. She watched the patrol's approach, counted to five, then leapt into the air, a dagger in each hand. A man and his wife spotted her attack, but instead of calling warning they shouted curses to the patrol. Veliana grinned as she fell, thankful for the added distraction. Their heads turned toward the shouting couple, they were unprepared for the vicious woman that fell atop them, her daggers stabbing and her feet kicking. She slashed open one guard's throat, spun about, and buried her blades into the back of the second.

Before the priests could cast a spell, twin projectiles of fire flew from the window, each the size of a fist. They struck the priests and exploded, bathing their bodies in black flame. Their pain-filled screams filled the street. The two remaining guards swung with their swords, but they were poorly trained, no challenge for Veliana's masterful daggerwork. She kept shifting, keeping one guard in front of the other so they could not work as a team. When the first thrust with his sword, she slipped aside, smacked the blade away with her dagger, and then rushed in. Her whole body slammed against the guard. Tip after tip of her dagger thrust through the creases in his armor. Blood poured from his neck, shoulders, and arms as he collapsed, his life bleeding out upon the ground.

She expected the last guard to flee, or call for help. Instead he rushed on, seemingly not caring if he died. Veliana felt her stomach knot as she danced about and kicked the back of his knees. As he tumbled down, another bolt of fire flew from the window. It burst around the guard's breastplate, charring flesh but not killing. Veliana rolled him over, stabbed her dagger deep into his shoulder, and then thrust her face to within inches of his.

"Whom do you serve?" she asked.

"I serve the lion," he said. Blood stained his teeth, and his voice was strained.

"What of your people?" she asked, trusting Deathmask to warn her if reinforcements arrived.

"My people?" the Lionsguard asked. "Karak's…followers. Those are my people."

The girl's stomach tightened. Not the faintest hint of a lie in those eyes. Religious fanaticism had taken over. There was no man left in that armor. She sliced his throat and left him to die. Standing up, she noticed over a hundred people had gathered around, watching their brutal, efficient work. She tried to read them, but was unsure. Too many looks of fear, worry, and sorrow.

She ran to the other side of the street, away from Deathmask, and catapulted herself up to the rooftops. Soldiers were finally arriving, their weapons drawn and waving uselessly about the air. As she ran, the people shouted at them, and her lips curled into a smile at what she heard.

"The Ghost will get you," they shouted. "Him and his Blade!"

So she was the Blade? That was a good nickname. She could settle for that.

Running her zigzag pattern, she went from roof to street to roof, to where 'the Ghost' waited.

⚜

The discussion soured quickly, for each had reached the same conclusion.

"The Lionsguard are so fanatical they might as well be hypnotized," Veliana said, yanking off her boots. She let out a little moan as she dipped her feet into a small kettle filled with water. With a brush of his fingers, Deathmask warmed the water and made it bubble.

"Such a meager use for my amazing talents," he said, removing the cloth from his face and tucking it into a pocket of his robe.

"There could be no greater use for your talents than making me happy," she said, her eyes closed. Glancing over her thin body with its tight, catlike muscles, Deathmask chuckled.

"Perhaps you're right," he said.

"About what?" she asked, opening her good eye.

"The Lionsguard," Deathmask said. "What else? But I watched that last guard attack you, even though all others were dead. Not the slightest hesitation. Hypnotization may not be far from the truth. Even trained soldiers will hesitate when they know their death is at hand."

"What about a spell?" Veliana asked, closing her eye and settling deeper into her chair. They were inside what had become their home, a modest but well furnished abode that had most likely belonged to a general, or similarly high ranking soldier of Mordeina's army. To their knowledge, that army was still heading east, joined with troops of Neldar to try and retake Veldaren and close the portal through which hundreds of war demons had flooded into Dezrel.

"A spell?" Deathmask asked. "As in, a spell forcing them to worship Karak and serve as a perfect, obedient soldier? Seems a little much. Any time a city is conquered, there are always hundreds of rats willing to show up and grab a slice of power in the newly established order."

"Rats run when faced with death," Veliana said. "Something else is going on here. If we're to have any hope of freeing this city, Melorak needs to die. You know that."

The man groaned and rubbed his eyes with his fingers.

"Yes," he said. "I know. But you've seen him fight, as have I. He sent Dieredon running like a little girl, and he killed Haern the Watcher as if he were an ant. And don't forget, he beat the two of us back with a single spell."

"Then we don't fight him," she said. "Not fair. That's not us. But he sleeps. He eats. He breathes."

"Not according to his followers," Deathmask muttered.

"He's human," Veliana said, her voice growing hard. "And if he's human, he can be killed. We've always boasted we can kill any man alive. Are you ready to take that back now?"

Deathmask walked over to the window. It was dark now. The streets were empty but for the hundreds of patrols. Every day they killed members of the Lionsguard, as well as priests and the occasional dark paladin. Every night, it seemed twice that number joined the patrols. They were recruiting from the populace like mad, and not just soldiers. Priests as well. Paladins, too.

"Let's say you're right," Deathmask said, turning to face her. "Now what?"

"We learn," Veliana said, removing her belt and untucking her shirt. "We watch, we learn, and we wait. All men have weaknesses. We find his, and we use it."

"So do you have an idea on how to do that?" Deathmask asked, enjoying the sight of her as she stretched.

"Now that you ask," the girl said, smiling. "Yes, I do."

"This is insane," Deathmask muttered, feeling naked without his gray cloth over his face. Nor did he have the hovering ash that inspired fear and dread in all who faced him. Instead he wore simple clothing of drab colors, the knees of his pants torn loose and the entire outfit intended for a much bigger man.

"Too late to turn back now," Veliana said beside him.

The two were near the bottom of the large hill the castle was built upon. They walked with their arms linked, their shoulders hunched and their steps staggered as if each were relying on the other for balance.

"It is not too late," Deathmask insisted. "No guards have spotted us, so don't lie to keep me from thinking rationally."

Veliana giggled, much louder than he anticipated or preferred. Her entire face and hair were covered with dirt. It was their best attempt to hide the long scar across her eye that might mark her as the vigilante Blade. She waved an arm wide, and sang a bad lyric about a peasant girl and a ruffian burglar who came upon her bathing. They had purposefully avoided patrols on their way to the many steps leading up to the castle, but no longer.

"Now it's too late," she giggled as guards approached. Deathmask counted twenty together in the pack and felt proud in knowing that he, 'the Ghost', was the main reason they travelled in such large numbers.

"Hey," Deathmask said, slurring his words and tugging Veliana forward. "Hey you guys!"

The patrol surrounded them, the Lionsguard swarming with weapons drawn. Three priests were with them, watching the events from a few paces back.

"What is your business being out this late at night?" one of the priests asked.

"We want to join," Veliana said, pointing a finger at one of the Lionsguard with a hand that just happened to contain a rather large and empty bottle. The guard yanked away the bottle, ignoring her whimper.

"Drunkards," the priest said after a quick sniff of the bottle. "You should be well aware this is illegal."

"Well, yeah," Deathmask said. He let his eyes focus and unfocus on the priest, but kept his smile locked tight. "See, we thought if we were you, then it would be legal, you know?"

"We want to join!" Veliana said again, rubbing her fingers across a guard's arm. "Be fun, right? Good money?"

She let her fingers slide from the guard's armor to her own chest and then giggled naughtily at the look he gave her.

"Fun?" he asked.

"Arrest them," the priest said. "No need to let such riffraff disturb our streets. A few days in a cell will teach them Karak's opinion on such distasteful displays."

Deathmask tensed while Veliana continued to flirt with the guard, completely oblivious to what the priest was saying. She sucked on one finger while hugging herself with her other arm. When the guards grabbed her, only then did she seem to react.

"Wait," she said. "What did we do wrong?"

A mailed fist struck the back of her head, and down she went. Deathmask shouted curses freely as two men held his arms. Another fist struck him, but it took two more times before he slumped, a limp sack of bone and muscle, ready for delivery to the castle prison.

When Deathmask came to, he opened his eyes, looked left, looked right, and then very calmly said, "Fuck."

Veliana was gone, which was already a deviation from their original plan. The two had expected to be placed together in a holding cell of some sort, where they could be kept under control while the imaginary alcohol in their system cleared out. The second problem, and the one that elicited the crude response, was that he was not in a cell at all. He was chained to a wall at the very entrance to the prison, in clear view of over eight guards. To his right were the barred double-doors leading up to the castle grounds. Across from him, tables of guards played cards and rolled dice. Along the wall behind them, rows and rows of clubs.

"I hear you," came a voice to his left. Deathmask looked over to see an elderly man with graying hair and half his original teeth, his arms chained to the wall above his head. When he talked, his voice grumbled and cracked. "You think, just one drink, right? Just one, and then you wake up in here, and the question, you see, the question is, is your splitting skull from the drink or from where those damn guards smacked you?"

"Yeah," Deathmask said. "Something like that."

"Name's Dunk," the man said while Deathmask shifted and checked his shackles. Thick iron, and painfully tight. His wrists were crossed above his head, the chains hooked into the low ceiling. He sat on his knees, and when he tried to stand, he found another set of shackles holding him immobile.

"Don't bother struggling," Dunk said. "Not even a bit of chain on your feet, just locks attached to the wall. You'll get used to it."

"Dunk?" Deathmask said, feeling his patience waning thin.

"Dunk the Drunk," the old man said, and he giggled as if it were the funniest thing in the world.

"Well then, Dunk," Deathmask said, his voice turning icy cold. "Shut…up…now."

"Shut it," said the man chained to Deathmask's right. "Your jabbering's worse than the chains."

There were five of them attached to the wall, and the other two chimed in their displeasure at Dunk's talking.

"You'll learn to appreciate me," Dunk said. "I don't recognize a one of you. Just wait. Third, fourth time you get tossed here, you'll love to see a friendly face. Wish I was seeing one now."

Deathmask smacked his head repeatedly against the stone wall behind him. They were bathed in dim light. Most of the torches in the windowless room were hanging beside the doors, with a few more surrounding the tables where the guards killed their time. One glanced back, distracted by all the chatter.

"Shut up, all of you," the guard said, rubbing his bent nose, "or I'll take a club and wail until my arms get tired."

"He's serious about that too," Dunk said.

"Quiet!"

Dunk laughed as the guard stood, reaching for a club, but the old man said no more, and for that, Deathmask was eternally grateful. He decided when they made their escape, he would do his best to spare that guard's life.

The thought of escape brought him back to the matter at hand. So far, he wasn't being closely watched, and that was good. What was bad, though, was how restricted his hands and feet were. He twisted his wrists, testing their give. Very, very little. One by one he listed off the spells he could cast with such a limited motion. They were not many, and even worse, there was still the matter of the guards less than ten feet away. If he started whispering verbal components to a spell, all it would take was one to know what they were and mash a fist into his mouth to end all possibility of escape.

That left Veliana. He looked about, realizing that of the five chained by the entrance, all were men.

"Where do they put women who are brought in drunk?" Deathmask asked. The others ignored him, but Dunk just smiled. Deathmask asked a second time, and as the guards glared over, Dunk just winked and made kissing motions with his lips.

"Damn it," Deathmask muttered. "Fine, Dunk, I'm sorry. Now, please, can you tell me?"

In answer, Dunk looked left and nodded his head toward a second set of stairs leading further into the prison.

"In chains like this?" Deathmask asked.

Dunk shook his head.

"Then like what?"

The old man shrugged his shoulders.

A roar rose from the tables as two men tossed down a week's wages, each convinced of victory over the other. Deathmask used that chance to cast a simple spell. A flicker of fire shot from his fingers, just enough for him to get a better glimpse at the chains around his wrists.

Dunk's eyes grew real big at the sight of the fire.

Another roar, coupled with laughter. The two guards had thrown down their cards, only to discover they each held the exact same hand. Deathmask tried a trickier spell, hoping he could manage the intricate movements of his fingers. Shadows curled down from the ceiling, swirling into his fingers and then pulsing into his veins.

"Dunk," he said. "Can you lean toward me?"

"What for, devil man?" Dunk asked.

"Just do it," Deathmask hissed. The rest of the guards were laughing and clapping the men on the back, congratulating both for the guts to bet such an amount, while both sighed with relief at knowing that, though they had not won, they had not lost. It wouldn't be long before the hubbub died and their attention refocused.

Shifting his wiry frame over, his shoulder leading, Dunk tilted his head as close as possible. Deathmask imitated the motion, and for the briefest moment their foreheads touched. Just a slight bump, but it was enough to pour all the dark energy out of Deathmask and into Dunk. The old man's body turned incorporeal, his muscle and bone replaced with shadow and magic. Dunk slipped from the bonds and laughed long and loud.

"I'm a ghost!" he shouted with glee. At this, the guards turned and saw the bizarre sight. They cried out in alarm, and several lunged for their weapons. Dunk wasted no time. He bolted straight for, and then through, the double-doors, vanishing into the castle.

"After him," they cried. In the confusion, Deathmask twiddled his fingers, wincing each time the sharp metal cut into his wrists. His own body turned translucent, and during that brief moment he fell forward, freeing himself from his chains. Still unnoticed, he stood, fire bursting from his palms. Half the guards had already unlocked the doors and hurried out. The nearest of the remaining four screamed as his body was engulfed in flame. The ash of his corpse floated through the air, settling into a faint cloud swirling around Deathmask's head.

"It's the Ghost!" screamed a guard, flinging his club and turning to flee. Deathmask brought him down with a word. Blood poured out of his ears, mouth, and eyes. The club struck by Deathmask's feet, doing no harm. Behind him, the remaining men chained to the wall gaped in terror. Magic flared in the small dark room, slashing the final guards to pieces with shadow blades. When the chained men continued to howl, Deathmask whirled upon them and pointed a finger.

"Quiet, or die," he said. Two obeyed. A third did not. Deathmask shot a single bolt of dark magic through his throat. The man quieted. Shaking his head, Deathmask rushed deeper into the prison. Halfway down the stairs he met a guard rushing up to investigate the confusion. Deathmask put a hand upon his throat and whispered two words of power. The guard collapsed, his throat constricted and unable to open for breath.

At the bottom of the steps was another door. As he reached for the handle he cried out in alarm. The door swung out, cracking him across the shoulder. He collapsed to the ground, muttering and promising death. Instead, a feminine hand reached down to help him up.

"I had to kill seven," Veliana said, pulling him to his feet. "What took you so long?"

"They chained me to a wall," Deathmask said. "You?"

"Holding cell with two other women. Nice gals."

The two rushed back up the steps, stepped over the dead bodies, and approached the double-doors to the jail. Against the wall, the remaining two prisoners closed their eyes and bit their tongues to hold in their sobs.

"Guards?" Veliana whispered, gesturing to the doors.

Deathmask nodded.

On the count of three, Veliana slammed them open. The two guards posted with their backs to them could only yelp in surprise before she slammed a club across their faces, shattering cartilage and splattering blood across the floor. Frowning at the club, Veliana dropped it and took the shortswords from the unconscious guards. She twirled them in her hands and whispered a word of magic. A soft purple glow surrounded the blades, strengthening them.

"We'll be near the soldiers' quarters," Deathmask said. "Where do you figure this Melorak will be?"

"The throne room," Veliana said, glancing up and down the hallway they had entered.

"I figured he would be with his priests," Deathmask said as he followed her.

"No," Veliana said, stopping at another intersection. They had been to the castle only a couple of times before, but that was enough for Veliana to have memorized the bulk of the corridors and winding passageways. So far, no sign of guards, and in that they were lucky, for Dunk had led most of them on a wild goose chase through walls and out into the streets of Mordeina.

Dead of night, three hours before dawn, and as they had hoped most of the castle was asleep. Veliana had been adamant: if there was any time to strike, it was at night.

"It doesn't matter how powerful he is," Veliana had argued during the creation of their plan. "All men are the same when they sleep."

The castle was incredibly well guarded on the outside, but within, other than the dozen at the entrance to the jail, it was unnaturally empty. Before, there might have been servants and nobles and all the miscellaneous characters of courtly life. Instead, there was silence. Melorak had executed everyone with the slightest hint of nobility. As for the servants, the cooks, the ladies-in-waiting, well…

Deathmask did his best to ignore the rotting corpses hanging from hooks hammered into the wall. For some reason they didn't smell, and he felt his fingers tingle with the proximity of magic. Not right, he thought. Not right at all.

"So we're here," Deathmask said, gesturing to the expansive and empty throne room. "Why are we here again?"

"Quiet," Veliana said, glaring at him with her lone eye. She pointed to a door at the far right of the throne. "In there," she said. "That will lead to several rooms for servants, and then the king's quarters."

Deathmask chuckled at the word 'king.' So far Melorak had been adamant no one call him a king, to the point of issuing an edict threatening pain of death to those who dared say it. He was a priest, a prophet, but not a king. It made no sense at all to Deathmask, but it did reinforce to him that whoever this man was, he couldn't possibly be sane.

"There will be a secret passageway out of the room," Veliana said. "So we have to strike fast to prevent him from fleeing."

"I don't think fleeing is something this guy does," Deathmask said. Still, he did his best to open the door quietly. In the days of old, several guards would have stood at attention through all hours of the day to ensure the safety of king and queen's possessions, so that no would-be assassin poisoned clothes or slipped snakes into the bed sheets. Now, though, it appeared Melorak feared nothing. No guards, not for him. Just the streets, and the exterior of the castle.

They crept down the hallway, silent as ghosts. They passed by two small doors, most likely servants' quarters, and then small windows opened up along the wall, revealing glimpses of the bedroom. Paintings lined the walls, and long curtains trailed from the ceiling before looping back upward. In the center was the gilded bed, and through the thin curtains both assassins could clearly see a sleeping form.

See, he sleeps, Deathmask said through quick motions of his fingers in an intricate language thieves had developed over a hundred years.

Silent, Veliana signaled back. *No pause. You right. Me left.*

At the end of the hall was the door into the bedroom. Deathmask grabbed the latch with his left hand and cast a spell with his other. When he lifted the latch, it made not a sound. He touched the hinges and again cast the spell. The door swung open without the slightest creak. In perfect unison the two stepped into the room. Their footfalls were softer and quieter than a gentle snowfall. Their clothes did not rustle. No light glinted off their possessions. A shadow of death, the both of them.

And it didn't matter.

Halfway to the bed, they stopped as the ceiling erupted in a cacophony of wails and shrieks. Veliana's eyes glanced up. Her hands shook, and her heart skipped. Hidden by the many curtains and hanging by thick nails and hooks were twenty corpses, every one animated by Melorak's dark magic. Their eyelids were peeled and gone. The corpses saw the assassins' entrance, and did exactly as they had been commanded to do: scream.

"Damn it," Veliana shouted, her strong legs propelling her forward. Deathmask trailed after, a spell on his lips. They still had a chance, if they could catch Melorak in the confusion. Deathmask's spell burst the curtains around the bed into flame, and through their dissipating ash Veliana leapt, her shortswords thrusting downward.

But for Melorak, there was no difference between dream and wake, for in both he dwelt in the darkness of Karak's embrace. A cocoon of shadows swirled from underneath the bed, entombing his body. Veliana's swords sparked at contact with it, and then the metal shattered. She screamed, the shards shooting back in all directions. Blood ran down her face and arms.

"Get out!" Deathmask shouted. He flung a bolt of magic, and in the brief flash of its travel a thin purple tail trailed after it like a comet. It splashed against the shadow barrier like water on stone. As Veliana retreated, clutching her face, the two felt icy shudders travel up and down their spines, for amid the din of undead shrieks they heard joyful laughter.

Melorak emerged from the cocoon with a smile on his face.

"The Ghost and his Blade," he said, his smile growing. "How I've ached to meet you."

His face was plain, his hair neat and trimmed. His teeth glimmered white compared to his dark skin and deep brown hair. If his face was plain, his eyes, however, were not. One shone a deep red, as if it were a window into the fiery abyss. The other was a milky white, victim to Mordeina's dying queen in a last act of vengeance against the man who had destroyed her kingdom.

"We've met," Deathmask said. His whole body straightened. "Bye now."

He clapped. Power rushed forth, and before Melorak could react, a wall of fire cut the room in half, separating him from the assassins. Hand in hand, they fled.

"Find them, my children!" Melorak shouted, and his voice carried throughout the entire castle on magical wings. He waved his hands, whispering a prayer to Karak. The fire died. Still smiling, Melorak threw on his black priestly robes. He would make an example of the two assassins, and he intended it to be very long, and very public. He needed to be ready, for he had no doubt that they would be captured within the hour.

❖

They had reached the throne room by the time Melorak's command rolled through the castle. At first they feared guards, but when they turned a corner, a hand reached out, fingers entangling Veliana's hair. She did not scream, only twist and kick. Her kick did nothing but sink into the rotten flesh of the corpse attached to the walls. It screamed and moaned, still reaching.

"Go back to death you mongrel," Deathmask said, shoving his fingers into the thing's eyes. His magic poured in, releasing it from its spell. Flesh peeled, and innards plopped to the floor in a soupy mess. Veliana broke two of its fingers off getting the rest of her hair free, then threw the pieces of bone to the floor. On the other side of the hallway, another corpse waved its arms uselessly and shouted again and again in a mindless roar.

"The guards—" Veliana said. She didn't need to finish, for Deathmask clearly understood as well. They fled down the hall, and with each turn, each step, their passage was tracked by the myriad of corpses shouting out their location. Calls of alarm from actual living guards soon joined their tail.

Deathmask followed Veliana with perfect trust. He slammed his fists to the ground at the first patrol they found, unleashing his fury into the stone. The floor cracked, and then spikes tore from ground to ceiling blocking them off. Veliana didn't say a word at their sudden change in direction, only sprinting the other way, bobbing and weaving as necessary to avoid the undead arms and legs. They passed a flight of stairs, and almost as if it were an after-thought, the woman turned back and sprinted up them, Deathmask quickly after.

"Height is our friend now," she said.

They travelled upward, into what appeared to be a tall defensive tower. They passed a few unused bunks for soldiers, along with many windows facing the steps leading up to the castle. Veliana peered through them, pondering.

"Time is *not* our friend," Deathmask said.

"No use going further up," Veliana said. "I hoped to avoid those damn undead, but there are no connecting bridges, no ladders, and no pathways. This is a dead end."

"Then down we go," Deathmask said.

As if in answer, they heard guards shouting, followed by the clanking of armor rushing up steps. Veliana kissed her palms with trembling lips. Purple fire engulfed them, making her deadly hands that much deadlier. Deathmask shook his head, realizing her aim.

"No last stands," he said. "Not for us, not ever. We kill, or we flee. There is no in-between."

"Then let's kill," she said. "For where else do we flee?"

"Come," he said, grabbing her hand without harm. "We climb higher."

Up the stairs they went. The rooms grew narrower, the furnishings more and more sparse. At last they were at the top, and Veliana held her breath at the view. There were windows on all sides, and barely enough room for the two of them to stand. She could see for miles in all directions. It felt like the entire tower shifted and swayed with the wind, and she clutched Deathmask for a moment as her fear got the best of her. At his smirk, though, she let go.

"Here is a much better place to kill," he said.

They stood on either side of the stairs. The first guard to emerge from below died before his head was level with the floor. The second died before he knew the first was dead. The third died when the bodies of the first two exploded in shrapnel of bone and metal. The fourth waited for more guards.

Deathmask rushed from window to window while Veliana hovered over the stairs, her clenched fists eager to deal more death.

"Veliana!" he shouted. "How scared of heights are you?"

"More than of dying," she shouted back. A cluster of undead had climbed up the stairs, and she repeatedly punched and kicked to topple them back.

"Is that your preference of those two options?"

Veliana glared at him.

"What have you got in mind, fool?"

Deathmask laughed, and without giving her any warning, he grabbed her hand and leapt out the window. So deep was her trust, so ingrained her discipline to follow her guild leader, she did not even hesitate. Out the window she jumped, still hand in hand with the laughing Deathmask.

Dark paladins were the next to arrive, and with flabbergasted looks they glanced around and wondered where the two could have possibly gone.

When they landed, and Deathmask let her go, Veliana promptly turned around and slapped him.

"Don't you ever do that again," she said.

Deathmask grinned. A large pair of bat-like wings stretched from his back to either side of the houses they were hidden between.

"You don't like heights?" he asked.

"I've never seen you use that spell before," she said, nodding to the wings.

"I never have," he said, knowing what she was doing but going along anyway. "Normally the spell creates a pair of arms with claws to help with climbing. I made a tiny change and hoped for the best. And, as you see, we're still alive."

She slapped him again.

"Never risk my life on such a wild guess again," she said.

"It was my life too, you know," he said, stalking after. But she would hear none of it.

6

Mira stood before the dead bush, watching it as it burned. Her hands slowly danced, her fingertips glowing with magic. With every twitch the fire shrank or grew, as if it were nothing more than a manifestation of the girl's smoldering emotions. Sadness crossed her face, and the fire shrunk, dwindled, becoming nothing but a faint hint of heat and light burning dull in the dim light of the stars.

"You all right?" a voice asked. Mira glanced back to see Lathaar approaching, his arms crossed as if he were cold.

"I'm fine," Mira said, looking away. She closed her eyes, and with every step closer the paladin came, the fire grew deeper.

"You've been quiet lately," Lathaar said, standing beside her. His arm wrapped around her waist. With a sigh, she closed her eyes and leaned against him.

"Something's happened," she said. "I'm not sure what it means."

"Something?" he asked. "That's a little vague. What's bothering you?"

Mira gently pushed him away, then lifted her arms to the sky. A soft sigh escaped her lips.

"My mirror," she said. "What happened to my mirror?"

The fire roared to life, higher and higher. It shot into the sky, a pillar of flame stretching to the heavens. Lathaar gaped at the sight, and without realizing it he stepped back as if afraid of the girl controlling the tremendous power. Then, with agonizing slowness, the fire lessened.

"Do you see?" Mira asked, her eyes closed and her head tilted back. The light washed over her in the gloomy night. "This is everything. My power used to ache within me, begging to be released. Now, the elements almost laugh at me, granting me their use for only a little while. My mirror...What happened to my mirror? Has Celestia abandoned us both? Am I to be punished for her actions? Or maybe this is my fault. I should be dead, Lathaar, dead and gone and with all of Dezrel better for it."

Lathaar's heart pained at hearing her words. He stepped closer and wrapped his arms around her shoulders, ashamed for having feared her presence, if only for a little while.

"You are as powerful as you are beautiful," he told her. "Never say such a thing. I need you here with me. I need to remember why this world is so precious, so valuable. Why we fight."

She turned from the fire and buried her face in his chest. His armor was cold. This angered her for some reason.

"Will you want me to fight with you tomorrow?" she asked.

Lathaar nodded.

"At my side. We know the demons overran Kinamn when they chased us west. How many still guard it, we don't know. If we're to have any hope of rest, we need to retake the castle. Within should be some supplies, and more so, we won't have to worry about them harrying us as we flee west."

"If we flee west," Mira said. "Many wish to stop and fight. Our numbers will grow no larger."

"That's not true," Lathaar insisted. "We have but a fraction of Mordan's troops, and our contact with Ker is limited. Antonil is their king, and both will muster forces so great in number even Thulos will fear our might."

Mira laughed.

"He'll fear nothing," she said, kissing his chin. "Not us. Not our power. We're playing his game, and as long as it is by his rules, we will lose."

The two fell silent. The bush burned away to ash, its heat vanishing, its light gone.

"Let's go to bed," he told her. "Tomorrow will be a bloody day."

"You go," she said. "I'll be with you soon. I wish a moment alone."

He kissed her forehead, then gave in to her request. Once he was gone, she looked to the stars, a prayer to Celestia on her lips.

"Tell me what is right," she whispered. "Tell me I have done no wrong. Tell me you love me, mother. Please. That's all I ask."

She went to Lathaar, having heard only silence.

❖

Harruq stood beside Antonil, the two surveying the city in the distance from their spot atop a gentle hill.

"So you want me, Tarlak and the others to go crashing in, kill a bunch of demons, and basically distract them while the angels open the gates?" he asked.

"That's the plan, yeah," Antonil said. "Ahaesarus seemed to think it was workable."

"Uh huh." Harruq scratched his chin. "Care to answer me a question? Whose banner is that flying above the towers?"

Antonil squinted, his vision nowhere as excellent as the half-orc's.

"I can't tell. What's it look like?"

Harruq frowned.

"Let me see…looks like a giant axe with a bloody handle."

"That's the White's family banner," said Antonil. "They've been flying that one for years."

"So not the demons." Harruq pointed. "So why is it up there above the city?"

This time it was Antonil's turn to frown.

"You know, that's a very good question."

Behind them stretched the remains of Mordan's army, preparing weapons and gathering into formations under Sergan's sharp commands. The angels circled above, also preparing. Only one angel, Ahaesarus judging by his size, remained earthbound, talking with Tarlak at the outskirts of the human camps. Antonil put his fingers in his mouth and whistled until the wizard finally looked over.

"What?" Tarlak asked as he approached, adjusting his hat on his head. Ahaesarus followed, curious.

"I need you or one of Ahaesarus's angels to fly over and survey the castle," Antonil said. "Either that, or you open a portal and sneak in to look around, Tarlak."

"I can send one of my scouts," Ahaesarus said.

"An excellent idea," said Tarlak. "As are all ideas that won't get me needlessly killed."

"You work for me, remember," Antonil said.

Tarlak winked.

"Still waiting on my pay."

They waited as Ahaesarus took to the air, called over one of his angels, and sent him toward the castle.

"So what's going on, anyway?" Tarlak asked as they watched.

"Something's strange here," Harruq said. "Just keep your fingers crossed."

"Toes, too," said Antonil. "I'd love to escape this morning without a battle."

A few minutes later the angel returned, a smile on his face.

"My lords," he said as he landed with a great rush of air and rustle of feathers. "I have a wonderful surprise for you."

⋈⊕⋈

The troops marched toward the gate, the men singing songs and cheering. The men on the walls cheered back in return, and sang their songs all the louder as the angels neared. Antonil led the way, Ahaesarus at his side. The Eschaton hung back, preferring to let the king handle the first introductions.

"You were the one here last," Harruq asked Tarlak. "What's going on?"

"Their king was dead," the wizard said as they walked, raising his voice to be heard over the throng. "Some lord named Penwick went to great pains to hide that fact, because the various other lords were going to tear themselves to pieces vying for the throne. When we left, Penwick was still in charge. I can't imagine he fared too well when the demons came flying in."

"Then who's this White guy?" asked Harruq. "Where'd all these troops come from?"

"That," said Tarlak, "is something I'm assuming we'll find out very soon."

Aurelia slipped her hand into Harruq's.

"I guess this is one of those times where you'll tell me to behave?" the half-orc asked.

Aurelia kissed his cheek.

"You're learning."

They passed through the gates to fanfare and cheers. Many troops lined the walls, but despite their numbers, there was no hiding the city's decimated state. No merchants filled the rows of broken stalls. No men wandered the streets to their smithies and bakeries. The walls guarded a ghost town, and that silence seemed to fight against the cheers of the defending soldiers.

An honor guard approached from the castle, banners held high, all of them of the axe with a bloody handle. Only one rode on horseback; the others were on foot with their shields polished and their hands on their swords. Antonil stepped forward, and at their approach he bowed low, then waited for their host to speak first.

"Welcome," said the mounted man. He wore armor but no helmet. His face was long, his eyes green and his hair brown. A long but well-trimmed beard grew to the bottom of his neck. "My name is Theo White, and I am king of Omn."

"Greetings," Antonil said. "I am King Antonil, lord of Mordan and Neldar."

"Then like me, you are king of nothing," Theo said, a bitter smirk crossing his face. "Come, let us return to the castle. Our provisions are few but should fill your bellies. But first, I must be introduced to your rather odd companions."

At first Harruq thought he meant him until Ahaesarus stepped forward. He chuckled, relieved to realize there were far stranger looking people than him now travelling with them.

"My name is Ahaesarus," the angel said as he bowed. "I offer you the blessings of Ashhur, and thank you for your hospitality."

"Keep your blessings," Theo said. "But I'll take your swords and spears. Come, to my castle. You have questions, I'm sure, and I'll do my best to answer."

He tugged on the reins. The honor guard pivoted, and back to the castle they travelled.

"Delightful fellow, isn't he?" Harruq muttered.

For once, Aurelia didn't jab him in the side.

※

Qurrah watched the procession enter the city, and with every cheer they made, his spirits sank further.

"Damn fools," he said to himself, for he was alone atop a small hill that looked down upon the fortifications. He sat huddled with his arms crossed over his chest, his chin resting on his forearms. He'd told no one he would stay behind, and no one had even noticed his departure, not even Harruq. Was he still so invisible to them?

"It's hard returning here, isn't it?" asked a voice behind him. Qurrah startled, then felt his cheeks flush.

"What would you know about that?" he asked.

Jerico sat beside him, his armor clinking. He put his mace on the ground to his right, away from Qurrah. In silence the two looked upon the town, each lost in their memories.

"They won't recognize you," Jerico said.

"That's because I killed them all," Qurrah said. He shook his head. "I once entered through those walls a conqueror. I won't do so now as if I am their savior."

"You were just one of many," Jerico said. His red hair blew in the soft wind. "You only opened the gates."

Qurrah laughed, the sound mirthless and tired.

"That is all I've done," he said. "I brought Tessanna into our lives. I cursed Aullienna. I retrieved the tome to open the portal for the demons. In everything I do, I open the door for death and torment. At least I killed Delysia myself. At least I can feel that guilt warm on my hands, just like her blood…"

He fell silent.

"Guilt is heavy," Jerico said. "You can pretend it's not there, but once you feel its weight, there's no easy escape."

"Why are you here?" Qurrah asked him.

The left side of Jerico's face curled into a smile, bitter and sad.

"This hill," he said, gesturing with his hand. "This is where Velixar nearly broke my faith. This is where I watched hundreds of innocents die. And this is where I slept with Tessanna."

"I promised to kill you for that," Qurrah said, feeling his whip tighten around his arm.

"You did," Jerico said, chuckling.

They both watched the city, watched the banners of the White family flutter in the breeze.

"Why?" Qurrah asked.

"Because I'm human. Because she..."

"No," the half-orc interrupted. "Not you. Her."

Jerico scratched at his chin, obviously uncomfortable.

"She felt you judged her," he said. "She felt with you she had to be strong. You were always taking from her, relying on her. If she broke, if she fell to sadness or despair...would you have been there for her?"

"Of course I would," Qurrah said, his voice a whisper.

"But did she know that?"

Qurrah had no answer.

"She wanted to break me," Jerico said when it was obvious the silence would stretch indefinitely. "She wanted to prove I couldn't be as forgiving as I claimed. She was right."

"Do you hate me?" Qurrah asked after shaking his head.

Jerico glanced over.

"Yes. At times."

"You watched me aid in the deaths of hundreds."

Jerico nodded. "I did."

"Yet I'm still alive."

Now the paladin had no answer.

"No one is as good as they claim," Qurrah said, standing. "But you've never claimed to be perfect, Jerico, only that you desire to be. Your failure does not deny that perfection. The fact that you haven't killed me is proof enough. But I think I know what it is Tessanna desired from you. What she'd never have gotten from me, for I'd never felt it myself."

"And what is that?" Jerico asked.

"Forgiveness. For Aullienna. It haunts her. Now Velixar's got her, he's twisting her, trying to break her like he tried to break you. Should I ever see her again, what will be left of her? A shattered thing? Will I even know her?"

Jerico clapped Qurrah on the shoulder.

"Come on," he said. "I'm hungry, and this hill makes for poor sleeping. Our friends await."

"I have no friends," Qurrah said.

"Don't be so melodramatic. Your family, then."

He offered his hand, and Qurrah took it.

"All right, but if anyone tries to kill me, you better protect me."

Jerico winked.

"We'll see."

They returned to the city.

The feast was meager, but Harruq was still thankful. It seemed like it'd been ages since he'd eaten in a chair at a table. They gathered in the great hall of the castle, with six long tables, three of them empty. Antonil and Theo sat opposite each other, with a few knights and angels between them and the Eschaton. Harruq absently chewed on some bread far too stale for his liking and watched the two kings talk.

"What are we missing out on?" he asked.

"Since when did politics interest you?" Tarlak countered.

"It might affect his food," Aurelia said. "That keeps him interested."

"I'm serious," Harruq said, clearly insulted. "We've marched in here expecting to fight, and instead find troops of some king that I sure don't know."

"You've barely been outside of Veldaren," Aurelia said. "Of course you don't know anyone."

"I recognize the name," Tarlak said. "That Pensely guy said that a baron named Gregor White was expected to become king, but then he died with no clear heir between his two sons."

"Sounds like Theo was the stronger of the sons," Aurelia said. She pushed away her plate, having no appetite for the light meal. "I wonder where the other son is. Dead, perhaps? Hanging from a branch by a rope? Maybe just jailed in a tower somewhere."

"Careful," said Tarlak. "You might be discussing a deep dark secret of this majestic White empire sure to rise in these final days."

Harruq rolled his eyes.

"Master of sarcasm, you are not."

"Better than you, oh master of the subtle."

Further down the table, Ahaesarus excused himself, stood, and then moved to sit with the Eschaton.

"I saw your stares," he said as he folded in his wings so they wouldn't brush against Tarlak. "I assure you, the plans being made are far less interesting than you might assume."

"Tell us anyway," said Aurelia.

Ahaesarus leaned back and crossed his arms as he thought over everything the two kings had said.

"We will remain here for a time," he said, figuring to start with the most certain. "I'll have angels patrolling all across the Kingstrip. Thulos and his troops won't get within a hundred miles of here without us knowing. Until then, we'll gather what soldiers we can and train them. As for what we do once the demons make their move…"

He gestured to where Antonil and Theo argued, their conversation having grown rather heated.

"That is still uncertain. I fear king White's desires are too fatalistic. He is convinced the world is coming to an end, and he seeks glory and blood to be his burial shroud."

"Who is this guy, anyway?" Harruq asked. "No one's told me anything. How'd he become king? How'd they retake this castle?"

"Did he defeat his brother after the city fell?" Aurelia asked.

"No," said the angel. "His brother was here when Karak's troops slaughtered everyone. Evidently only a token force garrisoned the walls. Once the barons discovered the destruction, they began mustering troops. The demons were careless, and instead of consolidating power they continued after us."

"Velixar wanted all of you dead," said Qurrah as he sat beside his brother. The table quieted immediately, broken only by Jerico's chuckle as he took a seat opposite him.

"Save the awkwardness for later," the paladin said. "Qurrah's information here is vital to our decision making."

"Go ahead then," said Tarlak, keeping his eyes on everyone but Qurrah. "Enlighten us."

"The demons were led by one named Ulamn. Velixar pressed him, kept him moving when he might have otherwise slowed. Both believed their supply of war demons limitless, and hoped to crush Mordan before they received warning they were even in danger. If the queen had time to gather her troops, the siege would have been far more dangerous."

"That rush left Kinamn here lightly guarded," Ahaesarus said. "And it also left the barons to prepare without danger or harassment. So months later, when the demons fled the other way, chased by us, Theo White gathered everyone under his banner. His army is the strongest, his command the wisest, and without his brother to compete for inheritance, he was an obvious choice for leadership. They stormed the walls only weeks ago, defeating the few demons stationed here. At the very least, Omn is now free of the demons' presence."

"But for how long?" Tarlak asked. He pointed a finger at Ahaesarus. "You know they're coming, and this time with a god on their side. Theo can't possibly think these walls will matter, or that we can hold them."

The angel shook his head.

"No, he doesn't," he said. "But his preferred defense for his country…it is careless. Dangerous. I hope in my heart your king Antonil can persuade him off such a course. I fear he won't. Until then, though, we must prepare. We do not know what Thulos will do, but I doubt he will come as quickly or as recklessly."

"He can't," Aurelia said. "The portal's closed. His demons are now limited, and with every death he grows weaker. He'll need men. Lots of men."

"That is Theo's thinking," said Ahaesarus. "Felwood Castle and Angelport are the two most likely places. It will take time to reach either of them."

"Will Thulos get them to switch?" Harruq asked. "Conquer them, make them serve his rule?"

Ahaesarus sighed.

"I don't know," he said. "Time will tell. I have little hope, though."

"Isn't that what your kind is for, hope?" asked Aurelia.

The angel smiled, but sadness hid in his eyes.

"I am here for this," he said, patting the sword at his side. "Nothing else. Come the battle, I will slay the enemies of Ashhur to protect the lives of this world, and will do so until my last mortal breath. I know of nothing else."

Harruq took a drink as the conversation quieted, worried by the strange chill that danced down his spine.

7

Tessanna watched the campfires flare to life across the plains with idle curiosity. The war demons were well practiced at their nightly duties, but this night they seemed tense. She knew they were approaching the lands guarded by Felwood Castle, but was it possible the creatures of battle felt nerves and doubt like everyone else?

She huddled closer to her own fire. She felt dirty and pathetic. What had happened to the goddess? At one time she had walked through the crowd of warriors proudly, almost daring them to lay a finger upon her pale skin. Now she quivered when they glared. She'd been afraid before, but not like this. She'd felt pain before, but not like this. She wasn't master over her fear. Pain came and went whether she allowed it or not. Through it all haunted the specter of Velixar, watching with his red eyes, touching her with his dead flesh.

It'd been six days since she'd last eaten. The simple wooden band, the one she'd worn on her finger nearly all her life, she'd cast aside during their march. Its magic had allowed her to eat only rarely, and very little when she did. She didn't want that anymore. Hunger stabbed her stomach, but she welcomed it. When she looked at herself, she saw a skeleton barely hanging on to life. Her hair was matted and unevenly cut. Not even when given the chance did she wash herself. She wasn't killing herself, but it was close. She was killing her beauty.

But it hadn't been enough.

"Your eyes," Velixar said as he sat beside her. He kept his arms crossed, his hands thankfully not touching her. "I've seen that look in dead men and women. You are still alive. What haunts you?"

"Rest your silver tongue," Tessanna said. "You know I don't believe a word it says."

"I never lie," Karak's prophet insisted.

"Your greatest lie of all."

He chuckled, anger lurking beneath the sound. He touched her hair. She didn't bother to hide her shiver.

"We are not far from Felwood," he said, gently fondling the dirt-streaked strands that fell all the way to her waist. "There will be servant girls, baths, clothes fit for royalty. This rough travel does not suit you."

"I am not your princess," Tessanna snapped. "I'm not your whore, either. I'm nothing. Even the weakest of men could gut me with a sword."

"I don't want you for your power," Velixar said. "A power that may or may not return."

"Then what is it you want?" she asked. She hunched her shoulders and looked away, unwilling to see that look in his eyes. The look she'd seen in so many men, though not always as frightening or dangerous.

"I want to break you," he whispered into her ear. "You were Qurrah's, but he never deserved you. You are the greatest woman of our time. You belong to the greatest man of all times."

"You are bones and rot," Tessanna said, but her voice lacked conviction.

His fingertips brushed her neck, then slid around her like a serpent. She was thin, so thin…

"I could snap your neck right here," Velixar said. Stars swam before her eyes. "I could strangle every bit of life from you, then raise you to be my queen. Qurrah is out there, my greatest failure. I will return him to Karak's fold. I will show him his error. When I do that, my love, I want you there. I want you to watch as he falls to his knees and begs me for forgiveness. I want you to see his tears and hear his wretched brokenness."

His grip relaxed, and she gasped in air.

He's mad, she thought. *Madder than me.*

"Will you want him, then?" Velixar asked. "When he bows before me like a beaten dog, will you still view him as your husband and master?"

Words of a spell came to her, so simple, so common to her former life. She grabbed his wrist and whispered them. Nothing happened. No fire. No magic. Velixar heard them and sneered, his ever-changing face a fluid mask of hatred and lust.

"You're abandoned," he told her. "My god is a god of order, and you know what goes hand in hand with order? Control. I have years, Tessanna. I know you are starving yourself. Keep that up, and I will have my undead force rotted flesh down your gullet. I know you shred your hair and dirty your skin. Come the castle, you will clean yourself, or I will give you to the men of Felwood, all of them. Perhaps even the demons will wish to partake. When Qurrah sees you, I want him to see everything he lost in forsaking me."

"He never lost me," she whispered.

Velixar flung her to the cold earth.

"Open your eyes," he told her. "You two are done. Should he beg for forgiveness and rejoin our faith in Karak, his first task will be to execute you. If he refuses Karak, then you will kill him for his blasphemy. There is no hope, not for either of you."

Tessanna heard his words and could hold back no longer. She sobbed, feeling the weight of the passing months crashing down upon her. She begged for Qurrah's arms, to hold Teralyn and feel life, to be a mother and a wife, to be powerful and beautiful. Nothing. She was nothing.

"Sleep alone tonight," he told her. "I have prayers to make."

He left her.

Tessanna slept deep into the morning. The war demons were already preparing to march out when her eyelids flicked open. Groaning, she touched her throat and wondered how bad the bruise might be. Velixar's words returned to her, and fearing his anger, she searched for something to eat. A couple of demons were rolling up their tent nearby, and she approached.

"Food," she said, as if she were a child. The demons ignored her.

"Please," she said. "I'm hungry."

One of them reached into his pocket, pulled out a small piece of bread, and threw it to her.

"Enjoy it, whore."

She caught the food and let the words roll off her.

"Thank you," she said as she nibbled on one end, her nose crinkling at the smell. Her hunger was enough to overcome its foulness.

She wandered north, following the march of the lead forces. Her bare feet ached, and often they bled. As she walked she remembered that initial flight with Qurrah, just the two of them fleeing west from the Eschaton. She'd been naked then, nothing to cover her feet, but despite that she'd felt comforted by Qurrah's presence. Only Aullienna's death had tormented her, but no wrappings could heal that. Only time, and only barely. She wondered if Aurelia still felt the pain as acutely as she did. Perhaps. Perhaps not. Tessanna felt herself an open wound. She was blood, bad blood. Maybe Velixar was Dezrel's leech, drawing her in, breaking her down, cleansing the world of her presence...

One by one the demons took to the air, until only the undead remained far ahead, having marched through much of the night to ensure they didn't fall behind the aerial troops. With the plains now clear, Tessanna saw Velixar approaching from ahead, a sickly horse trotting beside him, its flesh pale and gray with faded black spots across its back.

"I found a farm not far from here," Velixar said once he was close enough for her to hear. "This foal was let loose."

"A foal?" Tessanna asked. She thought of Seletha, the magical steed she had ridden across the land. A fiery, majestic horse from the netherworlds. Yet she was to ride this...foal?

"Do not worry about it bearing your weight," said Velixar. "Nor will it tire or disobey."

Tessanna noticed how still the creature stood, lacking the in and out of its sides as it drew breath.

"You killed it and brought it back," she said.

"Of course. It is more dependable this way."

Tessanna mounted the beast, doing her best to hold in her grimace. Riding beside Velixar atop a dead foal? What else could be more appropriate?

"How will you keep up?" she asked.

"You will ride alone," he told her. "I will catch up, but for now I have my prayers and my legs. The demons are tired of waiting for us. It was either this or ride in one of their slings. I prefer my feet on the ground. Sleep if you can, for we ride all day and all night until we reach Felwood Castle. And don't think of hiding from me. The moment you leap off, I will know. Stay seated unless you'd prefer to die crushed underneath hoofs."

"I'll need to eat, pass water," she said.

"Tell the foal," he said, sending her on her way. "I'll hear."

And so she rode, and for the first time in what seemed like ages, she was alone. The northern plains passed by as the foal trudged along, silent as the grave it no doubt deserved to be within. She rode, and rode, stopping only to urinate or eat the occasional berries growing low on rare clusters of bushes. Without a saddle or stirrups, she had to clutch her hands about the dead foal's neck. The smell made her sick. The touch made it worse. Her fingers ached, and her back screamed in protest.

And she rode, and rode.

Two nights later the foal stopped. Tessanna more fell than climbed off. The contact with the ground knocked the air from her lungs, and quietly moaning, she waited for her breath to return. Her back and fingers were a constant throb of pain. She stank of rotting skin and decaying horse hair. The plains were coming to an end, breaking into soft hills and trees that grew tall, their leaves a green so deep they seemed wholesome. She had touched them whenever possible, clutching them to her chest as the undead foal cantered on. They had a pure scent, a temporary counter to the stench of her mount.

"You're a bastard," she said, knowing Velixar could hear her. She wondered where he might be, how many miles away.

The foal remained perfectly still, not even swishing its tail to scare away the flies that buzzed about.

The nights were uncomfortably cold, a fire not needed to survive but needed to sleep well. So far, she'd had no fire, but now she saw the faint glow in the distance of many such campfires. The war demons were close. She'd kept up with them through the constant ride. Velixar had let her sleep only a few hours each night before the foal would wake her by pressing its snout against the back of her neck and nipping at her skin. The very thought of the creature's teeth touching her sent a shiver down her spine.

One of her favorite ways to start a fire, back when she still possessed her power, was to cut her flesh and set her blood aflame as it dripped upon the kindling. In memory of that, she clawed at her wrist with her ragged fingernails, feeling a burst of pleasure at the pain, pleasure that heightened when she saw the desired crimson flow begin. She had no real kindling, just a few twigs scattered about, but she piled them anyway. Drop by drop dripped down, and she blew upon them as they fell. No magic. No fire. Her tears ran down her face like the blood down her wrist.

A strange sound reached her ears. She looked up, and was mildly surprised to see Velixar flying toward her, a dark specter of the night. Giant bat wings stretched from his back, shimmering in their blackness. Her chest ached as they faded away like smoke. She'd once possessed wings like that…

"So much for your legs," she said.

Velixar stroked her face with his fingertips, a gesture that would have seemed loving if not for the wicked smile on his face.

"We reach Felwood sometime before tomorrow night," he said. "Thulos tells me a few scouts have spotted our approach, yet no army marches against us. They plan on hiding in their castle, which is perfect for us. The fewer casualties means the greater our army when they join our side."

"You seem so certain they will turn," Tessanna said. She tilted her head to one side and watched the blood drip down to her elbow. A curious look on her face, she licked it, then spat, unsatisfied.

"Your old ways are dying," he said. "Celestia has abandoned you. Your blood, your pain, it no longer satisfies. In time, you will realize your desire for something strong. Something controlled."

"Assuming Qurrah doesn't kill me."

Velixar narrowed his eyes.

"No matter what happens," he said, "I will treasure such a moment. You should as well."

She tried to turn away from him, but he grabbed her wrists. From her sitting position, she could do nothing as he forced her to the ground. He towered over her, the stench of death rolling down. Her heart hammered in her chest. His legs forced her knees apart. So cold, he was so cold...

"I will take you," he whispered. His face was beside hers, but no air moved across her. He did not breathe. There was no life in that being pinning her to the hard ground. "But when I do, it will be everything you could despise. It will be everything your fantasies cannot abide. Most of all, Tessanna...it will be *willing*."

"Never," she whispered back, tears running down the sides of her face. "I'll never."

"There are so many pieces of you," he said, rubbing his cheek against hers. "And how badly they've broken. Where is the animal? Where is the whore? And what of the child? You're more whole than you've ever been, Tessanna. Don't you realize that? I am what you need. I am the way to your salvation. Not Qurrah, and most certainly not the pathetic god he has turned to in his weakness."

Tessanna sobbed, thinking of the way Jerico had looked at her after she'd ridden him. All his love and mercy had turned to shame and disgust. She'd done that to him. By the gods, why had she done that to him?

"I hate you," she said. She felt her personalities swirling, a thousand colors blending together into some shapeless indecipherable smudge. Every single instinct inside her screamed to fall within, to retreat to another—the child or the being of apathy. But she couldn't. They had left her. Velixar's grip was tight, and her hands turned numb. She arched her back and screamed, once.

Karak's most loyal prophet struck her with his fist. The pain shocked her quiet. He glared down at her, an angered master, a ruling king upset with his servant.

"Thulos will make the men of Felwood cower to his name," he told her. "That is our way. Those who are strong will become weak, and their strength will serve that which they hoped to destroy. Your hatred means nothing. Your revulsions are pathetic. Go sleep in the cold."

And like a beaten dog, she did as she was told, crying herself to sleep and wishing she were in Qurrah's arms.

◁✦▷

Velixar woke her early that morning, the sun only a golden hint on the hills.

"Get yourself ready," he said. "I want to be there when Thulos reveals his godhood to the defenders of Felwood."

She urinated behind a tree, straightened her hair with her fingers, and then returned to him. He gave her nothing to eat. Instead, he nodded to the foal. After she climbed on, he joined her. If alive, the creature would have easily tired within moments, but its blood was still, and its strength dark in origin.

"Do not be scared," he told her as he wrapped his arms around her waist, so gently as if last night had never happened. "Time is of the essence. Let us see what this steed is capable of."

The foal galloped and Tessanna clutched its dead mane, every part of her trying to ignore the cold feel of Velixar's touch. The foal galloped at a startling pace, the wind blowing through their hair. The ride was brutal, nothing absorbing the shocks of the occasional uneven step. A miserable hour passed. Tessanna felt certain the foal would fall to pieces after a day or two of such riding, but all they needed was a few more hours. At the summit of a hill, she looked down into a valley filled with fog that appeared to creep out from the forest at its far edge. The war demons massed in the center of the fog, marching instead of flying. Tucked against the forest, its walls weaving through the trees, was Felwood Castle.

"They have rigged every tree to collapse," Velixar said as the foal slowed. "The ivy on the walls hides a thousand razors, deadly sharp. I once had a troop of orcs attempt to climb them. They bled out before reaching the top."

"Sad for them," she said, her voice an emotionless droll.

They rode into the demons' camp, then dismounted. After Tessanna leapt off its back, the foal collapsed. A wave of Velixar's hand and his magic left it nothing more than a long-decaying corpse.

"Come," he said, taking Tessanna's hand. "Let us find Thulos."

She fantasized plunging her hand into a fire to burn away his touch as she followed him.

Thulos sat on his throne, the fog swirling about him, hiding the feet of the chair and making it seem like he was floating. His armor shone even in the dim light, immaculately polished. He nodded to Velixar as he approached.

"I was hoping I would not have to wait for your arrival," he said. He tilted his head back, as if suddenly revolted. "Your relationship with that woman is baffling, prophet."

Tessanna felt her cheeks flush at being spoken of as if she were not there. It made her feel insignificant, invisible.

"One that should be of no interest to you," Velixar said, letting go of her hand.

"The girl is a daughter of the whore," Thulos said, looking to the castle. "She is powerless now. We would all be safer with her dead."

"Since when did you care for safety? Does conquest not have its risks?"

Thulos chuckled.

"So be it. I need your undead to circle the castle just outside the range of their arrows. Do not have them attack. Their presence is all I need."

"Fear is a powerful weapon," Velixar said.

Thulos looked over at him, then shook his head as if disappointed in a child.

"Fear? I will not cow them with fear. I will show them reason. Death, or honor. Serve me in life, or serve me in death. Temptations work better than threats, and it is all the better when they can see what happens should they resist that temptation."

"I bow to your wisdom," Velixar said.

"Just do your part, and quickly. I wish to start before the sunrise."

With a wave of his hand he dismissed them.

Velixar grabbed Tessanna's wrist and led them toward his undead, which were already marching into position circling the front of the castle. Fires burst to life along the walls, giant cauldrons of oil and pitch. Torches ran to and fro, held by frightened hands. Velixar could smell the fear even from his distance.

"Thulos is a fool," Tessanna said as she watched. "What could he possibly tempt these people with?"

"You dare call a god a fool?" Velixar asked, surprised.

"I do," she said. "And I call yours an abomination."

His punch split the inside of her lip. On her hands and knees, she spat blood and did her best not to cry.

"One more remark," he said. "One more blasphemy against Karak and I will make you an abomination so horrid men will pale at the very sight of your mutilated corpse."

She looked up at him, blood dribbling down her chin, and smiled.

"Yes, master," she said, but there was a wickedness in her tone. Velixar clearly didn't like it one bit.

They stopped before the front row of the undead, the castle gates looming ahead. It seemed the entire wall bristled with spears and torches. Tessanna was stunned by the amount. When they'd assaulted Mordeina, she'd thought the numbers impressive. It turned out that was nothing. Before her was a true army, one recruited with time and coin. At least a thousand men guarded the walls, and who knew how many more filled the interior courtyard.

"They will kill many before dying," she said.

"They won't kill a single demon," Velixar told her. "Show some faith."

She snickered again. A communal roar washed over her, the result of thousands of war demons shouting the name of their god.

"THULOS!" they cried as they took flight. In perfect formations they spread across the skies, carrying banners of the bloody fist. Thulos rode atop his throne, which the demons set down just beyond reach of the defenders' bows. The god stood. He'd timed it perfectly. The sun poured over the hills and shone upon his armor. He raised his sword high, and before the castle he seemed mighty, unbeatable. When he spoke, his voice thundered across the valley. It was as if storm clouds had settled above the castle and given their thunder to the giant before the gates.

"Warriors of Felwood," he said, so deep that Tessanna felt her heart quiver in her chest. "I come here bringing not destruction but instead the greatest treasure of any true warrior."

He pointed his sword south, and it was no accident he held the enormous blade with only one hand. It looked as if it weighed more than a man, yet he handled it with ease.

"By now you know of Veldaren's fate. By now you hear whispers of the men with red wings, war demons who burn and slaughter. What you hear are the childish cries of fear. You hear ignorance and cowardice. You are men of the sword and the spear."

He slammed a fist against his breast and then held it out to the castle.

"You prepare to fight," he said. "You prepare to die. I honor you! But your eyes are upon the ground, when you should instead look to the skies! There are a thousand worlds beyond your own. I speak no lie, for where else have I and my soldiers come from? Every single one offers a chance for glory. In battle you mortals find meaning. In war you understand life. List your vice. I will grant it to you! Gold, women, land, food, spice, drink…these are the spoils of war, and we are the Warseekers! Come down from your walls. Throw open your gates. Do not die here in a noble but shallow gesture. Reach higher. I offer you a life worth living.

"Think on my words. This world is ending. Do not end with it, but instead embrace a fate greater than any normal man's. In killing another, you assert your will. You declare to the heavens that you are greater. I offer you worlds to kill. A thousand men will die to each of your blades. Prove you are worthy. Show your power. Show your strength."

He held his sword with both hands and lowered his head. Tessanna watched, enraptured by his speech. Even she, a powerless captive, felt his words stir her heart. For a moment she imagined having her magic returned to her, and marching at Thulos's side as his queen, god and goddess. With a wave of her hand she would destroy thousands, burning them with fire and crushing them with ice...

"Most impressive," Velixar said. "His words themselves are magic. I can feel them weaving about me, like spider webs."

Light collected around Thulos's sword, the blade shaking as if it would explode from the energy within. His hair blew in an unnatural wind that swirled around him. It seemed the elements bent to his will. And then he swung his sword.

The shockwave sundered the castle doors, blowing chunks of wood and metal further within, filling the air with splinters. The crack echoed in the silence, breaking the spell Thulos's words had weaved. Now Tessanna felt fear and abandonment, and even knowing it was just the after-effects of the spell, she still struggled to dismiss it.

"The way is open to me," Thulos said. "All who would conquer, come forth. Kneel, and accept a lifetime of blood and honor."

"Unbelievable," Velixar said, total admiration across his ever-changing face.

They came by the thousands, kneeling in uneven lines. They were peasants and soldiers alike, and those with swords or spears cast them at their feet. Thulos stood before them, saluting. The troops atop the walls thinned, then altogether vanished. The god neared, and he paced as if inspecting them.

"Where is your lord?" Thulos asked.

"Lord Gandrem remains behind," said one of the soldiers. "He would rather die than serve."

"No," Thulos said, his voice a whisper, yet the magic in his voice ensured all heard for miles. "*I* am your Lord, and I stand before you."

He lowered his sword. The waves of war demons descended, the walls meaning nothing to them. Velixar thought to send in his undead, but Thulos turned and shook his head.

"Let my demons drink the blood of the unwilling," he said.

Tessanna listened to the screams of the dying who remained within the walls.

"Monsters," she whispered.

"Such hypocrisy," Velixar said, having heard her. "You aided me in conquering Veldaren. You watched as Kinamn fell. And here, we have granted reprieve, and life. Do you think the orcs spared any when they stormed through the streets at Veldaren? Yet now you pale and call us monsters. How is this so different?"

It wasn't different. He was right. The realization struck Tessanna like a thunderbolt. The last remnants of her apathy crumbled. The wildness inside her thrashed in its death throes. Her and Qurrah, they'd killed...they'd killed...

So many.

So very many.

She cried as the men and women of Felwood raised their arms to the sky in tentative worship of their new god.

8

The closest person to Melorak was the priest Olrim, one of the original seven who had remained when Queen Annabelle banished their kind from the capital. The man was elderly, with pinched eyebrows, pock-marked skin, and a dull sparkle in his eyes that paled compared to Melorak's fiery faith. Following his ascension, Melorak had appointed Olrim to minister to and train the newly recruited priests of Karak. While he was a grim and surly man, he also had an uncanny understanding of men and their thoughts. When it came to conquering a nation, that was exactly what Melorak needed.

One by one the many lords had come from their castles and bent their knee, pledging meager armies and always unspecified amounts of gold. Every time Melorak informed them of their duty, of their quota of men to give to Karak's service and the gold to fill Karak's coffers. Every time, the looks on their faces amused the dark priest.

"They're like children," Olrim said, pouring over long parchments tallying up their resources.

"How so?" Melorak asked.

"They forget their own wealth in a sulk as they ponder how much they must lose. That lord that just left, Hemman's his name, he controls a thousand acres, much along the Gwond River. Every acre is protected by our wall of towers, yet he mutters and thinks treason at giving up a mere tenth of his wealth, and only half his fighting men."

"Let them sulk," Melorak said, shifting in the throne as he waited for the next lord or baron to arrive and plead their allegiance. "This land is ours, and they know it. Who else remains against us?"

"The Craghills have pledged their loyalty, along with the Knothills and their surrounding plains, plus the villages upon Deer Lake. We've assumed total control of the Great Fields;

their harvest is too important to risk some idiot lord thinking to ransom leverage against us."

"And Hemman's pledged the rest of the northern rim," Melorak said. "What about the south?"

"From here to the Corinth River, we collect taxes, and the people pray to the name of Karak," Olrim said, rubbing his fingers together in a gesture of delight. "Only the Sanctuary remains untaken, but its priests have holed up in their mountain and repel our soldiers' attacks."

"Keep them harried, but do not press unnecessarily," Melorak said. "We will deal with them in time. They are a powerful foe. If we can keep them defensive and hiding, we will spread the faith of Karak unheeded throughout the land. When they finally emerge, let them find a world changed and moved on without them."

"That just leaves Ker," Olrim said. "Twice their king has pledged us loyalty, but I must say, I am skeptical."

"Are you really?" Melorak asked, surprised.

"Ker has been a nation most favorable to us, and much of the praise belongs on the shoulders of the dark paladins and their Stronghold. The people of Ker I trust, but their lord is an opportunistic man named Bram Henley. He treats faith as a weapon and nothing more. If he sees benefit in confessing allegiance to Ashhur and his angels, he will do so in a heartbeat."

"Then perhaps we should remove him."

"I would counsel against it," Olrim said. "He's popular, and worse, I hear constant rumors that he was given protection by Karak's prophet."

"Surely it is a lie."

Olrim sighed and rubbed a hand through his thin gray hair.

"There is no way to know, not without asking Velixar, who is currently on the opposite side of Dezrel."

"I can assure you that Karak will answer me if I ask," Melorak said.

"No good," Olrim said. "You aren't Karak, not to the people. All we have is my intuition that he is disloyal. The war still rages in the far east, and we dare not risk having a hundred revolts to stamp out."

"So we prevent a hundred small fires while risking one giant blaze?" Melorak asked.

"That sums it up well."

Melorak laughed, then stood from his throne.

"Come with me, then. What of my city? Is anything disrupting their worship of Karak, and of myself?"

"Our priests minister night and day," Olrim said, walking side by side with Melorak. "And more importantly, all traces of Ashhur have been thoroughly extinguished. We hang less and less each day for daring to speak his name."

"You hold something from me, friend," Melorak said, halting their walk. "What of the dark vigilante? What of the Ghost and his Blade?"

"A nuisance in the small scale," Olrim said. "But dangerous in the wide. All those hoping for rebellion do so because of those two pests. Until they hang from the walls, we will risk an uprising."

"Weeks have passed," Melorak said, his voice turning cold. "Over a hundred of my men have died at their hands. They came into my castle, *my room,* with murder in their hearts. They must be dealt with, Olrim, in a manner most fitting."

"And what would that be?" Olrim asked, clearly exasperated. "I have done all I can, from increasing the size and number of patrols to planting spies to watch for their passing, spies who always end up dead by morning, I might add. Other than having Karak point his finger and strike them dead, I see no way."

"So little faith," Melorak said, smiling. The priest-king pointed to the wall, where one of many corpses hung from hooks like macabre banners.

"Do you know who this is?" Melorak asked. When Olrim shook his head, the priest-king's smile only widened. "He was the Watcher of Veldaren, a rogue of such skill and danger that the king paid him a handsome sum to keep tabs on the entire network of thief guilds. He died when we conquered Mordeina, an act of mercy by a cowardly elf."

"Might he know where they hide?" Olrim asked, his hands rubbing together excitedly.

"Even better," Melorak said. "He knows who they are, and how they fight. You say Karak's hand must come down to smite these two interlopers? I say we channel Karak's hand through this shell."

Now it was Olrim's turn to smile.

"The shock," he said. "The surprise, the feel of betrayal, would be delicious to behold."

Melorak put his hand on the chest of Haern the Watcher, closed his eyes, and let his dark magic pour forth. He felt his magical mind crawling through the emptiness, searching for the thin white line that was Haern's soul. Muscles twitched, and tendons stretched and tightened as the shell was made ready for the host's return. Teeth clenched, Melorak's lips peeled back, grinning. Haern's soul was his. He rammed it into the corpse, layering it with spell after spell. He denied him memory of the Golden Eternity. He denied him choice and freedom. Instead, he bound his heart, mind, and soul far greater than any chain.

"Welcome back," Melorak said as Haern writhed on the hooks, shouting in horrendous agony. "And cease that wretched noise."

At once Haern obeyed. He glared down with slowly awakening eyes. His hands opened and shut, as if wishing for weapons.

"Such anger," Olrim said, clearly amused.

"Let it fuel him," Melorak said. He slapped the undead man across the face. "Listen to me, worm. You are mine. My word is law. I am god to you, is that clear?"

Haern struggled, but it did nothing to stop him from bowing his head and nodding.

"I deny you the right to speak," Melorak said. "For speaking has nothing to do with your task. There are two former acquaintances of yours I want taken care of. The man they call the Ghost. His eyes are mismatched, and he wears a gray cloth over his face. They even say the ashes of the dead swarm over him, masking his appearance. His robes are red, and his hair black. Do you know of whom I speak?"

Again, against all possible resistance, Haern nodded.

"Good. The other they call his Blade, a slender girl who wields daggers and sees through one eye. Do you know her?"

Another nod.

"Useful creature," Olrim said. "Will you dispose of him once the two interlopers are dead?"

"I will consider it," Melorak said. "It is a strain to keep him so controlled. Do well for me, Watcher, and I may free you."

He walked over a few feet, to where another corpse hung. Embedded into his rib cage were Haern's sabers. Melorak drew them out and handed them over. With a clap of his hands, the hooks detached from the wall, and the assassin fell free.

"Do not rest," Melorak said. "Do not hesitate. Feel no remorse, no pity. I do not care who else you kill in your quest, so long as they are not servants of mine. Keep your body covered so none know you are undead. Keep to the shadows. You have retained all your skill; I have made certain of that. Now go and spill blood."

Haern glared with naked anger, but his body was not his. Leaping soundlessly into the air, he sailed out a window into the courtyard and then ran, a blur of motion few could follow.

"Consider the matter of the Ghost and his Blade closed," Melorak said. "Now, about the matter of my growing army in Corinth…"

"What a shameful display," Deathmask said, reclining in a chair, his feet propped up on several pillows. "The lords and ladies of these lands lick Melorak's boots like he's a demigod. Any other usurper would have been beaten down by now. Where are the armies of Ker? Where are the troops of the northlands? The many guards at the wall of towers? Surely the homeland is far more important than keeping out a few emaciated orcs and goblins."

"The guards will not desert their post," Veliana said, "not even with all of Mordan in ruin. They will protect their land, their lives, and their posts, until they receive orders to the contrary. Such is the duty of all soldiers."

"Stupid," Deathmask said. "Who cares if you hold an inch of foreign soil if you lose your own damn throne?"

"They wait for orders," Veliana said. "Orders you know aren't coming. They're being told the priest-king Melorak is new ruler over Mordan, and that all the lords have sworn fealty. It's no lie. We've watched them come and go, wine on their tongues and cowardice in their hearts."

"Where the Abyss is Antonil?" Deathmask muttered. "He's still king, or at least he was if he's still alive. How many troops would become turncoats the second a true king, not some Karak-worshipping puppet, appeared and demanded his sovereign right?"

"Unless you plan on having Antonil magically appear—" she stopped mid-sentence. "Deathmask, do you feel that?"

"I do," Deathmask said, bolting to his feet and pulling on his boots. "Some undead abomination. It appears Melorak has brought Karak's magic against us."

They glanced around, scanning the window and the door, guessing where the undead creature might enter.

"This isn't right," Deathmask said. "I feel a stronger sense than normal. Veliana, it is no mindless drone!"

Veliana had drifted over to the window to peer outside and scan the streets. At Deathmask's call she jerked back, and with no time to spare. Twin sabers stabbed the air where she had been. Before she could react further, Haern swung in, his legs slamming her in the face and chest. With a small moan she fell back, breathless and dazed.

"Be still, puppet," Deathmask commanded, magical weight to his words. He could command undead as well as any priest of Karak, or so he thought. The attacker swayed, and it seemed like his motions took on a heavy, sluggish air, but still he pressed on, his sabers dazzling in the light.

"Shit," Deathmask said.

A bolt of black magic shot from his hand, connecting with Haern's chest in a solid hit that knocked him back several feet. The Watcher's hood fell back, and both members of the Ash guild felt their hearts plummet at the sight.

Haern, his eyes bloodshot and wild, snarled at them, his pale skin marked with rot. His once golden hair was matted and dull. In the center of his chest remained Dieredon's arrow, which had spared him torture at Melorak's hands when the city fell.

"Shit," Deathmask repeated.

Haern lunged again, but Veliana had recovered from the blow. Purple fire swarmed around her daggers as she batted away slash after slash. Haern towered over her, his feet dancing as Veliana swung her legs about, always failing to land a trip or kick. She remained completely defensive, her daggers a violet blur as they parried and cut.

A loud boom sent Haern retreating, even before the crimson fire erupted throughout the air where he had been. Veliana crossed her arms over her head to block out the heat and light. The fire rolled outward, never rising or falling, only staying in a rapidly expanding oval. A quick hiss of air, and then it slammed throughout the room, rolling across Deathmask without causing harm. The rest of the home, however, burst in flame, the walls charred black, and the curtains blowing out the window in fluttering ash.

Haern twirled, hooked a hand on the windowsill, and then hurled himself onto the roof as the fire exploded. As air sucked back in through the window, Haern came with it, charging headlong with his sabers at the ready. He went for Deathmask this time, leaping over the startled and prone Veliana.

"Hold!" Deathmask shouted, trying again to overpower whatever orders had been given to the undead assassin. Haern faltered in his steps, but still continued. That falter, however, was all Deathmask was hoping for. Silver chains appeared out of thin air, latching onto Haern's wrists and ankles. With a crumple of cloaks he hit the ground, rolling to avoid a second ball of fire that roasted the ground where he fell.

The clasps were magical, and much of their strength lay in the mental image of steel and the sensation of cold, hard metal.

But Haern cared not for either, and even if they had been real he would have struggled until his wrists broke and his rotting flesh tore. With his mouth screaming silently, he tore his hands free and slashed at the manacles on his feet. Unharmed, Haern glared at Deathmask, who was mere feet away.

Veliana's daggers buried into Haern's back, their purple flame searing flesh and gray cloak. Haern rolled with the blow, showing no sign of pain. He tossed Veliana to the side, one hand lashing out to cut Deathmask's throat, the other hurling his saber.

The sorcerer had one trick left up his sleeve. As Haern's blade struck his throat it passed right through, for Deathmask's flesh had turned to shadow. When his flesh returned to normal, he reached out, his hand grasping Haern's face. With every shred of power he forced a command into the undead man, keeping it as simple and primal as he could make it.

"RUN!" he shouted. Haern's entire body shook, and his eyes flared wide. When Deathmask let go, Haern turned and sprinted out the window, his long cloaks fluttering behind him in the wind. Exhausted, Deathmask crumpled to his knees and watched the assassin go.

"Please," Veliana said, laying on the ground to his right. "Deathmask..."

He glanced over, never realizing Haern had thrown his saber. Veliana was on her back, Haern's saber embedded deep in her chest.

"Vel," Deathmask gasped, crawling toward her. His hands passed over her wound, trying to assess it.

"Anything vital?" he asked, his hands closing around the hilt.

"No," she murmured, clutching his hands to keep him from pulling. "Please, it hurts, please."

He knew what she wanted. He couldn't bear to give it.

"You'll pull through," he told her.

"Haern'll be back," she said. "You only delayed him for a moment. Run, you damn fool, run!"

Deathmask felt his hands shaking. His mismatched eyes blurred, but no tears fell, so strong was his will.

"He'll pay," he said. "I will make Melorak suffer such pain he will beg for Karak's tender touch."

"Enough," Veliana said.

Deathmask pulled off his mask and kissed her lips. She kissed back, holding in a cough as she did. When the kiss ended, Deathmask slipped his fingers down to her heart. A single whisper and he stopped its movements. Her lungs went still. Her blood froze.

He stood and put on his mask. He reached into his bag and threw ash into the air so that it swirled about his face, locked into orbit.

He left.

When Haern returned moments later, he found Deathmask gone and Veliana still on the floor. A stone-cold look on his face, he yanked free his blade, sliced out Veliana's throat to be sure, and then left through the door, half his mission accomplished, the other half soon to follow.

9

King Bram Henley rode his horse into the center of the village, his keen edged sword held high. The lesser folk parted for their lord and his accompaniment of knights. A great fire waited to be kindled, and in the center of the wood stood three men tied to an upright log, their bodies stripped naked and bleeding from many thin wounds.

Bram slowed his horse as the last made way, revealing two priests dressed in the black robes of the roaring lion. They nodded their heads to their lord, but did not bow, which would have irritated him even if he hadn't already been furious.

"What travesty occurs in my realm?" he asked. His voice thundered through the clearing. He was an imposing man, with broad shoulders, long black hair, and a stern face marred by a single scar from eye to chin, self-cut in the tradition of his father's line. His naked blade revealed just how deep his fury went. He pointed it at the nearest priest, demanding an explanation.

"These men have defied the will of Karak," said the first. Bram recognized him as a high-ranking priest of Ker, a chubby man named Gill. His words dripped like honey but his fingers smelled of blood.

"And how have they done so?" Bram asked.

Gill puffed out his chest and gestured to the crowd, and it was to them he answered. The exaggerated movements of his arms rang bells attached to the bottom of his robes.

"We have but one lord in all of Dezrel, and he is Melorak, the lion of Karak, the voice of his thunder, the interpreter of his mighty roar. Who here would doubt Karak's power, or must his armies march through our nation once more?"

Bram's eyes narrowed, but he kept his tongue. Let the priest have his speech, so long as he got around to his point.

So far, the crowd was going along, but he sensed they did so not out of faith, but out of a desire to see the fire burn.

"These men would not swear oaths to Karak," Gill continued, his voice shrieking into a higher pitch. "They would swindle the good, meek people of this village, and then deny their god, spit in his face, and exalt a man above all. Who here could question their guilt, or their punishment?"

The priest beside him shouted, "Praise be to Karak!" and a dozen or so onlookers joined in. Bram urged his horse closer to the pyre and nodded to the centermost man, who did not seem afraid, only royally pissed.

"Is what he says true?" Bram asked.

"We're tax collectors, milord," the man said. "And that viper demanded a tithe. I told him we could not, for the money was not ours to give, but yours, and not even a priest steals money from his lord."

"Who is lord but our great lord, Karak?" Gill shouted. Bram turned on him.

"You would steal from my treasury, then murder those who would stop your thievery?" he asked. Gill's eyes widened in exaggerated shock.

"I am a servant of our great god, and am most humble to be in his service," he said. "You dare insult me, even you, King Bram, knowing that an insult to a high priest is an insult to Karak himself?"

Bram glanced about. The crowd was eating up every word, though many looked nervous at the implied threat.

Damn sheep, thought Bram.

"Perhaps these men did offer insult," Bram said. "But I know of no laws that decree death to those who might affront Karak. We are a free people, and have been ever since the brothers' war."

"There is a new law!" Gill shouted. "A law elevating the common man to equality among kings. A law of gods, a law of Karak, and let true justice cover Dezrel in its righteous fury!"

The crowd cheered. As they did, Gill spoke softer, so that only Bram could hear.

"Our judgment sweeps across this land," he said. "You would be wise to recognize and obey."

Bram sheathed his sword and nodded for his knights to leave.

"I have a message for your god," he said as he spun his horse about, and village men tossed torches onto the dry hay that surrounded the pyre. "Tell him that you, Gilliam Frey, are responsible for King Henley finally seeing the truth of Karak."

Gill beamed.

"Praise be to Karak," he shouted as Bram rode into the distance.

"Ride hard," Bram said to Sir Ian Millar, his most trusted warrior. "We must reach Angkar before dusk."

"What of the priests?" the knight asked as he kicked his mount's sides.

"To the Abyss with them," Bram said, hurling a curse to the wind as they rode across the yellow grass.

⊁⊰⊱⊀

"Wake Loreina," Bram said as he stormed through the door of his tower. "Bring her to the Eye. Oh, and Ian...be quiet about it."

The knight struck his chest with his fist and bowed.

"Everywhere the Lion has ears," the king muttered as he stripped off his riding gear. His room was poorly furnished, another relic of his family's many odd traditions. The rest of the castle was gilded, polished, and overflowing with pretensions of wealth. But there in his tower, his room, he had a bed, a chest, and a mirror, all made of plain wood and glass. He paced the room, trying to calm down but knowing he wouldn't. Too many were wresting control of his kingdom away from him. Four generations his family had reigned. He had no intentions of being the last Henley. Soon Loreina and Ian would be at the Eye, and he took several deep breaths to slow his heart and calm his nerves.

Bram kept his sword buckled to his waist. The world had grown dangerous as of late, and now he found himself on the side of the apparent loser of the spiritual war sweeping across

Dezrel. What if some mad priest tried to gain the favor of his god by coming after him?

"Everywhere," said the king, opening the door. "Goddamn everywhere."

The castle had three main towers built into the corners of its walls. One was the king's, another was housing for knights, and the third was the Eye. Its door was painted a deep red, and just above the door, ten skulls carved of stone leered down at any who might enter. He paused and looked up at them. They were relics of an older time, to give mystery and wonder to the tower and the proceedings within. How long until he'd be forced to carve the skulls into lions?

Bram shoved open the door and hurried inside. Immediately before him was a set of stairs, looping up and around to the only true floor of the tower: the Eye.

Inside the eye, paintings of men fighting angels, demons, trolls, orcs, and other types of monsters the artists' imaginations could conceive covered every bit of the walls. Torches burned throughout, casting strange shadows across the images. In the center, older than any living man, was a seven-legged table. Carved in perfect detail atop it was the world of Dezrel.

"We wait as you commanded," said Ian.

Bram was pleased to see he also still carried his sword.

"He might," said Loreina, walking around the table so she could kiss him. "I waited because I worry for you. Silly of you to think I'd sleep before your return."

Bram wrapped an arm around her waist and smiled down at her. She was a slender thing, her brown hair braided and falling down to her waist. Though her face dimpled when she smiled, her eyes remained hard, attentive.

"You know more than I what the rumors say," Bram said, taking a seat before the giant map. "So help Ian and me make sense of everything we are hearing."

"Not much puzzlement from the north," Ian said, crossing his arms and nodding toward Mordan. "Everything on the other side of the Corinth River is pledged to their new priest-king, Melorak. So far we've been lucky he hasn't sent a permanent envoy to keep an eye on us."

Loreina sat beside her husband, her hand in his.

"Their priests are doing a fine enough job on their own," she said. "I've watched them, listened to their whispers as they scurry about the castle. More and more they press for people to repent and confess their sins."

"We can't ban them," said Bram. His eyes lingered on Mordan as if he were looking for some hidden truth painted on the wood. "The moment we do, this priest-king will send an army to enforce his rule."

"Does he even have an army to send?" Loreina asked.

"Of course he does," Ian said, frowning. "He can't have taken Mordeina without one."

Bram crossed his arms and thought.

"It isn't as simple a question as it seems. With King Antonil marching east to retake Neldar, defenses must have been few. Whatever troops he has might be needed to quell rebellion and ensure the rest of Mordan's nobles swear their loyalty to him."

"They say he has an army of the dead," Loreina said. She shivered. "I don't like it. I hear the priests' whispers. This Melorak will come after us. Karak's pets are far too convinced of their ascension."

Gill's threat as the pyre burned echoed in Bram's ears. He told his wife everything, and she nodded as if not at all surprised.

"While you were gone, one of them came to me with another request for confession," she told the two men. "He said the same thing: that a new law is coming over this world, and that it would be dangerous for me to have sin in my heart."

Bram stood and flung his chair to the wall.

"Dangerous? *Dangerous!* I'll cut his heart out and show him just how bloody it is with sin. What was his name?"

"I don't remember," Loreina said.

"You lie. Who was it?"

"I said I don't remember."

Ian coughed from the opposite side of the table.

"An execution would only reveal our true feelings toward them," he said. "I don't think it'd be wise to give away our hand just yet."

The redness slowly faded from Bram's face, and he grabbed another chair so he could sit.

"Enough of them," he said, feeling childish beneath his wife's constant stare. "What of the east?"

"We've received hardly a word through any official means," said Ian. "The latest I've heard is that Theo White has assumed the throne in Kinamn, not that there was much to assume. The whole nation of Omn is said to be a wasteland. Those...demons...pillaged everything on their trek west. From what I've heard, at least half the nation is struggling to hold off starvation. Only those south along the coast have escaped relatively unscathed."

"Theo is a bitter man," Loreina said. "I've taken one of his former servant girls into my custody. She fled here when the demons first attacked, before Theo became king. He talks as if the sun will set tomorrow and never rise. With such thinking, he is unpredictable and dangerous."

"Where do his allegiances lie?" asked Bram. "They would normally be to Neldar, but with it in ruins, it seems he's free of any old ties."

"I'd say his allegiances will be only to Omn and himself," said Ian. Loreina nodded in agreement.

"There is one last strange rumor," said Loreina. She pointed to Kinamn on the map. "Refugees pour into our city every day, and I do my best to have the guards question them all. Those who might seem useful are sent to me. The hours have been long and tedious, but every now and then..."

She paused. Bram put his arm around her shoulder and kissed her cheek.

"What is it?" he asked.

"The angels," she said. "I hear men with white wings fly circles above Kinamn, and that Antonil is supposedly with them. If that is true, then his attempt to retake Neldar failed. He'll be coming back, hoping for safety in Mordan."

"And with an enemy to soon give chase," Bram said, following the logical path. "Even worse, he won't know that Mordan has fallen. He's trapped between two foes. Omn is his only ally."

"For now," Loreina said. Bram raised an eyebrow.

"For now?" he asked.

Loreina stood and gestured to the map.

"Enemies on both sides," she said. "Would you not say the same for us? Karak's law will depose us. The priest-king hopes to rule a unified Dezrel. We'll be lucky to have our heads on pikes instead of marching alongside his army of the dead."

"What do you suggest?" asked Ian.

"Theo is a dangerous man. That means he'd be a powerful ally. If he thinks his country is doomed, he will shed streams of blood without batting an eye." She pointed to the two rivers on either side of Ker, the Corinth to the north and the Rigon to the east, and then outlined her plan.

"Simple," said Ian. "But it could work. I doubt there's anywhere else we'd have such strategic defenses."

"But the angels are with Theo," Bram said, frowning at the map. "These religious zealots will overtake our nation, and I will not enslave myself to Ashhur just to free myself from Karak. I will not trade one set of chains for another."

"But those of Ashhur are desperate," Loreina insisted. "Defeat chases them, and they have no home, no hope. Whatever we wish, we can negotiate before we cast in our lot. As for Melorak…"

She crossed her arms and leaned against her husband. Her eyes lingered on the painted figurine of Mordeina.

"There will be no negotiating with that priest-king," she said.

"I'll send someone to speak with King Theo" Bram said, holding his wife tight.

"Let me be the one," Ian said. "You cannot trust this matter to anyone else. The fate of our nation hangs in the balance."

"Leave tonight, then. I'll begin mustering our forces."

Ian saluted and then left.

"What of the priests?" Loreina asked when he was gone. "They will question a sudden surge of recruitment."

Bram grinned at her, a bearish grin, one she had fallen in love with the moment she'd first seen it on their wedding day.

"Why, my dear, we have enemies of Karak right here on our doorstep. Is it not our duty to help defeat the angels in Kinamn?"

She kissed the scar on his face.

"That's my king," she said, smiling.

"The only king this nation shall ever have," he said. "I promise you this."

They kissed again, hungrier, wilder, the desperation hidden from their words escaping in their touch.

10

"Kick his ass!" Tarlak cheered, letting out a drunken whoop as the two combatants clashed their swords together.

"Trying!" Harruq shouted as he dove aside. Judarius's enormous mace smashed an indent into the packed dirt. Chunks of earth flew as the angel tore the mace free, swinging for the half-orc's side. Salvation and Condemnation blocked together, showering the ground with sparks.

"You're getting bolder," Judarius said through gritted teeth as he pressed the hit, pushing Harruq back. He flapped his wings, blowing dust into Harruq's eyes. Grumbling, the half-orc ducked, swinging wildly in hopes for a block. The swords missed. The mace smacked his skull, and he went down in a sudden delirious wave. All around, soldiers cheered or booed, depending on who they had wagered on.

Harruq rubbed his eyes as he stood and glared.

"That was cheap and you know it. First time you've won, the first time, and that's how you want it to be?"

Judarius gave him a curious look.

"A win is a win," he said. "Should I pretend my wings don't exist? Should you pretend your muscles are half their size when you train the other soldiers?"

"Quit whining," Tarlak said, pressing through the crowd and smacking Harruq on the shoulder. "You just earned me a nice bounty of coin."

Harruq raised an eyebrow.

"I thought you wanted me to kick his ass."

The wizard shrugged.

"I did. Doesn't mean that's who I bet on, though."

Harruq made a noise like a snarl and walked away.

"Only by cheating," he grumbled. "A cheating angel…What was that?"

"You're getting grumpy," Aurelia said, sliding beside him and wrapped an arm around his.

"Were you watching?" he asked.

She nodded. "Judarius thought you were being bold, but he's wrong, isn't he? You were impatient, frustrated. You've been like that for weeks."

"What are we waiting for?" he asked as he led her toward the courtyard well for a drink. "Instead of marching home to Mordan, we stay here and what? Hope Velixar doesn't crush us to pieces? The angels are out of their minds, and that White guy along with them."

"Theo's gathering his troops," Aurelia said. She dipped a finger into the bucket before Harruq could drink, chilling the water and flavoring it with lemon. "Besides, he has given you a great honor in training his new recruits."

"Training?" Harruq gasped after a long drink. "You call that an honor? I spend half the day fighting off clumsy strokes a child should know how to block, and the other half getting pulverized to a pulp by the ones that know what they're doing. Last time I was this exhausted was when I was training with Haern."

"At least you've been accepted," Aurelia said, dipping her hands into the bucket and taking a small sip. "The same can't be said for your brother."

Harruq sighed and shook his head.

"He still won't sleep inside the walls?" he asked.

"It's almost been a month. Tarlak's been joking that Qurrah will soon own the land he sleeps on. I wonder just how close to truth he is."

Harruq took another drink, then tossed the bucket and rope back into the well.

"Azariah told me he had an idea to help cheer Qurrah up," he said. "No clue what. Just hope it's soon. Never seen him like this."

"It's still an improvement," she said, rubbing her arms. "At least, over what he could be."

"I'll go talk to him," he said. "Almost makes me wish Tess was here to cheer him up."

"Don't say that name," Aurelia whispered.

Harruq kissed her forehead.

"No problem. Keep the bed warm for me tonight."

He trudged out of the castle walls and toward the hill overlooking the city.

Qurrah gathered the ashes together in his fists and concentrated. The words were the same, the well of power within him the same, but the spell was not working. Nothing was.

"I said *burn!*" he shouted, ignoring the pain in his throat. Flames licked around his fingers, the ash flared into orange embers, but the heat vanished. Qurrah cursed and hurled them back into the fire pit.

"Having fun?" Harruq asked as he approached.

"Don't be glib," Qurrah said, wiping the ash onto his black robes.

"Not sure what that means."

Qurrah rolled his eyes as his brother shifted uncomfortably. As if afraid to meet his eyes, he instead glanced about the meager camp.

"You staying warm at night?" he asked.

"I doubt you're here just to see if I need another blanket," Qurrah said. He knelt before the fire and closed his eyes. He felt the workings of a spell, but interlocked with them were traces of Karak, his thoughts, his desires. How much of his power had come from the dark god? Always there, always tempting…

"I'm just worried about you," Harruq said. He crossed his arms and shifted his weight from foot to foot. "You never come into the city. You never train with us. I'm scared to ask what you've even been eating these past few weeks."

"Squirrels and mud," Qurrah said, his eyes still closed.

"Stop joking. You're worrying all of us."

Qurrah stood, opening his eyes and glaring. He held up a fistful of ash.

"This used to be my life," he said. "Fire and destruction obeyed my whims like slaves. But it's gone. Every day I feel weaker, helpless. My mind is naked. My sword is made of wood, my armor cloth. Don't you understand? No matter what those angels say, I must atone for what I have done. I will face Velixar. I *must* face him, and if he wins, he might not just defeat me. He might...he..."

He flung the ash down. Every part of him shrieked for it to burn, to erupt in a flame equal to the fear and frustration in his heart. But instead it only flared a soft orange before scattering across the grass.

Harruq put a hand on his brother's shoulder.

"You won't lose," he said. "And even if you do, there's nothing *he* can do. There's no spell, no words, he can say to change who you are."

"Tell that to Jerico," Qurrah muttered.

"What?"

"Forget it."

Harruq pointed to the ash.

"What's the problem, anyway?" he asked. "I thought your spells were, well, spells. I didn't think turning against Karak would change anything."

Qurrah sighed. "Neither did I."

The two looked about, as if neither were sure what to say. During this brief reprieve, Harruq glanced skyward, and then his eyes widened.

"What?" asked Qurrah.

In answer, Harruq pointed.

Flying low in the sky, her white wings spread wide with each rhythmic flap, came Sonowin.

"Looks like the horse's wing has healed just fine," Harruq said.

"I should go," Qurrah said, putting the city to his back.

"Wait, where are you...ooooh."

Qurrah chuckled. "That's right. Last time I saw Dieredon, I was at Velixar's side. I'd rather not be the one to explain to him everything that's happened."

"Yeah," Harruq said, scratching his chin. "Remember back at the Eschaton tower? Elf nearly put an arrow through my throat. Aurelia's the only reason he didn't. Hmm. Maybe we should just let him land at the castle without seeing either one of us..."

Tarlak stretched out atop his luxurious bed, his hat resting over his face to block the light from his eyes. He'd been given the room once they moved in. He found bittersweet amusement in knowing it had once belonged to an advisor named Penwick, who had put off seeing them, then lied to keep the death of his king a secret so he might hold onto power. Sweet because the room was now his; bitter because, well, the whole city had been executed along with Penwick. Tarlak found that only a little depressing, but he tried not to think about it.

A knock on the door stirred him from his daydreaming.

"You know how much beauty sleep it takes to look like this?" he asked through his hat. To his surprise, the door opened, and no joke accompanied Aurelia's entrance.

"Tar?" she asked, something about her tone setting the wizard on edge.

"Hey, Aurelia. Something wrong?" He set aside his hat and sat up.

"Dieredon's here," she said. She bit her lip as she paused a moment.

"That's great!" Tarlak said, forcing a smile. His heart was in his throat. It couldn't be. He pleaded with Ashhur that it couldn't be. Aurelia's hesitation. Dieredon's arrival.

She stepped aside so Dieredon could enter. Tarlak moved closer so they could embrace, then smacked him across the shoulder.

"It's good to see you again," the wizard said, grinning. "I hope you weren't too bored. Things haven't gone so well for us, but I think we've got a…"

"Tarlak," Dieredon said. His voice chilled the room. The smile left Tarlak's face. Aurelia stood at the door. There were tears in her eyes.

"Karak's forces took the city," Dieredon said. "Their numbers were greater than we could withstand. Haern died saving my life. I'm so sorry."

For a moment, Tarlak only stared. His mouth dropped open.

"No," he said. He felt his hands shaking, and he couldn't stop them. "No. He can't. He's the last. Brug, Delysia, now...but now..."

He stumbled back to the bed and buried his face in his hands. Aurelia was there, her arms around him, her own wet face pressed against his neck.

"It'll be all right," she whispered as she held him. "We're here for you. We're here."

Tarlak tried to get it together. He tried to remember his friends, his newcomers, Harruq and Aurelia and the paladins. He tried to pretend the Eschaton mercenaries weren't dead and gone. He tried to stop his tears.

He failed.

❖

"How is he?" Dieredon asked once Aurelia stepped out. "As well as could be expected," Aurelia said, tucking strands of her hair behind an ear. She blushed a little, realizing how terrible she must look with her eyes puffy from her own tears. At her blush, Dieredon gently wiped below her eyes with his thumb and smiled.

"I need to tell Harruq," she said. "I don't know how he'll take it. They spent so much time training. Haern was always hard on Harruq, but only because he expected so much out of him. Seemed a little unnecessary at times, though. But those were happier days."

"It seems all the times of happiness are long lost to the past," Dieredon said.

"There is still happiness in each other," she said, accepting his embrace.

"He still loves you, and treats you well?" Dieredon asked.

"As best a half-orc can."

"Better than an elf?"

Aurelia elbowed him hard in the chest.

"Keep comments like that to yourself. He doesn't know about all that."

Dieredon chuckled.

"Secrets between husband and wife? As if your marriage wasn't shameful enough."

"Nothing shameful," she said. "You've thrashed him with that bow of yours. If Harruq thought he had to compete with you in anything else, especially *that*, he'd never have enough confidence to make it through the day."

"So does he compete?"

She elbowed him a second time, then pulled him close so their heads could touch.

"I missed you," she said, the momentary playfulness unable to last with the grief lurking behind the door to Tarlak's room. Her chest felt hollow and numb. Too much grief, even for her, who had lived through the exodus of her entire race from fire and swords.

"I have much to do," Dieredon said, gently pushing her away. "I need to talk with this new king here, as well as Antonil, so they know that no help remains for them from the west. I must also make haste for Quellassar. If Neyvar Sinistel won't give me the Ekreissar to fly against Karak's forces now, nothing will ever convince him to."

"Will it be enough?" Aurelia asked.

Dieredon kissed her forehead.

"Pray to Celestia it is," he told her. "Because without her help...No, I don't think it will be enough."

He left for an audience with the two kings. Aurelia leaned on the wall opposite Tarlak's door, her arms crossed. She chewed her lip as she thought of what to do. Harruq was outside the castle with Qurrah. She wondered if he'd seen Dieredon's approach, as well as how he would react. Poor Haern. He'd always been so kind to her, treated her like a beautiful princess. Dead and gone, and by Dieredon's own arrow. That part Aurelia had insisted Dieredon leave out of his tale to the wizard. The last thing they needed was Tarlak blaming yet another friend for the death of a loved one.

Time slipped away. She almost returned to their bedroom, but something kept her still. She wanted to be there in case Tarlak needed her. Her feet ached, so she sat, her arms across her knees, her forehead resting against her wrists. Eyes closed, she quietly cried.

"Aurelia?"

She looked up.

"Oh, Harruq," she said. She didn't bother faking a smile.

"What's wrong?" he asked, sitting down beside her.

"It's Haern," she said.

That was enough. He wrapped his arm around her and leaned her weight against him. Her hair spread across his chest. The weight of his body comforted her, along with the gentle touch of his fingers rubbing her temples. She kept her eyes closed as they talked.

"Who was it?" he asked after awhile.

"A priest of Karak. A powerful one, like Velixar."

"Did he suffer?"

Aurelia shook her head.

"No."

The half-orc sighed.

"At least we have that. I hope he killed a hundred of them before he died. No, a thousand. No one could beat him, not when he was lost in the dance, the cloak dance…"

He ran out of words. She took one of his hands and kissed his palm.

"Why do we do this?" he asked.

"What do you mean?"

"This. All of this. What do we have left? What are all of us dying for? This world is Karak's. We're the last tiny sliver of hope. Sometimes I just wish it was over, Aurry. I wish I could put away my swords and run away, just you and me."

"Live in hiding while the world burns?"

She heard him chuckle.

"You can't blame me. We've bled for this. We've given them everything. But Velixar's still out there, lurking, plotting. He's the last remnant of my old self, and until he's dead and gone I'll keep fighting. I just…I love you, Aurry. I'm terrified it'll be me next. That you'll be somewhere and Dieredon or Tarlak will show up to tell you…"

Aurelia kissed him to shut him up.

"Stop it," she whispered when their lips parted. "Just stop it. We do as we must. We helped create this war, and we'll help end it. And so you know, I'll kill you if you die without me somewhere."

He kissed her again.

"Sure thing," he said. He nodded toward Tarlak's door. "He going to make it?"

The elf frowned. "I hope so."

"No sense sitting here. Floor's freezing my butt numb. Let's go."

Just before they left, Aurelia knocked on the door, then slowly pushed it open. When she poked her head inside, Tarlak lay on the bed, his arms behind his head, his eyes absently staring at the ceiling.

"Get some rest," she said. "If you need anything..."

He didn't respond, didn't look at her. She left.

⋈

Despite his exhaustion, Harruq slept little that night. Memories of better times haunted his tired mind, and horrible nightmares plagued his sleep. Before the sun had even crept above the horizon he was up and about. He dressed in full armor, anticipating yet another long day of practice. He made his way to the courtyard, stopping only to grab a chunk of bread and wedge of butter from the mess hall. Once he finished eating, he swung his swords in lazy arcs.

After ten minutes, a commotion alerted him to the arrival of several men, all of them leading horses from the stable. One of them was King Theo, the others his private guard. Upon seeing Harruq, the king said a few words and then approached alone.

"We go to hunt," Theo said.

"I'm not much for hunting," Harruq said, halting his practice. "Hunting is for bows and spears. As you can see, I'm more of a sword man."

"You sound modest. Shame it is false. The people tell stories of you, did you know that? I'm not sure who started them, though many say your wizard friend told them first. I must say, I am a little jealous."

Harruq raised an eyebrow. "Jealous? Of what?"

Theo chuckled and leaned against his horse.

"You helped bring down an abomination that killed a hundred city soldiers. You stood alone at Veldaren, holding off a legion of undead so the people could escape. Others have said you spilled the blood of a thousand demons to keep a portal open from the hills of Neldar to the elves' forest. Some even claim you frightened away Karak's forces at Mordeina, and that your very prayers summoned the angels of Ashhur."

The half-orc sheathed his swords and did his best to look anywhere but Theo's face.

"I'm no hero," he said. "You hear trumped up stories, or people forgetting how many friends stood at my side."

"That doesn't matter. You stood against the many, and by your sheer will you endured. A last stand, giving no ground. What I would give to have been there, or to have guarded these walls when the demons first assaulted our nation. To kill protecting your land, your nation, your countrymen. To fall knowing you died for something, and that a hopeless cause can still be a noble cause. You have earned your status in these campfire stories, Harruq. In these dark times, I hope I have a chance to do the same."

Theo mounted his horse and then whistled for his guard.

"Are you sure you don't want to come?" the king asked. "If we're lucky, we may find a boar, and they give more than enough fight. Perhaps not for one such as you, but plenty for the rest of us."

"I'll stay," Harruq insisted. "I have your men to train, after all."

Theo frowned, as if deciding how upset he should be at the refusal.

"So be it," he said at last. "Train them well. Our nation of Omn may soon depend on the skill of those blades."

He joined his guard. As they rode out the gate. Harruq watched them go, thinking of what Ahaesarus had said about the king's fatalistic views. Theo didn't just expect to die; he wanted to. But not any death. A hero's death. A noble death. One worthy of legends.

"What do you plan, you crazy noble you?" the half-orc asked the courtyard. Wind blew through the air, but it carried no answers with it, only a chill that sent him back inside to warm himself before a fire until the sun rose and the training began.

※※※

When he returned, the peaceful calm had been replaced by a gathering of soldiers. At first he thought they were sparring in practice, but then he saw the stranger surrounded at the gate. Harruq muscled his way closer, curious to hear what was going on.

"I must speak with your lord," the newcomer was saying. "I bring a message from King Henley of Ker!"

"Ker's sided with Karak," shouted one chubby soldier Harruq recognized from their training. The guy couldn't block to save his life.

"What you hoping for, surrender?" asked another. That guy blocked well, but his attacks were painfully obvious.

"My name is Sir Ian Millar, and I bring a message of hope!" the knight shouted, repeating this again and again while Harruq watched. "I must speak with your lord!"

"He's out hunting," the half-orc shouted, tiring of the annoying spectacle. "I'm not of Ker, but I can assure you the hospitality has so far been much better than what these asses have shown."

Several turned on him, furious, but others quieted or even backed away in embarrassment. Harruq put his hands on the hilts of his swords, his glare daring anyone to challenge him.

"He's your problem then," said one of the soldiers. "Keep an eye on him, and keep him here in the open until our king returns."

"I'm already training your troops," Harruq said. "Might as well carry even more of your weight, eh?"

He grinned, but his hands closed tight on his hilts, ready to draw. The man backed down, though, and the others disbanded into pairs to spar. Only the knight remained, Ian was his name if Harruq remembered correctly, and each gave the other a funny look.

"You look strange for a knight," Ian said.

"I've got orc-blood, not noble-blood. You pick a strange time to arrive in a nation at war."

"I've nearly ridden my horse into its grave to arrive here, and I carry what is surely the first ray of hope to this war-torn country in months, yet my welcome is a band of thugs accusing me of being a spy, or worse."

The knight huffed and crossed his arms. Harruq chuckled.

"Not much for politics, are you?" he asked.

"Loathe them."

"Good. We might just get along."

Harruq caught the knight staring at something over his shoulder, so he turned around to see what. The two paladins were strapping on their armor and stretching. They'd taken to helping Harruq in training the men, Lathaar focusing on offensive drills and Jerico on increasing endurance, the both of them preaching or discussing theology with the men while they sweated and fought. The half-orc chuckled.

"You look like you haven't seen a paladin before," he said.

"We were told all paladins of Ashhur had been killed," Ian explained.

"You were told wrong, but only barely. Those two are the last."

"And you let them wander freely through your castle?"

This time it was Harruq's turn to look surprised. "Uh, what?"

Ian paused a moment, then coughed and looked away.

"Forgive me, I just…there are no priests or paladins to Karak here, are there? I am so used to Ker. Their kind is viewed as an unlawful presence."

Several men from the castle gates raised a call, and others took it up.

"The king approaches! All hail the king!"

"Come on," Harruq said. "Let's deliver your message, and then I can introduce you to the paladins. I assure you, they're a lovely couple, but I can't wait to hear them browbeat you about your country's wonderful laws. Oh, and if you think they're bad, just wait until you meet the angels."

Ian glanced skyward.

"Angels?" he asked.

Harruq only laughed.

⋈

Harruq had expected Theo to dismiss him once they reached his throne, but instead he ordered him to stay, sending away all others. Feeling oddly out of place, the half-orc listened as Sir Ian detailed his master's plan.

"We seek freedom from Mordeina's tyranny," Ian explained. "Their priests will soon rule if we do not stop them. Even now, my king gathers soldiers to fight, but this Melorak possesses a grand army, and is rumored to wield unmatched magical power. Soon he will march against us, but we will make our stand."

Theo's eyes seemed to sparkle at that.

"A valiant effort," he said, leaning forward in his throne. "But why come to me?"

"We will pledge our banner behind King Antonil, rightful ruler of Mordan. In return for helping him retake his throne, he promises our nation complete sovereignty. We will bow to no god, neither Karak nor Ashhur."

"A fair request, and one I am sure he will accept," Theo said.

Harruq wondered why Theo didn't bring Antonil in to listen. Surely this was something he should be present for?

"But not my only request," said Ian. "We ask for an alliance, good king. We hear rumors of a second army from the east. We cannot fight a war on two sides. If we are to succeed, then Ker must not fall. My king will defend the Bloodbrick Crossing. You must hold them at the Gods' Bridges."

Theo stood, and despite his best attempts, he could not hide his enthusiasm.

"Give me a day to prepare," he said. "I must discuss this with my advisors, and Antonil as well. I have servants waiting on the other side of the door. Go to them, tell them to give you my finest room."

"You are too kind," Ian said, and he allowed himself to smile. "If our nations may ally, then perhaps good will emerge from this darkness."

"But only if we are strong enough to fight for it," Theo said, dismissing the knight.

Harruq tried to decide whether to follow or not, but the king had not dismissed him, just Ian. Shrugging his shoulders, he waited and wondered.

"What more could we ask for?" Theo asked once they were alone. The king paced, too excited to remain seated. "An army coming from the east, to the only bridge into our lands. We have the place, and now the honor. If we win, or even delay, then Bram can destroy the usurper and retake Mordeina. We defend not just our homeland but the homelands of thousands of others!"

"It does sound like a good plan," Harruq said, doing his best to be tactful but feeling woefully inadequate. "But maybe you should discuss this with Antonil first? Or the angels?"

"I don't need to," Theo said, turning to him. "For I have you."

"Me?" Harruq's jaw dropped a little. "What do I have to do with anything?"

"Everything! If you stay, then your elf wife will as well. Then that yellow-robed wizard follows, friends staying with friends, and suddenly I have the heroes my men whisper of around their campfires. Even the paladins will join me. Among the company of heroes, my men will make their stand. Antonil would not dare interfere, nor is he stupid enough to turn down such unexpected aid in reclaiming his throne."

"Antonil might not be," Harruq said. "But what if I am?"

Theo paused. His eyes narrowed.

"Surely I did not hear you correctly," he said.

Harruq grinned. "Afraid so."

"But why? You have fought far more hopeless battles before. What is this but another part of your growing legend? You defended the people of Neldar, then Mordan, and now Omn calls for your aid. Yet you dare turn me down?"

"I like making my own decisions," Harruq said. "Besides, you think I'll abandon Antonil? You think I'll make everyone else stay to fight a god, all so you get your prideful death? You'll abandon this castle, your lands, the homes you're supposed to protect, all for one last desperate battle protecting Ker's border?"

The ensuing silence frightened the half-orc. Theo looked ready to kill him.

"Get out," he said. "Tomorrow my men march west for the Gods' Bridges. If you would be a coward, then so be it. I will build my own legend."

Harruq bowed and left, feeling the glare of the king burning into the back of his head. He went straight for the paladins, trusting their judgment on the matter. If any of his friends knew the politics and standings of the nations, it was they.

He found them sparring each other, lightly armored and sweating in the courtyard.

"Harruq!" Lathaar shouted upon seeing him. "Care for a fight? Jerico's not much sport; feel like I'm spending my time chopping down a tree."

Harruq shook his head, then blurted out everything he'd heard. The two paladins listened without saying a word.

"He's desperate for glory,' Jerico said when he was finished. "He probably spent so much time competing with his brother for his father's devotion that it's just become a part of who he is. Question is, do we think it is a good plan?"

"It's the best one I've heard so far," Lathaar said. "Granted, it's the *only* plan I've heard so far. I've gotten the impression everyone here is just waiting for Karak to make a move so we can react."

"Well, we'd be taking the initiative," Harruq said.

"But you don't like it," Jerico said, seeing Harruq's frown. "Why not?"

The half-orc shrugged.

"Not sure. But my place is with Antonil, don't you think? That's where we belong."

"We should prepare for travel," said Lathaar. "Either with Theo or with Antonil, we'll be moving west. There's no point in staying, not in an unguarded, unoccupied castle."

"Come," said Jerico. "Someone should tell Antonil. If all goes well, we might yet salvage his crown."

11

He'd spent almost two days weaving his way through the alleys and secret spots of Veldaren, but at last Deathmask was certain Haern had lost his trail. Under cover of night he slipped through the broken window, then snapped his fingers to summon a purple fire about his hand. He looked down at Veliana's body and frowned.

"You slit her throat," he said to the absent Haern. "Now why did you have to do that?"

Her eyes were still closed, her flesh pale and still. He put a hand against her face, the purple fire cold and giving no heat, only light. Carefully he looked her over.

"You seem no worse for wear," Deathmask whispered to her. "Though you're really not going to like feeling those maggots that I'm sure a few flies laid."

He set down his pack of supplies and rummaged through them. The cut on her neck worried him, and complicated an already delicate task. It hadn't bled, and the flesh had turned an ugly yellow where the wound had failed to seal. From his pack he found a small spool of thread and a single needle.

"You're going to have one nasty scar," he told her. "Hopefully you'll forgive me for that, too. Sewing is not one of my better skills."

Stitch by stitch he closed her throat, until it looked like she wore a grim necklace. After that he moved on to the stab Haern had given her, stitching it shut. That done, he stripped her naked and took out a bottle of alcohol from his pouch. He splashed it across her body, then began scrubbing. Anywhere she had a cut or opening he checked for bugs, eggs, and any other such vermin that was fond of the dead. He found plenty, but knew despite his diligence, he'd still miss some. Veliana was going to be so pissed...

"Cross your fingers," he told her, then grinned at his own bad joke. With a single word he removed the spell he'd cast two days prior. Her heart resumed its pumping. Her blood unfroze. Her lungs gasped in a long, painful breath. As she emerged from her stasis, her mouth opened in a single scream that lacked the force to express the delirium and pain she surely felt.

"Easy," he said, holding her in his arms as she shivered and thrashed wildly. "Don't scream. Don't talk. Haern cut your throat to make sure you were dead."

Her fingernails dug into his skin as she clutched him. Blood seeped from numerous cuts and bites, and he winced knowing they had to sting like a hornet because of the alcohol. Her jaw and hands trembled as her body endured wave after wave of jolts and shivers.

"If there's anywhere that hurts, point," he told her. "I need to make sure nothing is in you and…alive."

He carefully tilted her chin so she'd look up at him. Her good eye looked into his, and then pooled with tears. She nodded in understanding, then pointed toward her side. Taking out his knife, Deathmask knelt close and forced down any squeamish sensations. If Veliana was to endure, he had to be quick, thorough, and calm.

"This'll hurt," he said before slicing into her skin. A moment later he pulled out a thin white worm. He burned it with a spell before Veliana could see it. "Where else?"

She touched her ankle. Deathmask saw the bite, which had begun seeping puss once her body resumed its normal functions. Doing his best to ignore her choked cries, he pried it open. At first he saw nothing, but as the blood pooled he saw a ripple from squirming. The tiny grub died on the tip of his dagger.

One after another she pointed, he cut, and the intruder died. Dark blood seeped through the stitches and trickled down her neck, and any color slowly drained away from her face. Several times he thought she might vomit, but she never did. With every cut, he felt more and more proud.

"Any more?" he asked her after a very long pause. She bit her lip, then nodded. Her tears, which had dried up, started anew. With a trembling finger she pointed to her right ear.

"Inside?" he asked. She nodded. "Shit."

He put his hand against her head and closed his eyes. He let his mind focus on the essence of life. The touch would be so gentle, so weak...there. With a few words of magic he focused in on it, a threat, a feasting intruder, and without warning he cast another spell. The bug burst into flame. Veliana screamed at the pain, her inner ear burning. Deathmask held her tight against him, wincing at her sobs, but he did not end the spell. He burned and burned until there was nothing left but the tiniest pile of ash. He tilted her head to the side, leaned down, and blew with a soft breath tinged with magic. Out came the ash, sparkling as it floated to the ground.

"It's over," he whispered, holding her naked body against him. "It's all over. Your body needs to heal, and then it won't hurt anymore. Hopefully Haern's second cut didn't cost you your voice, but it might take awhile before we find out."

She whispered something, the sound wet and groaning.

"Yes, dear?" he asked, leaning closer.

"Bastard," she whispered.

"Love you too," he said, grinning. "And as enjoyable as this is, let's get you dressed."

Deathmask shook out her clothes, then helped her slide on the pants and shirt. Every movement hurt; he could tell by the winces she made and the little gasps that escaped her lips when he touched her. He talked to her the whole while, hoping the distraction would take her mind off the vast amount of aches and stings.

"I have a few people for you to meet," he said. "It's been two days since Haern, or whatever shell of Haern that was, attacked us. Since then, I've spent plenty of fun hours in undesirable locations I won't bother boring you by listing. There was one advantage, however, and that was in finding others who felt a similar need to hide. I also killed a few of the Lionsguard. Can't let them think the Ghost and his Blade are out of the game, can we? Anyway, it seems we've inspired some like-minded individuals. I'm sure you don't feel up to lively discussion, but it's with them we will be safest. Besides, there's someone there who I think you will be very happy to see."

Once dressed, he stepped back and surveyed her form. Her neck was yellow except for where the blood had stained it red. Her scarred eye was swollen shut, while her good eye still dripped tears. Every step she took, she winced, and it seemed she was unable to halt the tremble of her hands.

"Like a princess," he said. "Let's go, before daylight comes."

◑◉◐

Deathmask had no choice but to hurry along the streets. Veliana couldn't skulk or leap across the rooftops, so instead he looked every which way before leading her by the hand. Silently he begged whatever gods might be that Haern remained on the other side of town. If there was anything he wasn't prepared for, it was another duel with the undead assassin.

Twice he spotted a Lionsguard patrol approaching, but both times he led them into a side alley to avoid their torches. They steadily made their way south, away from the castle. They stopped once, for Veliana to catch her breath. With every rise and fall of her chest, she whimpered. Deathmask couldn't wait until they arrived. He hated seeing her in so much pain.

"Almost there," he told her. She looked up at him and mouthed the word 'good'.

The streets were calm and empty, the result of the many patrols and the viciously enforced laws the priest-king had enacted. For once, Deathmask was thankful. The unsettling silence made it easy to hear any patrols coming. Deep in southern Mordeina, he turned them down a street, waited for a group of priests and soldiers to get far enough away, and then led the two of them to a large house of stained oak. He rapped his knuckles three times against the double doors, paused, then three more. The door cracked open.

"Come in," said a gray-haired man.

The house had once been exquisitely furnished, but everywhere Deathmask looked he saw bright squares and circles where paintings and mirrors had once hung. The floor was bare, the long hallway empty.

"Follow me," said the elderly man. "You took much longer than expected. We'd all begun to worry."

Deathmask glanced back at Veliana and the stitch-grin on her neck.

"There were some complications," he said.

"Things are never as easy as we hope."

He led them through a parlor, past two bedrooms, and then down a set of stairs. Despite its lack of windows and thick stone walls, the deep cellar was well-lit by a floating ball of gold that shone like a miniature sun. Several men occupied the crowded space, kneeling on pillows or sitting on uncomfortable stools. Below the light, keeper of the spell, sat another elderly man wearing the white robes of Ashhur.

"Welcome back," he said. "It is good to see my prayers for your safety answered."

"Save your prayers for where they are useful," said Deathmask. He took Veliana's hand and pulled her to his side. "Veliana, meet Bernard Ulath, former high-priest of Ashhur."

"The temple may have fallen," Bernard said, a soft smile on his face. "But I am still a priest. Lay down, Veliana. I can see the pain all over your face, and I will do what I can."

Veliana sank to her knees, then rolled onto her back. She closed her eyes as Bernard began to pray. His hands shone white, filling with healing power. Deathmask watched with his arms crossed. He didn't share Bernard's sense of faith. He was a practical man, after all. But the priest's healing ability was superb, and his way with words and men skillful. For all of Deathmask's killing and scaremongering, it had been Bernard who had kindled the first true resistance against Melorak's rule.

"Did you encounter *him* while you were out?" asked one of the others in the room.

Deathmask switched his attention from Veliana to the man. He was a heavy nobleman, his face covered with a red beard. He tried to remember his name. Hocking, and first name with a K or a P...

"No, Hocking, I did not," he said, deciding first names weren't necessary.

"Thank Ashhur for that. A few of my men have seen him about, but he's never attacked. It seems he's got his eyes and swords for you only, though I fear what might happen if he succeeds."

"Yes, I'd hate to find out," Deathmask said, rolling his eyes. "Where are the others? I count five here, yet you promised at least ten."

"It's going to take time," said another, a wiry man with dark eyes. "Once we prove our goal is achievable, the others will come."

"Which means others now know of your involvement but have not yet committed to our cause," Deathmask said. "A potentially dangerous mistake, milord...uh..."

"Dagan," the wiry man said. "Dagan Gemcroft. You seem poor with names. Is killing all you are good at, Deathmask?"

"More than good. The best."

"Would you like us to introduce ourselves, maybe write our names on our foreheads to help you remember?"

"Enough," said Bernard, interrupting his prayers. "These times are difficult, but snapping at one another is childish. We have enough to begin our fight. That is all that matters. Now please, talk quieter so I might concentrate."

"I have over two hundred house guards ready to kill at my command," Hocking said, hitching his thumbs in his belt as if this number should impress him. Deathmask rolled his eyes.

"What else?" he asked.

"I have five-hundred mercenaries hired out from what's left of Neldar," Dagan said. "They're pretty damn angry at what's happened. They've cut their rates by half, just to get a shot at killing."

"Mercenaries and house guards," Deathmask said. "Such a grand army. Are they prepared to do dirty work? This won't be an honorable battlefield, gentlemen. We're going to fill the shadows with blood and fire."

"You won't burn our own property down, will you?" asked a man from the corner. He was tall but thin, giving him a stretched look that his wrinkled face only exacerbated.

"And you are?"

The man bowed.

"Lord John Ewes. I once owned half the great fields, until the priest-king took them from me at the edge of a sword."

"And what, you fear we'll burn your fields?"

"Damn right I do. That's my sweat and blood growing out there. For a century my family has toiled the fields, hired workers, dug and cultivated. Stolen, all of them!"

"You're yelling," Deathmask said, a dark grin on his face. "And what does it matter? The fire will make next year's harvest all the greater. As for this year…you have nothing. Better we give them ash to feed their armies than grain."

John crossed his arms and leaned back into the corner.

"How far are you willing to go?" he asked the assassin.

Deathmask looked down at Veliana's battered form, and he remembered his friends, the twins, who had died during Melorak's victorious assault.

"As far as my life will take me," he said. "You all must remember, we won't be heroes. No one will remember our names. If we're lucky, Antonil will show up, retake allegiance of the Mordan soldiers, and then crush this new priest-king dead. Until then, we starve them. We bleed them. We take their coin and bloody their noses. They've cowed the citizenry. We need to make them angry! Fire and hunger are our weapons now. And if any of you here aren't willing to give up everything, and I mean *everything*, to free this city from Karak's rule, then I suggest you leave right now and never let me see your face again, because the next time you see mine, it'll be covered with ash."

"We fight for our survival," Bernard said, standing and helping Veliana to her feet. Already her skin looked healthier, and the shaking of her hands had finally stopped. "Deathmask, you yearn for the bloodshed and destruction, but we are not the same. You are right, but I ask that we ensure our victims are only those sworn to Karak. I will not aid you in slaughtering innocents."

"There are no innocents in this war," Deathmask nearly snarled.

"Maybe so," Bernard said. His shoulders sagged, and he looked as if he bore a great burden. "But I still want you to try."

"So be it." Deathmask turned to Dagan. "Send your mercenaries to the Great Fields. They're harvesting the grain to feed his army massing north of the city. Burn the fields to the ground."

He shot a look at John, who sighed, then nodded.

"Burn everything," the lord said. "And may Ashhur have mercy on us all."

Deathmask laughed.

"Mercy," he said. "I've fallen in the company of fools. John, I assume you were paid a pittance when your lands were stolen from you? Take it and start distributing it among the poor under the condition they buy food and only food."

"What for?"

"When the fields burn, Melorak will need to obtain food from elsewhere. I want every spare loaf in the hands of Mordeina's people. If we're lucky, he'll get desperate and try to take it from them. Either that, or he buys it back, otherwise his army starves. No matter his choice, we win."

"You ask me to bankrupt myself," said John.

"No heroes, remember?"

"Already you burn my fields, and now ask for all my wealth? You're doing a better job destroying me than the priest-king."

"Quit complaining," Dagan said. "You think I haven't spent every coin I have keeping the mercenaries?"

"I have nothing left," Hocking said. "My house guards stay with me out of loyalty and a hope for revenge. At least you might one day retake your fields. Karak's priests have my fortune."

Lord Ewes threw up his hands in surrender. "So be it. This better work, rogue."

"Night will soon be over," Bernard said, ending the taut silence that had followed. "I will pray for your safety. Return to your homes. I will send a messenger for when we are to meet again. Go with Ashhur's blessing."

One by one the men left, until only Bernard, Deathmask, and Veliana remained in the cellar.

"You need to learn how to speak with subtlety and kindness," Bernard said, sitting back down and leaning against the wall. He let out a grunt of displeasure as his back popped. "These men are scared and desperate. Every day Karak's priests whisper in their ears, promising their wealth returned a hundredfold if they prove their loyalty and devotion."

"This is no time for childish handholding," Deathmask said. "We are at war, and they need to learn that."

Veliana tapped him on the shoulder, then tilted her head back and made a drinking motion with her hand.

"Do you have any wine or water?" he asked Bernard.

"Up the stairs," the priest said. "What few stores we have are in a cupboard to your left."

Deathmask left and came back with a wineskin. Veliana guzzled it down, even though she winced and clearly fought against the pain in her throat.

"This is some rebellion," Deathmask said, plopping down atop a stool. "Burning the fields will hurt them, but he won't disband the army. Melorak's been kind so far to the general populace, but I fear that will end soon enough. They'll pillage and tax like never before. We're about to make a lot of people unhappy on both sides. Are you sure your…fragile sensibilities will endure this? These are not times for grace and forgiveness, only blood and ash."

Bernard closed his eyes, losing himself in his memories.

"When Karak's army stormed the walls, my priests and I did our best to fend off the undead emerging through the tunnels. When the bulk of the army was trapped atop the walls, I sent my followers after them in hopes of freeing the soldiers so they might fight. Alone, I hurried to the queen, fearful of what her advisor, a priest of Karak named Hayden, might do. I arrived too late. Melorak and his priests were already there, singing Karak's praises. My beloved queen was dead. They scattered her ashes across the steps. As for my brethren, Karak's priests covered their heads with tar and put them atop spikes throughout the city."

He opened his eyes and looked at Deathmask.

"I am ready to do whatever must be done. I can endure no worse a day than that, hiding like a coward while my friends were tortured and killed."

Veliana knelt beside him, tapped her throat, then tapped his heart.

'Thank you' she mouthed.

"You will regain your voice in a few days," he told her, trying to smile. "Until then, you may stay down here and rest. I have cast many protections, and if this Haern is undead, he will burst into flame should he take a single step into the cellar."

They piled up pillows, and then Deathmask wrapped her in a blanket after she lay down. It wasn't long until she slept, unable to fight off her exhaustion. He kissed her forehead, then headed for the stairs.

"Where are you going?" Bernard asked.

"After today, I really need a drink."

"Drinking's illegal now. You know that right?"

Deathmask chuckled, then outright laughed.

"Then I'll drink twice as much," he said. "Fuck this priest-king and his laws. It's time we showed him the world isn't ready to roll over and die."

12

Tessanna watched the forest burn and cried.
"I know," said Velixar, standing beside her. "Isn't it beautiful?"

The smoke clogged the air for miles, blotting out the sky in a gray and black plume. Everywhere she looked she saw fire. The red haze made her feel trapped in a nightmare, one she could never wake from. She wore a sparkling red dress, her hair long and carefully cut. Velixar's dead queen, she'd begun calling herself. The bride of a corpse. Romance of the grave.

"Here come the elves," said a war demon standing beside them. He carried two flags, and he raised the red one above his head and then took flight. In response, a great patrol on horseback turned toward them, having ridden along the Erze Forest's edge waiting for the counterattack. They were over four-hundred in number, men that had bowed their knee at Felwood. Tessanna hoped the elves would see this and flee, but instead they raced out of the burning trees with their swords drawn. A single thin line of undead stood in their way, but Velixar appeared unworried.

The elves cut through the undead and continued on, but the distance was too great. The horsed archers unleashed their barrage. The first of many arrows landed, and then they fell like rain. Ten elves died, their corpses trampled as the archers rode across them before looping around in search of more targets.

Still Tessanna cried.

Thulos's plan had been simple. They'd scattered out along the forest's edge for several miles, then sent a thousand undead carrying torches in a single wave. The elves stopped many, but not all, and throughout the day war demons had flung pitch and torches from above. They'd started early in the morning, and after a day they'd burned hundreds of miles. As night approached, the fire only grew, devouring more and more of the forest. The elves couldn't fire their arrows due to the inferno between them and their enemy, and their swords meant nothing to the flying war demons and the patrolling archers on horseback.

"Look," Velixar said, pointing to the south-west. "Do you see the clouds? What spellcasters the elves have must be creating rainfall to protect Nellassar. The distance is too great, though, and they have too few. The fire will curl about them and destroy their great city. So beautiful. Tell me, Tessanna, does the goddess weep for the death of her children?"

"Mother doesn't speak to me anymore," Tessanna replied.

"A shame." Velixar smiled in the abyssal light and enjoyed the burning. "Perhaps your goddess is dead, and this night, we strangle the last remnants of her life."

Tessanna didn't answer. She only watched as yet another part of the world died.

><()><

Thulos's forces followed the forest to the south, rekindling fires where they dwindled and setting flames anew when they curled around the lower segments that had been beyond their original formation. They kept the task of burning to the undead, unwilling to sacrifice any fighting soldiers or demons to the suicidal task. After that first day, no elves dared attack. Velixar was certain they'd retreated back to their capital, and told Tessanna so. She said not a word back.

"I believe Jerico tried this trick on you," Karak's prophet said when he realized she was staying silent. "I don't remember it working too well for him."

Tessanna smiled bitterly.

They marched amid the thousands of troops taken from Felwood. Thulos had given Velixar command of them all, which he took to with eager joy. Before any drills or sparring, he enforced ritual prayers to Karak. The vast bulk said them without truthfulness or feeling, but he knew the frailty of men. Given time, they'd believe what they thought were lies. Given time, their souls would belong to Karak.

The collective army of Thulos halted for two days when it reached an ancient wall of rocks barely knee high, which marked the entrance into the Ramere. Tessanna was kept away from the proceedings, but Velixar always told her what transpired afterward. She couldn't decide if he was hoping to win her over with honesty and conversation, or if he were simply so confident of their success he wanted to gloat before it even transpired.

"The lords of Angelport have prepared for our arrival," Velixar told her the second night. "Thulos isn't happy that Ulamn left them alone the first time we travelled west, but never mind that. They cannot defend their lands against us. Have you ever been to Angelport, Tess?"

They sat beside a fire that seemed to offer her no warmth. She shook her head and scooted so close her toes were nearly in the flame.

"I have, back when their majestic ships were nothing but tiny little toys rowed by children. A great city, with many walls that stretch even into the water. There is but a single gate, not that it will slow us any. Wings and magic so ruin a lengthy siege…"

He stopped and stood.

"You still won't talk?" he asked. She kept her eyes down, her arms wrapped about her knees. "I thought so. You need a lesson, Tessanna. I am not surprised at your strength, but I thought in time you would have seen the truth in this life, the honor in our conquest. But it appears I must break you like I would break a mule."

Velixar walked to the nearest fire, one chosen at random from the hundreds that dotted the hillside. He came back with a rough looking man, his hair unevenly cut and half his teeth were missing when he smiled nervously at the two of them.

"Are you sure?" the man asked Velixar, who nodded. The soldier loosened his belt and took a step closer. "I'm a lucky man."

"That you are," said Velixar.

He knelt down beside Tessanna and moved to kiss her. When she pushed back, he laughed and grabbed her wrists. He was a big man, much bigger than her. She shrieked and clawed, but he held firm, and then his weight was atop her. When he let go of one hand to pull down his pants she slashed his face. In return, he struck her again and again, beating her chest and bloodying her nose. His forearm crushed her larynx, and she gasped for air as he pushed himself inside. He started out slow, then sped up, laughing and cussing as he held her down. At last he slowed, and he climbed off while trying to reattach his buckle.

"A pretty lass, but a bit loose," he said.

"Return to your tent," Velixar said. Tessanna lay on her back, her clothes in disarray. She kept her knees pressed tightly together, and they rocked left to right as if she were trying to force out the vile seed spent within her.

Karak's prophet knelt beside her and whispered into her ear.

"Every night I will find another. You know the diseases of men. Soon you will ache and blister and rot from within. No more silence. No more withering at my touch. My bride, or the army's whore. Choose."

She looked up at him, her face wet with tears.

"I'd rather be a whore."

Velixar stepped back and frowned.

"I make no idle threats," he said. "This is no lie. Every night, another man."

"And every night I'll thank Celestia that man is not you."

He kicked the fire, scattering it dead.

"Sleep well," he told her, seeking solitude for his prayers. She watched him go, and she did pray to Celestia, the first time since her childhood. Anything, she prayed, she'd do anything to have her power to crush Velixar and scatter his ashes to the far corners of the world.

Instead she fell asleep a cold, scared, powerless woman.

The next night, and every night after on the march to Angelport, Velixar kept his word.

The army pillaged as they traveled south-east to the coast, following the trade routes beaten into the hills from hundreds of years of wagons and merchants. Sometimes they'd send out squads to search further off the trail for more food. The delays and distractions made Velixar wish for the days when his army had been purely of the dead. Perhaps they lacked skill in fighting, but at least they didn't have to eat, or sleep, or waste precious energy fooling around with the steadily growing trail of camp followers. He'd nearly killed all the women, but Thulos ordered him to let them live. He seemed confident the constant rutting like animals would keep their nerves cooled and his men's tempers down.

They encountered the first few scouts as they neared Angelport, but before any could flee for safety, Thulos's advance patrols swooped down behind and took their lives. Unencumbered and with clear weather, they camped a mere day away to plan their attack.

"Thulos has kept his plan to himself," Velixar said as he started a fire and tossed Tessanna a scrap of bread. A red-bearded soldier was with him, and he leered at her hungrily. "Keep her company while I am away."

"Will do," said the soldier.

"What's your name?" Tessanna asked, nibbling on the food as if not the least bit worried or upset.

"Robbie." He crossed his arms and admired her form. From his vantage point she knew he could see straight down her shirt, and his pants bulged in appreciation. "Robbie the horse."

"They say that because you're smart?" she asked.

"You wish. You'll find out, girlie. That creepy man said I have all night, and I plan to use it."

Tessanna smiled at him.

"Touch me and I'll cut your manhood off."

"That so?" Robbie laughed. "How about you watch your mouth unless you want some black eyes and bruises to pretty up that face of yours? He didn't say nothing about being nice to you or leaving no marks."

"Beat me all you want," she said. "But rape me and I'll cut it off. Horsie."

"That's enough!"

He backhanded her. His knuckles bled from her teeth. Her smile seemed to grow at his anger.

"I've had worse than you," she said. "I've been fucked by six men at once, all while they beat me to make me scream. What are you? What does your tiny little prick matter to me? Listen to me closely, Robbie. You can tell the others what a great time you had, tell them I moaned like a virgin, but you won't touch me again. Now leave."

But Robbie didn't appear to have any intentions of leaving. His face flushed red, and he sucked his bleeding knuckles while wearing an expression more appropriate for an animal than a man.

"You think you're tough, bitch?" he asked her. "You see any around to help you? Any to save you? Take off your dress and maybe I'll play nice."

"What, you don't want it in my mouth first, or are you afraid I'll bite that little nub right off?"

He swung his fist, but this time she was ready. She ducked, the attack passing over her head, and then she had her dagger drawn and slashing. Robbie howled as she sliced the tendon in the back of his ankle, just above the heel. Tessanna rammed her weight against his knee, and his wounded leg lacked the strength to stand. As he fell she leapt atop him, her dagger stabbing into his arm. He struggled, but she rode him unbothered by his flailing. Again she cut, this time the tendons by his elbow.

"Shush now," Tessanna whispered, pressing her free hand against his mouth. The pain in his arms and legs was too great to struggle, so he relaxed and listened. "I warned you, didn't I? Now close your eyes. I promise to be nice and let you go, but you need to close your eyes. If you don't, you'll watch as I cut your other foot. I know it hurts, I can see you crying because of it. Imagine both your legs feeling like that. Imagine trying to march along. You think the war demons will let you stay behind? What do you think they'll do? Target practice for the archers, maybe?"

"No, please," he whimpered against her palm.

"Then close your damn eyes."

He did as he was told. Slowly she inched down his body, the dagger trailing against the fabric of his shirt, then his pants. It circled against his knee, then traveled upward. He flinched, and she laughed when he did.

"I did promise…"

In went the dagger, piercing his scrotum. He screamed and thrashed, but the pain was too great, consciousness fading fast. The dagger cut and cut…

When Velixar returned, he found Robbie splayed out by the fire, his lower body a disgusting smear of blood and gore. Tessanna sat on her haunches, licking the blade.

"I feel normal," she said, giggling. Velixar stood there, unable to react. He cared nothing for the man, but he'd promised her nightly torture. It wasn't much torture if she was the one with the blade.

"Perhaps it isn't rapes you need at night," he said. "Would you prefer a warm body to cut into, if your own no longer pleases you?"

In answer, she viciously slashed her wrist and bled it out onto the fire.

"You aren't fixing me," she said. "You aren't changing me. I'm still the same. I'm still me, the many pieces. You just broke me again. Send more men. I won't need the dagger. I'm a wild animal, wild and deadly."

She was laughing, seemingly delirious with joy. Whatever had stopped her from flitting between her selves, kept her sad and serious and tortured, had vanished. The blood dripped down, and she watched it oblivious to Velixar's presence. He took the dagger from her limp hand.

"Your magic," he said, suddenly hoping.

"Still gone," she whispered. "Mommy's still abandoned me. If you want a goddess as your queen, you won't ever get it. You'll only have me, broken, mad little me. If I'll have you. If Qurrah won't have me."

The necromancer felt his anger kindle at his former pupil's name.

"Tomorrow we will show Angelport the true power of the war god," he said. "And you can see what fate awaits Qurrah and his friends. Maybe then you'll realize how hopeless his life is."

He whispered words of magic, and Robbie's body stood, turned, and joined the ranks of the undead legion outside the camp. Thulos had given him specific orders to carry out, and while they were on the odd side, he had a guess as to what the war god planned. Strangely unnerved by Tessanna's dramatic shift, he left her alone, deciding he needed an extra hour of prayers to prepare for the coming siege.

Tessanna watched him go, wishing he hadn't take her dagger. Her smile faded, and with sudden vigor she wiped at the blood on her hands and face. It had been an act. The cutting, the laughing, the mad look in her eyes: all an act. She still felt broken, but strangely held together, bound by a force that frightened her and flooded her sleep with nightmares. But she'd also known Velixar's desires, and what he desired was the old Tessanna, the wild goddess who feasted on blood and lived like an animal. She'd given him a taste, all the while wondering what had happened to that older self.

Hopefully it'd be enough. She'd faked with many men before, and if she could fake well enough with Velixar, perhaps he'd keep away the men. She didn't need to be his queen; she wouldn't give him what he wanted just yet. She'd hint at it. Make him think the wild goddess was reemerging.

Tired and alone, she let out a sigh of relief and then bandaged her cut wrist with a ripped piece of her dress. For some reason, its pain was deep, an ache strangely comforting in its normality and lack of excitement.

Tessanna awoke to the sound of trumpets and shouting. She stood, wincing at the pain in her wrist. She felt a tingle in the back of her head, an assurance of something wrong or odd. When she removed the wrapping on her hand, she realized what it was. Her wrist was red, the cut swollen and angry. A thin line of black marked where the blood had dried. Never before had a cut lasted so long. She'd always healed quickly, no doubt because of Celestia's power within her…

She choked back a sob. Did everything about her have to vanish? Every unique piece of her fade away, rejected from her mortal form?

"We march in a few minutes," Velixar said, appearing from the chaotic mess of soldiers around them.

"I can see that," Tessanna said. Her somber tone must have alerted him, because his red eyes narrowed.

"Is something the matter?" he asked.

"Nothing," she said, lowering her hand and shaking her head to fling her hair across her face. As if hiding, she spoke like a child. "Must we go? I'll be scared."

Velixar chuckled. The sound sickened her stomach.

"We must. Now come."

He took her hand. It was cold, rough. She thought she'd vomit but held it down.

When they'd camped, Angelport had glittered in the far distance, just a twinkling of torches and patrols. No doubt they'd seen their camp as well, which is why Thulos had ordered them to build not one fire but two for every group. Tessanna expected the demons to fly in their tight formations to show off their numbers, but instead they marched along the ground, behind both the undead soldiers and men of Felwood. Only Thulos stayed at the front, issuing orders and urging them onward.

"Why do they walk?" she asked, hoping her tone was the right quality of curiosity and boredom.

"Thulos figures they've heard rumors of winged men," Velixar said. "Perhaps some there have even seen a few and lived. But if we delay revealing their presence, any defenses they've made in preparation for them might slacken or even be abandoned."

"We're to kill them all?" she asked. When he glanced at her, she giggled to hide her original unease.

"One strong display of power should be enough to convince the rest to surrender," Velixar said. "I wonder, though, why you might care either way."

"If you kill them all, where will I get my servants?"

"Servants?"

She batted her eyelashes at him.

"A true queen should have servants. Don't you agree?"

Karak's prophet laughed. "You're right. Perhaps we can find a servant girl or two, someone to clean and cook."

The morning passed, and they came closer and closer to Angelport. Tessanna looked over the defenses, praying they would hold. She didn't want to see another massacre. Even more, she didn't want to listen to the horrific chants as thousands more knelt and swore their lives to Karak. From what she saw, the defenders had a chance. They'd built several walls, concentric circles of wood and stone. The outermost wall stretched a great distance into the water, and all across the ocean waited an awesome amount of ships.

"Walls and water," Velixar said, catching her staring at the city. "They hope to stop a god's army with walls, water, and pathetic ships of wood. So foolish."

"They don't know any better," she said, feeling out of breath. Though Velixar had eyed her eating habits more carefully, she still had not regained enough weight. The hours of walking drained her, left her feeling empty. Velixar's constant presence didn't help, either. "But can you blame them for the defense? You seemed pleased with Veldaren's struggle."

"I had waited centuries to watch that city burn," Karak's prophet said. "Forgive me for wishing to enjoy the bloodshed. Angelport, though, is nothing more than a distraction. Thulos wants more soldiers, and he doesn't want an enemy at his back. I'd be happy to burn it down from afar before moving on."

The final mile was perfectly flat, the ground unsteady beneath their feet. Many times soldiers stepped onto what they thought was grass only to twist their ankles in a sudden dirt hole. Once Tessanna nearly tripped, but Velixar kept her steady. His arms wrapped around her waist, and she felt his thin, bony body against hers. She trembled, but not in the way Velixar surely thought she did.

"Soon," he whispered.

"Qurrah," she whispered back. "Not until he is gone forever."

A fire smoldered in his dead eyes.

"Soon," he said, and his ever-changing face grinned.

Architects had built the outermost wall thicker than the others, though not as tall. It'd been designed for many men to stand comfortably atop it, so Thulos led his army toward the imposing sight of several thousand archers standing ready. Velixar hurried her to the front so they might march beside him. As the god towered over everyone, he drew his sword and held it high so the sunlight might glint off it. His army halted.

"No doubt any army of this world would crumble against those walls," Thulos said as the two of them neared. "Yet to us it will fall in a single day. Keep everyone outside of arrow range. Prophet, are you ready to do your part?"

Velixar released Tessanna's hand and nodded. He closed his eyes, and with words of magic pouring from his tongue, he lifted his arms to the heavens and summoned all of Karak's power.

"*Shadows!*" he cried in a vile tongue Tessanna recognized as if from a dream life. The shadows before the outermost wall darkened to a black so pure it reminded her of the night sky, except with all the stars torn away. The darkness crawled up the wall, higher, higher, until it enveloped the defenders. Like a flood it poured into the streets, dousing torches and burying men. It did no harm, Tessanna recognized the spell well enough to know that, but the men within were certainly helpless and terrified.

"Let them wail about in their fear," Thulos said. A war demon waited beside him, ready to carry out his order to attack. Behind the wall of undead, his winged troops readied their weapons. Arrows fired in chaotic volleys toward them, as if the defenders believed an assault on the walls had already begun. The shadows remained, and slowly the arrows became only a trickle.

"Send your undead," Thulos ordered.

Velixar nodded, the changing of his features an imperceptible crawl. Tessanna knew the shadow spell weighed on him. Controlling the legion of undead would be no easy task. Whole body trembling, Velixar gave his orders. The undead broke into two lines, curling to either side of the city. Without sight, the archers didn't know of their approach and could not annihilate them like they should have. It wasn't until they were close enough to be heard that the archers attacked. Velixar winced as hundreds of his undead fell, their bodies pierced by many arrows.

But thousands remained, and one by one they plunged into the water.

"The boats," Tessanna said, daring to interrupt Velixar's concentration.

"Will see nothing," Thulos said, answering for him. "You were too busy…entertaining the men of this camp to know. I have made every one of them ingest stones on the march here. They will sink in the water, hidden and protected."

"You hope to assault the men whilst they are unaware," she said.

"Do not pretend to guess," he told her. "You are a child watching a master play a game you know nothing of. Enjoy the massacre, but in your place as an onlooker, not an equal."

She bit her tongue. If Velixar was upset at her reprimand, he didn't show it.

"The archers are focused on the undead," Thulos said to his demon lieutenant at his side. "Crush them."

They took to the air in a violent explosion of wind and feathers. They bunched into formations with expert speed, then flew straight for the front gate.

"Now," Thulos whispered.

Velixar lowered his arms. The shadows descended with them, just enough so that the archers could see the approach of the demons. Then the darkness rose again, and Tessanna could only imagine the archers' terror. Thousands of arrows sailed through the air, a desperate, blind defense against the attack.

Except the demons had broken to either side the moment the shadows returned. The arrows landed harmlessly in the grass while the two groups swung wide, gathered, and then swooped in perfect synchronization. They swung their glaives low, hurled their spears ahead of them. Tessanna watched them dip into the shadows, slicing and stabbing as they finally met above the gate. Not even needing a second pass, they curled back and returned to Thulos, who saluted them with his sword.

"Lower the shadow," he said.

Velixar opened his eyes, and the spell faded, blown away as if it were suddenly a dark mist.

Only hundreds remained of the original thousand, lucky survivors of a brutal massacre. They readied their bows, and to Velixar's disbelief, fired arrows toward the army as if to say they were not cowed.

"Most impressive," Thulos said. "They will prove useful to me after their surrender. Do you remember your cues, prophet?"

"I do," said Velixar.

Thulos approached the city alone, not bothering to stop even when he came within range of bowshot. He held his sword out to the side, as if ready to swing at any moment.

"Warriors of Angelport!" he said, and his voice carried for miles by the same magic he had used at Felwood. "You desire a fight, and in that you are commendable. I salute you, true men! But you have seen what we can do. You know the powers we possess. This is not your war. We come not to destroy, but to save. I want fighters, honorable destroyers of worlds to swear allegiance."

He glanced at Velixar, who nodded.

"Perhaps you think to flee to your boats," the god continued. "That is where your might has always been. But look to them now. Listen for their screams. Watch for their fire. You have no power, not against me, not against your god!"

Tessanna's mouth opened as one by one the ships began to list or ram one another. Sails tore, and others fled out to the ocean.

"What is going on?" she asked.

"They waited below," Velixar said. He seemed better now the shadow spell was gone, but still he spoke slowly, as if greatly distracted. "I had them tear out their innards so they might float back to the top."

Tessanna shivered, imagining the many rotting corpses floating up like monsters from the deep, crawling up the boats, their mouths flooded with water, their stomachs and chests ripped open.

"Those of you on the walls, step down and join me!" Thulos continued. "Those who wait further in, those of you with sword and axe, accept my offer. The lords of Angelport hold no power in this new world. This is a land of gods."

Several archers loosed their arrows, but only one was remotely accurate. Thulos smacked it aside with his sword. He waited, giving them time. He saw a scant few step down from the walls. Such a shame. He'd hoped to enlist them, but they were still stubborn, still resisting. It looked like he'd have to make do with the rest.

"There is no honor in your deaths," he cried to the city. "No salvation. No noble sacrifice. One way or another…you will fight in my name."

Velixar had begun casting by the start of his sentence, and by the end, his call to 'rise' thundered over the plain. The corpses atop the outer wall stood and attacked the remaining archers, burying them in their greater numbers. The last of the defenders died, torn to pieces and flung off the wall. When Thulos lifted his sword, the undead turned back toward the army, raised their hands as if in worship, and then cried out in unearthly voices a single name.

"THULOS!"

Several minutes later, the gate to the city opened, and the first of many bent their knee.

"Find out who their former lords were," Thulos said as he sheathed his sword and turned to Velixar. "Choose the most loyal and execute the rest. Use him to call back the ships. They might have goods that would be of use to us."

"As you wish," Velixar said, smirking as he bowed. The smirk hid his exhaustion, but Tessanna could see it by the dimness of his eyes. How many undead did he command, she wondered. How many thousands?

As the soldiers from Angelport flooded forward, eager to ransack the city, Tessanna listened to the worshipful cries that rang out, urged on by Velixar.

Karak! they cried.

Karak!

Karak and the War God!

Alone, seemingly forgotten, Tessanna cried as another city fell.

13

A ntonil's and Theo's men passed over the eastern of the Gods' Bridges, into the delta, and then camped before the western bridge, just outside the limits of Ker. There they trained and waited, waiting for confirmation from King Bram to enter. Two weeks later Theo received the order he'd been hoping for: prepare the defenses. The bridge was theirs to hold.

❖

"This is hopeless," Harruq said to Tarlak as they watched Theo's men dig trenches on both sides of the bridge. "Surely you see that."

"That's a mean thing to do, calling our only hope hopeless," said the wizard. He removed his hat and scratched the top of his head. "Shame you're right. I've been working on Antonil, but he's starting to get a bit of that noble calling in his blood. I think he's worried that, should everything go well, Theo will take all the glory and leave him looking the coward."

"Or Theo will die like we know he will, hardly slowing the demons."

Tarlak shrugged. "Yeah, that's likely. What's worse is we don't have a clue when this Thulos will even show up. Would be rather embarrassing if Theo's provisions ran out and he starved to death waiting to make his glorious last stand."

Past the bridge was a small cluster of trees that could just barely be called a forest, and the two Eschaton leaned against the trunks while watching the preparations.

"Been thinking," Harruq said. "You know we'll never get paid for all this. We're the lousiest mercenaries ever."

"Says you. I plan on marrying Antonil's daughter and becoming heir to the throne."

"Antonil doesn't have a daughter."

Tarlak gestured to the soldiers everywhere.

"If I can haul us from one side of the world to the other in hopes of surviving a horrendous war without having yet been paid a single coin, I think I have the patience to wait on Antonil to marry and have himself a daughter of suitable age. Either that, or get one disgustingly large tract of land donated to me after we retake Neldar. I might be all right with that."

Both shared a chuckle while the preparations continued. Harruq pointed to the ditches.

"Those won't do much against flying enemies."

"You feel like going and telling them that?" Tarlak asked.

"Not really."

"Telling them what?" asked Antonil as he joined them. He wore simple clothing, lacking his filigreed armor and helm.

"That this fool's errand will get us all killed," Harruq said.

"I disagree," Antonil said, crossing his arms and standing beside them. "They'll need to use this bridge if they're to march any soldiers into Ker. And even if they don't, they'll still try to crush them. He can't leave them at his backside, disrupting any possible supplies and threatening raids. Besides, I know a thing or two about pride. King Vaelor would never have let such a challenge go unmet, and I can't imagine a god having less pride than a man, king or not."

"A hard gamble to risk the lives of so many on," Tarlak said.

Antonil sighed. When he spoke, his voice had softened.

"I know. Which is why I will not make that gamble. My soldiers are going with the angels to Mordan. Those who wish to can stay, but I must retake Mordeina. Queen Annabelle entrusted me with the lives of her soldiers in hopes of saving my country, and in return her own city was conquered, her life taken. I owe her and her people much…more than I can ever repay. Let Hensley die, or even become a hero to be worshipped for all time. I just don't want to be known as a failure king, the one who left and lost his throne while suffering defeat after defeat…"

Harruq put his hand on Antonil's shoulder and shook him.

"Enough depressing chatter," he said. "We'll do what we can. That's all we can ever do, right? But I'll go with you, and if the world hasn't forsaken us yet, we'll plant your butt on that throne in no time."

"I'm going too," Tarlak said. "Can't let you get too far away, not with how much gold you owe me." He smiled a painful smile. "Besides, someone there killed Haern, and I want to make him pay. Fire. Lots of fire. Sound like a plan?"

Antonil stared into the distance, seeing nothing of his surroundings, just a horrific image of them trying to assault the enormous walls of Mordeina while priests and undead fought against them.

"Good a plan as any we have," he said.

◈

Antonil's men packed up their tents and bundled their belongings. Mira had little of her own to prepare, so instead she watched, strangely fascinated. Most looked relieved, though a few exchanged worried looks, always with others that were preparing to stay. Her path through the camp took her to the soldiers of Omn. There she heard whispers, curses, comments that confused her all the more.

"Cowards."

"Snake bellies."

"Why would you be a soldier if you're scared to die?"

"Antonil's not a real king. Wasn't born into it. Theo, he knows a king's true responsibility…"

Shouts reached her ears, and she turned to them. Several men had broken into a fistfight, and no one seemed eager to stop it. She thought of doing so herself, but then Ahaesarus arrived, thrusting the men apart and calming them with a word. He remained when the others separated, so Mira joined his side before he could fly away.

"They're so scared," she said to him. "Yet so many are angry as well. I don't understand."

Ahaesarus put a hand around her shoulder and smiled.

"They are right to be scared, and their anger is born out of that fear." He led her away from the noise and the shouting, toward the edge of the Rigon River. The water lapping against the sides as he folded his wings and sat.

"Why?" Mira asked, sensing he was ready to talk.

"Because those who stay behind expect to die, and those who leave know they are escaping that death, though they go on no less dangerous a path."

"And where am I to go?"

Ahaesarus seemed amused by the question. "Why, what you choose to do, as it is in all things."

Mira frowned. It seemed simple, but it didn't answer her question.

"The men who stay, are they truly doomed to die?"

The angel sighed. For a long time he stared across the water, as if mesmerized by something on the far side.

"Yes," he said.

"Why?"

"Because as long as Thulos is there, they will die. He is far too strong. Perhaps if my brethren stayed, we'd have a chance, but I do not wish to make this our final battle. If Thulos wants to conquer Dezrel, he will have to bring his spears to Avlimar."

Mira glanced back at the camps.

"If they know this, then why do they stay?"

"Because they hope to win, however little the odds. They are sacrificing everything in an attempt to hurt Thulos's army. Theo thinks they will slaughter so many men and demons that he will be named a hero, a legend of his time. If he breaks the army, forces them to stall or retreat, then Antonil might retake Mordan and muster enough men to defeat Thulos."

Mira thought of the men she'd seen in Veldaren, who had cheerfully given their lives to delay the attack of the orcs. It had been just a few, but they'd held a line, defiant against their certain deaths. This was the same, only grander, on a scale she'd never seen before. They would give meaning to their lives. Purpose.

"But that won't happen," she said, suddenly worried. "If the war god attacks, you are certain they won't succeed?"

Ahaesarus shook his head.

"Thank you," she said, kissing him on the cheek. "I think I do know which way I will go."

She rushed to tell Lathaar.

❖

"**B**etter get a move on," Harruq said to his brother. "I don't think too many will wait for you if you fall behind."

Qurrah's smile lasted only a fraction of a second before fading. They sat in what had been their combined camp. For once Qurrah had been willing to stay among the soldiers, and though he'd received many glares, none had confronted him. Progress, as the wizard would have said.

"Actually, I won't be going."

Harruq laughed, certain it was a joke. His brother's face immediately cleared up that assumption.

"What? Why?"

Qurrah crossed his arms and looked away.

"You know she's with them. This is my chance to see her."

"Well, yeah, but…but on the other side of the battlefield. You can't do this. You'll get yourself killed."

Qurrah nodded. "Perhaps."

Harruq flung what he'd been holding to the ground and grabbed Qurrah by the front of his robe.

"No," he said. "I just got you back. Tessanna isn't the only one that'll be there. Thulos, Velixar, and those winged demons, too. You're still weak. You're still confused. What are you hoping to do? What miracle do you think will happen to save you both?"

"The same miracle that brought me from Velixar's side to yours while demons and angels bled in the sky."

Harruq kicked a stone but had no reply. Qurrah stepped closer, and then awkwardly hugged him. Shocked, it took Harruq a moment to return the gesture.

"I must do this," Qurrah said, stepping back. "So much of this is my fault. If there is any chance of finding redemption, it is here, standing against him."

"You better live," Harruq said, his lower lip quivering.

"Same goes for you," Qurrah said. He smiled. "I'll be coming after you as a hero. Try not to disappoint me. Now please, you need to hurry. I don't think anyone will wait for you to catch up either, though you're a bit more loved than I."

Harruq grabbed the rest of his things, scooping them into a random pile in his arms.

"You're a bastard," he said.

"I know," Qurrah said.

They shared a laugh, and it felt good despite the sadness lurking behind both their smiles.

Since the men of Omn had no priests or paladins of Ashhur, Lathaar and Jerico led groups of them in prayer. They formed small circles, six or seven at a time, and prayed for strength, guidance, and the will to conquer fear. Mira walked upon the scene and stayed back, feeling like a trespasser. Men and women came and went, yet she lurked on the outskirts, willing to wait. At last Lathaar noticed her and smiled.

"Mira!" he cried, hurrying over to her. "Just trying to get a few last prayers in before we have to leave. They're good people, real good. This'll be tough. Is there something you need?"

She stretched on the tips of her toes, put her hands on his shoulders, and then kissed him. He stood shocked still as the kiss lingered, until at last he put his arms around her.

"I'm staying," she said when the kiss ended.

"What do you mean?" he asked.

"Thulos will kill all of these people if he comes here. Their valiant stand will mean nothing, no meaning or purpose. I can't let that happen, not when I can change it."

"What are you talking about? Mira, don't..."

"Please," she said, leaning her head against his chest. "Don't try to stop me. I saved myself once because of you, and now the whole world suffers. If you try, if you tell me you love me, I'll do it again. Please don't. Let me stay. Thulos hates me, hates mother. I will give him his chance to do something about that hatred."

Lathaar shook his head, and a thousand objections raced through his mind.

"He'll kill you," he said at last.

"A thousand times I've seen people risk their lives for others," she said. "It is only right I do the same."

"Please…"

"Don't ask me," she said. "If you love me, you won't ask me."

He kissed her, held her close.

"I won't ask you," he whispered into her ear. "And I do love you. So much, Mira. If there's any other way, you come back to me. Do you understand? You come back."

She was crying when she pulled away from his arms, and she wiped away the tears with her fingertips.

"Goodbye, Michael," she said, using the name she'd first learned from him deep in the Stonewood Forest, when she'd been a scared girl and he was a paladin of lost faith. A twirl of her fingers and she vanished, a spell stealing her away, far away, to where she could cry and no one would see her tears. In his mind, Lathaar felt her presence linger, and the ache nearly crushed him.

"Damn it," he said. He looked back to Jerico leading the prayers, and suddenly he felt like he had more pressing matters to attend. The thought of kneeling down in worship seemed unbearable now. Not with Mira going to her death. Not with him forced to let her.

"Damn it all to the Abyss."

◆◆◆

Qurrah did his best to get out of the way after informing Harruq of his plans. He'd fled to the small nearby forest, hoping for privacy amid the trees. By no means was he looking forward to enduring without his brother, but he saw no other way. His time of isolation did not last long, for an angel flew low and landed. The half-orc recognized him as their high priest.

"Come to offer me a prayer for good luck?" Qurrah asked, a bitter smile crossing his face.

"No," Azariah said. "I come bearing gifts, instead. Harruq told me of your decision. I find your choice admirable."

He gave Qurrah the bundle he held in his hands. The half-orc unwrapped it and held it up. His forehead creased as he looked back to the angel, obviously confused.

"It doesn't seem proper that you make your stand against Velixar wearing his former robes," said the angel. "You are no longer a servant of Karak, and you shouldn't dress as one. We have lost many of my brethren since coming here, but only one priest, a wonderful soul whom I loved dearly. I feel he would be honored for you to wear his robes."

Qurrah didn't know what to say. The thought of him wearing white, and not just white, a sparkling white shining with such purity...

"This isn't me," he said, offering it back to Azariah, who only shook his head and smiled.

"It could be, if you wished it."

Qurrah looked down at his dark robes, remembering how he had taken them from Velixar after Dieredon had temporarily defeated him and his undead. He'd felt betrayed then, determined to be stronger than his teacher. Did he still feel that? Was that who he still wanted to be?

He shook his head. Of course not. Not anymore.

He shed Velixar's old robes and donned the white. Azariah picked them up and folded them tight.

"When you feel ready, burn them in a strong fire," the angel said. "Let that end the last link Karak's prophet has with your soul."

Qurrah accepted them but held in his thoughts. No, the robes would not be the last. Tessanna was the last. As long as she remained at his side, he could never be free.

"Thank you," he said, bowing.

"Show the world who you really are," Azariah said. He kissed the half-orc's forehead and then took to the sky.

The angels led the way. Antonil rode horseback ahead of his men, who he encouraged the best he could. Aurelia found her husband waiting, watching the bridge and the men working at a feverish pace to improve its defenses.

"Will you be all right?" she asked him.

"It's like we're cursed to never be happy," he said. "Never to be together. Never to be peaceful and content."

"It does seem like that," she said. The dour look on his face hurt her, and she pursed her lips as she thought a moment. She had something to tell him, something she felt he should know, but wasn't sure how he would react.

"Harruq," she said. "I've been meaning to tell you…"

"Hmm?" He looked at her, but he wasn't really seeing her. His eyes were red, and he looked like he carried an anvil on his back.

"Never mind," she said. "Now is not the time."

He pulled her close and kissed her.

"Care to give me a bit of time alone?" he asked her.

"If that's what you need." She kissed his cheek. "I'm here if you need me. I always will be. You know that, right?"

He smiled at her. "Yes, I know."

She gave him his privacy.

The rest of the army moved on, but as Harruq watched, he was surprised to see he wasn't alone. Lathaar neared, lagging far behind the rest. He constantly looked back, as if hoping to see a glimpse of someone who was never there. Harruq changed the angle of his walk so that he neared, and eventually walked beside the paladin.

"Lose someone?" he asked, chuckling.

"I think I did," Lathaar said, and his tone showed he didn't think it a joke.

Harruq glanced back the same time Lathaar did, and he sighed when he thought of Qurrah. No, it wasn't much of a joke, was it?

"Sometimes life is a real bitch," he said.

"Amen," said the paladin.

14

B ram was sat in the Eye, staring at the enormous map of
Dezrel, when Ian arrived home.

"Ian!" the king cried, rising to embrace him.

"They agreed!" the knight said, and his face was all smiles.
"Theo and his soldiers will hold the bridge best they can
against the invading forces. As for Antonil, he will join us in an
assault against Mordan."

Bram smacked his arm and shared his grin.

"Well done," he said. "Now hurry, and bring Loreina to
me. We have little time!"

"Time for what?" asked the knight.

To this, the king only smiled.

M elorak seethed as his pock-marked friend and advisor
paced before him.

"Are you sure?" he asked. "Absolutely sure?"

Olrim nodded, his lips curled in together, as if he were
ready to bite them off.

"As sure as we can be of anything in this chaotic world.
Bram left only one survivor, a young priest named Joshua.
They cut off his hands and gouged his eyes out, set him on a
horse, and ordered him to ride. It's a miracle he made it here at
all."

"I want to hear it for myself," Melorak said, rising from
his throne. "Bring him before me."

"He is wounded and blind, my friend. Surely you cannot
expect him to be lying."

Melorak's eyes shone red with anger. "I said bring him
here."

Olrim acquiesced. A few minutes later he returned,
leading Joshua by the elbow. Melorak crossed his arms, feeling
his fury rising. The man looked hardly older then thirteen.
Acne covered his face. His bloody stumps had been bandaged,

and a long white strip of cloth encircled his head to cover his eyes.

"You are safe, Joshua," Melorak said. "You have endured much, and by Karak's strength you come to me, to where we may right the wrongs done to you. Please, tell me everything you saw before they took your eyes."

"It was the bells," Joshua said. Though he was tall, his voice was still young, boyish. "They started to ring the prayer bells an hour too early for service. We thought it strange, so we came. Edward—my teacher—he said perhaps there was an emergency, and we should hurry. But the guards were waiting. They were everywhere! I tried to kill them, but my faith in Karak was weak. Please, forgive me, I couldn't even slay a single soldier before they beat me down."

"That you fought at all is enough to assure you no punishment for any failings," Melorak said, hoping to comfort the boy. "Men fail. It is the very nature we embrace, and that Ashhur shamefully hides. Continue."

Joshua swallowed, and his body tensed as the memories continued.

"They bound our hands and gagged our mouths. One told me he'd cut out my tongue if he heard a single prayer. Surrounded by soldiers, they led us to the courtyard."

"How many soldiers?" Olrim asked.

"An army," Joshua said, turning his head in the advisor's direction. "Several hundred at the very least, and that was just with us. More searched throughout the nearby towns, finding every last priest and servant of Karak. Over a hundred of us, members of the faith. And then Bram came. He killed the first himself, and he wanted everyone to know it. Then the rest, they…they cut off their heads and tossed them in a pile."

Melorak felt his blood boil. Surely this pathetic king did not think he could commit such an atrocity and live, did he?

"Why did they let you escape?" he asked.

"I was to deliver a message," Joshua said. "But first they said they must make me look like what I was: a blind, worthless beggar."

"Your message," Melorak said, his voice low and quiet.

"It must have been the king," Joshua said. Tears ran down his face. "I recognized his voice. They'd already taken my eyes. It hurt so bad. He said to come to you, Melorak, and say that only the bodies of priests are welcome in Ker, and that he must politely send back the heads."

Melorak glared at Olrim, who bowed his head in shame.

"Three horses were with him when he arrived," he said. "Their backs burdened with sacks. I thought to tell you later, so that the goad from Bram would not affect your judgment."

"Affect my judgment? Are you mad?"

He calmed himself long enough to send for another priest to care for Joshua, then paced before his throne.

"This is just a desperate ploy for independence while we are still weak," Olrim said. "He knows he cannot stand against us given time. He hopes to act now, before your position has been established. How many revolts might break out if you leave? How many lords will suddenly grow a spine knowing you are not here to cow their men? You must remain here in the city! We must be patient, and wait for the voice of Karak to return with his demons and dead."

"How many of our friends live and preach throughout Ker?" Melorak asked. "Our brethren die at this very moment, hunted like dogs! Tell me, how many soldiers do we have at our disposal?"

"At last count, fifty thousand."

"Fifty thousand men, plus my priests, my paladins, and a veritable army of Lionsguard. And yet you would counsel me to be patient while my rule is challenged, and my vassal declares itself a sovereign nation beyond my control?"

"Avlimar floats above us," Olrim said. "The seeds of rebellion lay scattered throughout the city. The Ghost is not dead; you know that, for Haern still hunts. This is a trap. I urge you not to walk knowingly into it, no matter how great our advantage may seem."

Melorak approached his friend and put his hand on his shoulder.

"I won't," he said. "You will."

"My lord?"

"You are right about my leaving," Melorak said as he returned to the throne. "I must remain. My control over Haern would lessen given that great a distance, and I dare not let Ashhur steal away the hearts and souls of my nation just because some blasphemous king thinks he is above the judgment of gods. But your faith in Karak is strong, your knowledge of his teachings rivals my own. Take my priests and lead our army south. Cross the Bloodbrick into Ker and start burning. I want the whole country to be ash by winter. When you encounter this Bram, kill him and bring me his head. I will set it on a pike and give it life so he might scream for a year above the city gates."

"As you wish," Olrim said. "I am humbled by such a great honor, and will do all I can to destroy the challengers to Karak's reign."

"Go with the Lion's blessing."

Olrim bowed low, then turned to leave. As he exited the throne room, he shook his head and murmured to himself. Melorak's call stopped him at the door.

"Do not consider me rash, old friend," he said, his deep voice softening. "I have not forgotten the burning of the Great Fields. We lack the food to feed both our army and the people of this city. But Ker has plenty. Pillage and burn. Well do I know how precarious our position is until Velixar returns. Crush them all. I will be safe here among my Lionsguard."

Olrim bowed low, and this time the respect was honest.

"I will not fail you," he said. "For I could not bear the shame of kneeling at your feet when you have so nobly trusted me to succeed."

After he was gone, Melorak closed his eyes, letting his vision merge with that of another.

"Come, Watcher," he whispered. "The Blade is dead. It is time we find the Ghost."

⚜

Deathmask and Veliana had bounced from estate to estate, from Hocking's to Gemcroft's to Ewes's home. They'd waited for the riots to start after the burning of the fields, but to their frustration, they never came.

"The priests insist to the crowds that the fields are fine," John Ewes grumbled as they gathered before the fireplace of his home. "But I've had my men return twice in daylight. They're gone, all of them."

"Everyone is scared," Deathmask said. "No one will dare contradict the priests. The price of bread has risen only a little, and the coin you distributed only eased things for the city instead of burdening them greater."

"I have nothing now," John snarled. "No fields, no wealth. I've destroyed it all on your advice, and does the false king bat an eye? Does he squirm on his throne? Ruined, all ruined, and for *nothing!*"

They all looked about, but none could deny him.

"Perhaps he only stalls," Hocking offered. "He must feed his army somehow. They must eat."

"Unless he kills them all and brings them back," Dagan said, and his words cast a dark pall over the rest of the meeting.

"Come," Deathmask said to Veliana when the others disbanded. "Let us stay at Hocking's tonight. I don't think we'd have a warm welcome here."

She nodded and glanced about with her good eye.

"Broken," she said, her voice a painful croak.

Deathmask glanced back at John.

"Yeah," he said, sighing. "I know. And I'm the one who did it."

"No," she said. "Melorak. His fault."

He smiled. "Of course. Shame on me to forget that."

They slipped out the door and caught up to Hocking (whose first name was Aaron, Deathmask had learned through not-so-subtle attempts). The sun had long set, the moon bright and comforting. Hocking had two guards with him, burly men who clearly preferred honest combat to skulking in the shadows. One stayed at Aaron's side while the other hurried ahead, checking each street before waving them clear.

"We just need to give it more time," Deathmask whispered to the lord while they hurried along. "That John's a damn fool if he thinks we'll win this with a single act."

"None of us are fools," Aaron said. "But we are human. Leave us be for now."

Deathmask shrugged. "Whatever you say."

Up ahead, the guard turned to wave them along, then lurched behind a house out of sight.

"What happened?" Aaron asked, his voice a whisper. Beside him, his other guard drew his sword.

"Run," Deathmask hissed. "Run, now!"

Veliana drew her daggers and twirled them in her hands as Aaron hurried the other way. Deathmask pulled his cloth tight about his head and then sprinkled ash from his pouch. It wrapped about his head, floating, and through it he watched and waited.

"When?" Veliana asked.

"He alerted us to his presence," he said, looking every which way. "That was no misstep. But why?"

They couldn't stay frozen there in the street, not even with Haern lurking unseen. The thought kept nagging Deathmask that a delay was what he wanted, and that a Lionsguard patrol was already on its way. He thought of climbing to the roofs, but while Veliana might be comfortable up there, he was not near as limber or quick. Besides, up there was Haern's territory. He'd practically lived on the rooftops of Veldaren.

"Can you protect me?" he asked.

Veliana blew him a kiss in answer. He glanced at the shadows on the far side of the street, a good fifty yards beyond where Haern seemingly lurked. With that small a distance, perhaps he could make a shadow doorway. He hadn't created one before on such short notice, but the only way he saw them surviving against the brutal specter was by doing something unexpected.

He knelt there in the center of the street, putting his back to the moon so his hands pressed the stone in the center of his faint shadow. Words of magic slipped off his tongue with expert precision.

A single cry from Veliana was his only warning. Haern leapt off a nearby building, soaring through the air as if a pair of wings stretched from his back. His cloaks flapped in the wind but made no noise. His sabers curled downward, ready to strike. Deathmask closed his eyes, continued his spell, and trusted Veliana to save his life.

He heard the sound of steel striking steel disturbingly close above his head, then the heavy thud of what must have been two bodies colliding. The conflict traveled to his right, where weapons clanged against one another with horrific intensity. He dared not sneak a peak, not when a single errant word would ruin his spell. Faster and faster he spoke, risking the delicate weave for sheer speed. Veliana cried out once in pain, and he nearly lost his concentration.

"No time!" he heard her shout. He looped his hands about, the spell near completion. She'd just have to find a way. She might have erred, but he would not look. He'd die with his eyes closed, ash about his face, trusting her with all he knew.

Something sharp sliced his wrist, but he continued.

Veliana's firm body pressed against his back, and he felt her arms and legs jostle against him as the sound of melee combat rang deafening in his ears.

He continued.

At last, as he felt a saber curl across his face, looping down for his neck, he spoke the last word of the spell. The power rolled out of him, and clutching Veliana's shirt, he fell through the ground.

They reappeared in darkness, and finally he opened his eyes. Veliana spun, her daggers still drawn. She was clearly disoriented, so he grabbed her in his arms and held a hand over her mouth.

"Not a sound," he whispered. They were in deep shadow, but still potentially visible to Haern if they moved too much. He watched as the undead Haern kicked the ground where the shadow spell had been, then leapt to the rooftops to begin his search anew. His initial run took him south, the wrong direction. Deathmask breathed a soft sigh of relief.

"Mad," Veliana said, cracking a smile. Blood dripped from her forehead and arm. She had a wicked bruise on her cheek, but she seemed so beautiful to him when she smiled.

"Let's get out of here," he said. "And you're right. That was completely insane. I'll wait at least a year before trying that again."

They hurried north, deciding that perhaps Dagan Gemcroft's estate would be a better choice that night.

15

Mira walked with her arms huddled against her, as if afraid her beauty might attract the eye of a forceful and unfriendly man. She knew they were afraid of her; the men of Neldar had surely told them outlandish tales of her power…a power that was slowly fading. Celestia's world was dying. Her mother's heart had broken as her creations bled and died.

Very much a stranger at Theo's camp, she knew only one man there. The rest were polite enough, offering her meals and thanking her for staying, though they stared too long at her hips or her breasts. Her face, though, they ignored.

My eyes, she thought. *My eyes must scare them.*

She searched for the only man she knew. At first she'd thought he'd be at the outskirts of the camp, in self-imposed isolation, but that was not where she found him. Instead, the half-orc stood near the heavy activity around the bridge. He stayed out of the way, but he watched intently at the construction. Mira slid beside him, saying nothing, only wanting to be in the presence of a familiar face.

"They don't know how to defend against undead," he said after several minutes passed in awkward silence. "And they know nothing about fighting creatures that fly on wings and wield lengthy glaives. Velixar's magic alone will crush them, and who knows what the war god might do."

"Do you wish you had gone with your brother?" she asked.

"I do," Qurrah said after a pause. "Every minute of every hour, I do. But this is where I belong."

"Then help them," she said, gesturing to the bridge.

"What help can I be? They'd rather stick a sword in my belly than listen to my advice. My role is to give them a chance with my magic, and even that has turned against me. I once could devastate entire armies, yet now a simple spark of flame exhausts my mind."

"Your magic has left you?" Mira asked. "How is that possible?"

"I turned against Karak," Qurrah said. "That must be the reason."

She shook her head, then grabbed his hand. He gave her a surprised look but she ignored it. She was used to people not knowing who she was and what she planned.

"Come," she said. "Follow me."

She led him to one of the outlying fields far from the camp. With a clap of her hands she summoned a fire, a tiny little blaze that danced on her palm. A flick of her wrist and it burned the grass but did not spread.

"Do the same," she said.

Qurrah sighed. Had she not listened to a single word he'd said?

"I told you, I can't."

Mira crossed her arms and frowned. "Let me see for myself."

He turned to the fire. For a moment he felt embarrassed, for he'd seen the tremendous power both Mira and Tessanna wielded. Compared to them he was but a child, and that was when he'd been blessed by Karak. But now?

"You asked for this," he said, crushing his hands into fists. Words of the spell came naturally to his lips, but the power wasn't there. He should have felt it pouring out of him, like water bursting through a broken dam. Instead the fire flickered, grew maybe an inch, and then shrank back down. He sighed, and his head ached as if he'd put it through a great strain.

"Is that it?" she asked.

"I'm not faking this," he grumbled. "I've felt steadily weaker ever since I joined my brother. It's to the point now where even a ruffian with a dagger could probably kill me. If Velixar saw me like this, he'd laugh his head off his bony shoulders."

"It's not that, Qurrah. I can sense the power still within you. But you've forgotten how to use it because of your reliance on Karak."

Qurrah waved his hand, trying to summon a wall of fame. Only sparks flew from his palm.

"What would you know about it?" he asked. "You're the daughter of a goddess."

"Exactly. All my power comes from Celestia. As she weakens, so do I, but you aren't like me. You need to rely only on yourself. Think, Qurrah. Think back to before Karak! When were you strongest? When did your power seem limitless?"

Limitless…

The word struck Qurrah like a hammer, then looped around him like a vice dragging him backward years through time. When had he felt limitless? When had he felt that reservoir of power within him at its greatest?

The night he'd first encountered Velixar. When he'd *challenged* Velixar, ripping away his control of the skulls that circled Veldaren while his orcs besieged the city. Qurrah had been stunned by the strength within him, by how his limits were in fact nothing but self-imposed delusions.

And now here he was, a shadow of that strength, wondering where his power had gone.

"Try to hurt me," he said, snapping out of his introspection. Mira, instead of being surprised, only smiled.

"Fire or frost?" she asked.

"Both."

She hurled a bolt of fire, following it up with a lance of ice. The two attacks shot for Qurrah, who had his hands held out before him. He kept his mind focused on that memory, on that one moment where he'd dashed Velixar's magic and cut them like cheap threads. Within him, he felt something break. Shadows leapt from his hand, forming a barrier the fire and ice shattered against. He dismissed the barrier immediately. Sweat covered his forehead, and he felt like he might faint, but he'd done it.

"Like a muscle," he said, gasping for air. "Like a sore, unused muscle."

"Are you ready for more?" she asked.

He nodded. "Only one way to get stronger, right? We have only so long before Velixar arrives."

Magic danced around her fingertips. "All too soon," she whispered.

They trained for several hours, until Qurrah could hardly stand. That night, when they prepared for bed, he asked her to stay at his fire.

"For once, I'd prefer to not sleep alone," he told her. "I don't want to feel like a stranger to everyone."

She knew what he meant, for she felt the same. She spread her bedroll and blankets out on the opposite side of the fire, which burned through his magic, not hers, and then they slept.

A horrible unease woke Mira from her sleep. She lay still when she looked about, for she saw several men. They carried torches, and their light hurt her eyes. Her heart pounded in her chest. The men gathered around Qurrah, and they held naked blades that glinted in the yellow light. One man in particular seemed to lead them, for he stood directly before Qurrah and gestured to the others.

"Hold him tight," whispered the man. In the poor light his face looked haggard and long, a man carved of shadows and world-weary flesh. "Don't let him talk, and don't let him waggle his fingers, either."

Mira struggled for a course of action. They clearly meant to do Qurrah harm...was it right for her to stop them? Could she do so without harming them? And if she did, how would the others react? She couldn't fight off half the camp if they thought she and Qurrah were a threat. Confused, she watched and waited.

"Now," hissed their leader.

Two men lunged, each going for an arm. They yanked the half-orc from his blankets and pinned his arms behind his back. A third held a sword against his neck. Qurrah's long hair fell across his face, and through it he glared at his attackers.

"Say anything," insisted their leader. "A single word, and Rick here slices your throat. I hope you don't, though. I want to do that. I want to pay you back for everything you done."

Qurrah chuckled, so void of humor or fear that the others tensed. Mira ran a list of spells through her mind, trying to decide on one before the killing started.

"Payback for what?" Qurrah asked, unafraid of the blade pressed against the tender flesh of his throat. In response, their leader struck him, splattering blood from his nose.

"You got to ask?" the man asked. "You slaughtered thousands when you took over Veldaren, and you got to ask?"

"Make it hurt," said Rick. "Real bad, Jeremy. Make it hurt bad."

"Angels and kings have pardoned me," Qurrah said. Blood trickled down his neck from the cut made from his talking. "Must I now beg forgiveness from every commoner in the land? How have I hurt you, Jeremy? In some way, I have hurt every single man and woman alive."

Jeremy grabbed Qurrah's hair and lifted his head so they could stare eye to eye. Mira shifted in her bed, angling herself better for a spell. Someone was to die soon. She felt it.

"You don't deserve an answer," said Jeremy. "I don't care about kings. I don't care about angels. I know what you done to me, and that's enough. Don't you get it? To me, that's all that matters. And your blood's going to pay for all of it."

"Stop," Mira said, lurching to her feet. Her voice was calm, but it had a power to it. All of them turned her way, and one of the men even dropped his sword.

"Stay out of this," said Jeremy. "This has nothing to do with you."

"He's here to help you," Mira said, ignoring his protest. "He stands with you, ready to die when the demons come. Are you so eager he beat you to your twin fates? Is your hatred so great you'd deny him any chance at redemption?"

"He killed them," Jeremy said. "All of them. Don't you get it? You…you're just some witch; you're an elf in human form. You don't understand. You couldn't possibly understand!"

He shoved the others aside and grabbed Qurrah by the front of his robe, and he pressed his sword tight against Qurrah's neck. The half-orc refused to fight back, instead standing still and calm, though his eyes burned with anger and sadness.

"You wearing the white robes of an angel? A sick joke. I don't care how many demons he helps kill, he'll never atone for what he did!"

"Who was it?" Qurrah asked, his voice suddenly quiet. "Tell me."

"My little girl," Jeremy said, suddenly taken aback. "My wife, and...and Tasha. My little one. Butchered. Don't you get it? All of you, don't you get it? He deserves to die!"

He looked ready to kill. His hand shook, and tears streamed down his face. Mira felt her spells flutter in her mind, so great was his sorrow. Could she deny him? Their task was so hopeless, a fool's stand against an unstoppable force, might it be better for that one man to have his moment of peace in the last remnants of his life?

"I deserve it," Qurrah whispered. "You are right. I won't run from what I have done, and I won't pretend that your hatred is unjustified. But I will help you, if you let me, Jeremy. I will bleed and die beside you, all the while praying I might one day be worthy to stand in my brother's shadow. But you will not kill the one you wish to kill. The monster that took your beloved is already dead. He died holding his own stillborn daughter."

Everything slowed to a pause, a frozen moment in the night. Qurrah and Jeremy stared face to face, and there were tears in both their eyes. Slowly, the half-orc put his hand on Jeremy's wrist and pushed the sword tighter against his skin.

"Do it," he said. "Let this end. Every night I see a thousand faces come to haunt me. I have watched cities burn. I have watched loved ones of those dear to me bleed out by my hand. If your hatred is so great, then give me your blessing. Take it. If it'll ease your suffering, cut now! If not, leave me be so I can face the one who turned me into what I was. Let me see if I can bring a thousand demons with me to the Abyss that most certainly awaits me when I die."

"Fuck it," Jeremy said. He yanked his hand free and pushed Qurrah away. "I don't care how eager you are to die. You can wait like the rest of us."

"Such a kind gesture."

As the men departed, Jeremy turned back one last time.

"They claim you can summon the dead with a wave of your hand," he said. "They say you can clap your hands and bury an army in fire. That true?"

Qurrah nodded. "It is."

"Then prove you're not who you were. Fight with us, and fight like one of the damned."

Mira waited until he was gone, then put a hand on Qurrah's shoulder. "They're only…"

"I know what they are," Qurrah said, brushing her aside. "And they showed me more restraint than I ever could. If anyone killed Tessanna, or had killed Teralyn should she have lived…not even the gods would find their corpse. All the more proof of how wretched I am compared to the rest of the world."

"Must you be so hard on yourself?"

The half-orc laughed. "The world is ending because of my hand. Yes. I must."

He lay back down to sleep, rolling over so his back was to her. Mira stared at him while chewing on her lower lip.

"You won't win them over by how many you kill," she said. "You could call fire from the heavens and destroy every demon, and they will only fear you. Protect them. Struggle with them. Give everything you have, and then beyond, and they will see you are more than what you were."

She curled back under her blankets, and when he failed to respond, she was not at all surprised.

Qurrah was gone before she awoke the next morning. Preparations for defenses had already begun, but a few still ate. She stopped by one of the center campfires and accepted her morning rations. As she nibbled, she looked for Qurrah. Again she found him by the bridge, but this time he did not watch.

"Their undead have no balance," she heard him say as she neared. A group of men surrounded him, apparent leaders of the constructions. They all looked grumpy, but when Qurrah spoke, they nodded and didn't argue. "We need barriers every few feet, shin high. Your walls on the sides of the bridge need to go. Every dead body is a risk, and we must shove them off and into the water before they can bring them back to fight…"

She left for the nearby forest. She needed the solitude, for she had a message to send, one that needed to be absolutely perfect.

It was time to bait a god.

16

He thought himself beyond most human emotions, but Thulos felt a combination of eagerness and impatience as he led his army closer to the bridges. Since arriving on Celestia's world, he was yet to kill a man in combat. Nations had sworn their allegiance with hardly more than a shake of his sword and a promise of victory. He needed troops, yes, but everything felt too easy. As he walked, he thought of worlds where he'd encountered hundreds of mages in unified defense, or when elves had assaulted his legions while riding dragons of all colors. That was one of the few times he'd nearly 'died', in the mouth of an elder black wyrm, but he'd prevailed, and he bore the scars proudly on his body.

But this world? Pathetic.

Velixar assured him that in Ker, across the bridges, he would finally meet an army willing to fight. While resupplying at Angelport, they'd received word from several sailors arriving from Angkar, the capital of Ker according to Velixar, that their king had declared independence by executing hundreds of priests and paladins of Karak. The news had infuriated Karak's prophet, but only amused Thulos. So a king wanted to make a bid for freedom while the rest of the world burned? He'd heard of stranger things. The bridges across the rivers and into Ker were near, and within the kingdom's borders he planned on having himself a true siege. This time he would not recruit their strongest. He would not give them a grand speech about conquest and strength. No, he'd kill them to a man, so that the rest of the rabble they chased would hear of what awaited them.

He didn't sleep, so he was always the first about when morning came. Every dawn he inspected a different squad under his command, making sure they prepared for the day in an efficient, worthwhile manner. Sometimes he even stole over to the regular human troops, just to let his presence be felt.

They stared in awe of him, his size, his strength. It amused him, but he also knew that a few minutes there would keep the army disciplined better than a hundred taskmasters and their barbed whips.

Being in the presence of the war god suddenly made conquering worlds seem possible.

But that morning he oversaw none. Something nagged at him, like a worm burrowing into his brain. He kept hearing voices, but never decipherable, nor coming from any direction. Magic was at its heart, he knew, but from where remained unclear. He tried focusing on it, grabbing a hold of the invisible strands looping around his head, but they always broke like mist. More and more he thought he was being taunted. By who, though? Who was mad enough to taunt a god?

I am, said a voice, responding to his thoughts.

"And you are?" he asked, walking away from his army so he might have silence. The voice still sounded thin, and he didn't want to miss a word.

You come to my world, then ask who I am? Can you not feel my anger with every breath you take? Do not even the grass and trees ripple with fury when your demons pass?

"You sound unhappy, Celestia. Your memory must be as good as mine. I remember watching my demons burn this land centuries ago. How your precious creations cried."

You mock and insult because you feel victory is certain. You are isolated. You are vulnerable. You are not a god, not as you once were. Do you wish destruction? Do you desire to know fear?

"I fear nothing," Thulos said. He drew his sword and pointed it upward. "Is that where you are, Celestia? Must I cut a hole in the very sky to find where you hide?"

You must do nothing. I am coming to you, Thulos. That is, if you are not afraid.

Thulos felt a wave of anticipation flow through him, a sensation he had not felt in at least a decade.

"You would fight me?" he asked. "The world dies, and now you come to me in desperation?"

Death comes to the mortal, Thulos. So long as Karak and Ashhur remain imprisoned, I can destroy you. Eighty leagues south of here is a clearing sacred to me. Do not worry about finding it; I will guide you.

The spider webs of magic left, and the voice vanished. Thulos laughed.

"At last," he said. "At last a real challenge!"

He summoned Velixar, wishing to talk to him first.

"You seem joyous," said Karak's prophet as he joined him outside the camp. "Is it because the bridges are so near?"

"Celestia has come to fight," Thulos said. "And I have accepted her challenge. While I am gone, you shall be in charge of my army."

Velixar's red eyes flared with happiness.

"A great honor," he said, bowing low.

"One I expect not to haunt me when I return," Thulos said. "I will instruct Myann to follow your orders, but should you fail in your duties, or put my demons at risk, he will assume control."

Velixar did a poor job hiding his displeasure. He and the demon Myann had disagreed often when discussing plans at various intervals in their travels. It was that disagreement that made Thulos trust the war demon to protect his soldiers. Myann would not cow to Velixar, regardless of the prophet's power. If the lich risked his victory, he would stop him.

Though it might soon not matter. If he crushed Celestia, then his brothers might go free from their cages. For how slow things had moved, suddenly his victory rapidly approached. The god dismissed Velixar, relayed his orders to Myann, and then prepared for travel. Eighty leagues would take him several days to cross, and that was if he walked without rest. Which he would.

He would hate to keep a fellow deity waiting.

The trek had been quiet and tense, the result of the disagreement with Theo's men during their departure. Jerico soothed their worries and anger as best he could, but he felt like a damp cloth tossed upon a blazing inferno. He felt so drained by the day's end, he barely noticed Lathaar's absence.

It was only when they set up camp that he realized he was gone.

"Where's Lathaar?" he asked Tarlak once he found the wizard.

"Assumed he was with you," Tarlak said. "Check near the back. Perhaps he fell behind with a few others that weren't feeling too well."

The idea was as good as any, so he hurried through the ranks. Once free of the mass of bodies, he saw his paladin friend in the distance, kneeling in the tall grass. He walked toward him, feeling his stomach tighten with every step. Something was clearly wrong.

"Oh," Lathaar said, glancing up from his dead stare toward the ground.

"What's the matter?" Jerico asked.

"It's Mira," he said. Tears ran down his face.

"Is she...?"

But he didn't need to hear the answer. It was written all over his friend's face.

Seven giant oaks towered over the clearing, their leaves red and gold year round. Legend told that Celestia had stood in that very spot when she first created elves, and had taken inspiration from the trees about her. To reward them, she'd granted the oaks long life and health. Standing in the shadows of their branches, Mira found herself believing the tale Evermoon had told her.

She sang to pass the time. Solitude was an old friend to her, and while at Elfspire she had hoped for any sort of company, she now dreaded the arrival of another. She'd been fascinated with Lathaar, had found his troubled faith intriguing. Thulos reeked of pure, complete fanaticism for his goal. There was nothing to understand, only fear.

High above the trees, a silver star glimmered, guiding the war god toward her clearing. She'd chosen the spot not just for the close contact to Celestia, but also to give the men at the bridge the greatest chance that their combat would end before Thulos returned. Assuming she failed, of course, but she had already resigned herself to that fate. She was no different than them, no different from the soldiers and kings standing before the tide, and while she might not have a sword to lift against them, she had her magic.

Yes, her magic. She felt it growing, Celestia pouring all her power into her. The clearing was most certainly sacred. Even the trees seemed to lift their branches in awe of her, and the light glimmered on her skin. The days of waiting were soon to end. She felt time pass slow and steady, the sun falling and the moon rising in perfect, eternal rhythm.

And then time resumed its normal cadence as Thulos took his first step into the clearing.

"You look like her," he said. She thought he'd be angry, but instead he seemed amused. "But you are not. You are her daughter, her physical form in this world. Is she so cowardly that she will not risk her life as I have? What are you but a hollow shell for her to fill with her power?"

"I am enough to defeat you," she said, a comforting calm settling through her, traveling from the top of her head to the bottom of her feet. He towered over her, but she felt just as tall, just as powerful.

"Can gods die?" she asked.

"Everything can die, even gods."

She smiled.

"Then play the god, and I'll play the goddess. Let us see who dies."

She pushed her hands forward, her wrists touching. An enormous ball of fire roared to life, streaking straight for Thulos. Up came his sword, and a single swipe detonated it early. As the fire rolled around him he laughed. Twin strikes of ice followed, their lances sharp. One shattered against his armor, the other flew passed his head and buried into a tree. His smile grew.

"More," he said, lunging toward her with his sword leading. "Show me more!"

She whirled, and a funnel of air surrounded her, swirling higher and higher until it reached the sky. Thulos tried to stab through it, but a bolt of lightning struck the blade the moment it touched the air. He gritted his teeth and pulled back, refusing to let go of the weapon despite the pain. Thunder boomed, the elements seeming to grow angry at their battle. From within the vortex Mira's eyes shone white.

Unimpressed, Thulos slammed his sword to the ground. Its shockwave tore a giant hole in the funnel, and before it could close he slashed the ground, sending another forceful blast onward. Mira clapped her hands. The sound rolled outward with physical energy, disrupting his attack and pushing him back. The air funnel vanished. Lightning struck her uplifted hand, swirling around her body like a wild snake.

"Dezrel loathes your presence," she said. "It is time you suffered for the untold worlds you've destroyed."

"Stronger than you have tried," he said. He dodged the first bolt, deflected the second with his sword, and then accepted the third directly into his chest. He shook his head, disappointed.

"Better," he said, his voice nearly a snarl. "You have to do better!"

She ripped chunks of dirt from the ground and hurled them, but he slammed the boulders aside. The last one she threw he cut in half with his sword. Twisting it, he swung so the flat of the blade smacked the boulder back at her. She dropped to the ground, narrowly avoiding it. The chunk cracked the bark of one of the oaks, and leaves scattered down like an autumn rain. A snap of her fingers and every leaf burst into flame. Thulos winced in the sudden brightness, and then the fire erupted beneath him. He roared as he dove to the side. His skin was hard as stone, but faint black marks marred its perfection.

Mira thought he'd mock her, or congratulate her, but instead he attacked with such speed she had but a split-second to react. A defensive spell wrapped about her skin, and when the blade struck her side it failed to cut. Sparks flew, the powerful magic in his blade unable to sunder the equally strong defense. The energy still traveled through, and Mira cried out as she smacked against the trunk of a tree. The sword flew end over end after her. Shadows swarmed about her, protecting her. The sword flashed a bright red, then bounced off, unable to penetrate.

"Is this better?" she asked, stepping toward him while the shadows swirled. "Is this the power of the goddess you seek?"

White wings stretched from her back. The shadows faded, becoming streams of gold that formed a long dress, its skirt filling the clearing. Higher and higher she hovered, the ethereal wings showering the clearing with petals with each flap, petals that dispersed into wisps of shimmering light.

Thulos grinned at the display.

"About damn time."

A massive beam of power shot from her hands. Thulos rolled out of the way. The beam continued, exploding several trees as it blew a hole clean through the forest. A large gash remained in the dirt, carved by the blast. She unleashed another, this one angled lower. Thulos met it with his sword, all his power summoned into the blade. The magic enveloped him, surging into a dome that pushed the earth aside and bowled over the ancient oaks as if they were twigs.

When the light faded, Thulos remained. His sword shimmered with dark energy. His muscles bulged, every sinew in his body required to remain standing after the assault. Smoke wafted off his armor, and its edges shone red as if heated to near melting. Mira flapped her wings, and the feathers floated down.

"Such a pretty bird," he said, sounding out of breath. "Must I put you back in your cage?"

"Your strength is simple in its primal nature," she said. Her voice took on a strange, dual tone, as if two women were speaking. Thulos's eyes narrowed, for he knew that second voice well.

"Simple?" he asked. "Come now, Celestia. Must you insult what you cannot destroy?"

He swung his sword, and the shockwaves shone red as they travelled toward her. Mira batted them aside with her hands until she saw blood flick to the ground from her palms. Suddenly worried, she tried to soar higher, but the slashes continued, this time not for her but her wings. They tore through their ethereal nature, banishing their magic. The feathers poured into the sky like butterflies freed from a jar. Where she fell, Thulos stood ready, his sword raised heavenward.

Mira shrieked just before landing. Raw magic poured out of her, rolling across the land for miles in a destructive wave. Branches broke as their leaves ripped off their stems. Animals howled as their bones snapped. The ground cracked and heaved. Thulos screamed as his whole body shuddered. He felt his mortal form ready to give, to surrender to a death he could never imagine possible. Only his sheer rage kept him standing, kept him fighting against the power of the goddess he so vehemently loathed.

And then the wave was done. Mira fell limp to the ground before him, her golden dress fading to a simple green, torn and bloodied. With a shaking hand he pointed his sword at her throat.

"You could destroy the world and still not destroy me," he said, but his voice quivered with a newfound fear.

"It is the world that will destroy you," she said. Her eyes drooped, so great was her exhaustion. "Even now, mother sees your fate."

"Has she seen yours?" he asked.

She smiled. "She did, and she wept from the very moment of my birth for it."

He plunged his sword into her breast. No magic stopped it. No spell veered it aside. The blade pierced her heart, twisted, and then pulled free.

"Lathaar," she whispered as the blood spilled across her breast. "Please, remember…"

"I'll be waiting," Lathaar said, and his body trembled. "That is all she said. *Please, remember I'll be waiting.* Waiting. Which means she's gone."

Jerico wrapped his arms around Lathaar's shoulders as his friend cried.

"The Eternity isn't so far away," he said. "Our lives are but a spark from a fire. Stay with me, Lathaar. Stay with us."

Simple words, thought Lathaar. Honest, perhaps, and maybe true. But only words.

Only words.

17

In the light of dawn Thulos's army approached. The war demons floated lazily toward them, while in the vanguard swarmed the undead. Behind the lines of undead, making up the bulk of the army, marched the men of Felwood and Angelport. Qurrah saw the numbers arrayed against them and felt a tug of fear in his heart. They were outnumbered ten to one, at best, worse if he accounted for the undead Velixar was sure to raise as the battle raged.

"They'll be here in an hour," a man beside Qurrah said to another.

The land of the delta was flat and fertile, with no trees or hills to block sight of the army during its steady march. Murmurs and shouts rippled through the soldiers gathered at the bridge. A trumpet sounded, and then Theo strode forward, shouting commands. Men with shields lined the front, filling half the bridge with them tightly packed together. Spearmen wedged behind them. Along the riverbanks he lined up archers, far fewer in number than any preferred. Qurrah worried the archers might be vulnerable, but they had an excellent angle on the bridge.

Qurrah stayed with the archers, knowing the chaos at the front was not for him. He had one role, and he meant to play it well: counteracting Velixar.

"For the king!" shouted men all around him, and the half-orc glanced about to realize Theo had made his way to the back.

"I have my men in position," the king said. "It is such a shame your brother could not be here to bolster the front line."

"He has his fight waiting for him in Mordan," Qurrah said, hoping that would be the end of it.

"Perhaps," Theo said. "But instead I have you. Where should you be in this stand? What do I do with you?"

"There is a man with them, one who has walked the land for centuries. I will counter him as best I can until I drop from exhaustion. Otherwise he will slaughter your men from afar, and deny you the legend you so desperately desire."

Theo's eyes narrowed at the sarcasm in his final comments, but then he laughed and clapped a hand against Qurrah's shoulder.

"They say you unleashed this horde upon our world. Is that true?"

"It is."

"Then help put them back on their leash."

He motioned to one of his knights. The man stood beside the half-orc, his weapon drawn and his shield at ready.

"He will protect you from any wayward arrows or demon attacks."

Qurrah chuckled, hardly believing the audacity of the lie.

"And keep me from fleeing, you mean?" he asked.

"No one flees this battle," Theo said, a hard look crossing his face. "No surrenders, no deals, no peace. We die, or they do. The same goes for you, orc. You've told me your plan, and I approve. Fulfill your duties to me, to my men. You owe them. Time to repay it in blood."

He pointed to Thulos's army. "Their blood."

When he turned to leave, Qurrah spoke up.

"They will send their dead first," he said. "The barriers will make them stumble, but they will keep coming. Make sure your men are ready for that horror. And save your arrows for the enemies that still have breath."

"I'll keep it in mind," Theo said before turning back for the front line.

The knight assigned to guard Qurrah remained quiet, but the archers around them fidgeted and stared at the distance.

"I've never seen an undead," one asked. "What are they like?"

"Put an arrow through this knight and I'll show you," Qurrah said. He meant it as a joke, but neither the knight nor the archer found it very amusing.

"Never mind," he said. "They are like animals, slow, dumb animals. They won't feel pain, so an arrow does little to them other than adding decoration. Cutting their limbs and severing their spines works best, as does crushing their skulls...all jobs for swords and maces."

"Your role remains vital to this battle," said the knight to the archers while glaring at Qurrah.

"What is your name?" Qurrah asked.

"Osric."

"Well, Osric, would you prefer I lie, encouraging them to waste arrows and then encounter the shock of a foe immune to pain, to cold, and who will not bleed when stabbed and will not slow when wounded?"

Osric shifted his shield so it would be more comfortable.

"Sometimes a lie prepares a man better for battle than the truth."

"And what truth is that?" Qurrah asked, fighting a grin.

"That when a demon comes for your head, I'll lift you up so he has an easier target."

Qurrah laughed, and it felt wonderful. A few of the other archers chuckled along, but most clutched their bows and wished for the battle to start, or for it to never arrive at all.

"At least a thousand men," said Myann. "Perhaps even two. It seems they no longer trust their castles and walls, and now come to us in the open."

"Not open," Velixar said. "They make their stand on a bridge. Foolish. Water means nothing to the dead, nor a bridge to those that can fly."

"Then dispose of them quickly," the war demon said. "That is, if you view them so pitiful a challenge."

Velixar glared. He held Tessanna by the hand as the two marched at the head of the army, surrounded by the undead. She snickered at him, and he wasn't sure if it was mockery or honest amusement.

"Very well," Velixar said. "I will send my dead first. While they press the enemy front, you fly over and crush their archers, then take them from behind. They won't have a chance."

Myann shook his head. "Risk the lives of my men, all to spare you a few more of your dead puppets? I don't approve."

"Our victory will be assured," Karak's prophet insisted.

"Victory is already assured. We can always recruit more men, raise more dead. How many villages await us along the coast if our numbers thin? But we of the Warseekers are limited until the portal reopens. Find another way. Crush them with your magic and your dead. Or should we wait for Thulos to return, so that he might see how wrong he was in placing you in charge?"

Velixar looked beyond him to the bridge. A single spell increased his vision to that of a hawk, and he analyzed its defenses. Rows of stone barriers lined the bridge's path. In the very center a V-shaped wedge faced outward, crafted of wood and reinforced with stone. Any attackers would be funneled to either side, creating obvious chokepoints. His undead would be shoved off the bridge by the hundreds. As for his human soldiers, the archers on the far side would decimate those on the bridge who had not yet reached the front lines.

"Our army will lose thousands all because you will not risk losing a few demons," he said.

"I would rather sacrifice every one of these humans than have a single soldier of my own die," Myann said. "Have I made myself clear?"

Velixar's shifting face slowed, his eyes burning with anger.

"Perfectly," he said.

The bridge was close. It was time to act.

"They're just the dead," Tessanna said, watching him closely. "Send them in. Test the defenders' mettle."

"Archers first," he said. "Bury the bridge in arrows."

"As you command," Myann said, offering a mocking bow. The demon relayed the orders. Hundreds of men carrying bows slipped through the ranks to the front. Upon call, they nocked an arrow, holding it for the briefest moment until the release order was yelled. In a great wave they sailed, raining down upon the defenders and their shields. Velixar frowned as he surveyed the damage. Too few were damaged, and only a handful of dead bodies fell from either side of the bridge, pushed off by their comrades.

"Again," he said. More arrows sailed, but the wall of shields was thick, and the sides of the bridge aided in protecting them. After the fifth wave, Myann made a sound like the cross of a laugh and a snarl.

"Now you're just wasting arrows!"

"Enough!" Velixar shouted. "If you want my legion destroyed, then so be it."

He closed his eyes and sent out his orders. The undead surged forward.

"For Karak!" they cried with their mindless voices, a thundering roar that accompanied their charge. That charge slowed to a crawl when they hit the first of the barriers. The undead stumbled over them, the bones in their feet cracking. Some of those in worse condition toppled, their knees or hips tearing from their bodies as they continued on. The rest crushed the fallen, and a small bridge made of the dead formed over the stone. Velixar muttered at the simple, basic defense. His undead could slash and bite with their arms, attacking with a basic primitive sense, but gingerly lifting a leg over a barrier, followed by the other? Absurd.

Beside him, Tessanna giggled.

"Your dead look funny," she said.

The farce repeated at the next barrier, and then the next. Beside him, Myann laughed.

"Perhaps you do need our aid," he said. "Your minions seem eager to kill themselves without any help from the defenders."

Velixar did his best to ignore them both.

"For Karak!" his legion shouted. Even as they stumbled and fell, they still moved forward. The sounds of snapping bones and trampling flesh had to be horrific. Soon they would reach the defenders at either side of their wedge in the center. He closed his eyes and began casting a spell. He wanted to make sure their initial surge dealt significant casualties, otherwise the fight might drag on forever. He outstretched his hand, and from his palm shot several purple balls of fire. They rotated as they flew toward the bridge, but instead of exploding amid the defenses like he hoped, they veered low and crashed into the water, their trajectory ruined.

"Have you lost your aim as well, now?" asked Myann.

"Someone is there, protecting them," Velixar said. "And I know who it must be."

"It's Qurrah," Tessanna said, the amusement gone from her face. "He's here."

"To try and stop me?" Velixar wondered, hardly believing his former pupil's stupidity.

"No," she said, her voice a whisper. "He's come for me."

"And he will meet you," Velixar said as his undead crashed into the defenders. He watched them slam their fists into the wall of shields. Spears lunged over the shields, and swords stabbed between them. "Though when he does, it will be with a dagger in your hand, ready to take his life."

Osric felt frustrated as the fight began without him. He wanted to be in the front, where his shield might do some good. Instead he was stuck playing wet-nurse to a mixed breed who dabbled in foul, cowardly magic. Then he heard the half-orc chanting something, and in the distance several circles of fire winked into existence, approaching at frightening speeds.

"What are those?" he asked, shocked. They looked like tiny meteors, and they were heading straight for the bridge.

"Quiet," Qurrah said. He pointed with three of his fingers, whispered something strange and sickly sounding, and then flung his hand downward. The meteors sank with his hand, plunging into the Rigon River in a great explosion of steam and smoke.

"You saved them," Osric said, struggling to believe what he had just seen. The half-orc only shook his head, an amused smirk on his face.

"He is just warming up. Ensure that my concentration goes unbroken. Soon you will see his full strength."

"He? Who is he?"

Qurrah ignored him. His eyes remained on the far side of the river. His fingers trembled, not from fear but from excitement. More globes of fire soared toward them. Qurrah made a fist and clenched it tight. All of them, seven in total, detonated halfway to the bridge. The shockwave blew Osric's hair back across his face. Lighting followed the fire, but the half-orc crossed his arms and said another of his strange words. The lightning stopped mere feet from Theo's men, curling about as if striking an invisible sphere.

"Is that you?" Osric asked, still not believing. How could the wiry man be stopping such power? He looked barely strong enough to lift a sword, and only if he used both hands.

"I'm giving your men a chance," Qurrah said. "Now no interruptions!"

Spell after spell fired from riverside, and each of them he countered. Arrows of shadow splashed across a defensive sphere. Spears of fire dipped to the water, unable to keep flight. When boulders hurled into the air, Osric felt his heart leap into his throat.

"Uhh…" he said, then silenced himself. Nearby the archers cried out in warning, but still the half-orc remained calm. He closed his eyes, lifted his arms above his head, and then hooked his fingers into strange shapes. One after another the boulders shimmered black and then exploded. Harmless pebbles rained down upon the soldiers, pinging off their armor.

"Forward!" Osric heard a man shout over the chaos, and he recognized it as the voice of his king. The defenders pushed, shoving the undead back with their shields. With nowhere to go, they plunged off the sides and into the water.

"Foolish," the half-orc said. "Doesn't he understand? The dead don't drown!"

Osric pushed through the archers, curious about his words. Sure enough, the dead thrashed like children learning how to swim, but despite the wildness of the strokes, they still pushed forward, although the river carried them far. Soon they would climb ashore.

"Shit," he muttered. He sheathed his sword and rushed ahead, to where several hundred men waited for their turn on the front.

"To me," he shouted, grabbing men by the shoulder and pulling them after. "To me, to me! Attackers at the rear!"

The few that argued saw his rank and obeyed. He pulled the hundred back and stuck fifty on either side of the bridge, guarding their flanks.

"Watch for movement from the banks!" he shouted. "Some might make it before the river takes them!"

Sure enough, the first of many undead appeared, those weighted by armor or heavy possessions when they died. They emerged like ghosts of the river, the water pouring from every orifice of their bodies. They tried to chant out the name of the dark god, but their mouths garbled water and slime. The soldiers struck, hacking them down and shoving their bodies back to the river. Osric cheered them on but stayed at the half-orc's side. As a blast of lightning curled around another protective sphere, he realized just how important his mission had suddenly become.

"Into the river," Qurrah said as he gasped for air. Sweat covered his brow, and already dark circles formed underneath his eyes.

"What?" asked Osric.

The half-orc braced as if expecting a blow. His body shook as bolt after bolt of shadow splashed harmlessly against a defensive ward about the bridge.

"Shove any dead into the river!" Qurrah insisted. "Our dead. He'll raise them!"

The casualties at the river edge were few, but some had fallen to the strong blows of the undead or died with blood gushing from gashes in their throats or chests. Osric winced, horrified to commit such a dishonorable act on his fellow fighters, but so far the half-orc had proven wise.

"Push them in," Osric said, pointing his sword at the dead soldiers. "Take their armor, then let the river have them."

The soldiers obeyed without question. In between waves of attacks, they found their dead and shoved their corpses in.

Without their possessions they floated along, coloring the muddy river red as they vanished downstream.

"He's getting angry," Qurrah said.

"Who is?"

Osric received no answer, but he didn't expect one, either. He was already getting used to hearing only half a conversation. When a massive beam of shadow soared not for the bridge, but directly at them, he figured Qurrah meant the strange attacker from afar. The knight braced his shield, feeling a bit ridiculous at the protection it offered compared to the attack, but it felt natural. Qurrah crossed his arms and roared out in pain. The beam slammed into a defensive barrier of magic that cracked and twisted with a sound akin to glass. The beam flared white at its contact, so close Osric thought he could reach out and touch where they met.

When the beam ended, Qurrah collapsed to his knees.

"No!" Osric shouted, dropping his shield and putting an arm underneath each of Qurrah's. "Get up! We need you, now stand!"

Lightning crackled in the sky just before the clouds unleashed their fury. Blast after blast struck the bridge, killing groups of men at a time. The front line weakened and then broke, the undead pushing past the initial wedge and into the greater mass of soldiers behind. A trumpet called out twice, and the defenders pulled back to thick barriers running perpendicular to the bridge. They hopped over the carved tree trunks and turned. Fire erupted throughout the bridge, swarming upward in pools that grew underneath the men's feet.

"Hold me," Qurrah said, sounding intoxicated. Osric kept him steady as the half-orc slurred a few words and then waved his hand. The fire rippled and weakened but did not die. Screams of the burned reached them despite the distance. The half-orc grumbled, looped an arm tighter around Osric's neck, and then tried again. The fire faded, just in time for them to beat back the undead that surged around either side of the wedge. Orbs of darkness shot from the riverside. Qurrah blocked half, the others slamming deep into the ranks and exploding. Their death cries sent shivers up and down Osric's spine.

"Who is on the other side?" he asked as shadows curled around the dead bodies. "Who wields such horrible power?"

"Velixar," the half-orc said. "His name is Velixar."

"Well, I think you were right,' he said. "I think you did make that…Velixar…angry."

He grinned, and Qurrah shared it.

"Do our men hold?" he asked. Osric glanced up.

"They hold. For now, until more of that lightning hits."

"It won't. Not while I still have strength to stand."

"Looks like you have a moment to breathe, though." Osric pointed to the undead, who had pulled back from their assault. While the defenders watched, they grabbed the broken bodies and flung them off the bridge to clear the way. "He'll surely wait to attack until the rest of the army does."

Qurrah bobbed his head up and down but kept silent. He seemed too busy catching his breath to say much of anything. Osric felt more and more of his weight lean against him.

"How long can you defend us?" he whispered, quiet enough so none of the nearby archers might hear.

"An hour, maybe two," the half-orc said. "He's stronger than me. Older. Wiser."

"That's not enough," he said. "We need days, not hours. You must do better. That's an order."

Qurrah raised an eyebrow.

"An order?" he said, the corners of his mouth fighting a smile.

"Direct order," Osric said. "You remember that."

Qurrah laughed, and when lances of ice fell from the sky, he shattered them with nary a thought. Meanwhile the undead resumed their attack, flailing at the shields and swords with their arms. The entire weight of the thousands pushed them forward, hoping to topple over the barriers. The wedge was too wide, though, and too few could press through. The minutes passed as the dead piled up, until at last they stopped again to clear the way. Osric had lost count of how many spells Qurrah protected them against during that time. Only a few had made it through, each mistake costing the lives of many men.

Again Qurrah leaned against him as the break came. His hands trembled, and his eyes drooped from exhaustion.

"Water!" Osric called to the younger men that ran about the army. "Bring me water!"

A man hurried over with his waterskin, and Osric poured a long draught into the half-orc's mouth.

"Wine would be nicer," he muttered.

"So would a thousand mounted knights. We make do with what we have."

Qurrah stood and popped his back.

"Aye. And what you have is me. I pray you make do."

Osric looked to the men bunched along the bridge, methodically shoving off their dead. The vast bulk had died not from the undead but from that strange Velixar's spells. The casualties would have been tenfold without Qurrah to protect them.

"We're better off than you think," he said.

The minutes passed, yet the undead remained back. The enemy archers returned, firing off a volley that clacked against the arches of the bridge or thudded harmlessly into their shields. Theo climbed onto the wedge and shook his sword toward Thulos's army in blatant mockery of their assault.

"They aren't attacking," Osric said. "What are they waiting for?"

"**C**an you not see the need for your demons now?" Velixar asked, gesturing to the bridge. "They are too well entrenched. I cannot overwhelm them with numbers, and our archers are wasting arrows, as you so elegantly put it."

Myann rejected the idea without a moment's thought.

"We have lost nothing," he said. "Your dead are toys for us, nothing more. They are not real fighters. Send in the humans."

"The casualties will be enormous," Velixar insisted.

"Not if your magic broke through," the demon said. "Who is this stranger that keeps besting you? I wonder how weak Karak must be if you are his greatest prophet."

"Do not blaspheme his name!"

"Then do not give me reason to!"

Velixar turned and glared at the bridge. A brute force method was not going to work. They'd held his undead off for several hours now, and even worse, they'd dumped the bodies off the bridge and into the river below. Within minutes they were out of his reach. What he'd give for a single demon to find Qurrah among the crowd and shove a spear through his heart! Even if the half-orc wished to repent, Velixar knew he would refuse the display. Qurrah had cast his lot in with the damned, and nothing would save him from their fate.

"Prepare the mercenaries," Velixar said, referring to the men from Angelport. "They seem the more bloodthirsty of the lot. Until then, I want fires burning all along the riverside. When we make our move, I don't want them to have any notice."

"As you wish," Myann said, his voice full of mockery.

The undead pulled away from the bridge. Velixar oversaw the fires, and he set the men from Felwood to cut giant piles of grass to burn atop the little wood they had. Once wet, the smoke would billow in giant columns, exactly how he wanted it. He also thought to try an occasional spell, but instead he saved his strength. When the real assault began, not his humoring of the demon with his undead, he wanted to unleash everything he had. Qurrah had stopped many of his strongest spells, but he hadn't pushed himself, hadn't stretched to the very limits of his power. Tonight he would, and the half-orc would break against the strain.

As the fires grew in strength, he joined Tessanna by the water, staring off to the other side.

"Is he looking for me?" she asked. "Do you think he can see me from where he stands?"

"You will see him soon enough," Velixar said. "Are you so eager to kill?"

She glared at him with such anger that he stepped back, stunned.

"I will not," she said. "I will *not*. If you want him dead, then do it yourself. I'm not your puppet. I'm not your plaything. I was Qurrah's, and I still am. I think I forever will be, too. Sick your little men on me, or threaten my body. I will not break, not to you. Not ever. Do you understand, you wretched abomination?"

He slapped her, but the act was more reflex than conscious. Instead of being afraid, Tessanna grabbed his robes and pulled herself closer.

"Again," she cried as tears ran down her face. "Again! Beat me, rape me, do whatever you want. Everything shows how Qurrah was so much better than you!"

He wrapped his cold fingers around her throat and lifted her off the ground. His eyes seethed red as he held her close enough for their noses to touch.

"I can't break you because you are already broken," he said, his voice deathly calm. "But I will make you mine. Have you been playing with me, little girl? Have you been pretending? You should have continued the act."

His fingers crushed her larynx. Her lips pulled tight against her teeth, then slowly started turning blue.

"I won't kill you," he whispered. "But I will bring you to death's edge, over and over again. I will make you beg for the reaper man's scythe. Qurrah is not better than me. He never was, and he never will be. When he bleeds out in your lap, you'll finally understand."

He dropped her. When she landed, he kicked her twice until she rolled away.

"You there," he said, pointing at a passing soldier. "Stay here and keep an eye on her. If she tries to leave, or swim into the river, or anything at all, cut her throat."

"Yes, sir," said the soldier.

Velixar stormed away, needing space to clear his head. He didn't want to think about the enigmatic girl, her lies and her mockery.

Please, he prayed to his god. *Calm me down. Give me strength. This is our finest hour, and our greatest challenge. I must meet it. I must crush the wayward son.*

He heard no response, but he felt his inner turmoil cease. Such chaotic emotions had no place in him, not for the prophet of a god of Order. When he stood directly facing the bridge, Angelport's mercenaries behind him, he felt at peace. He'd been too far from the battle. In the thick of things was where he belonged. If Qurrah was to stop him, then let him come to the front. Let him try to maintain control amid the chaos. None could challenge Velixar. None could beat him. He was the voice of the Lion, and it was time they heard his roar.

"Are the men ready?" he asked.

The mercenaries' commander saluted. "We are ready," the burly man said.

Velixar raised his arms heavenward, giving thanks to his beloved deity.

"Go," he said. "Sing your war cry just before you reach their lines."

"Angelport!" the mercenary roared, and then they rushed forward, to the gap in the fires leading to the bridge. A silent order from Velixar and his undead marched, but not to the bridge, but far upriver, beyond the reach of the fire.

"Even without you I will attack them on two fronts," Velixar said to the absent Myann. "Karak does not need your cowardly wings to achieve victory."

18

O sric sat facing the river, his armor feeling twice its normal weight. He felt ragged and thin, and though he needed sleep, it felt painful to close his eyes. To pass the time he grabbed nearby stones, rolled them in his hands until they were clean of dirt, and then skipped them across the water. His previous record was nine jumps, but that night the best he could do was four.

"Not many sleeping," he said as he searched for another rock, one he hoped to do better than the paltry two skips his last one had made before plunking below the surface.

"Velixar should have sent his human forces in first," Qurrah said, lying beside him, his white robes easily visible in the starlight. He watched the smoke in the distance. "He could have pressed us all night with his undead, but now they're such a pathetic remnant there would be none left in only a few hours. Come daylight, we would have been too exhausted to fight the well-rested soldiers. He's playing games, putting his pride before strategy. He did this before, though, when he attacked Veldaren. My brother crushed thousands of orcs and undead, all because the damn fool didn't blast holes in the walls like he should have."

"Could he crush the bridge with all of us on it?" Osric asked, suddenly feeling anxious.

Qurrah nodded. "If I let him, yes. A few powerful spells could break its foundations, and then it would come crumbling down."

Osric shivered, hating how every deeply ingrained idea of warfare seemed futile or foolish in the face of that strange Velixar's power.

"What is he?" the knight asked.

"Who? Velixar?"

"Yes. Him."

The half-orc fell silent for a moment. Osric found a stone and cast it into the water. Five jumps. Not bad, but it was more a product of the stone, not his throw.

"He was my former master," Qurrah suddenly said. "He taught me, and I was eager to learn. Ever since the first generation of man he has lived, preaching the word of Karak. He is a twisted, decaying wretch of bones and rot. Every word he speaks is false, though he swears he has never spoken a lie. He's determined, deceitful, and dangerously intelligent."

"But he can't be that perfect. He hasn't done what you say he should. He's kept his demons close. He's given us rest. And you've held his spells at bay."

"For now," Qurrah said. "But he doesn't sleep. He doesn't tire. Soon I won't be able to lift my head while he's still…"

Osric glanced in his direction when he suddenly stopped.

"What is it?" he asked, reaching for his shield.

"The clouds," Qurrah said, pointing. A great blanket swarmed over the stars, hiding its light. Only the fires on the riverside remained visible, and just barely through the smoke billowing in great pillars. "He errs again. He thinks to hide his movements, when the very act of hiding them gives him away."

The two climbed to their feet.

"Alert the others," he said. "They'll attack soon."

Osric sent one of the archers to relay the message, but there was no need. Already he heard Theo bellowing orders from the front, and those orders relayed again and again in a deep echo from the rest of the soldiers. Osric shifted his shield so it hung comfortably from his left arm, then stabbed his sword into the dirt by his feet.

"Stay strong," he said. "That's another order."

"Your orders are starting to irritate me."

Despite their exhaustion, Osric nudged him with his elbow.

"You have permission to be irritated, so long as you obey."

Qurrah chuckled. "Smug horse-humper."

"Strong words from a twig I could break with two fingers."

The half-orc winked at him. "You'd need at least three fingers, jackass."

Osric laughed, but cut it short when the sound of combat reached their ears. He winced, trying to see. Something sounded different. He heard steel hitting steel. The human forces had come to play.

"Archers!" he screamed. The men scrambled for their bows and grabbed their arrows. Osric frowned at their poor coordination and wondered where their commander had gone.

"Loose those arrows like mad," he shouted as many waited for a group volley. "No time. Go, go!"

The arrows began to fly, gradually growing in number. In the darkness he struggled to see where they landed, as did the archers. No doubt many splashed into the water, but he trusted their accuracy even in the night. A steady barrage landed on the far side of the bridge, safely away from any of Theo's men. As he watched their quivers empty he wished they had a hundred thousand more arrows ready. At this rate, they'd be done within a few hours.

Frustrated, he flung his last rock into the water, watching it skip twice…and then vanish amid the soft churning of the surface.

"The water!" he screamed. "Swords to the water!"

There were only twenty or so soldiers nearby, but he yelled for them all. The undead arrived, just dark silhouettes in the light of the fire on the other side of the river. At first the soldiers cut them down with little difficulty, but the water heaved to and fro as hundreds more emerged, their bodies bent, their arms dragging along the surface. This was no random assortment like before: it was a tightly packed group numbering in the hundreds.

Osric screamed for Qurrah to help, but the half-orc was too busy hurling small orbs of fire to counteract similar orbs of a much greater size flying in from Velixar. Desperate, he grabbed one of the archers.

"Bring men from the bridge," he said. "Tell them we've been flanked. No arguments. You make them send help!"

"Yes sir!" said the archer before racing off. Osric grabbed his shield and stood between Qurrah and the water. If any undead wanted to gnaw on the half-orc, they'd have to go through him. Sadly, it didn't look like that would take too long. The men at the water fought valiantly, but the dead grabbed at their arms and legs and dragged them back in, clubbing them while they thrashed and struggled for air. The archers, realizing their vulnerability, dropped their bows and drew short swords from their belts. Without armor or proper training, Osric knew their defense would crumble fast.

"We need to get you somewhere safe," Osric said as his fellow men-at-arms died.

"I thought you had orders that I not flee," Qurrah said, his voice sounding distracted.

"I did. I'm overruling them." Osric didn't have the authority to overrule orders from the king, but he had a feeling Theo wouldn't mind. He could always beg for forgiveness later…assuming any of them survived.

He grabbed Qurrah's arm to pull him along, but the half-orc jerked free.

"Wait," he said

"But we have to…"

"I said wait!"

Osric felt his heart pound in his chest at the sudden look of fear that crossed Qurrah's face. The half-orc crossed his arms and braced his legs. High above, the smoke swelled with lightning that shone an eerie red. A crack of thunder boomed down, shaking the grass. Osric startled at its massive volume.

"He'll destroy the bridge," he cried as the first blast of lightning arced down. The half-orc held his arms upward, surrounding the entire army with a shield that sparked into existence with every touch of the lightning. With every blast, Qurrah winced. The thunder crashed, its volume rising, its anger growing.

"Not good," Osric said, looking to the river. The undead were pushing through. They'd be on Qurrah in moments.

Seeing no other choice, he smacked his sword against his shield and waited for them to hit. His ears ached from the thunder. The dead shone red in the evil light, with blood on their rotting fists and great lipless grins.

The archers broke, overrun.

"Stand your ground!" Osric shouted, despite knowing they would neither hear nor obey.

The undead surged up the banks, half chasing after the archers, the other half curling around to trap the defenders upon the bridge. A handful charged directly for him, and he met them with his shield. Their slimy fingers reached, and he beat them back with chop after chop of his sword. He decapitated one, removed both hands from a second, and then slammed a third back down the bank, to where it rolled until it splashed into the water.

Too many remained. He felt one sink its teeth into his forearm, crunching the metal of his vambrace while simultaneously shattering its own teeth. Another shredded its own skin pulling on the top of the shield, its dead eyes staring at him. Hungry. Vicious. Unstoppable.

"He can't win," Qurrah cried behind him. At some point he'd fallen to one knee, yet he kept his arms skyward toward the storm. "You can't let him win!"

Osric flung them back and then slashed wildly with his blade. He remembered what Qurrah had said earlier, and did his best to cut their necks or slam his sword through an eye socket and into the brain matter. Their fists beat against him, hurting even through his armor. He felt his flesh bruise under their assault. He tried to push, but his weight was off—there were too many. He fell onto his back, his shield pinned against him by putrid bodies. Too many...

"Be gone!" Qurrah screamed. He grabbed one by the wrist, igniting its rotting flesh. He waved a hand at another, flinging it back with an invisible force of magic. Two more died, their spines ripped out of their backs.

"No!" Osric yelled, smacking away the half-orc's offered hand. "Them! Not me, them!"

He pointed to the bridge, where the red lightning was tearing through Theo's ranks, killing tens at a time.

"I'm sorry," Qurrah said, and Osric could barely believe the words he heard. "I couldn't sit here…I couldn't just watch as they killed you."

Once more he lifted his arms, shielding the army. Shouts echoed over the sound of thunder, followed by combat far too close to be on the river. Half the army had abandoned the bridge and come to their defense. Steadily they pushed back the tide, forming a solid line along the bank at either side of the bridge. Osric cleaned his sword on the grass and then sheathed it. He thought to check his wounds but lacked the time. Qurrah's arms shook with every breath, and his skin had taken on a sickly color paler than his normal shade of gray. The storm he weathered was incredible.

"Second wave!" one of the knights along the riverside shouted. A fresh surge of undead came roaring forth, gurgling the name of their deity. Osric wished he could join them, but instead he stayed before Qurrah, making sure none jostled or interrupted him while they rushed from the bridge to join the battle. More and more he wondered if the half-orc would endure. The lightning flared so bright it seemed a bloody sun had risen. The translucent shield shimmered and bent under the assault. Sweat ran down his face.

"I can't!" he screamed, a cry of horrible despair.

Osric grabbed his shoulders and held him steady. "You will! You must!"

"Too much," he said, his voice dropping to a whimper. "Please, I can't. He's too strong…"

And then the storm ceased. Qurrah collapsed into the knight's arms. Osric held him, struggling to see in the sudden darkness. One by one the fires along the far bank faded and died. Trumpets signaled the retreat of the men on the bridge. They'd held, but for how long, he didn't know.

"You've got another chance to recover," Osric told the half-orc. "Just rest, relax. They've run out of tricks. How many dead you think we've killed? A thousand? Two? We've made our stand, Qurrah, and we're not done yet."

Qurrah laughed. "You haven't even fought the demons."

He lifted his hand, looped it around twice, and then pointed a single finger toward the sky. A soft ball of light shot upward, and after rising to the clouds, it exploded into a great flare.

"This darkness is no accident," he said. Hundreds of winged silhouettes filled the air, rising from behind the army. Osric felt his blood chill, and then the flare died, hiding the war demons from their sight.

"Can we survive their attack?" he asked.

Qurrah glanced at him, then shook his head.

"Soldiers with wings, ancient armor, and skill beyond any man here? No. We won't." Osric felt despair, but then the half-orc clutched his wrist and used it to steady himself. "But it doesn't matter. We'll take as many of them with us as we can. You with me?"

"Until the end," Osric said, and slapped the half-orc's shoulder.

The defenders on the bridge saw the demons' approach as well, and they braced their shields and wondered in what way they would attack.

"We're vulnerable here," Osric said, glancing at the archers. "What do we do?"

"Onto the bridge," Qurrah said. "Hurry. Even the archers."

Osric started shouting orders, motioning over any nearby knights he saw.

"To the bridge!" he shouted to them. "Hurry, we have no time. Get to the bridge!"

The men that had lined the water's edge backed away, then stopped when another wave of dead emerged.

"Ignore them!" Osric shouted. He led Qurrah by the arm amid a great throng flooding the back end of the bridge. "Form up ranks. Protect the front lines!"

About half of them had made it when the demons arrived in a hail of spears. Some archers fired arrows in random directions, but most flung their bows down and rushed for safety. A few made it. The rest died as the demons flew low, their glaives sweeping down to slash their throats and cut off their heads. The undead curled around, now free to exit the water without difficulty. Steel rang out from the front lines, a fresh assault from Thulos's human soldiers.

"Stay calm!" one of the knights shouted, trying to organize the defenses. Qurrah looked uncomfortable there in the center, with combat on both sides. There was hardly any room to breathe, but Osric did his best.

"They'll seek me out," Qurrah said. "Velixar will make sure the spells he casts reveal my presence."

Men screamed as the demons made another pass, their long glaives slashing while they remained far beyond retaliation. Those at the sides kept their shields high, but the following wave dipped low, taking out their legs. Blood spilled across the stone and into the water.

Balls of fire hurtled in from the riverside, and Qurrah countered them with orbs of frost. Mere seconds from casting his spell, a spear thudded into the stone, missing him by inches. The half-orc, instead of appearing frightened, laughed at the night sky.

"Still alive!" he cried.

Velixar's spells looped in, more fire and darkness that the half-orc countered. He seemed re-energized, though Osric feared it a last gasp, a second wind that would soon run dry. Demons scattered about, but in the darkness they were impossible to track.

"Can you give us light?" Osric asked him.

Qurrah was busy flinging bolts of shadow to counter similar bolts, and without missing a beat, he flicked his hand in a circle. Fire erupted along the tops of the massive supporting arches that lined either side of the bridge. In their light they saw the war demons circling like vultures. One was in mid-dive, and Osric flung his shield in the way. The glaive scraped off, and then they crashed together in a pile of wing and armor. Nearby soldiers hacked the demon to pieces and pulled the corpse off him.

"Thanks," he said once he stood.

"Make way!" a burly man screamed from further up the bridge. "Make way for the king!"

The men parted, and a squad of five knights arrived carrying Theo, who bled from a vicious wound on his shoulder and chest. His armor had been split in half, and Osric shuddered to think what such a blow would have done if the protection had not been there.

"Osric," one of the knights shouted, recognizing him. "At our side! We must protect him from these winged devils."

"Come!" Osric said, grabbing Qurrah's arm and pulling him amid the circle of knights.

"Get that wretch out of here," said one at the half-orc's intrusion.

"We protect the king, not him," said another.

"No!" Osric bellowed. "We protect them both. He is just as important, perhaps more. Guard him from the demons' spears!"

A squad of demons flew low and flung their spears, but the knights saw their approach and shifted their shields together to form a wall. The spears dented the metal, and one splintered through, but none pierced flesh.

"I cannot see," Qurrah insisted. Two balls of fire detonated among their ranks, his vision blocked to their approach. The knights did their best to give him room. Shadows leapt from his palms, forming nine-fingered hands that grabbed an incoming barrage of boulders, crushed them to small stones, and then flung them into the air. Demons fell, the stones snapping bones in their wings or knocking them unconscious. Qurrah smirked, clearly enjoying the sight of their deaths.

"West!" one knight shouted. Another barrage of spears thudded into their shields.

The undead pressed against the rearguard, who lacked the numbers to fight them off effectively. Without the solid line and barriers to hide behind, the dead gradually pushed them back, clawing and beating the defenders to death one by one.

"How fares my army?" Theo asked. He lay on his back, his arms crossed over his chest.

"They fight bravely," one knight said.

Osric wished he could say they were winning. The battle on the front was turning against them. The rearguard had begun to crumble. The demons circled, slashing at any vulnerable defender. Only Qurrah kept them safe from the terrible Velixar, and the half-orc's eyes shone with a feverish madness.

"Unto death," Theo said, a smile creasing his bloody face. "They'll sing songs of our stand."

"If there any left to sing," Qurrah said. He pointed a finger at where he thought Velixar stood watching the fight. He felt the last of his strength draining away. It'd been too many spells, too little food, too little rest. But if he was to die, he'd give them one last show. One last moment of defiance against Karak and his pets.

"You cherish your demons above all else," he said. A fireball soared in directly for him, but it crashed against a magical barrier and detonated early. "So let this burn far beyond my death."

He lifted his arms. The fire on the arches brightened, changed to a deep purple hue, and then erupted before any of the demons could retreat. The fire bathed the heavens. It streaked through the clouds like an army of molten wyrms, searing flesh and devouring wings. The demons fell by the hundreds, the rest retreating. Throughout the display, Qurrah laughed.

"Unbelievable," one of the knights whispered when the half-orc collapsed beside the king.

"You're not done," Osric said, kneeling down beside him. Everything he saw about the man showed he was wrong. His eyes rolled in his head, his countenance hardly alert. His extremities trembled, and a cold sweat bathed his body. Osric clutched him in his arms and held him.

"You must stand," he said. "You must defend us."

Fire roared in from the riverside, and unheeded it swarmed over the front line of the defenders, killing friend as well as foe.

"I can't," Qurrah whispered.

"You must!"

"I can't!"

A meteor slammed into the bridge a few yards away, blasting through the stone. A group of men fell through with it, doomed to drown in their heavy armor.

Osric shifted the half-orc's weight to his left arm, then clasped his hand in his.

"You did us proud," he said. "Until death, I'll defend you."

Qurrah smiled, and it seemed a great weight left his shoulders.

"Thank you," he said. "And I'm sorry."

Osric stood and turned toward the front line, which wasn't much of a line anymore. Men of Thulos rushed ahead, cutting down the defenders. Without their king, and helpless before the steady barrage of fire and shadow that tore through them, they could not continue their stand. The knights gathered tight, and they rallied as best they could. The spells stopped for a moment, and in that reprieve they fought back. Osric himself killed five, building a pile of dead at his feet. They shouted praises to their homeland, daring the mercenaries of Angelport and soldiers of Felwood to charge.

Instead they stepped back, and a man in a black robe approached. His eyes shone red in the darkness of his hood.

"Velixar," Osric said, and he breathed the word like a dark omen.

The specter lifted its bony hand and pointed. Fire burst from his fingertips, swarming about the knights. Osric screamed as he felt his flesh bubble and peel under the tremendous heat. He tried to stand, to swing at the damned thing that had broken their defenses, but his pain was too great. He coughed, and he tasted blood on his tongue. Again the man raised his hand. Osric glanced back to Qurrah, who knelt beside the king.

"Forgive me," said the half-orc. Then came the fire, the pain, and then nothing.

19

Tessanna staggered across the bridge, pulled along by Velixar's icy grip on her wrist.

"At last they have broken," he said, pushing toward the front. "In the end, Qurrah could never withstand my strength."

She bit her tongue and held in her retort. Velixar seemed far too unhinged to argue with. His eyes flared wide, and the changes of his features advanced at a rapid pace. More than ever he seemed like a monster loosed upon the world, and his touch filled her throat with bile. He cleared his way through, casting fire on the defenders. Her head swam from the heat and the smoke. Horrible as it seemed, she hoped Qurrah was dead. She wanted to find a body, a cold corpse that Velixar could not torture, could not harass, could not try to make her…

But then he was there, kneeling beside another wounded man. Velixar killed the knights with him, and with a wave of his hand, sent his troops swarming past, to overwhelm the men behind.

"Who is that with you?" Velixar asked, tilting his head to the side.

"King Theo White," said the wounded man. "Go burn in the Abyss, you demon. We crushed your army. We slaughtered ten for every one of us that fell."

"A king?" Velixar asked. "Amusing. You died for nothing, cretin. And I shall rule in the Abyss, not burn. Perhaps I'll meet you there in another age."

He ripped rib bones from a nearby body and flung them through the king's eyes. The man convulsed for a moment, then lay still.

"You were a fool to abandon us," Velixar said. "I must say, I never expected such weakness. From your brother, perhaps, but never from you. And those robes? White? Is this a joke, Qurrah? Do you really think they accepted you? You were a pawn for their defense, nothing more. It is easier to have you as a friend than an enemy."

Qurrah chuckled, but his grim laughter died when he looked past Velixar to Tessanna. Their eyes met. Tessanna felt her heart flutter, and Velixar's grip tightened on her wrist.

"Don't," she said, but it didn't matter. He flung her to her knees and shoved a dagger into her hand.

"You know what you must do," he hissed into her ear. "He has abandoned you, and he has abandoned me. There is no place for him in Karak's world. Cut his throat. Spill his life across your hands. There was a time you reveled in the sight of blood. Remember that. Become that same beautiful creature once more."

She looked at Qurrah. A thousand emotions swirled within her breast. She thought of his bitter words to her for sleeping with Jerico. She thought of the times they'd shared alone, their lovemaking vicious and desperate. They'd clung to each other through the most horrible of tragedies, and she'd clawed his chest when Aullienna died. There had to be good times, though, moments of sun and warmth. That time by the rose, they'd declared each other husband and wife, more than lovers. Had they lived up to such a promise? Who was she to judge? She'd let Thulos into the world, dooming them all, and why? Because she'd been hurt? Because she wanted to punish Qurrah?

He was looking at her, and when she looked back, something in his eyes quivered. What did he think of her? Could he forgive her? Could she forgive him? What madness had separated them? What dire need had broken them? The dagger in her hand, could she do it? She couldn't. She couldn't!

"I'm sorry," Qurrah whispered. "For everything."

Tears ran down her face, and his too. She clutched the dagger so tight her knuckles turned white.

"I never wanted to hurt you," she said.

"I know."

"I've missed you so much."

"So have I."

"I love you, Qurrah."

"I love you too, Tess."

She tried to drop the dagger, but then Velixar was there. His hand was ice, and it was strong. He pushed forward, and she fought, she screamed, but in went the blade. It pierced through his ribs and into his heart. He gasped once, then fell to the side. Blood spilled across her hands. His blood. Qurrah's blood.

He said something in his raspy voice. She leaned closer, clutching his white robes now stained red.

"...not mad..." he said. "Not...I'm not mad. Tess..."

She shrieked as he died. His body went still. No breath. No life.

"Please," she sobbed, beating her hands against his chest. "Please, no, I'm sorry! Please, Qurrah, I'm so sorry! Don't leave me alone, I don't want to be alone. I can't. I can't, please..."

She felt Velixar towering over her, lurking like the damned reaper-man he was.

"You sick fuck!" she screamed. "I hope you burn!"

She tried to stab him, but he slapped the dagger aside. It skidded off the side of the bridge and vanished. Her flailing did nothing to him, but she kicked and clawed anyway until he grabbed her wrists and held her back.

"He deserved nothing less," he said to her.

"How could you?" she asked amid her hysterical sobs. "How could you make me? Put his blood on your own hands, you damn coward! Your hands! Your guilt!"

The words seemed to sting him, and he let her drop. The bridge was slick underneath her feet, but she crawled toward the body of her lover and put his head in her lap. Gently she stroked his face, smearing blood across his forehead. Her tears fell down, mixing with the blood. She looked up at Velixar, who watched the display as if torn.

"He was better than you will ever be," she said. "I felt it when I held your damn portal open."

One of the war demons landed beside Velixar. He gave her a strange glance, then dismissed her.

"A third of my soldiers," the demon said. "I send them under cover of darkness like you insist, and I lose a third!"

"And I lost nearly every single one of my undead, and half the mercenaries and men of Felwood!" Velixar shouted back. "Are you happy now, Myann? Thulos will have both our heads, all because you wouldn't crush them when the battle first started."

"The blame is on your head, not mine," Myann said. He flew away, crimson feathers floating in the air after his departure.

Tessanna fled, wanting to be anywhere else, to think of anything else. She thought he'd follow, but Velixar remained behind. For a moment she thought he was as broken as she was, but that seemed impossible. She felt apathy sliding over her, returning like an old friend, and she welcomed it.

❖

Velixar knelt beside the body, a strange stirring in his soul. He'd killed thousands before. He'd even felt regret, such as when he'd sacrificed Harruq's daughter to reveal the brother's true loyalties to Qurrah. But this was different from them all. Kneeling before Qurrah's body, he felt a complete and total failure.

"You were my greatest disciple," Velixar whispered as he carved runes into stones with his forefinger, which glowed red with fire. He'd taken the body and with tenderness surprising even to himself, set it down to the cold earth beyond the bridge. "How is it you fell so far? And how is it that I never saw it until now?"

He did his best to put Tessanna out of his mind. He'd broken her, perhaps worse than she'd ever been broken. The separation should have lessened her hurt. Qurrah's betrayal and anger should have been enough for her to realize how inferior he'd been at the end. But whose fault was that? Who had let such a promising disciple become nothing but an enemy? He'd spent hours tormenting Jerico, revealing his lies, proving his faith false. Yet he'd failed. His war was not just for land, for gods, but for the souls themselves. Tessanna refused him. Jerico denied him. And Qurrah betrayed him.

Failure after failure after failure.

He wouldn't fail this time. When he'd first found the two brothers, he'd told Karak that Ashhur had made his greatest failure in letting them fall into his hands. Yet who had them now?

"Ashhur will not keep you," he said as he put down the last stone. "You are not his. Your soul belongs to me, Qurrah. To me it was promised, to Karak it was sworn. You won't escape this. You won't deny what you know is true. I don't know what you were told that made you change your allegiance. I don't know the promises and lies of your brother, or what sentimentality stayed either of your hands."

He sensed someone approaching but kept his eyes focused on the body.

"I know what you're thinking," he heard Tessanna say.

"You never know your own thoughts. How could you know mine?"

Tessanna sat opposite him, and she let a hand rest atop Qurrah's cold chest. Most were disturbed by corpses, but Velixar shouldn't have been surprised that Tessanna would not be upset by their touch…

"I know because it is written on your face, and on these runes," she said. "Why must you do this? What do you hope to gain?"

"I failed Qurrah in life," he said. "I will rectify that failure. Help me, or leave me be."

"He will only be a puppet, a lifeless shell of who he was. You rectify nothing."

He glared at her. She looked haggard and tired, dark circles making her face look sunken and hollow.

"What do you know?" he asked. "This spell is one of the strongest in existence. His soul will be trapped inside his body, and bound to my command. He was swayed by his emotions and unreasonable expectations. He cast blame on me when it belonged to Celestia. But now we will walk side by side for eternity. We will travel through the realms, him and I, master and disciple."

"Don't do this," Tessanna said. She pulled her hand back and shivered. "Don't condemn him to such a fate."

"Condemn?" he asked. He felt his exasperation grow. "Are you really so blind? He is condemned *now*, having turned his back on Karak. Do you think Ashhur's Eternity is beyond our reach? With Karak freed, we will storm even there, and cast down the great host. Into Karak's fire he will go, if things go unchanged. I must save him. I must bring him back so he can learn the truth of Order and Justice. Leave me be, harlot. You are just a slave of the whore. Go worship the wilds and the trees and leave the true matters to me."

She stared at him, her red eyes dripping tears, her lips quivering. He could almost feel her hatred rolling toward him.

"Whatever you hope from me," she said, "you will never get it. And whatever you seek from him, you will not find it. You play with bones, Velixar, and you know only shadows."

When she was gone, Velixar sat on his knees and went over the words to the spell. He'd used a variant of the spell on an elf such a long time ago, and Qurrah had been there to witness the display of power and control. The bitter memory stung. Never could he have guessed then that he'd be using that same spell on his most beloved disciple. This was his moment of triumph, damn it all! The world was theirs! Why must he suffer over such a wayward son?

An hour crawled as he prepared. It must be perfect. He must have Qurrah back exactly as he was, or the entire act would mean nothing. Cries came from the bridge, but they were muted and tentative. Thulos had returned, and every soldier there feared his reaction. All but Velixar. He could not care less. Let the god be furious. He'd done his best, and been foiled only by his own demon he left in charge.

Thulos's heavy footsteps alerted him to his approach. He felt a wry smile come over his face.

"To think you thought the defenders of Ker would prove poor sport," Velixar said.

The war god crossed his arms and frowned down at the body.

"What is this?" he asked. "Myann has told me much of the battle, and while he does his best to deflect the blame, I know it was him that cost you dearly. I do not blame him in protecting my demons, but it was foolish to sacrifice your soldiers and undead instead."

"We won," Velixar said. "Every defender died, with no surrender offered, nor accepted. The land of Ker is yours. Nowhere is there a city to stand against us. Now please, leave me be. I have matters I must attend."

"Yes," Thulos said, his deep voice booming his disapproval. "You consort with the daughter of the whore, and now you seek to bring back he who stood strongest against you. Bury the swords of your enemy, Velixar. You never know when they might turn against you."

"My control is complete," Velixar said, his anger flaring.

Thulos chuckled. "We will press men into service as we travel toward Mordan. Those who refuse will join your ranks of the dead. As for your *control*...tonight is a night for humility, not pride. Remember that."

He left, and Velixar was thankful for it.

"He thinks this is for control," he said to Qurrah's body. "What arrogance. What single-mindedness. What does it gain me if I lose your soul while conquering this world? I never lie. I swore that to you time and time again. I will not let your entire life equal a lie."

The moon rose higher, and he felt comforted in its light. Despite his long dead state, he still found the night sky beautiful. It was the time of Karak, a time for escape from the blaring, persistent sun. Peaceful. Calm. Order.

"Rise, Qurrah," Velixar whispered.

The runes flared. The magic poured out of him, and he felt a pull on his chest. His reservoir of magic drained at a frightening rate. Sparks flared from the stones. A sheen of violet hovered over the body, gradually spreading into the cold flesh. From death to life...how could anyone deny the beauty and majesty of such a nature? Velixar knew that he served the miracle worker, the conqueror of death, not Ashhur.

The culmination of that proof lay before him. Qurrah's eyes opened, and deep within his irises shone a red glow.

"No," he said, his voice a cold whisper. He lifted a hand, and it shook. "No!"

"Welcome back," Velixar said, feeling his lips spread into a smile. "I have missed you, my disciple."

Qurrah screamed. Not an uncommon reaction, really, though he was still disappointed in how easily his disciple seemed to lose control.

"Enough," he said. "You are not some frightened peasant or stubborn elf. You are Qurrah, servant of Karak's dark throne. You should have enough presence to endure the transition from the hereafter to now."

"What...what have you done to me?" Qurrah asked. He looked at his hands as if they were foreign to him.

"In time, you will understand the new way your senses work," Velixar said. "Touch and smell will come to you as if from a distant room, though you will hear and see better than when you were alive. As for your..."

Qurrah extended his hand, a spell on his lips. Velixar was too shocked to defend himself. He flew back as the lance of ice pierced his chest. When he landed, the ice shattered, leaving a gaping hole in his robes.

"You will obey!" Velixar roared, every shred of pity leaving him. He poured his will into Qurrah's undead body, denying it free will. The half-orc struggled, and his body quivered with exertion, but still he went down on one knee with hardly a pause.

"That is better," Velixar said. He glared at the hole in his chest. That would take time to mend. Thank Karak he didn't have to breathe...

"Why?" Qurrah asked. Given the commands flooding him, Velixar was impressed by the effort that single word must have taken to say.

"Why did I bring you back?"

The half-orc nodded. Velixar shook his head, again disappointed. Was it no so obvious? Was the world so muddled and gray that only he saw the truth clearly? He knelt before Qurrah and put his hands upon his face.

"Because you are my son," he said. "You once loved me, for I rescued you from a fate of obscurity and powerlessness to become something greater. Something more. And I will not let you die here, that promise unfulfilled. At my side, Qurrah. That is where you belong. Tessanna, your brother, the elves…all conspired to keep you away. No longer. You are mine."

Velixar denied the half-orc a chance to respond. He knew in his confusion he would not understand, not yet. But he had made magnificent progress on the paladin, and that had only been over months. With Qurrah, he would have centuries, if not the rest of eternity.

"I know you wish to see her," he said, switching the subject. "For a while, your emotions for her might linger. Go to her. Let her see your true form, and see if she will still cling to you."

Velixar gave his disciple his control back, though he still remained on edge in case he did something rash. Instead Qurrah stood and looked about.

"There," Velixar said, pointing to a distant fire. "She is there."

Without a word, Qurrah left for her.

><

Tessanna shivered although the fire was warm. It seemed like the heat could not penetrate her skin, and no matter how close she scooted, nor how badly her skin burned under the heat, she could not feel its warmth seep in. She thought of plunging her bare hand within the embers, to watch her flesh peel away, all to see if ice coated her bones. She cut herself instead, though the comfort was meager. It helped her slip away into apathy, though, and compared to the torment she felt, it was divine.

But then Qurrah approached, and the apathy revealed itself a lie. She felt her love and hatred swirl through her, and lost for words, she sat there as he joined her at her campfire. Long minutes passed as they both stared at the fire. It seemed neither knew what to say. At last Qurrah stood and turned to leave.

"Wait," she said. He stopped and looked back over his shoulder.

"What?" he asked, his voice so soft, so tentative.

"Are you still who you were?" she asked.

He paused as if to decide, and then nodded.

She flung herself against him, wrapping her arms around his neck as she buried her face in his bloodstained robe.

"I missed you so much," she cried. She let her tears bathe his chest. His hands wrapped around her waist. They were cold, but the warmth came from the act itself, the love that guided them. They said nothing as she cried, only held one another. She thought to say sorry, but didn't know for why or if it even mattered. She wanted to tell him of everything that had happened, of the abuse by Velixar, the rapes by the men, and of how every single night she'd prayed for his touch before she could even think to fall asleep. But instead they held one another.

"What do we do?" she asked once she regained her composure.

"My life is no longer my own," Qurrah said. "I do only what I am allowed. I'm sorry, Tess. You don't deserve this."

"I don't deserve anything," she said. "Please, just stay. I don't care what he's done to you. Just stay with me. Don't leave me, not ever again. I'm sorry. I'm so, so sorry."

He kissed her forehead, and his lips were like ice. Compared to Velixar, though, he was a comfort, and that night she lay down with his arms around her, and though his breath did not blow against the back of her neck, she still slept without a single nightmare to ruin her rest.

20

Bram rode northwest with his vanguard when they first saw the men flying in the sky.

"What in the gods' name is that?" asked Ian riding beside him. They had just passed through a gap in the Southron Hills, and before them spread the green plains of Ker.

"Either angels or demons," said Bram. "Though I see them flying no standard."

"They are too far away," said a soldier beside them. "I see only birds."

"Damn lot of birds," said Ian. "And I never knew a bird that wore armor that glinted in the sun."

They pressed on, now on edge and clutching their weapons tight. Their numbers were far from impressive, only five hundred knights and two thousand footmen. The rest of his army waited at Bloodbrick Crossing, guarding the entrance from Mordan into Ker. The southern lords had already been preparing for war before Bram ever contacted them, for they feared the covetous eye of Karak's priest-king in the north. If it came to battle now, and Antonil's men had fallen at the Gods' Bridges, then they were already too late. Against such a formidable host, they had little chance.

Their fears were unfounded, though, for as the army approached the standard of the Golden Mountain shone from winged banner carriers. The ground forces also came into view, and they were clearly not dead but alive, men of Mordan and Neldar.

"Several thousand," Ian said as they veered off course to meet the approaching army. "At least a thousand winged. Might it be enough to take Mordeina back from Karak's devil?"

"We need only one man," said Bram. He veered his horse around a deep patch of grass that grew like a tall pillar, sprouting from a muddy stretch where a spring surfaced. "If

Antonil is there, the rest of the northern lords will turn to him, at last finding a unifying name to rally behind. Despite how thin his grasp, he is still their true king."

"Some king. Within days of his crowning he was riding east with all of Mordeina's troops to take back his real homeland. He cares nothing for Mordan and her people, and while he was away, he lost everything. Are you sure they will welcome him so openly?"

Bram shrugged. "He was Queen Annabelle's husband. That is good enough for me. Thrones have been taken for weaker claims than that. And I'd prefer you guard your tongue when we meet him, Ian. We need his aid, not his scorn. If that is how you speak of one king, I fear to know how you speak of your own."

Ian accepted the reproach and let the subject die. Behind them, their army buzzed with excitement. Many were eager to see the angels, for while a few had seen the demons, none but Ian had seen Ashhur's celestial warriors. As they neared, their gold armor shining, the noise increased.

"Here is far enough," Bram said. "We'll have broken legs with how distracted everyone is. Too many animal holes in the grass."

A scout approached, lightly armored and swooping low on the wind. Bram remained mounted, and he raised his sword high so the angel might see him among the rest. Beside him, Ian raised the standard of Angkar, a wolf in profile, its eye a bloody red. The angel saw this and banked lower, and then with a great beat of its wings and scattering of feathers, it landed.

"Well met, king of man," said the angel. His voice had a strange accent to it, as if his vocal chords were not flesh but glass, so clear was his speech. "Are you King Bram, who we have been instructed to meet?"

"I am," said the king. "And what name may I call you, angel of Ashhur?"

"My name is Horon, and I speak for Ahaesarus, our worldly commander. Would you meet with us, and with our friend, king Antonil of Neldar?"

Bram held in a smirk. What a poor way to introduce the man. Why not king of Mordan, of a land that truly mattered and was friendly to them?

"Our agreement has already been made with King Theo. Bring your men, Horon, and your angels. Let us break bread and share stories, for unless Antonil has changed his mind, we are still allies."

The angel bowed.

"I will send them forward," he said. "May Ashhur watch over you, King Bram."

As Horon flew off, Bram rolled his eyes.

"Only person I want watching over me is you and your sword," he said to Ian.

"Honored."

Bram waited for Ashhur's army to arrive while Ian set about ordering the soldiers, getting tents pitched and fires prepared. They circled the wagons together in the center, preparing to cook what salted meat they had so the few livestock that followed might last several days longer. At least they had plenty to drink, though. Bram personally felt he could live on wine if the need arose. Might even make him a better fighter, given how he over-analyzed everything about his opponent come a battle.

His eyes kept returning to the skies and the winged men. Winged men…how strange. What changes to a siege did that mean? He'd known of lengthy battles, castles held by a mere hundred that fought off thousands. But without walls, without moats, without thick gates of wood and iron…what then? Might Ashhur's angels fly right over the walls of Mordeina and open the doors for them? He shuddered to think of the demons that approached from the east. He'd kept Loreina back at Angkar where he hoped the castle would provide her safety. Perhaps it would have been better if she'd come with him, or at the least, found a secluded home somewhere along the coast.

When the human army neared, Bram dismissed such thoughts and rode to greet them. He was curious to meet this Antonil. He'd tried to learn what he could, but his stay in the west had been too brief. Antonil had been in charge of Neldar's forces prior to its destruction, and after the death of their king, Edwin Vaelor, he'd assumed the role of lord and protector over the survivors. His claim to kinghood had been tenuous at best, but then he'd married Annabelle, solving that problem. Bram had thought the man a potential opportunist, taking advantage of the war and destruction to claim control over two kingdoms, but every story he'd heard seemed to indicate Antonil was an almost unwilling partner to the marriage, reluctant to assume his role.

Bram sighed. He wondered which was more dangerous: an egomaniacal, greedy king reaching for everything not his, or a hesitant king unsure of his own rule and forced to accept the responsibilities he should have been raised since birth to endure.

"Find Ian," he told one of his guards. "I want him near me in case something goes wrong."

The guard returned with Ian just in time to meet a small group hurrying ahead of the rest. Bram saw one angel flying low, and the rest seemed a strange assortment. One was clearly Antonil, an adequately imposing man (and thankfully older than some of the stories had claimed). Beside him, though...

"Is that an elf?" asked Ian.

"A beautiful elven lass," said Bram. "Does he have their aid, I wonder? And who is that beside him?"

"Orc blood's in the giant," said Ian. "I'd recognize that gray curse anywhere. This Antonil fights with the banned and the cursed. I don't like it."

"Angels, too," Bram said. "Don't forget them."

Ian smirked. "I fear they'll be the worst of the lot. Keep them to their promise. I bow my knee to you, not Ashhur."

Antonil stepped ahead of the others, and he bowed low but bent neither of his knees. A nice touch. Bram returned the bow, and felt mildly impressed. He waited, deciding to let this new king say the first words.

"Greetings, King Bram. My scout has told me you welcome us with open arms. After so many leagues of travel, I must say those words were a blessing to hear."

Bram smiled. "And with an army marching toward my northern border, your winged soldiers are an equal blessing."

He caught the orcish blooded one start to say something, then stop after the elven woman elbowed him. Good, he thought. At least one of the two knew their place.

"I have enemies on all sides," Antonil said. "Are you sure you desire to welcome my company? I might doom your country, not save it."

"Will you bleed to defend it?" Bram asked.

"To my dying breath," said Antonil. "Mordeina is my right, my city to protect. Aid me in retaking it, and I'll slaughter a hundred men with my own sword to keep your lands safe."

Bram felt quite pleased. Not the best with words, but the man's emotions showed plain on his face. He was honest in his desires, and sincere in his ability to kill. The man might be useful after all…

"Come," he said. "Let us eat! I can't claim it a feast, but it is a meal, and a chance to rest your tired feet…"

He glanced at the enormous angel that stood behind Antonil.

"…and wings," he added.

❖

"An unusual man," Ian said later that night, when the fires were burning low and the few remaining men not drunk off their feet had begun heading to bed.

"A simple man to understand," Bram said. "He's guided by ideals and a loose notion of nobility, yet not bound to them. He'll be easy to guide our way, so long as we don't directly contradict his sense of morals."

Ian tossed another log onto their fire and started smoothing out his blankets.

"And that orc fellow?"

"Brutish. Plays dumb, but he's not. Oblivious to proper manners, though."

They shared a laugh. The orc-blood had interrupted their conversation twice, and after the second time, Antonil had sent him to another table. On his way, the elf had zapped his rear with a thin bolt of electricity.

"And the wizard, that mercenary leader...Tarlak?"

Bram settled into his own blankets and shifted back and forth so the grass smoothed out below him.

"Thinks he is far funnier than he really is. Held his liquor better than anyone else there. And he's a total ass."

Ian lay down and scooted closer to the fire.

"Think he'd really turn me into if frog if I had kissed the elven lady?" he asked.

"Probably. I might have paid him just to see it, so long as he could reverse the curse."

Bram laughed at Ian's incomprehensible grumble. They remained silent for a moment, both staring up at the stars.

"What of their men, and the angels? Do you think we stand a chance?"

"They've fought more battles than our own have," said Bram. "And they're driven on by desperation and ideals...a potent combination. They will defend, and kill without remorse. Ker will survive. I am certain of that now."

Ian thought a moment, and Bram knew that was a sign the man was trying to say something he thought he might not like.

"Their ideals," he said. "You mean their faith? It's infectious. With the priests of Karak gone, they'll pour into Ker once this war ends. We may not owe them loyalty through any official means, but neither were we sworn to Karak. It took slaughtering all of their priests and paladins to free us from their grasp. I would hate to do the same to them. These people are better than that. They deserve better, especially if they stand with us as allies."

Ian paused again, and Bram inwardly sighed. Couldn't he just be quiet and go to sleep?

"You know," said the knight. "There was one other thing that struck me as odd. They have no camp followers. None at all!"

Bram broke out into laughter.

"Sleep well," he said. "Tomorrow we march for Bloodbrick."

They left early morning, traveling west. They reached the Corinth River by midday, and from there they followed it upstream until they arrived at the bridge. Already the defenses were in full construction. Bram met the nobleman responsible, a Lord Peleth who had provided over two thirds of the initial builders and defenders, totaling near two thousand. After their rushed greeting, they went to survey the defenses while the rest of the arriving army set up camp.

"We've heard many wild rumors," Peleth said as he walked ahead. He was a large man, his belly round and his pants held tight by an over-extravagant gold buckle. While they walked, he gestured wildly with his right hand and massaged his goatee with his left. "Men and women fleeing Mordan have told us their priest-king holds sway over the dead, and that his soldiers fight with a fanatical zeal. We've tried to build our defenses accordingly."

He led the king through a maze of tents leading to the bridge. Just before the bridge they stepped into and then out of a deep trench.

"In case we have to fall back," Peleth said.

"I'm no simpleton," said Bram.

Peleth shrugged and continued on. The bridge itself was a pale imitation of the Gods' Bridges, but the Corinth was no Rigon River, either. Neither top nor bottom had arches: instead there were seven columns on either side propping up the flat crossing. Despite its name, the bricks were a faded gray.

"We've built several lines of defense," Peleth said, pointing to the palisades of wood wrapped together with rope. "Just a few, and kept them low enough to strike over the tops. It'll be tough climbing over if we have to retreat, though."

"Then I suggest we don't retreat."

"I don't expect us to lose the bridge," Peleth said. "Only reason why I didn't make a retreat any easier. Like I said, I've been talking to these people, and I know what'll happen. If they're that damned certain to win, they won't try to crush us on the bridge. They'll wade right through the water and to

Karak with the casualties. Rain's been low, and it'll only go up to their chests."

"Do we have the men to protect the riverside?" asked Bram.

Peleth gave him a smug grin. "Just you wait until you see what I've got waiting for them should they try to cross."

They left the bridge and went to one side. Bram looked about and was sorely disappointed.

"Where are the palisades along the banks?" he asked. "We have time, and wood from the forest nearby. Why leave the riverside defenseless?"

"Look closer into the water," Peleth said, his smug grin not at all lessening.

Bram leaned over, but saw only mud and his frowning reflection.

"Nothing," he said.

"Exactly. I've been wanting to try this since that Moore the Red pulled a similar tactic on me up near Lake Cor. Brought me a whole mess of smiths. Follow me."

He led them back into the camps, toward the heavy sound of hammers. Sure enough, ten master smiths worked around hastily constructed forges, their helpers hurrying to and fro. Bram saw them working on either square plates of iron, or thin spears of metal.

"I don't like riddles," Bram said. "What is all this?"

"Here," Peleth said, reaching past one of the smiths and grabbing a strange object. "Take a hold of this."

Bram accepted it, and he turned it over in his hands. It was an iron plate, flat and twice the size of his hands. Attached to its center was a four inch barb.

"Watch," said Peleth, taking it out of his hands and placing it on the ground. He hovered his foot above it, gently letting the tip press against his boot.

"You hope to hamper them when they charge," said Bram.

"Not just hamper them. I've had them working on these nonstop for weeks now. The ore's low quality, had a stockpile of it for ages wondering what to do with it. These'll work perfect. They'll be rushing ahead, all hollering and hoping to catch us by surprise, but then they'll plant foot on these beauties. They'll *drown*, Bram. These won't let go, and they're not light. Get a whole mess of men behind, pushing and shoving to move forward, and they've got nowhere to go but down into the water. Best of all, no one will have a clue what's going on until it's too late."

Bram grinned at the simplicity.

"Not bad," he said. "Though I think we should still set up some palisades. How many do you have of these devils?"

"Over a thousand," said Peleth. "My men have been shoving them into the water night and day."

"A thousand?" He looked at the contraptions with a whole new respect. "Damn. I'm glad we're not the ones trying to cross."

"And don't you worry about holding that river side," Peleth said. "I may not look the warlord, but you've been treated with silk gloves down in Angkar. Up by the lake, we have the real bandits. You get your knights and hold that bridge, where the fighting is bloody and honorable. Down here in the mud...I got my own plans. My men'll be ready. I promise you that."

Bram smiled, clasped the man's wrist, and pumped it twice.

"This works, I'll make sure your lands double in size," he said.

"The other lords won't like that," Peleth said.

Bram picked up one of the spike traps and held it before his face.

"The other lords didn't give me these," he said.

❧❦❧

"So where are you going?" Harruq asked as he neared. Jerico winced, and he was glad the half-orc couldn't see his guilty reaction.

"Was hoping to do this quiet," he said. "But you're not one to cooperate just for the sake of being nice, are you?"

Harruq laughed. They stood at Jerico's campfire near the outer edges of the camp. His tent, however, was conspicuously absent. Instead, all of his supplies were on the paladin's back, including his shield. Harruq pointed and then waggled his finger.

"I'd say you were trying to run from trouble, but that isn't like you or Lathaar. So how about you tell me what's really going on before I start yelling for soldiers to lock you in some stocks until you change your mind."

"Friends of mine are in trouble," Jerico said, shifting his pack so it hung more comfortably from his shoulders. "I spoke with several men from Mordan in between their prayers, and let's say I didn't like what I heard. People dear to me, people I nearly failed to protect once, are trapped and in danger. I have to help them."

"And the fight at the bridge?" asked Harruq.

Jerico shrugged. "I'll try to make it back in time. If not, you'll have to kill double for me."

He winced, waiting for a reaction, but instead the half-orc laughed again.

"Far as I know, you haven't sworn yourself to any king here, so get going. I'd recommend going really, really far south before crossing the river, though. You hear about them spike things they've been laying? Not a time for a casual swim, but neither do I think they'd be too keen on you walking over the bridge."

"Thanks," Jerico said, and inwardly he sighed with relief. He'd worried Harruq would call him a coward or bring too much attention to his leaving. Even worse, he thought he might run and tell Tarlak. He bowed awkwardly due to the pack, then hurried off.

Of course, he didn't get far. Less than five minutes later a blue portal swirled open, but instead of the wizard, Lathaar stepped out. Without a word, Lathaar punched him in the chest, hoisted his own pack, and then trudged west.

"That's for trying to leave me behind," he said without looking back.

"You were needed back there," Jerico insisted, feeling like he'd done something wrong even though he was sure he hadn't. "Someone needed to preach the light of Ashhur to the soldiers before battle."

"Keziel is my friend as well," said Lathaar, slowing a little so they could walk side by side. "I know that's who you're hoping to rescue. The question is, why? What is going on at the Sanctuary?"

"Two different men told me that Mordan's priest-king had sent soldiers and priests of Karak to surround the Sanctuary, effectively trapping them inside. They've held out, so far as they know, but as for food and water…I won't let them waste away, not when I have my mace and my shield."

"And my swords," said Lathaar. "Those at the crossing will have to make do without us. You're my brother in arms, Jerico. Don't try something like this again."

"Will you punch me again if I do?"

"Yes. And much, much harder. Here's far enough. Let's wade across."

Holding their supplies above their heads, they pushed across the river and into the land of Mordan, where Melorak ruled.

21

"Keep it quiet," Deathmask said as he and Veliana watched the wagon roll toward the enormous gates of Mordeina. He glanced back, saw her scarred neck, and then chuckled. "I guess that won't be much of a problem for you."

She jabbed him in the side with her fingers.

"Fuck. You."

He grinned. Her voice was steadily coming back, but still she spoke in broken sentences. Every word was pain to her.

"Watch your mouth, little lady. And keep it down."

They peered over the small hill, through the heavy grass atop it. The wagon lumbered slowly, as if the oxen pulling it were tired from a long journey. They saw two riders at the front, only one of them visibly armed with a blade. The wagon itself was covered, but the time and size accurately matched their expectations.

"It's loaded with grain," Aaron Hocking had told them at their last meeting. "Just the first of many coming in from storehouses along the wall of towers. You want to starve the city? You burn those wagons down to the very last grain."

Deathmask had volunteered him and Veliana for the task, not that there had been much choice. Time and money, or more importantly the lack of money, had dwindled down their forces. They still had a token force, but they were scattered about the city, killing the stray guard and whispering words of rebellion. Besides, the day he and Vel couldn't handle a single wagon was the day he hung up his mask and took up farming.

"You want the driver or the guard?" he asked.

"Guard."

"Take all the fun." He put on his mask and then scattered ash into the air. "Loop around. I'll distract him. On three."

He lifted his fingers, then counted down. On the third, he rushed out, moving silently in his red robes. The sun was setting, the sky a dark blue. With neither of the men up front wielding a torch, he reached the wagon before the driver spotted him out of the corner of his eye. It was that same eye Deathmask hurled a bolt of shadow into. His body convulsed as the power rolled throughout, exploding his brains inside his skull. The guard drew his sword and shoved the body aside.

"Don't be foolish, just surrender the wagon," Deathmask called out to him. The guard lifted his sword as if to surrender, then jerked forward. Veliana pushed him off and hopped atop to grab the reins, not bothering to clean her daggers before she slipped them back into her belt.

"Easy," she mouthed to him.

And then the wagon's covering collapsed, revealing twenty soldiers inside, plus Haern, who lunged before she could even react.

"Vel!" Deathmask screamed, his hands a blur. Dark lightning arced through the men, killing two. He saw Haern land atop Veliana, his feet blasting the air from her lungs. She tumbled off the side, and Haern followed, his cloaks flapping behind him as he fell.

Deathmask killed another soldier by striking him with his hand, the magic pouring through his armor and into his heart to stop it. He tried to cast another, but something hard struck the back of his head, and he collapsed. His vision darkened, and he fought to retain consciousness. He couldn't fade out now, not with Veliana in danger, not with her alone against that undead freak that was Haern...

When he opened his eyes, Veliana lay beside him. If he'd been a religious man, he might have praised a god that she was still alive. They both lay on their stomachs, their arms bound behind them. He felt more than happy, however, to blame all the deities for such a horrible predicament. As he made a list of spells he could cast without somatic components, he felt something sharp press against the base of his spine.

"I wouldn't try anything," someone said behind him. "Melorak's pet has his eye on you, and he's a fast one. You'll be dead before you get off the first syllable of a spell."

Not good. Not good at all. Haern had a saber against his back. There weren't enough gods for him to curse. He looked to Veliana, whose look back said it all. They were dead, and they both knew it.

Time dragged on, and in no hurry. Deathmask kept his breathing loud and steady. Veliana knew a little bit of magic, and she was far more nimble. If he kept Haern's gaze locked on him, perhaps she could think of something, because he sure hadn't yet. He breathed heavily through his nose, hoping the volume might become a drone they stopped listening to. Some of his spells were just a few syllables, and if he could get one off before a saber ran him through...

For a moment he thought of trying the same trick as before, and faking his and her deaths. He chuckled. Doubtful that would work. Not this time. Besides, Haern was too thorough. He'd cut off both their heads to make sure.

The mood of the men suddenly shifted, and he glanced to his side to see many legs approaching, one in particular wearing flowing black robes ornately decorated with silver and gold.

"Excellent," he heard the vile voice of Melorak say. "Tell Aaron he shall have his wealth returned in full, and his estate removed from the priesthood."

Aaron, thought Deathmask, feeling a thorn in his gut. *Aaron Hocking? That spineless weasel sucking...*

A foot crashed into his side, and he groaned as he rolled over. When he looked up, he saw Melorak glaring down at him with his single good eye.

"Do you know how much trouble you've caused me?" he asked. He reached down with a pale hand, his fingertips sparking with magic.

"Not near enough," said Deathmask. "How about you send your little pet somewhere else, and we can discuss this like civil men?"

Melorak brushed his fingers against his mask. It caught fire and burned. Deathmask screamed as he felt his flesh blacken, the smoke stinging his eyes despite how tightly he clenched them shut. He howled as he flailed against his bonds. A foot pressed hard against his chest, and he could only assume it was Haern's. Once more he felt the tip of a blade on his skin. His jaw trembling, his eyes hopelessly watery, he did his best to smile.

"That was my mask, you asshole."

The blade pressed into his flesh. It was quick, in and out, and not deep. Just enough to draw blood and send more pain spiking up his spine. He tried not to scream. He did. Damn body felt like screaming anyway.

"You have information I need," he heard Melorak say. "You've done well, tormenting my guards and fostering rebellion, but it ends tonight. But I know you are not alone. The leader of Ashhur's priests was never found when I conquered this city, and I know he lives. Where is Bernard, Ghost? Where is he hiding?"

"Why don't you ask your snake-bellied friend, Aaron?"

Another stab, higher up. The blade scraped against his rib bones on its way out. More screaming.

"I have, but Bernard was not there. Perhaps Ashhur warned him, or he sensed deception. Where are your safe houses? I know your kind. You never would have trusted Aaron with every secret. You'd keep one or two to yourself, as leverage should things go ill. Well things have gone ill, you miserable wretch. If you want a quick death, you'll tell me where he might have gone."

Deathmask's mind raced. Bernard wasn't supposed to have moved positions, but it wasn't unheard of, given how careful they'd been. But where could he have gone? Where might he hide that Aaron would know nothing of? And even if he did remember...would he tell? Since when was he so hopeful for a clean death? With his life, a messy, brutal execution seemed more appropriate anyway.

He forced open his eyes. His skin felt like a leathery mask shrinking in on itself. What his face looked like, he didn't even want to know. Through the blur, Deathmask saw Melorak leering down with his arms crossed, while Haern stood nearby, his foot on his chest, his sword hovering just above his heart.

"Fuck you," he said.

No sword. No stab. Instead Melorak knelt down beside him and grabbed his neck. In his cold grip, he held up his head and forced him to stare into his red eye.

"You may think you'll never tell," he said. "But the dead will always talk to me. You don't have a choice in this matter. Tell me now, or after I kill you and bring back your ghost. Perhaps I'll even leave you in that state. You certainly deserve it."

Deathmask felt a sliver of doubt pierce through his pain. Melorak was most certainly not bluffing. He'd seen the rows of corpses hanging from hooks throughout the castle. The man was a master of death, while he himself was only a dabbler. Should his soul be wrenched back into this world, he would tell everything.

"Go ahead," he said, making up his mind. "I'll give you nothing."

"Not yet," Melorak said, rubbing a finger against Deathmask's face. He bit his teeth to hold in the scream. "See, when you're dead, you won't feel the pain. Oh, there are ways I could make you uncomfortable, perhaps terribly so, but nothing this fierce. Nothing this *intense.*"

Deathmask screamed as Melorak's fingers dug in so tight he thought he'd claw his face off like a mask. His blisters pulsed with agony. Blood seeped down his jaw and neck. Any thoughts of spells or escape fled. All his mind knew was overwhelming suffering.

Perhaps he passed out. He didn't know. But Haern no longer stood atop him. He rolled to one side, forcing his eyes open. Veliana was on her back, Haern's sabers against her throat. She remained strong, refusing to even whimper.

"What of you?" Melorak asked her. He gestured to the soldiers around him. "Would you prefer a clean death? Or should I give you to the men? You'll be anything but clean afterward. Normally I'd frown upon such lewd methods, but you are the Ghost's Blade, after all. Out of every sinner in this world, I cannot imagine anyone more *deserving* of such a fate."

"Besides yourself?" he heard Veliana ask. He winced when Haern kicked her in the face, probably breaking her nose, but he'd never felt such pride. That's my girl, he thought. Show them you're not afraid, either.

"Your wit is childish and unimpressive," Melorak said. He crouched beside her and gently brushed her hair from her face. With his own robe, he cleaned off some of the blood dripping from her nose. "The time for pettiness is over. You know I cannot let you live, not after how many you have killed. Karak demands punishment, and I must give it to him. But it need not be lengthy. It need not be one of pain and blood. A simple spell, a gentle touch of your breast, and I can stop your heart. Tell me where Bernard is. I assure you, no matter my frustration, I would never let these men defile your corpse after your death. Save yourself from them, from everything. Please. Where…is…Bernard?"

She looked to Deathmask, and in her good eye, a bit of dire humor sparkled.

"You want to know?" she asked. "I think you're about to find out."

Sunlight exploded amid them, as if a nova had burst into existence there upon the road. Deathmask thought to free himself, but he'd stared directly into that light, and his mind reeled in confusion. He struggled, but his bonds were tight, and the words to spells seemed slippery in his mind, elusive things he couldn't grab a hold of. Hands wrapped around his chest, and suddenly he was up and moving, his legs running as if on their own accord. The ground shifted unevenly below him, and he started to fall.

"Keep running," he heard Veliana say. He clutched her tighter and did his best to resume. He glanced back only once, and through the orange and yellow blobs blotting his vision, he saw Bernard standing between them and Melorak, a halo of light circling his feet. Golden lances slashed from his hands, cutting down guards.

"Help him," Deathmask muttered as they neared the top of the small hill from where they had spied the wagon's arrival. "We should…"

"He knows what he's doing," Veliana said. "At least, I hope so."

They half-ran, half-stumbled down the hill. Deathmask felt his vision returning, and his steps grew in confidence.

"North," he said. "We have little time."

"Time for what?" she asked.

"Hocking…"

◁◈▷

"Everything?" Aaron asked the messenger.

"Due to your cooperation and show of loyalty, Melorak insists we return your estate despite how great Mordeina's need is for taxes to support its people," said the young man. The symbol of the lion hung from his neck, small and carved of wood.

"When will I receive payment?"

The messenger smiled as if his patience were already tried.

"In time, we will send appropriate funds from our coffers to your estate. Until then, I bid you good night."

"Excellent. Tell Melorak I am most thankful for his kindness."

The messenger bowed and left. Aaron shut the door behind him and then pressed his back against it. At last, it was over. He had his mansion, his wealth, and his reputation, all restored. His house guards wouldn't have to live like beggars in the nearby homes of farmers. His possessions, which had been ransomed off in the name of taxes and fines, would return. His paintings of distant lands, his family heirlooms, his swords and chests and dressings…all back.

Perhaps he'd been a fool to challenge the priest-king, and a bigger fool for trusting Bernard. They'd sacrificed everything for a hopeless task. There was no point. No honor. As Deathmask had made perfectly clear, they would be no heroes.

He poured himself a drink, one of his few luxuries he'd managed to hide from the collectors. It was illegal now, and therefore exponentially more valuable to the right people. With lord Ewes and lord Gemcroft arrested, and Bernard soon to be executed, he felt he needed the drink more than he might need the extra bit of coin.

"To broken dreams," he said as he toasted his empty parlor.

"And shattered memories," came the traditional reply from the door.

Aaron's glass fell from his limp hand and shattered. Deathmask limped through the door, Veliana helping him along. His face was a blackened, scarred mess, but his eyes were alive, bloodshot and furious.

"But how?" he asked, taking a step back and glancing for his sword.

A dagger flew past his head and thudded into the wall, an inch above where his sword rested upon a table.

"Bad idea," Veliana said. "And better question is: why?"

She let go of Deathmask and lunged. Before the thought to dodge had even entered his head, he was already falling to the ground, her heel smashing his teeth. Two daggers stabbed either side of his sleeves, pinning him. He turned to the side and spat blood.

"Why?" he asked. "Because somehow Melorak saw me. Whatever that pet assassin of his sees, he sees. His priests came to my home. I had one choice, you have to understand. I either helped them or died."

He felt himself start to cry, and humiliating as it was, he couldn't stop. Veliana leered down at him, her scarred eye milky white and hovering so close. Even it seemed swirling with fury.

"We were ready to die to protect you," she said. "Bernard, Dagan, all of you. If not for Bernard's arrival and those soldiers' inability to tie a real knot, we *would* be dead. You expect us to forgive you for succumbing to what we did not?"

He closed his eyes and shook his head.

"I had no choice. This happens, don't you see? Kings fall, new rulers take their place. We lost. What does it matter? In time, another will replace the priest-king."

Veliana chuckled, and her daggers pressed tight against his neck.

"Another?" he heard Deathmask say. "The man is death made flesh, Karak's new prophet and ruler. He is not some normal usurper. He is not part of the ebb and flow of politics and kings. He is a blasphemy to our world, and must be destroyed. You've nearly ruined our only chance at overthrowing him. Damn fool. It's a shame they'll be coming for you soon. You deserve hours of torture, if not days. Count yourself lucky I have only minutes to make this worthwhile."

Aaron's eyes shot open, and he saw Deathmask kneeling beside him. He tried to rise, but the daggers held him, and Veliana sat upon his knees, locking them down. The only thing he accomplished with his struggles was to fill Deathmask's face with disgust.

"Such cowardice," he said. The words burned whatever remained of Aaron's pride. "You never deserved my aid."

Aaron winced as the man's hand pressed against his forehead. It was feverishly warm.

"Lord Hocking," Veliana whispered. She'd crawled atop him, one hand holding his hand down, the other tight about his neck. "You are a turncoat, lowest of the low. You are less than the worms, and a worm you will become."

He screamed as she drew another dagger and thrust it into his bicep. When she cut, no blood flowed. Instead he felt a strange numbness spread with each stroke, until by the time she was severing bone it was as if it were the arm of another. Aaron looked to the mage in horror, whose charred face smirked with pleasure.

"At once," he said, gesturing to the stump at his shoulder. "The pain will come all at once, as will the blood. Time is now your enemy."

Veliana leaned over and began on the other arm. Aaron squirmed, but she held firm, as if he were nothing more than a nuisance. Unable to stop himself, he watched as her dagger sank into his flesh. The pain dulled, nothing but phantoms of what he knew he should feel. At last she pulled free his arm and tossed it aside.

"Almost there," she said, blowing him a kiss.

Next came his leg. He felt strangely light-headed, and his struggles were nothing but spastic shakes. It took several minutes before she cut through all of his thigh. When his leg came free, she stood and carried it to his fireplace. She dumped it unceremoniously in the pit, kicked a bit of ash over it, and then returned for the final leg.

"I'm sorry," Aaron said, or at least he tried. His tongue had grown thick and dry. He still felt phantom sensations from his limbs, the touch of the wood floor, the soft spread of the ash, and the gradual chill overcoming them as the blood within slowly cooled. When she pulled free the final leg, she grabbed the two arms and carried them to the fire. One by one she set them inside, then turned to Deathmask.

"Do you want the honor?" she asked him.

"Many good men died today," Deathmask said as he approached the fireplace. Every step seemed slow and gingerly taken. Aaron wondered just how badly his face pained him, yet still he hid it. Could he handle pain so well? He had a feeling he was about to find out.

"Not just a good man," Deathmask continued. "One of the best. Bernard may be dead, sacrificed to save us from the fate you created. My mask has become my own face, and my own flesh will soon rot to ash. But you…you deserve the fire of the Abyss. It's coming for you, but not yet. Let the angels and demons wait. I have my own fire for you."

He spat onto the bundle of arms and legs. When he reached down his hand, flame burst about it. When it touched the saliva, it roared to life as if it were lamp oil. Aaron's eyes widened as he realized he could still feel sensations within his severed appendages. He writhed and screamed as he felt every inch burn and blister. The fire spread, consuming his fingers, his toes, his thighs and arms and elbows. A pathetic, bloodless stump, he screamed and cried.

"All at once," Veliana whispered into his ear. "That is when the pain will come. Beg for mercy. Beg for it, Lord Hocking. Beg for it, *worm*."

"Mercy," he cried, his head rolling side to side. "Please, mercy, kill me, I beg you!"

Deathmask reached into the fire and pulled out a handful of ash. A gentle throw and it floated together, once more becoming a mask to hide his face.

"I don't know the meaning," Deathmask said.

He snapped his fingers.

The blood burst from every cut across Aaron's body. He howled until there was no air in his lungs, no sound from his throat. He felt every single cut Veliana had made, slicing, chopping, and cracking his bones and joints. The blood pooled about him. He felt it stick to his face, seep into his clothes, and still the pain, still the burning. It didn't seem possible. He should have passed out. No one could endure such pain. But he did. While Veliana and Deathmask watched, he sucked in another groaning breath and screamed again.

Veliana placed her dagger above his left eye, its tip dripping blood.

"We'll make sure everyone knows of your death," she told him. "We'll let everyone know the fate awaiting those who betray the Ghost and his Blade."

The dagger thrust, and in the last fleeting moments of thought remaining, Aaron thanked the gods for the end.

<hr>

Melorak stood beside the empty wagon, his hands wet with blood. The blood of a priest. Bernard's blood.

"You were lucky," he said. "Bear the scars proudly, fool. Ashhur has so few followers left, he must have given you every scrap of his power, and it was still not enough."

He looked to his dead soldiers, slain by the supposedly peaceful sect of Ashhur. After the blinding eruption of light, he'd seen little, regaining his senses in time to protect himself from a barrage of spells that shimmered gold but stung like fire. Every last one of his guards had died in the onslaught. One on one, Melorak versus Bernard, they had battled. And when he should have had victory, when he at last held Bernard's robes in his fist and cast a spell that would explode the blood out of his chest, the priest had vanished in a sudden shimmering of silver.

"A cowardly escape," he said. He'd thought to hunt for him, but the act was pointless. He wouldn't know where to look, hadn't even known where to look prior to the attack. But with both the Ghost and his Blade escaping, he knew his last link of discovering their location was gone. Dagan Gemcroft and John Ewes both rotted from chains in their cells. He'd personally cut their throats. He could summon back their souls, but the stubborn rebels would not remain in any safe house they'd used prior to that night. They were intelligent, resourceful, and dangerous.

"This is not over," Melorak said as he stared at the blood on his hands. "I will find you, priest. Your kind has no place in my world, not anymore. Karak's time to reign has come. When Olrim returns victoriously, my soldiers will scour every tiny nook and crevice within the city. Be with me, oh mighty lord. Hear my prayer. Let his death be mine, and mine alone."

He looked to the wagon, where the body of Haern lay still. Bernard had waved his hand, paralyzing him with a single word. Melorak focused, seeing the sparkling chains in his mind's eye. One by one he broke them.

"Your mission is not done," he said as the undead assassin stood and retrieved his swords. "This is your last chance. Whatever remnants of you are in there, understand that I will keep you here for eternity should you fail. You'll hang from the hooks, feeling them pierce your flesh. The maggots will feast, the worms will crawl, and still you'll await my orders like the obedient slave you are. Find them, and kill them. No rest. No mercy. Go."

Haern left without a single remark or sign of understanding, only a lifeless sprint that was frightening in its speed.

"Guide me, oh lord," Melorak prayed to the stars. "The time is almost come."

He returned to the city, to where his throne awaited. If all went as planned, he'd have his army back in a few months, fresh from the slaughter of the nation of Ker.

22

Aurelia endured their awkward stares as she walked across the bridge. While the men of Ker hadn't been completely responsible for the elven exodus to the east, they'd certainly done nothing to stop it. Even worse, they'd turned down every request for aid throughout the trek from Bloodbrick to the Gods' Bridges. She knew her kind, already exotic to humans, was even rarer to the men in the land between the rivers. They treated her politely, and she smiled back in return. A few even offered clumsy bows or hurried out of her way. No doubt they knew of her magic, her vital role in defending them. Would she earn their respect? Even with its walls, doors, archers, and Eschaton, Veldaren had fallen to the onslaught of Karak. Would they do any better, here with a shallow river and a bridge?

"Lovely as ever," said one of the men in charge of reinforcing the bridge's barricades. His smile grew underneath his lengthy mustache and beard.

"Thank you," she said, tilting her head slightly and curtseying to the compliment. The man blushed and returned to his work.

Beyond the final barricade she stood alone, staring off to the distant fields. She knew, if she followed the river northeast, she'd reach Lake Cor, and then, nestled against it, the burned remnants of her homeland. For a fleeting moment she considered visiting those ruins of Dezerea, to walk where she had been raised, to put her hands on the charred trunks that had once held aloft her home. Perhaps enough time had passed for new trees to begin sprouting, and the grass to return to the forest floor. But what point was there in hurting herself with memories? The past was a flood of pain and sadness. Her homeland, her parents, her only child…

"Please," she whispered, though to whom she did not know. Perhaps Celestia. "Don't forget about us now."

There, at that bridge, her parents had made their stand alongside the greatest spellcasters of their time. Tens of thousands of troops had marched against them, held back for days by the slaughter. The rest of the elves, herself included, had escaped because of their sacrifice, and a heavy one it had been. The magical bloodlines of elves, already thin, had nearly vanished. She was one of the rare few remaining with the gift, and now here she stood. Once more the gift of elven magic might die upon the Bloodbrick.

She'd heard the stories about that battle years later, always filtered to them through humans that had survived. Part of her still regretted never coming back to help them. She'd been young then, especially for an elf. Perhaps she could have tipped the balance. Perhaps she could have held the line long enough for some to escape, her father, her mother…

"Uh, miss?" said one of the builders, breaking her thoughts. "Miss, your husband's looking for you."

She glanced back to see Harruq on the far side of the bridge, and she heard him call out her name as he spun about. One of the soldiers pointed him her way, and she crossed her arms and looked to the distance as he approached.

"Started worrying you'd left me," he said as he slid his arms around her.

"Just hoping to get a bit of quiet," she said.

"So you stood near the men with hammers and saws?"

She kissed his cheek and hoped he'd let the matter die. He did, but switched it to something just as upsetting.

"This is where they died, isn't it?" he asked.

She tensed in his arms, then felt ashamed. He held her tighter, and she relaxed and put her head against his neck.

"Ten against thousands," she said. "If only I were as strong as them. In a single day I could send our enemies fleeing back to Mordeina."

"Wasn't there," Harruq said. "So I can't say whether or not that's true…but I know you're as brave as they were, as noble, and most certainly prettier."

"You never saw my mother," she said, but she kissed him for the compliment anyway.

They both quieted and stared to the distance. With their sensitive eyes, they saw the smoke of many campfires drifting lazily to the sky.

"Less than a week," he said.

"If that."

"We'll defeat them when they arrive. We've faced worse and won."

She chuckled.

"When?" she asked. "Kinamn was massacred. Veldaren crumbled. The angels are the only reason we survived at Mordeina."

"Well this is rather gloomy, especially for you."

He kissed the top of her head, and she sighed. He was right, of course. Normally she tried to keep her emotions above such pessimism, but this bridge was different. It remained a symbol throughout her race, of how they were forever outnumbered, forever persecuted, and doomed to die no matter how strong they might be and how many they might kill. They lived in mankind's world. Celestia's blessing was slowly leaving their clerics, and her gift of magic had dwindled in their bloodlines. Was there any future for them in Karak's world?

"We have to win," she said. "We fall here, and our hope is gone. The angels are just a reprieve. No more miracles await us. Come Karak's paradise, men and elves will be slaves at best. How did we come to this, Harruq? How did we sink so far? What happened to this world?"

"Questions with no answers," he said.

"No," she said, wrapping her arms around his and holding him tight. "Too many went unstopped: King Baedan, Velixar, Tessanna, King Vaelor. The cowards have ruled, the strong have remained silent, and Karak's pets ruin everything they touch. Your brother was the first, don't you see that? He was the first we've saved."

"You're wrong," he said. "I was the first. And because of you. Only you. And you'll save us again. You'll stand here with us and show mankind the strength and honor of the elves.

Now come. Tarlak's prepared some sort of game for us to play to help get your mind off all this drudgery."

"Shouldn't we help them build?" she asked.

He laughed, and the warm sound soothed her fears and pushed away her sadness to the past.

"We'll help enough," he said. "When the blood starts to spill, we'll be there in the thick of it. I may not wield magic like you and Tar, but my blades will drink their fill."

<hr/>

Nothing could have prepared Olrim for the bittersweet joy in controlling Karak's army. The thrill he felt in planning, sending out scouts, and giving orders to his generals was undeniable. Matching in its frustration, however, were the conflicting reports, petty squabbles, struggles for food and supplies, and the overall headaches induced by cramming so many different men into a single cohesive unit.

"We're ready to march," said Gregor Black, one of his generals. He was the most insistent in his abilities to aid Olrim. No doubt Gregor felt him unprepared for his new position.

"We were supposed to be ready twenty minutes ago," Olrim said. "What excuse do you have this time?"

"It's the damn men from the Craghills," said Gregor. "They'd sheathe their swords in their asses if I let them."

Olrim sighed. Of course, Gregor had been born on the opposite side of Mordan from the Craghills. He'd heard plenty of opinions from both geographic areas while listening to confessions prior to the war. It seemed war did not unite like he had hoped, only invited more reasons to use the excuses.

"I don't care," Olrim said. "Get them marching. We're almost to the Corinth. Once we cross the river, we'll set up camp while the rest of the wagons catch up. From there we'll scorch the earth on the way to Angkar, and pillage whatever food we need until we reach the ocean. Then we'll see if Bram is willing to talk peace, or if we must starve him out of his castle."

"Of course," said Gregor. "Ker has rarely rebelled against us, and never have they survived a siege by the Mordan army. There is little to fear in their military might. Only their angels might give us pause, damned winged men. No place on a battlefield for the likes of them."

"Give the order to march," Olrim said. "If there are winged men to fight, you let me worry about dealing with them."

In their second hour of march, they saw the first angel scout. The angel hovered high above, his golden armor glittering in the morning light. There was little doubt that he came from the crossing.

"Keep the men tight together," Olrim told Gregor. "I don't want anyone vulnerable to an ambush. With their wings, they might strike from anywhere."

"Of course, sir," said Gregor.

By the third hour, Bloodbrick Crossing was in view, its surface covered with fortifications and soldiers. All along the opposite bank stretched several thousand men. Into the air went battalions of angels, flying in steady circle formations that greatly exaggerated their numbers. Olrim joined his priests, seeking their opinions.

"Save our spells for Ashhur's warriors," said one of the elders. "They are our only true threat. We set a trap for them, yes. A trap they will never expect."

"We cannot delay," said another. "If Antonil is with them, he might foster rebellion in our own troops. Our generals might turn to this former king in hopes he will be a weaker ruler than Melorak."

"And what of our paladins?" Olrim asked.

"Wait until the first great bloodshed has ended," said the elder. "Then send in our paladins to lead the way."

The wisdom seemed sound, and the others agreed. Olrim returned to the front and ordered them on. They marched with one eye to the sky, always wary of a surprise attack by the angels. No attack came. They reached the crossing without incident. Only five hundred yards away, they stopped and set up camp.

"I've got the other generals preparing their groups," Gregor said. "If we pelt the bridge with arrows, we can charge while they clear away the dead. Then our archers can rain upon their reinforcements. Once we push through to the other side, nothing can stop us but those angels."

"We outnumber them fivefold," said Olrim. "Why should we bottle ourselves up on the bridge?"

Gregor harrumphed as if he were asked a question by a child.

"The bridge might be rough going, but it is still an even fight. What else might you suggest, wading across the water? Nonsense. They can kill us no faster than we can kill them on the bridge, but the river is a different game, priest. Wet and helpless, they'll cut us down by the hundreds as we try to emerge on the other side."

"They don't have anywhere near enough to guard both sides," Olrim said. "How long can they hold the bridge? Two days? Three? The angels only complicate things further. We must win, and now."

"Why this mad rush?" asked Gregor. "Why sacrifice certain victory days from now for a costly risk today? This is foolishness."

Olrim dared not mention Antonil's name. Melorak had spread word to the land that Antonil had perished. For him to return…where might Gregor's loyalties lie? What of the other generals who served under him, or the other nobles fighting with him?

"This army is under my command," Olrim said. He pointed to the crossing. "Send in our men. When there is no room at the bridge, send the rest into the water. Let them see the full might of Karak."

"As you wish," Gregor said, slapping an arm against his chest and bowing. Olrim felt the disrespect dripping off him, but he let it slide. Melorak trusted him with victory, and victory is what he would bring. With such a massive assault, there was no way the angels could tip the scales in their favor. They would be too few, and with him and his priests assaulting their every move with spells, they would accomplish little.

Feeling the excitement building in his chest, he smiled and laughed. Let it all out, he thought. The battle approached.

Ker would fall to the Lion, and he would be the one to reap the honor and spoils.

❖

They'd been given the basics of King Henley's plan, but Ahaesarus had an inkling that the king kept something hidden from him. He hovered just above the bridge as the rest of the angels flew in their circular formations. Mordan's army prepared so close, and he watched the great mass of soldiers sharpen their swords, polish their shields, and ready their bows.

"So many," Judarius said, hovering beside him.

Ahaesarus nodded in agreement. He didn't feel fear, not for death. He'd seen the other side, had felt the light of the Golden Eternity on his skin. But for the humans? For those slowly dying in Karak's fist? He feared for them. He knew the price they'd pay for a loss at the crossing. Thulos had conquered a thousand stars. If he escaped from this one, he'd continue on with his destruction. It needed to end. If Ashhur was kind, he would be the one to end it.

"They wish us to ensure they hold the bridge," Judarius said. "What a waste. Without open spaces, our skills are limited. Why not crash into the rear of our enemy's formations? Or the priests, why not kill them?"

"They've proven resourceful and clever when it comes to warfare, Judarius, more so than us. We are not perfect."

"Neither are they."

Ahaesarus stretched his wings, falling a short distance as he did. A single powerful thrust and he shot back up to Judarius.

"If we cannot trust them, how can we expect them to govern themselves, protect one another, and live the life Ashhur desires them to live?" he asked.

Judarius shrugged. "Forget it, then. We will follow their orders, though I wonder how we became their servants instead of the other way around."

He flew over to join in the formations of flying, and Ahaesarus let him go without saying a word. He understood his frustrations, even if he did not approve. Judarius was the strongest and most skilled angel when it came to warfare. To have him obey the orders of men he could defeat without effort, and who had not once set foot in Ashhur's presence, surely burned. It was no secret he had been terribly upset by his repeated defeats by the half-orc warrior, either.

"Not perfect," Ahaesarus said as he drew his sword. "Such a terrible lesson to learn."

He thought the priest-king's army might send someone forth to negotiate, but as the front lines tightened, and the soldiers funneled toward the crossing, it seemed they were too eager for war.

"Banner carriers!" he shouted. Three angels flew beside him, each holding a colored banner to issue instructions to the rest of the angels.

With them ready, he waited and watched the fight begin from his vantage point in the sky. Footmen charged the foremost barrier near the edge of the bridge, using their shields to protect them from the swords that lashed out above the barricade. Bram's defenders fought well, and they held their ground in the bloody chaos that erupted. The few who fell were immediately replaced, their bodies shoved into the water.

Ahaesarus frowned as he watched a twin blast of fireballs leap from their side of the river toward Karak's forces. The work of Aurelia and the yellow wizard, Tarlak, he was certain. But instead of erupting in a great devastation of fire, the spells sizzled and puffed, their power gone. The angel looked further back, to the line of priests behind the approaching soldiers. They held their arms high and wailed prayers at the top of their lungs. No doubt they'd cast protections of some sort. If the priests countered their magical assault, one of their few advantages was gone.

"Ready Judarius's squad," he told his banner carriers. Two of the three raised their banners high and waved them side to side. One of the larger groups pulled free from the formations and like a river of gold and flesh dived for Ahaesarus.

"The priests!" Ahaesarus shouted as they neared. He pointed to the line, protected by dark paladins. "Take them out, or distract them until our casters go unchecked."

Judarius saluted, an enormous grin on his face. Into the most dangerous part of battle he was being sent, and against the original plans of the humans. No doubt for him, this had been the best outcome possible.

"For Ashhur!" Judarius shouted, lifting his two-handed mace high and then leading his hundred into the fray. They looped once and then dropped, swooping with near reckless speed. Ahaesarus crossed his arms and waited, a strange worry stirring in his gut. The priests were in the open, unguarded. He saw dark paladins nearby, yet they did not protect their most valuable leaders. Something was wrong, but what? Why did they not cast a spell as Judarius approached?

And then the angels hit. They shredded the robes and tore through the priests…who were not priests at all, but illusions of dust that scattered at the mere touch of their weapons. The angels started to bank into the air, but they were still low to the ground, and now in the open. From within the ranks of the footmen, men in plain clothes stepped out, their hands outstretched. The worry in Ahaesarus's gut turned to full blown horror.

A barrage of shadow flew toward them, compacted into bolts that seeped into their skin and sent their muscles into wild spasms. As they tried to bank around, the ground cracked, and fire erupted from the deep chasms of the world. The first few barreled straight through, and the screaming bodies that emerged on the other side were terrible to behold. The rest streaked higher and higher. One by one angels fell, their wings withering to dust. By the time they reached safety beyond the river, the soldiers of Karak were cheering. Of the initial five-hundred, only four-hundred returned.

"Where is Judarius?" Ahaesarus asked as they rejoined the ranks.

"I am here," said Judarius, curling in his wings and dropping down so they could speak face to face. Ahaesarus put his hand on the warrior's shoulder, then let him go.

"Such cowardice!" Judarius snarled.

"They are clever, devious, and vicious," Ahaesarus said. "Catch your breath, and combine with Ataroth's angels. Go swiftly. We are still needed!"

The proud warrior accepted the orders, then flew away. Ahaesarus turned his attention back to the battle. During the brief skirmish between the angels and priests, it seemed Aurelia and Tarlak had managed to score a few good hits. Fire burned along the far riverside, and amid their forces he saw a gap, and in its center was a great boulder of ice. Their latest attacks fizzled and dissipated, however, the priests' protections once more established.

Meanwhile the fighting intensified against the first barrier. The footmen had to climb atop their own dead, but the height was enough so they could stab over the wall, and several leapt across, knocking down men and pushing aside a small space that others could follow. The defenders always surrounded and slaughtered them, but each time it took them longer, and each time more made it over. If they were to hold instead of retreating to the second wall, they would need reinforcements soon.

"I want Ataroth's assault to be against the..." he started to tell his banner carriers, then stopped. A collective roar swept across the river, and then en masse the entire army surged forward, splitting into two groups, one on either side of the bridge. When they reached the river they never even slowed.

"Milord, your orders?" asked the banner angel to his left.

"Wait," he said. "We watch and wait. If either side, or the crossing itself, falls then all is lost. Find where we are the weakest, then descend. Make sure they are ready!"

Feeling every muscle in his body tighten, he watched the soldiers wade across the river. To make matters worse, the footmen attacking the bridge pulled back, and onward came twenty paladins of Karak, their blades burning with dark fire as they held them high.

"With me!" he cried, seeing the turn of events. "Ataroth, watch for a break in the lines. Terah, Solom, with me!"

He curled his wings in and dived, trusting them to follow. The priests were ready for the attack, for a barrage of over thirty bolts of shadow crackled through the air toward them. Ahaesarus spun, narrowly avoiding them. From the screams of pain behind him, he knew many were not so lucky. The paladins also saw their approach, and they braced themselves for the crash. Ahaesarus let his sword lead the way, and then with a horrific screech of metal, they collided.

The black fire burned his flesh, and he felt pain spike up and down his wings. He swung his sword in circles, hacking and cutting. More and more angels slammed in beside him, some even rolling through the lines with their wings curled against their bodies. Such valiant sacrifices…Ahaesarus blocked a chop of an ax, stepped closer, and then rammed an elbow into the face of the paladin. Down came his sword, finishing him off. An arrow of fire struck the blade as he pulled it back, and he looked up to see the priests approaching. Fire and shadow flew in waves, and the angels had no protection against it.

"Retreat!" he cried, taking to wing. He felt a blast of fire roll across his arm, only for an instant before he was soaring through the air, but long enough. He gritted his teeth to hold in a scream as he flew to the river. A glance back showed Terah's group had endured the worst of the assault, losing ten men under the attack. The dark paladins were destroyed, however, which meant the bridge still had a chance.

He flapped higher, then risked a glance at his arm. Patches of his skin were black, and pieces of his armor had melted against his flesh. Come nightfall, the pain would be immense trying to remove it. Assuming they were still alive by nightfall. Fearing the worst, he looked to the river, but was stunned by what he saw. Hundreds of bodies floated in the water. The enemy soldiers attempting to cross clearly struggled against something, and as he watched he saw many drown, pushed underwater by the men behind them. Those defending the river, while lightly armored, proved more than a match. They wielded long spears and thrust them into the water, stabbing Karak's soldiers long before they might reach the edge.

Ataroth was yet to join a side, so Ahaesarus flew to him in his position high above the bridge.

"Might they hold?" he asked.

"The humans put traps in the water," said Ataroth. He pointed to the bank. "They're too slow wading in their armor. The spearman are finding them easy prey. Already the rest retreat. Such poor tactics were a gamble, and we have made them pay dearly."

"How many?"

"At least two thousand," said the angel. "Perhaps more. We choke the river with the dead."

Ahaesarus looked to the camp stretching for hundreds of yards on the other side of the river.

"Not enough," he said. "They'll push back to the bridge and forsake the water. With all their might pressing forward, we will find...Archers! Get back!"

They retreated as arrows sailed into the air, traveling much farther than he ever could have expected. Several angels fell, while others dripped blood atop the bridge's combatants as they flew to safety. Over a thousand archers readied for another barrage, safely surrounded by footmen and guarded by the priests of Karak as they chanted and worshipped their dark god.

"Shields up!" came the cry from the men on the bridge. Arrows rained down upon them, and the noise was terrible to hear. Shouts of pain and anger followed. The army pushed into the bridge, emboldened by the archers' success. Another rain came down, and the beams of magic that shot toward the archers hit a spherical shield and splashed against it, unable to penetrate. More thuds, more wood and steel hitting shields, and more cries of death and blood.

"They can't hold against that," said Judarius, joining Ahaesarus to watch. "We have to take out those archers!"

"The priests guard them," he said. "And they have footmen around them in a wall. The moment we charge, those arrows will turn on us, not them."

"But why else are we here?" asked Judarius. "We do what they cannot. We bleed so they might live. Hundreds of us will die. So be it. What chance do they have if the archers go unchecked?"

He watched as another volley fell upon the men on the bridge. What choice did they have?

"Get ready to give the order," he said.

Banners lifted and spun. As the angels gathered, another volley descended upon the shields of the men. Footmen climbed over their own dead to cross the first barrier. Trumpets called below, and then the defenders abandoned the first wall. The attackers did not chase immediately, instead waiting for one more volley to land. Ahaesarus winced, but the expected slaughter did not happen. Instead the arrows bounced back as if hitting a clear wall of glass.

"Delay the order," Ahaesarus said.

"Why?" asked Judarius. In answer, he pointed to where Aurelia and Tarlak stood side by side, their hands glowing a soft white.

"They've begun to protect against the arrows instead of wasting their energies attacking."

"Then what of the priests? Might they begin their own attack?"

Ahaesarus crossed his arms, and his body rose and fell as he thought.

"They'll test the defenses and watch us, and we'll do the same. They suffered greatly because of their haste crossing the river. Let us see if they try such a gamble again."

With his excellent eyes, he watched the fight on the bridge. It seemed Karak's soldiers were struggling worse against the second wall than the first. Then he saw the half-orc in the thick of things, and he understood why. Harruq raged like a beast, his swords red blurs as they tore through armor and flesh. He'd seen him spar his angels, but never in full fury. He glanced at his own two-handed sword and wondered how he'd fare in straight combat against that berserk. Not well, he thought.

Harruq bolstered those around him, and they did their best to keep up with his relentless assault. From behind the front lines came Lord Peleth's men with their spears, no longer defending the riverside after the disastrous attack upon it. They stabbed over and between their allies, braced tight so the attacking surge of troops continuously impaled themselves on the spearheads. Only Harruq went without aid, for he needed the space to hack and swing.

"The wall is impeding him," Ahaesarus wondered aloud. "What could he do in open battle?"

Judarius smirked and said nothing.

Bolts of shadow splashed across the Eschaton's shield, making it shimmer momentarily into view. Men rotated in and out from the front line, Bram doing everything he could to keep them rested. Karak's men surged forward without hesitation, never once slowing. Ahaesarus shook his head. The crossing was certainly earning its name this day.

"The priests," Judarius said, pointing to where they gathered. "They prepare a spell, but what?"

"Whatever it is, the cost is tremendous," said Ahaesarus. Twenty bodies lay slain before them, soldiers sacrificed so their blood might be used in the casting of the spell. "They can't break their concentration. Our time to attack is now."

"I will take the archers," Judarius insisted. "You lead against the priests."

"Very well. Go quickly, and may Ashhur protect us both!"

Beside him, his banner carriers relayed the orders. In moments they had split into two groups, branching like rivers toward their respective targets. The archers saw, and Ahaesarus twirled through the barrage that met their charge. Arrows pinged off his armor, and two sliced his flesh, but none pierced deeply. Saying a prayer for those behind him without such luck, he led the dive toward the priests. With his sword leading, he aimed for the closest and swung.

The angels crashed through the priests, and this time they were no illusion, no phantom magic. Blood soaked the ground as they pulled up toward the sky, arrows chasing them. When he reached safety from the arrows, he glanced back to see the results.

Half the priests lay dead, but the other half had finished their chant. Lions made of fire and shadow leapt from the sacrificial dead, pawing the ground and snarling eagerly. Ahaesarus thought they would leap for the bridge, but then long, bony wings stretched out of their backs, their feathers billowing strands of darkness like smoke. Nearby Judarius continued his assault on the archers, encircling them and hacking down their footmen guards.

"Retreat!" he screamed. The lions leapt to the air, trails of smoke billowing behind them as they flew for Judarius's angels. Ahaesarus took his men to the air above the bridge and set up a perimeter.

"Wait until they arrive," he shouted. "When they do, the lions shall not pass. They shall not!"

His angels saluted with their weapons. Hovering, waiting, they watched as Judarius turned, his hundred angels attempting to follow. The lions slammed into them, raking their chests with claws and biting at their vulnerable wings. With the combined weight they could not fly, and the lions roared as they slammed the angels to the ground. The few that survived the fall died instantly after, swarmed by footmen.

The lions leapt again, chasing after Judarius and the rest.

"Wait!" Ahaesarus screamed. "Wait for them!"

The angels flew past the line. Ahaesarus readied his sword. The lions neared. They were enormous, twice the size of a man. Fire shone from their eyes, and when they opened their mouths to roar, they saw lava burning deep within their throats. Closer. And closer.

"Now!"

They met the lions head on, swords and maces swinging. Molten blood splashed across them. Fangs tore into flesh. Ahaesarus's blade pierced the belly of one, and as it fell it roared up at him, breathing fire. He twisted his blade, protecting himself against most of it. That which got through splashed across his neck, and he screamed at the pain. Channeling it into strength, he turned and slashed another in half, kicking the lion's head away so that its final death roar burned only air. Holding his sword in one hand, he clutched his charred neck with the other and struggled to breathe.

"Azariah?" he cried out. He felt his head start to swim, and was unsure of where he flew. "Azariah, where are you?"

"Come with me," said an angel, grabbing him by the arm. Together they flew, back to the riverside. Ahaesarus felt his knees tremble, and upon landing he lacked the strength to stand.

"Cursed blood," he heard another say. A hand pressed against his neck, and the pain stabbed deep into him, far greater than any mortal wound. White light flooded his eyes, and he let that sight soothe him. The sickness left him, the strength in his legs returned, and, feeling made anew, he stretched his wings and took in his surroundings.

They were behind the human forces. Azariah's priests walked about the clearing, tending to the wounded that came to them from the front. Azariah himself attended him, and he looked to his leader with guarded worry.

"I am fine," Ahaesarus said, seeing that expression and wishing nothing more than to banish it. "Do not worry for me."

"The lions' fire is a foul creation of Karak," said Azariah. "You are lucky Ataroth brought you to me in time."

Ahaesarus realized who it was that had brought him back, and he saluted the angel.

"You'd have done the same for me," Ataroth said.

"Who commands your angels?"

"I left Zekiel in charge. It should have been Judarius, but…"

He pointed to where the angel lay. Ahaesarus felt his heart shake. Judarius had been bathed head to chest by the fire, his armor melted to his flesh, half his hair gone. His eyes were closed, and even the lids were scarred black.

"He lives?" Ahaesarus asked.

"For now," said Azariah, glancing at him. "I will attend to him when I can, but there are too many, and more come even now."

Soldiers carrying friends and comrades approached, the wounded bleeding and sobbing in their arms. Ahaesarus's heart went out to them, even though he knew he should numb himself to their pain. There was too much about him, too much blood, too many wounds, and far too many dead.

"How many archers?" he asked Ataroth.

"We killed a third before the lions came, not counting the footmen that fell before us to protect them. Come, let us survey the battle, if you are strong enough to take wing."

Ahaesarus wasn't sure, but he knew he could not show weakness, not now. He grabbed Ataroth's wrist to be sure, and then together they flew above the crossing. Indeed, half the archers had fallen, and those that remained had gathered farther back. They'd ceased their volleying, no doubt because of the Eschaton's shield. The priests looked to be discussing something, though what he could only imagine. As for the soldiers, they had pulled back. For now, the battle had ceased.

"Both sides have suffered tremendous casualties," Ataroth said. "They suffered greater, but I fear they have far more than we to lose."

"The river runs red with both our blood," Ahaesarus said. "This is no victory."

"Nightfall comes. Perhaps we can assault under cover?"

Though the idea might be worth considering, Ahaesarus winced at the thought. He'd lost so many angels already. Could he risk losing more?

Of course he could. They were all dead men, clinging to a desperate hope for a miracle.

"Tonight we rest," he decided. "We need to be ready, though. They might try an assault of some sort at night. And what of the elf and the wizard? Can they protect us all through the night and day?"

Ataroth's look said enough. Of course not. And Karak had enough men to harry them every hour. They would get no rest. Sheer exhaustion would defeat them.

"What else is there to do?" he asked. "We kill until we die. That is our fate."

Feeling defeat tugging at his heart, he watched as the elf slipped through the lines until she stood before the first wall, which the attackers had surrendered during their retreat to safety.

"What is Aurelia doing?" he asked. "What if the priests…"

He stopped as the very ground seemed to groan.

"What is going on?" asked Ataroth.

"I don't know," said Ahaesarus. They could only watch and see.

Lightning crashed, so bright that spots swam before his eyes. The earth cracked before Aurelia, and the sound was as if the spine of the world had broken. Karak's soldiers readied their weapons as the priests prepared spells, no doubt protections against the sudden onslaught. Fire leapt from the river, crawling as if it were alive. It took shapes, those of strange beasts with four arms and no faces. The creatures crawled upon the ground, burning everything beneath them. A wind tore in from the south, gusting so strong that Ahaesarus feared he might fall.

"This isn't possible!" Ataroth shouted. "She can't be that powerful!"

The elf raised her arms. The ground heaved, cracking and splitting in a thousand places. Onward the fire creatures crawled. All around the lightning struck, each bolt the size of several trees lashed together. The thunder boomed, strong enough to make his heart quake. It seemed the very end of the world had come, focused before the army of Karak. The sky opened, and from it great blasts of white magic struck the ground, tearing open chasms that stretched to the very depths of the Abyss.

Against such an onslaught, the various generals did what any sane man would do: they gave the order to retreat.

The fire rose higher from the river, a great wall that seemed to stretch to the sky. It rolled forward, sweeping up the flame creatures and carrying them on. Horses panicked and fled. The priests cast protection spells, but their magic failed to even alter the path of the destruction. Great boulders of ice slammed into the gap between the armies, forming craters that stretched for hundreds of yards as the ground roiled beneath. Further and further the army fled as the spells gave chase. The last to leave were the priests, who hurled bolts of shadow behind them as they fled, which did nothing.

"What manner of devilry is this?" Ahaesarus asked. "No mortal is that strong. Come with me, Ataroth. I must find out."

The angels dived, then eased up carefully onto the bridge. The soldiers cheered, but it was subdued, as if they too were in awe of the broken wasteland before them. Aurelia stood before them, her arms raised. Tears ran down her face from her closed eyes. Ahaesarus opened his mouth to speak, then closed it. He felt as if he were witnessing something terribly private and feared to interrupt.

"Awesome, wasn't it?" Tarlak asked, pushing through the soldiers and joining them on the bridge. Harruq ran with them, and he hurried to his wife. When he wrapped his arms around her, she looked to him and smiled. Her hands lowered. Throughout the crossing, a gentle breeze blew.

"I must hear an explanation," Ahaesarus insisted.

"The memories," Aurelia said, but her tears overwhelmed her again. She clung to her husband.

"It was my fault, really," Tarlak said, jumping in to help her. "When we couldn't penetrate the priests' defenses, I remarked how I wished we could have had her parents and their kin to help us. And that's just what she did."

"Memories," Aurelia said again, composing herself. "Just the memories of the past."

A breeze blew again, stronger, and as if blowing away sand from a glass, the illusion before them broke. The shattered ground became smooth. The ice and fire faded like stars before the sun. Broken trees became erect, and the chasms unearthed closed and were made whole.

"It wasn't real," Ahaesarus said, stunned.

"I wasn't here," Aurelia said, wiping tears from her face. "But the memories lingered. I finally saw, felt the power they commanded. I let everyone see what had transpired. I let everyone see what we once were capable of, before mankind slaughtered our strongest and best. I'm what's left, and I am nothing compared to them. Illusions and smoke, that is all."

"But they fled!" Harruq said, and he squeezed her in his arms. "Surely you can take pride in that."

"She should," said Ataroth. "We will prepare just in case they return. Let's clear the dead, rebuild the walls, and perhaps add a trench or two on the opposite side of the bridge."

"If they return, they won't fall for such a ruse again," said Ahaesarus.

"Then we'll give them a taste of Aurelia's real power," Harruq said, and he smiled through their worry and sorrow for the dead. "None can stand against us, right?"

"Sure thing," Tarlak said. His look to Ahaesarus said otherwise.

23

"Quiet," said Jerico as he led the two of them toward the forest's edge. "Wait here until I say."

Lathaar frowned but accepted the order. They'd marched toward the Sanctuary at a steady rate, and at last they'd come to the shallow forest that grew beside the Elethan Mountains. They'd come for their friends, but they had the slight problem of the siege. For the first few miles in the woods they heard and saw no sign of life, but as they approached the end, they'd seen tracks and heard occasional shouts in the distance.

Jerico vanished behind a line of trees. Lathaar sighed and drew his swords. He felt eager to kill, which seemed wrong when he realized it. Of all the times he'd felt abandoned by Ashhur, he'd never enjoyed hunting and killing the servants of Karak. Yet now, with Mira dead, he wanted nothing more than vengeance. Vengeance…was that Ashhur's will?

"Be with me," he prayed. "I'm lost. I'm confused. And I really, really want to kill someone."

"Amen," Jerico whispered, startling him.

"Bastard," he grumbled.

"Such language for a paladin. Come on. We've got our work cut out for us."

They reached the last of the trees without difficulty. Beyond them camped a small army of soldiers, their tents spreading out in a half-circle surrounding the Sanctuary. Only its front half was made of wood, the rest built deep into the mountain rock. Torches burned in its four towers, and Lathaar felt relief at the sight. Survivors still hid within, not yet defeated by the siege.

"How many you think?" Lathaar asked, careful to keep his voice at a whisper.

"At least two hundred footmen," Jerico whispered back. "Another hundred archers."

"You realize there's only two of us, right?"

Jerico winked. "You're right. We should give them fair warning before we attack."

He dropped his pack of supplies, readied his shield, and then drew his mace. Lathaar looked at him like he was mad.

"We're not that good," he said. "They'll kill us with arrows alone."

"I'm not an idiot, despite evidence to the contrary," said Jerico. He pointed toward the Sanctuary's door, which was burnt and cracked, yet still holding together. The soldiers that milled about maintained no strict lines or attention. Lathaar doubted they'd seen any combat since the first day or two, when they'd obviously tried, and failed, to breach the door.

"You want us to make a run for it?" Lathaar asked.

"I've got my shield," Jerico said, giving it a pat. "We push through, then bar the door behind us. Once we're inside…"

"Once we're inside, we'll starve with the rest of them. Are you out of your mind? We'll be no use in there."

"Well, we're not doing much good standing *here*."

The two looked upon the few hundred and struggled for a plan.

"I wish the mage was here," Lathaar said at last. "What I'd give for a few of his fireballs on their tents."

"That's it!" Jerico said.

Lathaar smacked him to keep his voice down. A quick glance around showed none had heard him, but they backed into the forest just in case. He listened as Jerico outlined his plan, which while truly insane, at least made more sense than joining the starving priests inside the Sanctuary.

"They'll have only a token guard," he said when Jerico finished. "It could work if we move fast, and strike a few hours before dawn, when they'll be their most tired and inattentive."

"We have little time," said Jerico. "Hurry. I want them to have one vicious wake up come the morning."

They took turns sleeping to make sure they didn't miss their chosen time. Lathaar was already awake when he felt Jerico nudge his shoulder with his foot.

"It time?" he mumbled.

"Close enough. Get ready."

Lathaar reattached his armor, with Jerico helping him with the buckles. Once ready, they said one last prayer and then split. Jerico made for the forest line, while Lathaar wrapped a thick branch with cloth soaked in what little lamp oil they had. He set it ablaze and then counted to two hundred. Beside them was one of many piles of kindling pushed up against the trunks of trees, also wet with oil. At two hundred, he set it ablaze and then ran.

Prior to nightfall, they'd made over twenty such piles, and he dashed from one to the other, lighting them and then continuing. Some burned too weak to set their tree aflame, but he only needed a few to start the fire he wanted. The trees were lush and full, plenty of fuel for their needs. When he reached the last of the piles, he looked up to the sky. Smoke blotted out the stars. Good. At least several had grown strong, and the kindling piles lined all around the camp, forming a nice U-shaped goal for the fire. Now he just needed to wait for the fire to grow and then…

Shouts came from the camp, first a few, then many. From far to the side, he peeked out to see. The men were rushing to the edge, carrying whatever tools they could find. The fire wasn't evenly spread yet, but growing. Without any source of water, the men did the only thing they could: they began digging a trench so they fire would not spread beyond the forest.

"Go get them, Jerico," Lathaar whispered, thrilled at how smooth their plan was working. The light of the fire made it difficult for him to see the Sanctuary. Only the torches in the towers shone clearly, the rest a dark haze. If all was well, Jerico had sneaked inside without notice, and at worst, killed a few before dashing in. Well, not the very worst. Very worst, he lay dead on the ground, an arrow in his side. Lathaar had a feeling it'd take a lot more to bring down Jerico than a few inattentive guards.

The smoke billowed higher, and all attention was now on the fire. Time for him to act. He curled around to the side of the camp. No guards. He took a few deep breaths and then burst into a full sprint, heading for the far side of the trench where the people were at their fewest. At the last moment he drew his swords, and one man glanced to the side and shouted just before he crashed through the line. He spun and cut without any finesse and thought, spilling blood across his armor and knocking bodies into the shallow trench. Unarmed and unprepared, they had little chance. The rest scattered, crying out for aid.

"Fear the wrath of the elves!" Lathaar screamed before turning and racing back into the forest, figuring any sort of misdirection could only help. He kept his head low and curled around the outer line of the fire, which was still growing at a pace that worried him. He thanked Ashhur it wasn't fall, and the leaves dry and brittle. His armor was hot enough as it was. Last thing he wanted was to be baked inside it.

He followed the fire, keeping it to his right until he emerged on the other side of the ditch. Some of the soldiers were armed, and many on the lookout. Not enough, though, not to deter him. Gasping in the clean air, he waited until he felt ready and then charged. This time they saw him just before his arrival, but the bulk only tried to flee, not fight. He cut down the nearest, who wielded an axe, two more who swung their shovels at him, and then gutted a fourth before he could escape. The smoke drifted over them, so that only his glowing blades shone in the confusion.

"Eyes on the forest," Lathaar muttered as he turned back to flee.

The fire still burned strong, but the wind seemed to be keeping it from pushing deeper into the center. He went to the middle of the line, but once there he felt his bravado fade. The fire licked off every thin trunk. The ground shimmered red, and it seemed more liquid than solid. The heat gathered in a great wall, one he could feel growing stronger with every step. Could he do it? Could he really?

But Jerico was relying on him. Lathaar needed to be the reaper from the flame, to keep all eyes on the forest, all backs to the Sanctuary. When the priests made their escape, any who happened to notice would fall to their spells and Jerico's mace.

Only a concentrated effort by the army could stop them, and if they were scattered, exhausted, and unaware a battle had started...

He ran, his eyes barely able to stay open from the heat. He felt his armor grow warm, then excruciatingly hot. Sweat soaked him beneath his inner layers of padding. His lungs burned from the smoke. Step after step, he forced himself through step after step. When he burst into the fresh air, he laughed, stunned to be alive. The men digging the trench were in no way prepared for his maniacal approach. He cut them down, a swirling death of glowing swords. This time men closer to the inner parts of the camp noticed him and came running, their weapons at the ready. Lathaar barely saw them in his oxygen-starved delirium. He swung in wide arcs, clumsy maneuvers that better opponents might have easily defeated. But they were tired, confused, and poorly armored.

Even with such advantages, and far more years in training, he felt himself slipping. Blades rang off his armor, and one cut through the padding at his elbow, slicing all the way to bone. His breath came with difficulty, and either blood or sweat, he didn't know which, ran from his forehead to sting his eyes. More soldiers swarmed about him, trapping him against the burning forest. He laughed, knowing he had to look like some horrific demon from the Abyss. He sheathed his short sword, held his long sword in both hands, and screamed out the word to unleash the full power of his faith.

"Elholad!"

The blade remained the same. He felt doubt tug on his heart, and his dire grin spread wide. It had to be Mira, he thought.

Damn her, she's got me doubting.

He kept swinging wide, taking step after step back toward the forest. Might he burn within? He felt its heat blowing against him from the wind. It was growing, the fire still spreading. He couldn't fight them off, couldn't defeat them. His faith was weak, Ashhur's greatest gift denied to him. They must have seen the weakness in his eyes, for they pressed closer, wielding swords and shields that blocked every counterattack.

In the distance, he saw flashes of white. Someone shouted his name. The priests were coming, or were they fleeing? Would they rescue him, or leave him to die? He didn't know. He felt weak and lightheaded. Swords cut in, and he parried best he could. Any thoughts to counter vanished. Another step back as a blade missed gutting him by an inch. Another step as he braced to block a powerful overhead chop. More light, closer, brighter. Men turned, a few raised their weapons, but then Keziel burst through. He spoke a word, though strangely Lathaar heard not a single syllable, only felt its power roll across them. The enemy soldiers fell back as if struck by a battering ram.

"Come, my son," said Keziel, grabbing Lathaar and wrapping an arm around his waist. "Into the fire."

Lathaar didn't understand, but he was too exhausted to question him. Together they rushed into the forest, the flames licking behind them. Light glowed from his skin, and he saw it lift off in waves. They were not consumed. He couldn't even feel its heat. Step after step they walked, Lathaar leaning much of his weight on the older man. At last they came out the other side. The light faded.

"Next time think of a better plan," Keziel said as they both sucked in air. "I don't want to ever do that again."

"Where's Jerico?" Lathaar asked.

"With the others. They ran about the southern edge of the fire. We must keep moving. It won't be long before the rest of the army comes in pursuit."

"How will we find them?" Lathaar asked as they walked deeper into the forest, where the flames were but a frightening red haze in the distance.

"Once we're outside, it shouldn't be hard to locate them. Of course, the same goes for Karak's men. Step it up. A young man like you shouldn't be outpaced by an elder like me."

Jerico was waiting for them not far away when they emerged. Sixteen priests were with him, and they held their hands upward, shining as if they were torches. Keziel responded in kind, and then they hurried over.

"I take it all went well?" Lathaar asked when they neared.

"I made it inside without notice," Jerico said, smacking him on the shoulder. "Getting out was a bit trickier. Saw you fighting out there. Would have terrified even me. A few soldiers caught us sneaking about, but they were too scattered to stop us. Of course, Keziel had to run off like the madman he is to save your hide."

"It's much appreciated," Lathaar said, and he chuckled despite the heat and terror that moment had inspired. "Where to now?"

"We've heard only rumors of the outside world since Melorak's ascension to the throne," Keziel said. "You should know our destination better than I."

"Are there really angels?" asked one priest, a younger man with just a shade of stubble on his chin.

"Aye, there are," Jerico said, grinning. "I guess that's where we'll head…assuming they're still alive."

The man smiled, but then he caught the troublesome meaning at the end.

"What do you mean, still alive?" he asked.

"What of Neldar?" asked Keziel. "Do we not have aid from there and Omn?"

"For now, we head to the crossing," Jerico said. "We'll explain on the way."

⊰✺⊱

They traveled for several hours that night. Keziel detailed the events of the siege the best he could, with the other priests chiming in should he forget something. They'd heard of Antonil's marriage, though after the event, otherwise they would have attended. When the priest-king slaughtered Annabelle and took over the city, again they'd heard only rumors from the occasional traveler seeking guidance or merchants bringing in their weekly wares.

With Karak in control, they figured it was only a matter of time before an army came for them. They'd stored up food and supplies, then barred the door and waited. Over five hundred had come at first, and they'd showered the towers with arrows and prepared their battering rams. The first and only assault had been brutal, but the priests had defended through the broken cracks in the door and from the various windows and towers. They'd killed over a hundred, though lost many priests in turn. After that, whoever had been in charge changed tactic, preferring to starve them out. They'd been dangerously low on food when Jerico made his rather surprising entrance.

"We nearly took off his head," said another priest who held an ornate sword in one hand.

"You would have tried," Jerico said, shooting him a wink.

After that, Jerico told their tale, of their horrible defeat at Veldaren, the war god's arrival, and the planned defenses at the crossing and the Gods' Bridges. Through it all, Keziel shook his head and frowned.

"Surely these are the end times," he said when the paladin finished.

"Sure does seem like it," Lathaar said.

"Nonsense," Jerico said. "It's only the end if we lose. I don't plan on it. We'll hold the bridges and the crossing. Just you wait. You'll meet the angels, all of you, and then we'll head to Mordeina. Karak won't know what hit him!"

Lathaar glanced back at the forest. He couldn't tell, but he swore he saw men in pursuit, just shades and illusions in the pale moonlight.

"If you say so," he said, hurrying them on.

24

D uring the day they marched, and it was then that Tessanna had Qurrah to herself. It was at night, when she slept, that he became Velixar's.

"You will stop feeling the need for sleep," Velixar told him.

Thulos's army camped in the heart of Ker, just outside a small village with a name Qurrah didn't know and doubted any would ever remember. They had resisted the war god's call for allegiance, so now they marched among the dead, yet more soldiers for Karak's mad prophet. The half-orc glared, seeing no need to hide his hatred.

"I need no advice from you," he said. "Just put me in the ground and give me death."

"Your heart is not ready for death," Velixar said.

Qurrah felt like striking him, but even the thought came with difficulty. He felt spells latched about his body like chains, denying him any vicious action against his new master. He could speak how he wished, but only speak. Everything else was a struggle, unless so commanded.

"My heart doesn't beat anymore," he said. "It is more than ready."

Velixar smirked. "Your soul, then. It is good to know the transition back to life has not dampened your sense of humor."

Qurrah looked to the distance, where the last remnants of the village burned like a great torch in the starlight.

"More lives you've ended," he said. "When will you have enough?"

"All lives end," Velixar said. "Don't be sentimental. I have given their shells reason and purpose. I could do the same to you, but you deserve better. You served once, faithfully, and with love. Surely you remember that as clear as I."

"I remember it like a nightmare upon waking."

"Don't bore me. Those were grand times. Had you ever felt so powerful? So in control? The anarchy of this world is a burden we must endure until the great cleansing comes. In death, we find order, so death we bring to the rest of Dezrel. They no longer suffer. They no longer toil endlessly to provide a meager respite from the pain in their bellies. They no longer pray to false gods that provide no comfort, no strength. Ashhur and Celestia die in the coming months, Qurrah. It is time you learn of the only god that matters."

"I know enough of Karak. Too much, even."

"Is that so?" Velixar asked. "Do you remember that quaint little village, Cornrows? Stay still. I command you."

Qurrah turned rigid. He couldn't lift a single rotting finger if he wanted to. Velixar's cold fingertips pressed against his forehead, tingling with magic. A spell came from the prophet's lips, and then Qurrah gasped. The pale green grass of Ker changed to the golden fields of the Kingstrip. The stars shifted their positions. He moved not as the dead but as the living. Beside him walked his brother, his muscles bulging, his swords awkward and new in his hands.

"So we'll do what he says?" asked Harruq. "We'll kill the villagers, all of them, without reason?"

Qurrah tried to answer, but the past answered for him.

"You have done much for me without question, without pause. This is different. Velixar has given us the power and privilege to do what we were always meant to do. I need you to embrace this. Velixar's reason is the only reason we need, that we will ever need. It is in our blood, our orcish blood, and that is a weight even your muscles cannot hold back. We are killers, murderers, butchers, now granted purpose within that. That is our fate. That is our reason. Do you understand?"

The ghost of Velixar shimmered into view, hovering behind them as the memory froze.

"Do you hear the truth you once spoke?" he asked. "The truth you now deny?"

"We are more than killers," Qurrah said. "I swallowed a lie, and now this world suffers for it."

Velixar shook his head, and it seemed the red in his eyes dimmed.

"We are killers," he said, sad, almost wistful. "Murderers, butchers, *now granted purpose within that.* You have lost your purpose. You have your place. It is at my side, learning, growing, becoming my greatest apprentice, my worthy disciple, my only friend. Do not deny the strength you once wielded. Do not deny the certainty you once felt, now thrown away for vagaries and promises that you cling to with childish faith. Go relive your proudest moment."

The phantom of the prophet vanished. The memory resumed, and no matter how hard he tried, he couldn't stop speaking. He couldn't stop approaching. He couldn't stop himself from readying his whip and eyeing the town's defenders as targets for practice and nothing more.

"We've come for you!" Harruq screamed.

Blood spilled by his blades. Qurrah killed a young man with his whip, burning his neck to the spine. More fell to bones he flung from his pouch. Every second of it he fought against the memory, the sight and sounds were terrible. Worse, though, was how the feelings then returned to him: total elation.

Just the past, he told himself, wishing he could close his eyes and make it all go away. *All in the past. You made mistakes. He can't condemn you for them. They aren't who you are, not anymore.*

But it was hard to remember that as he made a man wither away as if the blood in his veins had turned to dust. Hard to remember as he froze his arm and mocked his attacker. Such superiority…such power…

He heard a cry from his brother. He remembered it well, a cry made after butchering two little girls in their home. He'd thought it one of battle, a victory howl from the primal depths of his brother's soul. But now, though, knowing the compassion his brother had hidden, the love he'd felt for the elf, he heard something else.

He heard torment. He heard horror and pain. His brother screamed against everything that he represented, suffering through to bury it down. That was what it had taken for

Harruq to become what Velixar had wanted…what *Qurrah* had wanted. At one point he'd felt pride, but now he wanted nothing more than to silence it. His vision shifted as everything became liquid, and then he saw darkness, then stars, and then the rest of the world as he emerged from within the memory.

"You never understood then, but I did," Velixar said, his deep voice almost a whisper. "Your brother's love for you was so great he buried his true self, despite the pain, despite his revulsion. You are no different now. I know what you are, and it is a brilliant man, skilled in necromancy and driven by logic. You know this world is corrupt. You know it brings pain, hunger, and despair. But you have let out your own brutal cry, and buried it for the sake of your brother."

He crossed his arms and stood at his side. Together they watched the last of the distant village burn.

"It is beautiful," he said, "watching fire cleanse away the last bits of hurt and chaos. Remember, Qurrah. Remember not just who you were, but who you really are. Don't deny it. Don't hide it. It took incredible strength to do what your brother did, and it has taken you great strength to do the same. I am no blind fool. I know the trials you have endured. I know the struggles of faith your stillborn brought to you. But let us persevere. Let us become the reapers. This world is aching for the harvest."

He turned to leave.

"Think on that," he said. "And think on your own words. Purpose. What is your purpose now? What has it ever been?"

He left, and with no other choice, Qurrah stood there and let his mind whirl around and around, feeding on itself like a snake consuming its own tail. He wanted nothing more than certainty, but all he felt was doubt. Could Velixar be correct? Could he really? For hours he waited, memories flooding him, good and bad. What was their reason? What was that purpose? He thought of the battles he'd fought with his brother, and the ones against. Who was right? Who was wrong?

When the sun rose, he felt miserable and broken. Its heat was a strange, muted sensation on his skin, yet he wished for nothing more than it to blaze hotter and hotter until his body was consumed and his mind finally put to rest. He wanted to cry, but his eyes could produce no tears. He wanted to weep, but his heart refused to break, for its beat was dead, his throat was dry rot, and his mind knew nothing but ache and desire for death.

"Qurrah?" he heard Tessanna ask. He glanced back. She stood slumped, her hair covering her face, her eyes looking to the grass as much as him. Behind her, Thulos's army prepared for another long day of marching or flying. Qurrah felt anger burn hot within him, wild and sudden. She was responsible. She'd killed Aullienna, turned him against his brother, led him down dark paths that he'd have never…

No. Lies. Cowardice. He wouldn't cast off his blame to her, not when she still so clearly loved him.

"Yes, Tess?" he asked once he regained control of his emotions.

She slipped her hand into his and stood beside him. Together they stared at the sun rising in the east.

"Was it bad?" she asked.

He nodded. "Velixar torments me without end. I don't know what is truth or lie anymore."

She smiled. He sensed a bit of the shy side of her, the one more like an innocent little girl instead of the deadly daughter of the goddess with blood on her hands. Still, it wasn't complete. She seemed more together, more whole.

"Then think outside yourself," she said. "Think of someone who you trust. What would they say? Does he lie? Or does he speak truth?"

Qurrah thought of Harruq, and what he'd say to Velixar's honey-coated words.

"He'd say Velixar's words are poison, and I'm an idiot for even listening," he said, and a bit of a smile tugged at the corners of his mouth.

"Good boy."

She pressed against him, but pulled away only moments later.

"Am I cold?" he asked. She didn't answer, but she squeezed his hand and looked at him so sadly he thought his heart might break, if it wasn't broken already.

"You used to be the only warmth I knew," she said. "Velixar took that from me. That is why you must never believe him. That is why you must forever hate him. He didn't just take your life, Qurrah. He took it from *me*. Should Celestia ever return her blessing, I will destroy him. I'll cast his ashes to the rivers so he's washed away forever from the land of Dezrel."

Qurrah winced.

"He'll make me stop you," he said. "I won't have a choice."

"You always have a choice."

He looked down at his wretched dead body.

"Not like this. Not anymore. And for that I hate him most of all."

A ntonil ate with a few of his trusted soldiers and generals, all of Neldaren blood. The soldiers of Mordan still honored him, but he found it difficult to relax with them around. The men of his home country had been with him as he struggled to accept his appointed role. They knew his faults, his weaknesses. But Mordan? They expected him to be a king, and many blamed the loss of their capital and the death of their queen squarely on him. Most kept their mouths shut about it, but every now and then, while he wandered throughout the campfires...

"At least we're back on Mordan soil," he said.

"What's so great about Mordan soil?" asked Sergan, his long-time friend.

"It means that most of my men will now feel they fight to reclaim their homeland instead of defending and retaking the homes of others. Besides, it means we're almost at the end. I'm not sure I could stand walking another mile."

"Plenty of miles ahead of you," said Bram, who bowed as they turned to address him. "Care to make room for me by the fire?"

Sergan reluctantly scooted over, letting the king join them in their little ring.

"I'd rather pretend we'll be at Mordeina tomorrow," Antonil said. "Must you play the realist among us?"

Bram laughed. "Someone must, I should say. We've won a victory, but let's not fool ourselves. The elf's magic was illusion, nothing more. They still vastly outnumber us. How are we to retake a walled city when the defenders outnumber the attackers?"

"The angels make light of any walls they meet," Sergan argued.

"And they even make light of most of our troops. But what of us? Do you think the few thousand angels we have can retake the entire city? Don't be foolish. If our opponents simply turn around and come after us tomorrow, when we no longer have the river to help us, we'll be dead."

Antonil shifted uncomfortably, and he wrapped a blanket tighter around his shoulders.

"We've done what you asked," he said. "We've defended Ker. Will you now turn back on your promise to help us retake Mordeina?"

"Don't get nervous," Bram said. "I have no such cowardice in me. But only a few miles away sleep the soldiers of Mordan. Think on this, Antonil...who is their king?"

"That priest-king, I suppose."

"No," Bram said, shaking his head as if correcting a young student. "That is their current ruler, but who is their *king*? Who have they sworn their swords to for generations? Who can trace their bloodline back to the early days of Victor the Grand?"

"It's you, you daft fool," Sergan said. He elbowed Antonil in the side. "You do realize that, right?"

"What are you playing at, Bram?" Antonil asked.

The man leaned in closer, as if he were to tell a secret.

"You and I are brothers, Antonil. We both wear the crown. We both know thousands live or die depending on our choices. But sometimes we must endanger our own lives. We must risk everything in a last throw of the dice, because sometimes, the greatest victories come only with the greatest risks."

"I'm still waiting for an explanation," Antonil said.

"Take wing with the angels. Come with me to their camp. The sellswords and commoners may not care who they fight for, but the lords themselves? Who knows how they have been treated, or where their loyalties lie?"

"You're asking him to walk right into the enemy's hands!" Sergan nearly roared.

"Keep your voice down, fool," Bram said, and with such authority that Sergan immediately obeyed. "And I will be right at his side. This no trap, and no pointless gesture. Think of what they have just seen. Do you remember the tempest that broke the rock and rained ice and fire across the grass? They must think the gods themselves have come to retake Mordan. We must use that. Let them see their king has returned. Let them bow their knee once more to the true bloodline."

"A thin bloodline," Antonil said, his tone carefully guarded. "By a short marriage to Queen Annabelle, and nothing more."

"Far better than the priest-king who threatens to overthrow the lords and nobles to establish a theocracy."

"Maybe," grumbled Sergan. "But who is to say they won't turn him over to the priests the second you two show up?"

"We're kings," Antonil said. He stared into the fire, deep in thought. "They must respect us. We'll represent life before the priest-king took control. How many will turn to us in hope? How many will turn to us in fear? Bram's right. While they sleep, we might steal half their army away. Thousands of soldiers…"

He stood and nodded to Bram.

"Have you told Ahaesarus about this plan?" he asked.

"Not quite," said Bram. "I told one I felt might be more…open to the idea. And don't worry about his safety, Sergan. You're coming with us."

Azariah led the way, while behind him, three of his most trusted carried the humans in their arms. The fires of the enemy camp were easy enough to see, red dots among the moonlit darkness. Azariah angled lower, and they dived to the far side of the encampment.

"Are you sure you can do this?" Antonil asked Sergan once they landed.

"Not at all," Sergan said. He grabbed his axe and shifted its belt so it hung more comfortably from his waist. "But I'd rather it be me going in there than you."

"Be calm, certain, and authoritative," Bram said. "Act as if you are asking a question where only one answer will please you, and the rest will cost them their heads. The slightest hint of fear will betray you. Remember the display the elf put on. The illusion of power is often greater than the real thing."

"Can't we just kill them all instead?" asked Sergan. He rolled his eyes at their glares and shifted his belt a second time.

"I look fine?" he asked.

"You look fine, and you'll do fine," Antonil said, smacking him on the shoulder. "Now go, and do me proud. And come back alive."

Sergan nodded, wiped his brow, and then trudged for the camp. He ran a hundred sentences through his head, trying to think of something that sounded appropriate. Both kings had tried giving him lines to say, but they fumbled on his tongue so they'd given up. He was on his own.

"Damn stupid kings," he muttered. "Claim they'll risk their own lives, then send me in to do the dirty work. All I have to do is start hollering as they chop off my head and they're gone, safe in angel arms while I find out how many ways they can twist my insides into knots before I pass out from…"

He stopped, for before him stood a guard looking as perplexed as Sergan felt. Before he could even shout warning, Sergan saluted, a single smooth motion perfected over many years serving the kings of Neldar.

"Well met, soldier!" Sergan said. He felt proud at how sharp his voice came off, not at all horrified. "I'm here to speak for King Antonil Copernus, husband of Queen Annabelle Copernus. I wish to speak with your lord."

The soldier stammered. Sergan recognized his sort. He looked freshly conscripted, his servitude in the military one step up above slavery. Perfect.

"My lord is asleep, but I take orders from…"

"Don't try telling me you don't take orders from your lord," Sergan said. "Who else would you take orders from? Now go wake him, and don't you worry about him being mad. This is a diplomatic matter, you see? I ain't waiting until morning to make my offer."

"Diplo…but, sir, please stay here so I can…"

"I will not sit here while you run off to find a wet-nurse to change your soiled underpants, boy! Who is your lord? What's his name?"

"Hemman. Lord Hemman of the north."

Sergan rested his hand on the handle of his axe and delayed speaking for a second to make sure the conscript noticed.

"Then, boy, I suggest you bring him to me at once. No delays, or else you can explain to them why the elf goddess decided to no longer parley."

"But I can't leave here unguar…"

"I said go!"

The young man saluted and then rushed into the tents. Sergan chuckled despite his heart pounding like an orc wailing on a drum. So far so good. Once he got the audience of a lord, any lord, then his chances of succeeding went up tenfold. He waited just beyond the light of the campfires, hoping no one else would spot him. He was not so fortuitous.

"Halt!" shouted a guard, and by the growl of his voice, Sergan knew he had found no wet-eared conscript.

"I'm armed but not dangerous," Sergan said, lifting his hands upward as two soldiers approached, both with their swords drawn. "I'm here on behalf of King Antonil, and I need to speak with your lord."

"You're a spy," said one. "On your knees, now."

Sergan fixed his most brutal glare on the man. "I would rather die with an axe in my hand than bow one knee to the likes of you."

They circled him, one to his back, one to his front. So far he kept his axe at his side, and in truth he wouldn't dare draw. He just needed to delay. Every second was precious.

"One last chance," said the guard before him. "On your knees, now, and hand over your axe."

"I've come to speak with your lord," Sergan said. "I've come with an offer of…"

The guard behind him struck the back of his neck. Vision swimming, he fell to his knees. A sword pressed against his throat as the other took away his axe and cast it several feet to the grass.

"Where's Gideon?" asked one of them. "Where'd you hide his body?"

Gideon?

"You mean that little boy pretending to be a soldier?" he asked. "He went running for Lord Hemman. Still, he's a smarter man than either of you."

The older struck his face with his fist. Sergan spat blood and chuckled.

"Now that's the welcome I was expecting."

A sword hilt struck his side, followed by a boot to his stomach. He coughed and beat the grass with a fist.

"What is going on here?" he heard a gruff voice ask. He glanced up to see a raven-haired man glaring down. He wore a thick coat of fine leather and a thin silver crown across his forehead. Several soldiers surrounded him, their belts bristling with weaponry.

"Hemman?" Sergan asked.

"Arthur Hemman, lord of the north. Step aside, both of you. I will not have a man who comes here in peace to be treated in such a manner."

Sergan accepted an offered hand to stand. He glared at the men who had beat him, and they glared right back.

"A fine welcome for a man who comes offering a deal," he said.

"They will be punished accordingly. Put them out of your mind, and please, tell me your name."

Arthur had a nice baritone to his voice, and he stood with his back straight as a pole. Perhaps they might just get along.

"Fine then," he said. "I'm Sergan Copperson, and I've served Neldar's military since I was out of my diaper-cloth. I speak for Antonil Copernus, rightful king of Mordan."

It was as if a lightning bolt shot through the surrounding soldiers. It didn't seem possible, but Arthur stood even straighter.

"We serve the priest-king," Arthur said. "It is treasonous to speak of loyalties elsewhere."

This is it, Sergan thought. *Tread carefully, like you got porcupines for socks.*

"Loyalties forged in blood, protected in battle, and trusted for centuries shouldn't be tossed to the wayside, nor ever be spoken of as treasonous," he said.

"How can we trust he's even alive?" asked one of the soldiers. Arthur held up a hand to silence him.

"Rude, but true. How has Antonil survived? Where has he been while another sits on his throne?"

"You can ask him yourself. He's hardly a minute's walk from here, just awaiting my signal that it's safe."

Sergan enjoyed the second bolt that ran through the soldiers. They were gathering now, at least thirty in the vicinity. He hoped it stayed quiet, though. If the priests caught wind of what was going on, matters would turn dire.

"He would come here, into the very camp of his enemy?" Arthur asked. "Surely he is not that foolish."

"Not foolish," said Sergan. "But he is brave enough to do so. Or would you come out and meet him, as is proper for a lord come to pay respects to his king?"

The tension thickened at once. Sergan stared at Lord Hemman, refusing to break eye contact. The man was thinking, tossing and turning over ideals, loyalties, and practical matters of fortune and standing. He'd thrown the dice. Time to see if it was a seven or the reaper's eyes.

"I will go to him, as is deserving of his standing," Arthur said. "But I will not go alone, nor unprotected. I do not question Antonil's honor, but only those who might use his name for their purposes."

"And the other lords?" Sergan asked. He felt the tension drain out of him and was beyond thankful. "Will you bring them, too?"

"I would rather not risk it," said Arthur, and Sergan realized there were a hundred ways to interpret the response. "I will speak for the others in matters I am most comfortable, and relay to them anything beyond that. Now lead."

Sergan glanced back into the darkness. He'd been instructed to bring Antonil by sending a messenger with a password. Seemed like it was time for a little deviation from that. Hopefully neither would get mad...or end up dead.

"Follow me," he said. "Bring as many as you like, but keep your swords sheathed. They're not alone or helpless, either."

He turned to go, and Hemman followed with a group of ten soldiers. Sergan wasn't entirely sure where Antonil waited. He'd been told they would move about, keeping to the skies and watching for any messenger or stranger wandering out in their direction. Such a large group as they were, he figured they'd find him with little difficulty. So he walked, keeping silent and glad those behind him did the same. He'd done his part. He'd talked, and did a damn fine job of it, too. At least, he thought he had. He wasn't dead yet. Surely that counted for something.

"This is far enough," Arthur said as they reached the end of the campfires' light. "You say he is waiting, then where is he? I will not venture into the wilderness to await an ambush."

Sergan glanced upward, then chuckled.

"He's here," he said. "Look to the stars, boys. We've got men with wings."

Azariah landed first, a spell already glowing on his fingertips. Arthur's soldiers stepped closer to their lord and readied their weapons. A single flap of the angel's wings, and they tensed, preparing for an attack.

"Lay off 'em," Sergan said. "I'm no prisoner, and they're no ambushers."

Azariah nodded. He lifted his mace to the air and waved it once in a circle. Down came the rest of the angels, the two kings in their arms. Antonil stepped free, and when he saw Arthur, he smiled and bowed low.

"Welcome," he said. "I am honored by the courage it must have taken to meet me."

"How do we know he's the real king?" one of the soldiers whispered a bit too loudly.

"Because I remember him from his wedding," Arthur said, pushing the man aside. His eyes never left Antonil's. "Welcome, King Antonil. I would embrace you, but sadly we find ourselves on opposite sides of this war, and I fear the dagger that might find my back."

"Then let us remove that fear," Antonil said. "Come. Join my army. Your allegiance to the true king of Mordan has not changed. You strike me as an honorable man. You know you belong at my side when I reclaim what was taken from me."

"Your army?" asked Arthur. "I watched the chaos at the Bloodbrick. You fight with angels and elves and ruffians of Ker. Where are the men of Mordan? Where are the men of Neldar?"

"They are among the ruffians," said Bram as he took a step forward. "Though I must say I disapprove of such an ignorant name."

Arthur's eyes widened as he realized who stood before him.

"King Bram," he said, bowing. "You both honor me. I am not worthy, two kings come to visit just myself."

"We'd prefer all the lords of Mordan," Bram said. "Where are the rest?"

"They do not know of your arrival," said Arthur. "We live in dangerous times. There are those in power who would frown on such a meeting, and the fewer here, the better."

"So be it," said Antonil. "I do not know what lies you have been told. I do not know what wrongs have been committed by the hand of the priest-king. I left to free one nation, and in return find another enslaved. I have come to free you, all of you. Let the nations of Ker and Mordan unite.

Whatever oaths you have made, they were false and forced at the edge of a sword or in the darkness of a dungeon cell. I am your king. Lend me your swords."

Arthur crossed his arms. His men about him grew quiet, and they stole glances at the angels, afraid of their exotic beauty and strength. No doubt they were pondering what chance they had if their lord rejected his duty and it came to blows.

"When Melorak took rule, he took over a hundred acres of my land," Arthur said. "Land that had been in my family's hands since my father was a babe. He went through every coin I had and took what he called a tithe. These things come and go, and all matters are dangerous when new blood takes the throne. But he also sent a priest to my house, and under penalty of death, he must remain. My wife and children bow to that wretched lion idol day and night, and that burns far worse than the loss of coin and soil. I worship neither god, my king, though now I wonder as I see the angels of Ashhur before me. To not have a choice, though..."

He drew his sword and knelt.

"King Antonil, King Bram, I offer you both my allegiance."

His soldiers beside him immediately followed suit, many with bewildered looks on their faces. A few, though, grinned with an eager light in their eyes, as if they had suddenly become unchained.

"What of the other lords?" Antonil asked, biding Lord Hemman to stand. "Will they do the same?"

"Our time is short," Arthur said. "I must go and find out. If we join you...can you promise victory? I've seen the wrath of your angels, and I saw the power of your elven goddess. But what of men? Can we turn the tide?"

"We will," said Antonil. "This world will not become the terror Karak wishes it to be."

"Return to your camps," Arthur said. "If you would allow, wait for me at the Bloodbrick, and pray to your god that all goes well. If it does..."

"Go with Ashhur's grace," Azariah said, clenching his fist to his chest and bowing.

Arthur gave him a look, then chuckled. "Just make sure he doesn't get forced into my house when this is done, either," he said before returning to the camp.

When they were gone, the others lingered for a moment, as if hardly believing their fortune.

"Well," said Sergan. "I think that went well. Great, even. Now let's get back to camp so I can get some damn sleep."

"**W**hy aren't we moving after them?" Harruq asked the next morning. "Figured we'd want to keep on their heels so they don't start thinking of another attack."

"Too close to their heels and they'll see we're just a little yapping cub instead of a bear," Tarlak said, sitting down next to him and handing the half-orc a chunk of bread smothered with butter. "And I couldn't get much out of Antonil. He's spending more and more time with that Bram guy. Can't decide how happy I am about that."

"Oh no, he's spending time with a king instead of you. How will you endure?"

Tarlak laughed, loud and open-mouthed despite the chunk of bread he'd just bitten into.

"I'll mope and cry into Aurelia's bosom. I think that'll cheer me up just fine."

Aurelia smiled at him but held back any normal retort. She'd been subdued since her display at the bridge, but Harruq hoped that she'd be back to her normal self in time. He frowned. Now that he thought about it, she hadn't been her normal self for a while. Something was off, but what?

"Just wish we could get back on the move," Harruq said.

"You're never happy, you know that Harruq?" said Tarlak. "If we're chasing armies, you grumble about the travel and your back hurting and how the angels like smacking you into trees, yet if we decide to take a single day's rest, you're at it again."

"Don't make me stab you," the half-orc muttered.

Tarlak feigned fear, then took another giant bite.

"You know," he said, staring north. "Maybe it's me, but that looks like a big army coming our way."

Harruq stood and squinted. "Huh. I think you're right."

Aurelia lifted an eyebrow. "Should we be worried?"

"Something's up," Tarlak said, staring off toward the front of the camp. "I see Antonil and his little buddies gathering up, but they sure don't look ready to fight."

"Then what's going on?" asked Harruq.

Tarlak shot him a grin. "Well, let's find out, shall we?"

A few words of magic and a portal opened before them. Tarlak beckoned them in, then followed after. When they stepped out, they stood beside Antonil and a rather surprised looking Bram.

"I don't recall inviting you three to join us," Bram said.

"That's how they are," Antonil said, adjusting the crown on his head. "They're more useful disobedient, anyway. I'd probably be dead twice over if they bothered to listen to orders."

Bram snorted, his mouth locked in a frown. Harruq grinned at him and offered a salute.

"Just here to protect his royal ass," he said. "Don't mind me."

"So what's going on?" Tarlak asked, sliding between Antonil and Bram while the half-orc kept his attention the other way. "Did we miss out on some fun?"

"You might say that," Antonil said. "You can listen, but remain quiet and behave."

Harruq surveyed the approaching army. They marched with their heads low, their backs slumped as if their shields and weapons weighed more than them. A few banners flew from spears and poles, but not many. His quick estimate, though, was massive. Thousands of men, come not to fight, but to...what?

"This is the reward for your bravery," Bram said. "This is your rightful respect as king. Do not just expect obedience. Demand it. When they bow before you, do not heap praises upon them. They have done their duty. Their reward is their renewed honor in the eyes of their lord."

"Surely the right path to be a beloved king," Tarlak muttered.

"Says the honorless mercenary," said Bram. "Do not pretend that you know how to rule. You control a pitiful few with coin. Nothing compares to being law and judgment for thousands."

"Enough," said Antonil. "They approach, and I don't want them to see my friends squabbling amongst themselves."

"Let them come to you," said Bram. "Make them remember their place."

Four men rode at the front of the great river of troops, dressed in exquisite armor no doubt handed down their family line for generations. Beside each of them rode a younger man wielding a banner. The colors and symbols meant nothing to Harruq, but he knew a lord when he saw one. They rode up to Antonil and then dismounted.

"Lord Hemman," Antonil said, nodding his head slightly. "I am pleased to meet you again, this time in light of day."

One of the men stepped closer and bowed. He was tall, and when he spoke, his voice was deep and firm.

"Only a few tried to stop us, and they backed away when we drew blood," said Hemman. "We have come to offer our allegiance to the rightful king of Mordan. Antonil Copernus, will you accept my sword?"

He drew his sword, knelt, and offered it up. Antonil smiled.

"Of course," he said, saluting with his own.

Hemman stood, but when he turned to go, he stopped and looked back over his shoulder. His deep voice dropped lower in volume, possibly the quietest the man could whisper.

"They know we have left," he said. "All our families are in danger. Our name is nothing without you. Will we win? Tell me, Antonil. Let me hear the words. Can we win this fight?"

Harruq looked to Antonil, and he was not the only one. Tarlak crossed his arms and waited. Bram's eyes narrowed, as if ready to judge the new king by his answer.

"Both the grave and the throne await me," Antonil said. "And by my sword, the wings of Ashhur, and the magic of my friends, I will seek them out, and run from neither. Let the priest-king fear my name. I come for what is mine."

Hemman nodded. Worry still filled his eyes, but the answer seemed acceptable. He turned to the other lords and let them introduce themselves as the thousands crossed the river. As they bowed to their lord, Tarlak took his Eschaton and left.

25

Village after village fell. At Thulos's insistence, they made for the Corinth River, seeking an entrance into Mordeina and meeting with the rumored priest-king.

"If his allegiance is true," the god told Velixar, "then the last of the angels stand no chance. At worst, we find them already dashed upon the walls. It would be a shame, though. My sword desires blood, and this world has proved rather elusive in providing worthy opponents."

"At least you killed the daughter of the whore," Velixar said, stepping out of the large tent.

"Just one of them," said Thulos. "Another remains."

Velixar glared but kept his mouth shut.

On and on they travelled until they reached the Bloodbrick. Thulos led the way, and he stopped before it to survey the area. On both sides he saw communal graves burned with fire. Blood soaked the bridge. High above hovered a legion of crows, no doubt having feasted well the week before. Many bodies still floated, caught against the rocks, their bodies pale and eaten away by the fish and the birds. Distressingly few bore the wings of Ashhur's angels.

"Who fought here?" he asked.

"It must have been Ashhur's men, for I see wing bones among the pyres. But against who? I don't know. Perhaps an army from Mordan marched south, hoping to subdue Ker and her king."

"Then they were defeated," Thulos said. "An ill sign. We must continue on. If Mordeina has fallen, then our task grows that much greater."

Their supplies thinned during the weeks following. The villagers who surrendered instead of joining Velixar's dead told of how an army had come from Mordan and taken much of their food, and then even more on the way back. Ashhur's army had given chase only days behind. Thulos's mood soured at that, and they rushed after with even greater speed.

Through it all, Velixar poisoned the night with his words. Through it all, Tessanna brought Qurrah back from the edge during the day.

"You know he lies," she told him while they travelled yet another day north toward Mordeina. "What is it he says to you that tortures you so? What lies could he possibly have that you cannot outright dismiss?"

Qurrah didn't answer immediately, but Tessanna was used to this. Often now Qurrah took a moment or two to think. It seemed every question he felt duty-bound to answer truthfully, no matter how terrible it might make him seem. She waited him out, part of her dreading the answer, part hoping she might help him in any way.

"He sends me into my past," he said. "He forces me to live the life I would rather forget existed. You say I am not my past...but how can I deny what I must endure every night? I feel the pleasure in the kill. I remember my pride, my power. All the guilt I feel, it vanishes as I hold myself above the wretched that I murder. It's so heavy, Tessanna. So heavy..."

She took his hand in hers as they walked. It was cold, but she had grown used to it, as she had his awkward pauses, his deathly pale skin, and the horrible silence in his chest. His eyes, though, they still had life. His voice might be a hollow reminder of what he had been, but his eyes told her how much he still loved her. As long as she could hold onto that, as long as she could cling to it so tightly that pulling them apart would spray blood and kill them both, then she felt hope.

"After Aullienna died," she said, hesitant. She had never told him this before, but perhaps it might help. "After...you know. I dreamed of it. I saw her plunge into the water. I could even see what she saw, these little faeries dancing about her in a world so beautiful. Every night I watched her die. It was peaceful, in a way. She never knew the danger, not even at the end. She saw something I could only see the faintest glimpse of, something golden and wonderful. And then all would go dark, her body just a shell floating in the water. Every night,

Qurrah. And when I'd wake up I'd hate you for casting the spell, and hate myself for ever asking you to do it."

Qurrah's lower lips spread tight across his teeth. She knew that meant he was struggling to keep his emotions in check. If he still had a living body, perhaps he'd even be crying. She kept going, needing to tell him. Needing him to know.

"I nearly killed you while you slept," she said. "I tried to convince myself I didn't need you. I'd lived without you before, and while it was lonely, I never hurt. But you hurt me, so bad, so deep. I held my dagger in my hand and imagined your blood on my fingers. It didn't excite me. It didn't ease me in any way. I hated you so much, Qurrah, but I couldn't do it. Despite the dreams, despite my horror, despite being afraid and lost and clinging to you so desperately…I couldn't. I loved you too much. I tried to imagine my life without you, and I couldn't."

"Why are you telling me this?" he asked.

She clutched his hand in hers and stared up at him. A deep ache swelled in her chest as she wished to kiss him but could not. She couldn't even stand the thought of feeling his lips against hers, now dry, cold, and lifeless.

"Because now you endure the same. Velixar forces you to relive the hurt. He tries to glorify what you regret. I held on because of you…and you…can't you do the same? I thought, just maybe, you could love me. Maybe if you love me enough, you'll endure. Can't I help? I want to help, Qurrah. I want to feel that I've at least helped one life, because all I do is ruin. All I do is destroy. Mother made me broken, and all I do is break."

She was crying, and she couldn't think of anything to say. She felt she had a thousand things to tell Qurrah, to ask him, to beg for forgiveness or understanding. But instead she pressed her head against his bloodstained white robes and sobbed. All around them the soldiers of Thulos marched on, giving them strange looks but not daring to speak.

As she cried, she felt his hand gently rest atop her head. Part of her tensed, afraid of what he might say, afraid that he might be angry at what she had once thought. The other part was glad she no longer hid it from him, even if he had never known the secret existed.

"I don't know if it will work," he said. "But I'll try. For you."

"I love you," she said. "Even like this."

"I know," he said. "How, I will never understand."

She smiled and wiped at her tears with her palms.

"Maybe because I'm insane."

Qurrah laughed. It sounded so warm, so *alive*, that she laughed with him and momentarily forgot the army about them, the demons above them, and Velixar marching ahead of them, just waiting for night to fall.

✦

That night, as she lay down for bed, Velixar came to her. "Come with me," he said, his red eyes barely visible underneath the hood of his cloak. "Tonight, I want you to see what I have always known."

"And what is that?" she asked.

He smiled but did not answer. She accepted his offered hand and followed him out of the camp, beyond the light of the campfires, and to a collection of runes carved into the dirt. Qurrah stood in their center, his head tilted back, his vacant eyes staring at the sky.

"What is going on?" she asked. Velixar pressed his finger to his lips and shushed her.

"He is lost in his memories," he whispered. "Do not disturb him. I have chosen a very special memory, one I want you to see."

"I don't want to see it," she said, looking away.

"But he is your beloved," Velixar said, grabbing her jaw and forcing her to look at him. "He is the one you yearned for while you were with me. Should you not know everything about him?"

He pressed his fingers against her forehead. Images poured in, smoothly and expertly taking over her senses one by one. She found herself watching a frozen moment in time, that of a dark alley where the two Tun brothers stood before one another. Pain and anger covered their faces. She hovered between them for a moment, and then plunged into Qurrah. She saw what he saw, felt his emotions course through her. Time resumed.

"I will kill again," Qurrah yelled. She felt pain in her throat, and a slight trickle of blood. "I will kill children, women, elders, elves, Tarlak, Brug, I'll kill any I wish, whenever I wish. Aurelia, Aullienna, their lives are nothing to me, nothing to you. Have you grown too blind to see it?"

Aullienna...

The name echoed as time once more slowed. Beside her, a phantom of Karak's prophet laughed.

"Do you feel his anger?" he asked. "Do you feel his honesty? Nothing to him. Nothing! Children, women, elves, Aurelia...Aullienna...does your name fall on this list? View your beloved as he truly is!"

He yanked her back and out, so that she stared at the brothers. Harruq was in mid-swing, the back of his fist ready to slam into Qurrah's face. Still the name echoed. Nothing to me. Nothing.

Nothing.

"You clung to him in your darkest despair," Velixar whispered. "But who is it you cling to? You bed a monster. You romanticize him into an ideal, a perfect master to fulfill your perverted desires. Look at him. *Look at him!*"

His face was curled into a sneer. Rage filled his bloodshot eyes. She still felt his emotions perfectly synced with hers. His absolute certainly nearly overwhelmed her. He meant it. Every word. The girl she adored, the one floating face down in the water...nothing?

"There is another memory," Velixar whispered.

"No," she said, terrified of what it might be. She wanted out. She wanted back to the now, to bury the past and think of it no more.

The world shifted and changed. She stood in their old home, her lover before her. Qurrah looked stunned and confused. Her hands moved of their own accord, her lips spoke with a mind of their own.

"What is it?" he asked. His arms moved about her, but the reaction was calculated, cold, a placating attempt.

"The girl is dead," she sobbed, clawing at his chest. "I saw it, she's dead. You killed her, you killed her!"

She felt herself tear into him. Her fingers passed through cloth and raked his chest. All her old anger roared to life, as absolute as Qurrah's had been. She felt rage, pure, mindless rage. His blood ran across her fingers, and she thought of her words only hours before. His blood on her hands...and this time it did excite her.

The memory slowed, and she felt Velixar hovered nearby, laughing. Tears ran down her face, but then she felt anger, her own, not the memory's. He was stopping the remembrance? Why? With her thoughts, she pushed ahead, surprising Velixar by the sudden willingness and acceptance of Qurrah's torture. She felt her anger return, her clawing at Qurrah continuing, but then his arms tightened about her. He stood still, in total shock. Her thrashing stopped, and she pushed her head against his neck and sobbed. Despite the pain she'd inflicted, he stroked her hair. Still no words. What had they done? What horror had they committed?

Deep down inside her she felt a part of Qurrah connect, the part trapped there with her in the memories. He felt that same ache, that same communal pain. She could almost imagine his arms around her still as the memory twisted and turned a murky gray.

Not yet...

The words came from everywhere. She felt Velixar burn with rage, but now Qurrah forced his memories aside. Linked with Tessanna, they found another shared memory, though she had always thought it secret.

◆◈◆

Qurrah stood outside their house, that same night Tessanna had felt Aullienna die. He stood with his arms at his sides, his hood pulled back. His hair blew in a soft breeze. With his head tilted back, he stared up at the stars.

Tessanna crept out of the house, careful not to make a single noise. Like an animal she crawled on all fours, almost wishing she could be a prowling cat, to live a life without complications and love. Closer and closer she came to Qurrah, watching him stand there like a statue. How could he be so heartless? How could he leave her there to weep alone in their bed? She should kill him. She had her dagger, and he was unaware, unprepared.

But then she was close enough to hear. The sound was strange. She almost didn't understand it, and then when she did, she didn't believe it. Could he?

Alone and broken, he stared at the stars and wept. Confused and scared, she watched, too cowardly to interrupt a moment that private.

Nothing? she heard the phantom voice of Qurrah ask. *Is this nothing? Are these the tears I cried for nothing?*

She felt Velixar raging against them. Once master, now he fought for control, lost in the world of Qurrah's memories. She remembered those tears, and she felt Qurrah's pain bleeding into her. He'd wept for Aullienna, but not just her. He'd wept for the loss of his brother. He'd wept for the pain he'd caused her. He'd bared his soul to the stars, because he trusted only the stars to understand, to not judge him, and to give him peace.

At last she returned to the house, crawled into the bed, and laid there for hours unable to sleep.

"You can't steal this from me," Tessanna whispered, feeling her senses returning. The dream world faded, and then Velixar's cold fingers left her forehead.

He immediately struck her. Blood splattered from her mouth as her lips cut against her teeth. She fell, but Velixar grabbed her hair and yanked her back to her feet. His hand wrapped around her throat and squeezed. She grabbed his wrist and pulled, but she was nothing to him, nothing without her magic. As she gasped for air, she saw Qurrah standing in the center of the runes, watching.

"Do you think you will prove me wrong?" Velixar asked his former disciple. "Do you think a single weak moment of tears will wash away years of certainty? Enough of these stupid sentimental falsehoods. Is she why you remain terrified of embracing Karak's perfection? Is she why you stumble? Always remove a thorn, no matter how deep. Those who make you stumble must move or be destroyed."

Tighter and tighter his hand closed around her neck. Tessanna gasped, and she felt terror creeping up her spine. Was this how she would die? Strangled while Qurrah stood there, forced to watch, bound by Velixar's will to remain still as she kicked and twisted until she suffocated? Spots floated in her vision, purple embers with red centers. His hand was cold, so cold...

And then it was gone. She landed some distance away, flung as if she were a dirty rag. As she retched, she looked back to see Velixar pressing his forehead against Qurrah's, his hands wrapped around his neck as if they were lovers.

"I am no fool to your desires," she heard Velixar whisper, just loud enough for her to overhear. "I feel them much the same. Do not let them control you. Do not let your pathetic mortal notions of morality and conscience decide your actions. It was her hand that took your life."

He looked back to Tessanna, who glared.

"And it must be you to take her life. When you are ready, Qurrah. When you are ready for Karak's true embrace, for you to fully understand...do the same to her. Take her life, and if you like, I can help you bring her back. She can join us in perfection, freed from the goddess's taint."

Qurrah stood still as a statue, but he had enough control to speak.

"Leave us," he said.

Velixar smiled.

"Do the right thing," he whispered, then returned to the camp. Tessanna ignored him, kept her eyes only on her beloved.

"Will he make you?" she asked as he stood there.

"He's left me the choice," Qurrah said. "For now."

"Then will you?"

Qurrah walked over to her, fell to his knees, and then wrapped his arms around her.

"Never," he whispered. "I never could. Please, Tessanna. Kill me now. While he's gone, find a stone, a dagger, and tear out my heart. He'll make me do it soon. I know him. His patience is almost gone, his mind with it. Don't make me endure that. Please."

She shook her head.

"So you'd make me kill you instead? Velixar tried that once. I won't, Qurrah. We'll find a way. Together, we'll find a way."

She nestled against his chest and closed her eyes.

"And if there isn't?" he asked.

She clutched him tighter.

"Then we'll make one."

26

Melorak was executing a sympathizer of Ashhur when Olrim returned.

"Olrim?" he asked, pulling the dagger back and wiping it against his clothes without thinking. He'd been alone with the screams in the dungeon cell when the door opened, and he squinted against the light.

"Forgive me," the other priest said. "They told me you had strict orders not to be disturbed, but I must speak with you."

"You've returned months before expected," said Melorak. "I imagine we have much to discuss."

He gestured to where the bloody prisoner hung upside down from chains. If he was conscious, he didn't show it. Pieces of his intestines hung down past his head.

"I will be done shortly. Wait for me at the throne."

He sliced a few more tendons, but his mind was no longer on the task at hand. Olrim had already returned? What possibly could have happened? He'd seen the carefully guarded fear in the priest's eyes. Whatever he was to hear, he doubted he'd like it. Frustrated, he cut the prisoner's throat and stepped back from the blood. If only all of Ashhur's followers could suffer such a fate, he thought. The meager resistance he fought would vanish altogether.

He left the man hanging and exited the cell. Two guards waited, one holding a change of clothes, the other a clean towel and a small basin. Melorak washed his hands and face, changed his robes, and then went to the throne room. Olrim waited as expected, kneeling in prayer at the foot of the ornate throne.

"Such passionate prayers," Melorak said as he sat down. "I doubt even Karak has the strength to ignore such a plea."

"I have failed him in terrible ways," Olrim said. "Even with all my years, my faith is that of a child."

"A child's faith is both great and weak," said Melorak. "Great in its strength, yet weak in its malleability. Such are our current failings. We must ensure the children hear Karak's word from a very early age, before they even think to question what they are taught. But enough of that. I see you desperate to explain, and I am eager to hear. Tell me of this great failure."

"An army waited for us at the Corinth," Olrim said. He kept his head bowed while he talked, as if afraid to meet Melorak's eyes. "It was them, my friend. The angels of Ashhur fought alongside men of Ker. Not just Ker, either, but the soldiers sent with Antonil from Mordan. They'd prepared, and I led us right into the trap. Some devilish spikes covered the river, and I watched hundreds drown. Many more died to the pikes that awaited on the other side. They built walls upon the Bloodbrick, and we paid dearly to cross each one. The angels killed many of my priests, and we slew few in return."

"How many did they have?" he asked.

"Ten thousand, my lord."

Melorak felt his anger flare.

"Ten thousand against your fifty, and you lost because of a few traps and the failed god's angels?"

"Please, forgive me. But there is more than I have told. We lost several thousand, yes, but victory still would have been ours, if not for the elf."

Melorak felt a sting of worry. "The elf?"

Olrim nodded.

"While we pulled back to regroup, she stepped before the bridge and began to cast her spells. Never before have I seen such power, Melorak. She tore the ground apart, sundered the sky, and sent such devastation toward us I lost all control of my men."

"You had nearly my entire host of priests with you!" Melorak seethed. "How could a single elf defeat your combined might?"

"Even Karak might have felt fear at this display!" Olrim said, a bit of his stubbornness overcoming his shame. "You know me, Melorak, long before you took your new name and became Karak's favorite. I would never lie, and if I say that it seemed Celestia herself had come to crush my men, you know I say so without lie or exaggeration."

Melorak sat back in his seat and forced himself to calm down.

"How many have you left?" he asked.

"After the battle, nearly the entire host. But my failures do not stop there. Word spread of Antonil's return, though how, I do not know. Come morning, I found nearly a third of my army on the march south. As I returned to Mordeina, my numbers dwindled even more. I posted guards, but it never mattered."

"How many are left?" asked Melorak, stunned by the news. How could things have fallen apart so quickly?

"Fifteen thousand."

Melorak sat there on the throne, running the numbers through his head. No matter what, he was suddenly outnumbered, facing Ashhur's angels, the returned king, and some strange elf wielding the power of the goddess. The Lionsguard that remained in the city were only a few thousand, many of them recently trained. Would the great walls matter against such opponents? How many more might cowardly turn to Antonil and abandon that which promised to make them great?

"This cannot be," he said. "We must inspire the people to loyalty. We must let every man and woman in the countryside know of Karak's power."

"But how?" asked Olrim. "Our time is short. We may have quelled the resistance here for now, but it will gain new life when word of Antonil's return reaches the public's ears. Our priests work night and day to spread the word, and our Lionsguard have executed hundreds if not thousands. Every week I send out more to the farmlands and homesteads to purge Ashhur's taint. What more can we do?"

Melorak closed his eyes and offered a prayer to Karak for guidance. What could they do? Was there something missing, some vital task still before him? Or perhaps this was his trial of faith, his turn to make a stand and prove that they were the true way?

And then he heard Karak's voice in return, and he had his answer. He looked to Olrim and told him what had been demanded.

"A dragon," he said.

"But they don't exist," said the priest.

"Then I will make one," said Melorak. "Double the patrols. Send every priest we have out into the streets. I want prayers made to Karak nonstop for the rest of tonight."

"Where are you going?" asked Olrim as the priest-king hurried down the hall.

"I will be in the gardens," he said. "Ensure no one interrupts me. And make plans for a grand revealing tomorrow. I want the whole city to witnesses the full extent of Karak's power."

"As you wish," said Olrim.

Melorak went to the gardens, not for their tranquility, but for the large open space they provided. He would need all of it. The creation would be grand, and deep down he felt a sliver of doubt. He brushed it away. Of course he might fail, but that didn't mean he would. His faith was strong, his loyalty unquestionable. He was the heir to Velixar. No longer did the world need a prophet. It needed a ruler, and he would show them his authority.

First he paced the gardens with a long stick in hand. He carved runes into the dirt, the words for faith, control, worship, and domination repeating in a pattern. An hour later he went to the center of the garden and removed the benches. The fountains he struck with his hand, his flesh flaring black with magic. The old stonework shattered, and the water spilled across his cloth. It was cold, but he embraced it. The cold gave his mind focus. Feeling strangely proud of his solitary work, he put the stones into a pile, then began picking through them. One by one he realigned them on the ground, forming a great rune, the symbol of the lion.

"Be with me, Karak," he whispered.

He spent the next hour in prayer. All throughout, the words of the spell came to him. They were simple, despite the complexity of the creature he wished to create. It seemed it would rely on his faith and strength of vision. While he prayed, the sun dipped below the walls, and as the shadows stretched across his body he gave thanks to his beloved deity.

It is time, he heard Karak say, his voice like a whisper breathed against the back of his neck.

Melorak stepped to the far side of the garden, turned to the center, and then lifted his arms to the heavens.

"In your name, I do this," he shouted. "In your name, I pray. I am a weak, earthen vessel. I am clay. Make something of me, my god. Give me your power. Hear me! See my faith! The time has come, oh Lion of the World. May the weak bow, may the proud tremble, and may the followers of the false god be blinded by the truth!"

The words of the spell came to his lips, and he spoke them as if he were possessed by the will of another. The shadows curled and danced, and the moon raced along as if lost in time. Hours were but seconds as the spell crashed out, the power so great wisps of smoke and darkness puffed from his lips. His lone eye shone a violent red. He felt his body tremble, and sweat rolled down his neck. In his mind, the creature became more than just an image. It was alive, a fierce and mighty thing demanding release. He gave it its desire.

The ground cracked, the rune in the center bursting with fire. The shadows poured into the chasm, like water down a drain. All throughout the city lanterns and fires darkened, as if their light were an affront to the creature's arrival. Wind blew in a swirling torrent, its howl deafening. His body trembled, but the spell was near completion. A name, that was all that remained. He must give it a name!

"Rakkar," he screamed. "I give you life!"

Rakkar's roar seemed to shake the very walls of the castle. Olrim arrived not soon after, and Melorak smiled at him despite his exhaustion. His friend's mouth opened wide, and he fell to his knees and held his palms outward in a display of complete devotion.

"I have never seen such beauty," he said breathlessly.

"The city is ours," Melorak said. Even speaking took much concentration, for only his constant will and focus kept Rakkar under his control. "Prepare the great revealing while I rest."

"Praise be to Karak," said Olrim.

Melorak smiled as behind him Rakkar softly growled.

"Praise be, indeed."

"What do you think he's planning?" Veliana asked as they weaved through the crowd.

"We've heard rumors of Antonil ever since Melorak's army returned," Deathmask said. "I expect nothing more than some fear mongering and lies, but it is best we hear all the same."

Veliana shrugged and kept pushing closer toward the steps of the castle, where Melorak was supposed to make his appearance. They wore cloaks with deep hoods, and had even smeared dirt across their skin and hair to make sure Haern didn't spot them among the crowd. The rapid arrangement smelled of desperation, and given how poorly their own resistance was going, both she and Deathmask were eager for any sort of victory. If they could perhaps prove what Melorak promised was false, maybe they could leverage that, along with the rumors of Antonil, into something workable. As it was, their resistance had become nothing but the two of them plus Bernard. The house guards had disbanded since the rest of the lords were hung from the gates of the city.

"Here is close enough," Deathmask said.

They were several rows back, but still within easy sight. The people swayed and jostled, but they endured it with practiced ease. They'd come early, expecting an enormous crowd. All throughout every quarter the Lionsguard carried naked swords, ordering attendance. Hardly a soul in sight seemed happy to be there. If he started shouting words of revolt, he wondered if he'd spark a massive riot then and there. Given the sheer amount of priests and Lionsguard that roamed about, perhaps not. Still, the thought amused him, and he imagined scenarios of the destruction as they waited for the priest-king to show.

An hour later, Melorak stepped from the castle, flanked by priests and dark paladins. He wore his robes adorned with silver and gold, and atop his head, a newly fashioned crown glittering with sapphires.

"Rather over the top for one such as him," Veliana whispered into Deathmask's ear.

"Is it an act?" he asked. "Or is he trying to appear more kingly?"

Veliana shrugged, not having an answer.

"Men and women of Mordeina, your ruler!" shouted one of the dark paladins. His voice carried far by the careful design of the stairs and curved wall stretching to either side. The noise of the crowd lessened, but was by no means silent. When Melorak lifted his hand, an eerie calm swept over them. No sound, none at all, came from the crowd. Curious, Deathmask clapped his hands once. Nothing.

"People of Mordeina," said Melorak. He sounded tired, old, but his voice remained deep as ever. "My beloved people. I know you hear rumors. I know your hearts are weak, and turn to thoughts better left unspoken. I am human. I am Karak made flesh, and I understand these weaknesses. But now is not the time for doubt. Now is not the time for cowardice. The world has changed, and we must change with it. I am not alone with Karak, nor am I his only voice.

"Throughout the night, I heard your prayers. They strengthened me. They gave me hope. And now I give to you a gift in return. Look to the castle, and look to the sky! View what your faith hath created. View the power of Karak. Let it sweep across you, burn your heart, and set you on the true path. Rakkar! Come forth!"

A great roar swept over the crowd, seeming to explode from within the castle. Deathmask felt his heart chill at the sound. It seemed to shake his bones, it was so loud. A blade of pure shadow tore into the sky. Smoke billowed behind it, a trail that looked like a scar across the blue. It circled once, kept aloft by enormous wings that were reminiscent of a bat.

Beside him Veliana murmured something in shock, but the spell across them stole it away.

"Rakkar!" Melorak cried again. The beast turned and landed between him and the crowd, its wings curling about itself. The creature looked reptilian, its scales made of deep shadow. Violet eyes shone from the sides of its head, possessing a frightening intelligence as it surveyed the crowd. It walked on all fours, with enormous claws, each the size of a man. Its long neck lifted, and then it roared. The nearest rows collapsed to their backs, while the rest fell to their knees, pushed down by a compulsion even Deathmask struggled to resist. From deep within its throat fire burst in a great pillar, as if the creature were attempting to burn the very heavens. At last the spell ended, and the murmurs of the crowd rumbled to life in deafening waves.

"A dragon?" Veliana asked, having to press her lips against his ear to be heard.

"It's not possible," Deathmask said, shaking his head. He seemed to be trying to convince himself. "It just can't be possible."

Melorak lifted his arms in praise.

"Let the bastion of Ashhur fall to Karak's might!" he cried.

Rakkar spread its wings and took flight, heading straight for where Avlimar floated above the city, a constant reminder of the angels and their absence. Deathmask swallowed, feeling a lump in his throat growing. Any chance of a rebellion died before them. No one would resist such a creature. A legend come to life. A dragon made of shadow, smoke and flame.

"What do we do?" Veliana asked.

"I don't know."

The creature flew closer, closer, soon just a trail of smoke as it neared the golden city. Deathmask watched, unable to look away. Just when it was to land, it pulled back, and he heard its wail of pain all the way from there. A thin smile spread across his lips.

"It can't stand its light," he said, suddenly laughing. "Watch it squirm!"

The creature breathed fire at the city, burning some of the outer pillars, but it could not draw any closer. It circled once or twice, and as the murmuring grew throughout the crowd, it turned back toward the ground. Deathmask looked to Melorak and felt greatly amused at how the priest-king seethed.

"Let's go," he said, grabbing Veliana's wrist. "We need to see if Bernard has any idea how to defeat that thing."

"He hoped for a far greater victory today," she said as they cut into a side alley away from the crowd.

"Yeah," Deathmask said, glancing upward to where a great trail of smoke led to the castle. "I think he's accomplished enough. Long as that thing lives, our chances are nothing."

"Then we kill it," Veliana said.

He stopped and looked at her. In response, she laughed.

"You once prided yourself for accomplishing the impossible," she said. "Have you really changed so much?"

He ran a hand across his horribly scarred face, burned by Melorak's fire.

"No," he said. "And so be it. Let us talk to Bernard, and find out just how to kill a dragon."

27

The Eschaton met, fully understanding it might be their final time.

"Glad to have you all here," Tarlak said. They gathered around a bonfire built far from the camps, for they desired solitude and privacy for their meeting. Some stood, and some sat on the grass. The wizard turned to each of them in turn as, high above, the moon waned.

"Glad to have you back," he said to Lathaar and Jerico. The two paladins sat beside one another, and they saluted him half-heartedly. "I can't imagine it a real meeting without some paladins to tell us what we're doing is morally wrong."

"Always happy to help," Jerico said, and he smiled.

"And you brought a friend," said the wizard.

"I will do my best not to interfere," said Keziel, brought to speak for the rest of the priests.

Tarlak nodded to the Tun couple, Aurelia snug in Harruq's arms. He felt glad Qurrah was not at their side, though he also felt guilty for such thoughts. With a sigh, he brushed them aside and did his best to keep his smug grin going.

"Of course, we must be honored by our beloved king's presence, since he is only an honorary member of my Eschaton."

Antonil nodded. He'd said not a word since joining them. Tarlak wondered if he missed Bram's presence. The two had become inseparable as of late. With Mordeina only a day away, his nerves had moved beyond eating him up inside. They seemed ready to devour him whole.

"Last, but not least," Tarlak said, gesturing to his left. "Thank you for coming, your wingedness."

"I've come as you requested," Ahaesarus said, but he saluted nonetheless.

Tarlak smoothed his robes and shifted his hat. His grin slipped, just a little.

"As you all know, well, this is it. This is the end. Tomorrow we reach Mordeina's walls, and this time we're not going to enter as Annabelle's guests. Archers will line their tops, and arrows will be our greeting. But far be it from me to make things sound easy. We need a strategy. This is no normal military siege. We have enemy walls before us and an enemy giving chase behind. There is no retreat, no bargaining, and nowhere else to go."

"We will make no assault unimpeded," said Aurelia. "Thulos and his demons have rushed like mad to catch us. They will attack while we are in the midst of our own."

"Have you seen them with your magic?" Antonil asked.

Aurelia rolled her eyes. "I can see their fires from here, as can all of you. The south glows from it."

"We could turn to face them," Lathaar offered. "Fight in a place of our choosing, and then if we succeed, we'll have all the time we need to lay siege to Mordeina."

"We cannot stand against them," Ahaesarus said. "Not with Thulos amid their ranks. That is what I have come to tell you all. There is but one place where we shall have even a shred of hope, and that is within our city of Avlimar. Ashhur's strength radiates from every hall, and within them, Thulos will feel weakened. Not a lot, but enough so that we might strike him a mortal wound."

"But how will you get him up there?" asked Tarlak.

"We go and wait for him," said the angel as if it were obvious. "He desires nothing more than combat against worthy opponents, and who is more worthy than Ashhur's handpicked guardians? We will draw him and his demons into the sky. As for the battle on the ground, we will leave that to you."

"I was hoping we could use your help to fly over the walls and break open the doors," Tarlak said. "But it appears you have made up your mind. So onto my second plan. Keziel, if given time, do you think you could break down the first gate to the city?"

The priest rubbed his chin as he thought.

"If we combined our strength? Perhaps. It wouldn't be a quick process, and we'd be vulnerable."

"I'll be there to help you," Tarlak said. "I have a few tricks of my own."

"If you can break open the gates, we can rush through," said Antonil. "Can you force a hole straight through the second wall?"

Tarlak gave him a wink.

"I remember the defenses. That sharp hook and that narrow gap between the walls would be a horrific killing field. We'll plow straight into the city, assuming our priest friends can hold up. From there, I say all of Antonil and Bram's men rush in."

"We'll have our strength divided in two," said Harruq. "Is this really wise? Why not have the angels fly us all to Avlimar and we make our stand there?"

Ahaesarus laughed.

"You are many thousands, and we are but a few. It would take days to bring everyone. If you remain outside the walls, Thulos's troops will destroy you. Better we attack."

"What of his ground forces?" asked Antonil. "He will have more than the demons. Do you really suggest we fight them on two fronts?"

Tarlak shrugged. "Yes. I'll be with the paladins in the back, and we'll have several lines set up to meet them. Ahaesarus will divert the demons and the war god to Avlimar, and the priests will help Antonil punch through the walls and into the city. So I guess you're wrong, Harruq. We'll be dividing our strength in three, not two."

Harruq rolled his eyes. "I feel so much better. And where will me and Aurry be in all this?"

"That…I don't know. You have a preference?"

"I do," he said. "Where will Velixar go?"

"He will be at Thulos's side," Keziel said. "Of this, I am sure. I have never met him, but read much. Always he will be with the commanders, keeping his grasp tight on those who rule. Who wields any greater power than Thulos?"

"Then I'll wait for him in Avlimar," Harruq said. "After everything he's done, it only seems right that I get to be the one to cut off his damned head."

"You make it sound so easy," Jerico chuckled.

"I hope it is."

"Does our king approve of this mad plan?" Tarlak asked. Antonil nodded.

"Very well then," Tarlak said. "We all know our roles. Get some rest. Tomorrow will be long and bloody. We may never see each other again, so just in case, I have one thing I wish to say: Antonil, you'll be paying me even in Eternity, so don't think dying gets you out of your considerable debt."

Several chuckled, but the humor was forced, and they all knew it. Tarlak looked about the fire, and his heart ached for those who were gone. His sister, who would have sat to his left, always ready to support him if he felt lost. Brug, who should have been guzzling down some ale and telling him how stupid their plan was. Haern, who would have mocked the demons' blades and smiled underneath his gray hood. Aullienna, who would have bounced on her father's knee, unaware of the dangers facing them, and the blood they would spill to protect her home. Even Qurrah and Tessanna's absence was felt, though by the look in Harruq's eyes, none felt it more keenly than him.

"Seriously," he said, suddenly feeling quiet and awkward. "It's been a pleasure to know all of you. Stand tall now, and may we meet each other once more, be it in this life or the next."

"May Ashhur watch over us," said Keziel.

"Amen," said the paladins and the angel.

"Dismissed," Tarlak said, waving his hand. "Go drink or talk or make love. We've got one last night. Spend it well. Come the dawn, we must forget ourselves, and let killing be all we know."

❁

Make love is what Harruq and Aurelia did, once they found a secluded spot far enough away. He kept his movements slow, and his touch tender. Afterward he lay beside her, her arms atop his chest and her face nuzzled into his neck. He felt her tears against his skin, and he shifted so he might hold her tighter.

"Don't worry," he whispered. "We've faced worse before and came out all right."

"That's not it," she whispered back. "I've something to tell you, but I'm scared to say it. It might just be a cruel joke, or an unfulfilled promise stolen away from us by such a pitiless world."

Harruq stared at her, and he felt the gears in his head slowly turning.

"You're not," he said.

She nodded, then broke into nervous laughter.

"For about two months now," she said. "We'll have another child, should we endure. You'll be a father, and I a mother."

He kissed her again and again, then pressed his forehead against hers as he felt his own tears building.

"We'll endure," he said. "And you should have told me sooner."

"I know. I love you, Harruq."

"I love you too, Aurry."

✥

"There are just so many," Lathaar said as Jerico sat beside him.

"Let them learn to pray for themselves this night," Jerico said in return. "You have your own prayers to make."

He chuckled as Lathaar nodded, as if reluctantly accepting the wisdom.

"How many of them die tomorrow?" Lathaar asked, gesturing to Antonil's army around them.

"All," he said. "None. Some may die tomorrow. Some the week after. Given enough time, all will die. At least they'll die fighting for something greater than themselves."

"Cold comfort to those they love."

"It is for those they love that they fight."

Lathaar threw up his hands in surrender. Jerico chuckled again, feeling like he dealt with a stubborn student.

"Will you be ready for tomorrow?" he asked.

"Of course."

"I'd prefer an honest answer, not the expected one."

Lathaar pressed his face into his palms and rubbed. He looked so exhausted...

"Ever since Mira died, I've found myself doubting. Where is Ashhur's strength? Where is the god I have put so much faith in? Our order is destroyed, with only you and me remaining. Everywhere his priests have been butchered. Hundreds of thousands have died in the past few years alone. So much death. So much loss. How do I trust Ashhur to protect me in the face of such tragedy?"

He fell silent and waited for his answer.

"I don't know," Jerico said at last. "Do we judge him by this world's failings? Is Ashhur wrong to ask us to forgive? Is he wrong when he asks us to help others? I know he's not, for a world where kindness and mercy are seen as weakness and folly...that is a world I don't want to live in. So I fight for the one I know. I fight for the one I love. We know little of the past and nothing of the future. In this bleak darkness, we must be a light even when others would fade. Don't blame yourself for doubting, Lathaar. Your question is honest, intelligent, and true. I wish I could give you a better answer."

Lathaar leaned closer toward the fire and stared at the burning embers.

"Yours will do for now," he said.

Tarlak scanned the distant walls of Mordeina with eyes magically enhanced by a spell. When Ahaesarus spoke beside him, the disorientation made him stumble, and with a quick jerk of his hand, he ended the spell.

"You will see nothing on the walls to prove your plan brilliant or folly," the angel said, offering the wizard a piece of bread. "But I think a warm bit of food will do you wonders."

Tarlak accepted it with a smile.

"Thousands of men about the camp, yet you come to me. Should I be flattered?"

"If it would make you feel better, then yes."

Both laughed.

"You seem remarkably human, once you get used to the wings and the fact that your arms are as big as tree trunks."

Ahaesarus smiled. "We were men, Tarlak. Being here on Dezrel…it brings back many memories, not all of them good, but most. I'm reminded of my sins as much as my triumphs. Truth be told, I miss the Golden Eternity. This world is cold and painful."

"I can imagine." Tarlak took a bite. "I bet the food is worse down here, too."

The angel tilted his head a moment, then nodded. "You're right. It is. Perhaps I think too much, and merely miss eating well."

Tarlak chuckled. "Good to know I'll still get to eat after I fall off this mortal coil. Wine, too? I mean, what's the point of eternity if I can't get tipsy every now and then?"

"Is this the closest you come to discussing theology, Tarlak?" the angel asked.

"Probably."

He broke the bread in half and shared it with Ahaesarus. As they ate, Tarlak stared once more to the north, remembering the walls he'd seen, the many torches and guards.

"It doesn't look good," he said. "Starting to think I'll be seeing my sister by tomorrow's end."

Ahaesarus put a hand on Tarlak's shoulder.

"I hope you do not mourn for her still. She is much beloved, and many she touched were there to greet her upon her arrival."

Tarlak's cheek quivered, and he no longer brought the bread to his lips, his appetite gone.

"You met her?" he asked.

"I did. She's beautiful, Tarlak, the kindness within her shining bright in a way your earthen eyes cannot see, nor understand until you've been there."

"If you die before me, I want you to tell her something. You owe me that. I want you to tell her how much I miss her, and that I can't wait to see her. And I want a hug when I get there, damn it, and I…"

"Enough," Ahaesarus said, gently shaking him. "You'll tell her yourself, dear friend. A day from now, a year, or twenty, it matters not. You'll tell her."

Tarlak forced himself to smile.

"It might not matter, but between you and me, I'd still prefer it to be twenty years from now rather than a day."

"Given how many of my own men are risking their lives, it seems inappropriate I be left out of your planning," Bram said to Antonil as they marched through their ranks. They offered shallow compliments as they passed, hoping to use their presence to keep morale high before the coming battle.

"I gathered with my friends, nothing more," said Antonil. "Our plans on the ground have not changed."

"Then you let your friends rule through you, instead of you ruling them."

They complimented several men still sparring despite the darkness, then continued on.

"I would be a fool to not heed their advice," Antonil said. "And though I command the men, the angels are no subjects of mine."

"Then whose are they? What lord do they swear to?"

"Ashhur, I guess."

Bram saluted a few times, then lowered his voice as he spoke.

"So in service to Ashhur, they are in service to no one but themselves. What if my soldiers decide that is the lord they would prefer? The priests already wield great influence. Karak's paladins held sway over our kings for over a century. My father was the first to defy them, and it nearly cost him his life."

"What are you saying, Bram?"

Bram remained silent for a moment, realizing he was letting his emotions get the best of him. He smiled and chatted with a random soldier, then continued.

"You've promised my nation independence, and I trust you to keep it. But what of your son, or your son's sons? With angels in the sky and priests guiding your decisions, how long until it is Ashhur who rules the land, not a king? Those who claim to speak for him will become rulers in all but name."

"Ahaesarus has no desire to rule, nor the priests."

"How do you know?" asked Bram. "The angels have been here but a short time. How many texts of Ashhur talk of a new kingdom created on the land of Dezrel? I will not have my home conquered in a holy war."

"That won't happen!"

"Then swear to me," said Bram. "Swear that for a hundred years, no angel enters my land. Give me your word now, and should we both survive the morrow, let it be entered into writing and declared to an entire court of witnesses."

"How can I swear for angels that I do not rule?"

"Then swear I may defend myself, and you will recognize my right to rule. I will not become a pawn of a theocracy."

They reached the edge of the camp, and Antonil kept his back to his soldiers as he frowned.

"You bring a foul temperament to what should have been a peaceful night," he said.

Bram grabbed his arm and forced him to turn and face him.

"I do what I must for my kingdom," he said. "What if I die, but you survive? I must hope your honor is great enough to carry through your promise and protect my wife. And what if you die? You have no heir, and the one chosen will most likely bear white wings. Must I beg to them in hopes they honor your promise made to me? No chances. No risks. I do this for my home, my family, my soldiers, my nation. That is the role of a king, Antonil. You are too trusting to put your back to your friends and your life in their hands. You will find a knife there one day, carved with jewels and bearing the symbol of the mountain."

"Enough!" Antonil said. "You have my word, still as true as when I first gave it to you. Now leave me be. I've heard enough insults to my name this night. Do you think I am a fool? Do you think I don't understand the great dangers to everything I hold dear? I will die a glorious king, or as the greatest failure to rule in the history of our nations. Now either unhand my shoulder or draw your sword."

They exchanged cold stares, neither moving, neither blinking.

"I'd always thought we could be close allies," Bram said as he pulled back his hand.

"We still could be."

Bram shook his head.

"Long as you hold council with paladins and angels, you are compromised. Forgive me, Antonil. You have impressed me with your courage, but after tomorrow, we are kings of adjacent nations, and nothing more."

For once, Velixar was too busy planning and praying to spend the night tormenting Qurrah, so he and Tess fled to the far reaches of the camp in hope of solitude. Without a fire, they cuddled together. So glad to have him there, she did not mind the chill of his skin.

"They are not far," Qurrah said, staring north. In the distance burned the fires of Antonil's camp, tiny spots glowing among the hills. "I wonder if Harruq is among them. Will I sense his death, if it happens? Or was he among the dead floating in the water when we crossed the Bloodbrick?"

"Your brother will find a better death than that," Tessanna said, gently stroking the dried blood on the front of his robe. "Though I fear he finds it tomorrow."

They fell silent, but Qurrah could not let the thought hang in the air unspoken.

"And at my hand," he whispered.

Tessanna closed her eyes and tilted her face into the cloth of his robe.

"We are slaves, you and I," she said. "What freedom is there for us? Can you fight him? Should he give the order, could you stay your hand?"

"I don't think so," he said. "Velixar has ruined me. He drove a wedge between us, helped kill Aullienna, and will now complete his work. As long as Harruq lives, he knows I will hold to hope. One by one, the pure moments of my past die.

You will be the last, I know it. I know it, and I can do nothing to stop it. This is the Abyss, Tessanna. Swords and fire cannot compare to my torment now. To know and yet be powerless to stop the sins I have been commanded to commit. What will I say when Harruq bleeds before me? What can I hope for other than my own death, and at his hand? A final death…"

She clutched him tight, and her sobs grew loud enough for him to hear.

"Don't talk like that," she said between sniffles. "Don't talk like there's no hope. There has to be. Damn every god and goddess if there isn't."

He felt his anger flare at her words, but she was right, and he wished that he had something, anything, to say to convince her things would turn out all right. But what could he say? What lies did he know that she would believe?

"I love you, Tess," he said. "Everything else is cold and frightening. But I do love you. Please know that."

She curled into a ball on his lap and shivered as his arms surrounded her.

"If only your body was as warm as your words," she said. "Dead or alive, Qurrah, I'll always be yours. Never forget that."

"I promise," he said.

28

There was only one plan Bernard would accept, and he told them of it that morning.

"Everywhere people whisper of Antonil's return," he told the two assassins while they gathered within the small basement of an Ashhur sympathizer. "And you yourself saw the many fires in the distance. Whatever chance they have, it dies against the dragon Melorak has summoned."

"You don't know that," Veliana insisted.

"How many soldiers could they have?" Bernard asked. "Even with the angels' help, they will die by the hundreds against that beast. It must be destroyed. You saw how weak Melorak looked. The strain of keeping that dragon in existence must be a heavy toll. Against him, I have a chance."

"Then let us come with you," Deathmask said. "He'll have guards, paladins…"

The priest shook his head.

"He'll have his undead, and they are nothing to me. The rest will be at the wall. This is the last battle, and he knows it. Even if he has a few guards, I must rely on his pride to accept a challenge. I am a priest of his most hated enemy, and to refuse would be a sign of weakness, a direct insult he will not dare allow. You two must find a way to get Antonil inside the city."

Deathmask rolled his eyes.

"We meet here in a dark cellar, just the three of us, so you can tell me and Vel to go open the massive gates to the two walls? Have you lost your mind, old man?"

Bernard smiled. "Perhaps. But Haern is still out there, and as long as we are separate, he will hunt for you. I need him far and away, unable to help Melorak should the duel turn to my favor. The city is ripe for rebellion. The oppression is too heavy, too brutal. Find a way to get Antonil into Mordeina's streets, and the Lionsguard will be crushed beneath their heels."

"Reckless and stupid," Veliana said. "You ask for the impossible. Thousands of soldiers and archers will line every inch of that wall. Deathmask's magic is strong, but even he can't pulverize doors that enormous."

"I have faith you'll find a way," the priest said, placing a hand on each of their shoulders.

"And I have faith in nothing," Deathmask said. "Other than that we're all going to die if we do this."

"I'd hoped you'd have a bit more faith than that," Bernard said.

Deathmask slipped the gray cloth over his scarred face and scattered ash into the air.

"I do," he said as the ash revolved around his head. "Faith that I'll kill plenty before I meet the reaper-man. Go with your god, Bernard. If he's not too far gone, maybe he'll send us a miracle. Right now, we need one."

Ashhur's army marched for the capital before dawn had fully bloomed, determined to lose no distance to Thulos's chasing army. The Eschaton stayed with Ahaesarus and his angels, who walked upon the ground in an attempt to give hope and cheer to the many soldiers.

"How far back are they?" Tarlak asked after a half hour's march.

Ahaesarus motioned for one of his few scouts in the air. The angel swooped low and gave his report.

"Two miles at most," said the angel. "And gaining fast."

"They'll come upon us before we can even reach the first of the walls," Tarlak said, frowning.

"Then we have little time to spare," said Ahaesarus. "When the battle starts, we will fly to Avlimar and set up formations. The display should be enough to goad Thulos into battle."

"Don't forget to bring us with you," said Harruq. "I want my crack at that Thulos."

"You had one back in Veldaren," Aurelia said, her frown showing what she thought of the idea. "You ended up with a horrible wound in your chest."

"Still breathing, though," Harruq said. "And now I've got something to pay him back for!"

Twenty minutes later they crossed through a thin collection of hills, weaving through them along a well-worn path in the grass. Mordeina came into view, banners waving from her walls. High above, Avlimar glittered like a second sun.

"Urge them on," Ahaesarus said to Antonil after receiving another report from his scout. "We might not reach the walls at the pace they chase!"

Onward they marched, the great city of Mordeina growing ever closer. Harruq felt his nerves gather in his throat, and he started wishing the battle would begin at any moment. Their run to the city didn't feel like an attack; it felt like a desperate retreat. Perhaps it even was. Most likely they would die crushed against the walls. Still, if they were lucky, they might take a god with them before the end.

The city loomed nearer. The banners flapped in the soft breeze, close enough now for them to read their sigils. They saw the many archers lining the walls, more than enough to make the half-orc shiver. They would assault under a rain of arrows, of that he was certain. He looked back to the thousands that followed, a collected force from Neldar, Ker, and Mordan. Armies of three nations, come together against the might of Karak. And that wasn't counting the angels and war demons...

"This is going to get bloody," he muttered, shaking his head.

Aurelia squeezed his hand, showing she heard. He kissed her cheek and continued on marching.

They were trampling the short grass upon the fields before the walls when the scout returned once more, this time looking frightened.

"A quarter of a mile, if that," he said. "They have thousands of what appear to be undead, plus many more soldiers travelling behind them. Thulos himself must be whipping their tails given how fast they march."

Ahaesarus spread his wings. They were mere minutes from the wall, and slowing down to form ranks. The battle was upon them.

"Come with me," Ahaesarus said, offering his hand to Aurelia. Judarius offered his arms to Harruq, who grudgingly accepted.

"Don't drop me, eh?" he said.

"I'll try," said the angel. "Though all those losses in sparring might have loosened my grip a little."

Harruq glanced to Tarlak, who only shook his head and laughed a hollow laugh.

"Be safe you two," the wizard said. Then they were gone, soaring into the air in the arms of the angels. Harruq felt a momentary spell of dizziness at the sudden height, followed by exhilaration. That exhilaration turned to fear when they turned to see the great host giving chase. The war demons fluttered into ranks, hovering over the lines of warriors. Harruq craned his head to watch Antonil and Bram rearrange their own forces into two lines. One enormous line moved toward the city gates. A much smaller line remained put, and it seemed like it would be only a stumbling block against the attackers.

Harruq said a quick prayer for those chosen to be in that last line, then looked to the sky. They climbed higher and higher until they were far above the city, and the battlefield below looked like a collection of ants scurrying toward one another. Avlimar glittered before him, stunning in its golden beauty and pearl walls.

"Wait here," Judarius said as he set the half-orc down on one of the large clearings along the outer edges, designed for the angels to easily land and take wing from. Ahaesarus arrived with Aurelia moments later, and she smiled at Harruq as she stepped onto the comforting stone.

"We will fight only a little while in the air," Ahaesarus said as Judarius flapped his wings and took off. "Then we will retreat further in. Ashhur's blessing permeates every single brick and hall. It is within here we will make our stand."

"If you see a demon carrying a priest of Karak, you let him land, eh?" Harruq said. "I want the privilege of killing Velixar, not some very, very long fall."

"I will consider," said the angel before joining the rest of his kind.

Suddenly they were alone, the city calm and empty behind them. Only the angels flew circles about, spread wide to exaggerate their numbers. Aurelia took his hand as they stood to watch.

"Stay with me," she said. "Please, just stay with me until the end."

He pulled her fingers to his lips and kissed them.

"Until the end," he said.

◆◆◆

"They flee to their golden city," Thulos said as the angels of Ashhur took flight. Velixar watched as he strode alongside the war god at the front of the army.

"Just the angels," he said. "What plan do they have?"

"The height," Thulos said. He pointed to where the rest of the army hurried toward the walls. "If we assault the ground troops, they will dive down atop us. In aerial combat, this is equivalent to us putting our backs to their blades. Too great a risk for a fight we are set to win. Let them choose their place of combat. Their blood will stain gold as well as grass."

Velixar nodded as he watched the angels fly. He cast a spell to enhance his vision, hoping to better see their numbers. As they flew, he felt a smile spread across his ever-changing face. There, hanging in the arms of one of the angels...

Harruq. It had to be.

"Who will command the ground troops?" Velixar asked.

Thulos gave him a surprised look. "I presumed it would be you."

"Give the honor to Myann. He has been cross ever since our failure at the Bloodbrick. I wish to go with you."

"And why is that, prophet? Do you desire to slay angels? Are mere mortals no longer worthy of your judgment?"

Velixar made sure he answered in total calm.

"There is one among the angels whom I have long sought after. I wish him to join me, or die at my feet. He helped bring you into our world, and he deserves a chance to repent."

"Repent?" asked Thulos. "You are a strange one, Velixar. So be it. I will give Myann control. You may come with me in the arms of my demons. Just do not get in my way, nor presume my warriors will give any reprieve. If your...friend dies at their hands, do not bring the matter to me."

Thulos raised a fist and shouted orders. Velixar ignored him, instead pushing through the ranks of his undead until reaching where Qurrah and Tessanna marched hand in hand. He frowned at such contact, and a single thought to the half-orc forced him to let go.

"We go to the golden city," he said, unable to contain his joy. "We go to end this once and for all. Your brother and your lover, Qurrah; they will both be there. Let us see just where your heart truly lies."

He flagged down a demon and ordered others to be brought with him. The demon cursed him but obeyed. Two more arrived, and in their arms, the three soared with the rest into the air, flying higher and higher toward the angels of Ashhur. Velixar gave his undead a single order, one they would follow until they beat their fists against the walls of Mordeina: slay the living before you.

"A glorious day," he shouted to Qurrah, who was too far away to hear due to the roaring wind in their ears.

The three carrying them stayed back as the forces collided. The demons swung their glaives and flung their spears, spilling blood like rain to the ground far below. The angels weaved and cut just as viciously, and Velixar felt the exhilaration growing within him. He wished to help but could not, not until they were closer and he felt firm ground beneath his feet. The angels merged from their spread out pattern into a thin stream of warriors, and they sliced through the demon ranks like cloth.

Then Thulos arrived. An enormous pair of crimson wings stretched from slots in the armor on his back, and he cut angels down left and right, tumbling their severed bodies to the battle below. After he killed a score, the rest retreated into the city in a stream of feathers and gold armor. The demons carrying the three closed in, and on one of the many landing platforms set them down.

"Stay with me," Velixar said to the two. Shadows sparked off his fingertips, as if unable to contain the killing magic he so desperately wished to unleash. "Aid me in killing the angels, Qurrah. Let us put your strength to good use."

⊷⊶

Tarlak stood between the paladins, watching the army approach. They were but a thousand, a thin line to catch the brunt of Thulos's strength. All around the men stood with grim faces and naked blades.

"I can slow and disrupt the charge," Tarlak said. "Once they're here, just keep me alive and my spells will tear them to pieces. Oh, and don't die yourselves, all right?"

"We'll try our best," Jerico said. He saluted the wizard. "But try to keep us alive as well. It only seems fair."

"What, I have to kill great hordes of attackers *and* babysit you two? Now you're asking too much."

Lathaar started chuckling, but not at Tarlak's joke. When he couldn't stop, Jerico asked him what was so humorous.

"Don't you see?" he said, pointing to the coming throng.

"See what?" asked Jerico.

"His army. Nearly half of it is undead."

"More undead?" Jerico's face spread into a wicked grin. "Is that so?"

They lumbered closer, poorly armed and armored, and only a few hundred yards away.

"Personally, I'm sick of killing undead," Tarlak said, fire bursting around his hands. "But you two have the time of your lives."

He hurled balls of fire, which soared across the distance and detonated, roasting tens at a time. He followed up with a pair of boulders he ripped out of the ground behind him, sending them crashing through the ranks. All around, the soldiers saw Tarlak's display and cheered.

"Getting close," Jerico said.

"I know," Lathaar said.

He sheathed his shortsword and held his longsword with both hands. With his eyes closed, Lathaar prayed to Ashhur, hoping his faith was not lost. He still felt doubt clawing at him, but in this he felt certain. In this, he knew his place.

"Elholad," he whispered.

His sword turned to a blade of purest light, the white rolling off it in thin waves like frost off a pond in the morning. Lathaar let out a breath he didn't know he'd been holding and then looked to the charging undead.

"Don't let them pass!" he cried to his allies, his voice carrying to the thousand. "Do not retreat a step. They are dead. They are mindless. We are the living. We are the strong. Slay them, men of Dezrel! Show the gods your strength!"

Tarlak punctuated his sentence with a bolt of lightning, the boom rolling over them matched only by the roar of the undead crashing into the line. And hold they did, slamming their shields and stabbing their swords as the undead fell, and fell, until they formed a barrier for their own.

Clamoring over the pile of dead, they lunged at the defenders, clawing and biting at their armor. In the very center, Lathaar and Jerico fought like the paragons they were. Lathaar's sword sliced through the throng while Jerico's shield exploded their bodies into bones and dust with every slam. Tarlak did his best to aid the rest, hurling bolts of lightning up and down the lines.

Hundreds died, but as the wall before them grew, Thulos lost far more.

"No fear!" Lathaar cried, and his words carried the blessing of Ashhur. "Feel no fear, no sorrow, no pain!"

The line, which had begun to weaken, suddenly surged forward, cutting down the undead. Blood soaked their armor, and rot coated their blades. The ground rumbled as Tarlak summoned a few more boulders, rolling them just behind the pile of dead to crush hundreds, giving them a moment's breather before the rest hit. The assault continued relentless, but they gained no ground. A thousand fell, their bodies robbed of the false life given to them by Velixar.

But a thousand more pressed on.

Jerico let out a cry to Ashhur and shoved his shield forward. Light burst from its surface. The nearest undead collapsed, unable to endure, while hundreds more in all directions stumbled as if suddenly robbed of sight. Lances of ice plowed through their ranks, and the defenders surged forward yet again, cutting them down.

"We've got them!" Tarlak shouted, leaning over as he caught his breath. The undead were scattered and few, easy prey for the defenders. A quick estimate showed they still had seven hundred standing against Thulos's men…all four thousand of them.

"Well," Jerico said as the first wave approached. "At least we built a wall."

Tarlak laughed and cracked his knuckles.

"Time for another…"

He stopped as a great roar echoed through the valley, so powerful that even Thulos's conscripts halted.

"What the abyss was that?" he asked, and then he turned and saw it.

The creature soared out of Mordeina, black smoke billowing after. It flew a single circle above Antonil's troops, then plummeted, scattering men like they were playthings.

"That's not good," Lathaar said, and Tarlak couldn't contain his laughter at the greatest understatement he'd heard in years.

"No," he said, turning his attention back to the conscripts resuming their charge, hesitant as if they also were afraid of the great beast slaughtering men by the hundreds. "No, I think I can safely say we're all fucked."

❈

Bernard left for the castle, and Deathmask and Veliana moved for the wall. But instead of going straight for it, Deathmask veered them back to the castle and found a large mansion with a gently sloping roof.

"Why are we here?" Veliana asked as Deathmask looked for a way to climb up.

"I'm tired of being hunted," he said, grabbing a windowsill and pulling. "Now help me before I embarrass myself."

She boosted his foot so he could plant it on the sill, then grab a hold of the roof and climb up. Veliana used a similar maneuver, though she needed no help, and her lithe body landed atop the roof with a soft thud.

"Show off," Deathmask said, winking.

"What is it we're waiting for?" she asked. "Can't you see? The battle is about to start!"

She pointed to where the demons flew toward Avlimar in diamond formations. Deathmask ignored her, for he kept his gaze to the castle.

"Just wait," he said.

"For what?"

He glared at her through the gray mask. "I said wait."

Minutes crawled. With her arms crossed, Veliana watched the battle in the sky vanish into the interior of Avlimar. Deathmask knew she wondered why they hadn't made for the wall like Bernard asked them, but then Rakkar announced its presence with a great roar that shook the city. It tore into the sky, breathing fire and spreading smoke with each beat of its wings. It sailed right over them, the passing of its shadow chilling both to the bone.

"Go," Deathmask said, suddenly urging Veliana toward the castle. "Help Bernard, and quickly!"

"What? But he asked…"

"I don't care what he asked!" Deathmask shouted, grabbing her wrist and pulling her close. "He is a fool if he thinks the two of us can get that army inside. This city lives or dies by Melorak's hand. Go, while the dragon is gone!"

She pulled her wrist free and glared.

"And you? What will you do?"

Deathmask pointed far down the street, where Haern ran along the rooftops toward them.

"There's a reason we're up here," he said, grinning. "Like I said, I'm tired of being the hunted. Go. Kill the priest-king, and I'll deal with our stalker."

She kissed her palm and then blew it to him.

"You better live, you bastard," she said before leaping off the roof.

Deathmask cracked his neck and looked to Haern.

"Planned on it," he said as the assassin landed before him, his sabers drawn. He leered up at him with his dead eyes. Deathmask saw a hint of recognition in them and wondered just how loose Melorak's control had grown. With both the dragon and the assassin to dominate, he had to be stretched thin. Perhaps that would gain him an advantage. Or perhaps it would let more of Haern's skill return, and he'd die in seconds. Only one way to find out.

"An age ago, you and I dominated an entire city," he said as Haern remained crouched and ready to lunge. He kept a spell ready, the single word of power eager on his lips. "It is such a disgrace to see you like this. Let me end it, Watcher. Let me send you to the grave, free from the priest-king's taint."

Still Haern remained, watching, waiting. Deathmask gave him no sign of attack. He would not be goaded into making the first move.

"Can you even understand me?" he asked. "Or is your brain rotted and worthless, your soul just a mindless ghost following orders…"

In the distance, Rakkar roared, and Haern lunged with it, his movements a sudden blur. Deathmask cast his spell. Fire burst in a circle around him, soaring twenty feet high in a great circular pillar. Haern twisted to the side, pulling back from his killing lunge. He was just a half-seen shadow but Deathmask tracked him best he could and then guessed at a landing. When the fire lowered, he slammed his hands together. The pillar exploded anew, this time further down the roof. Haern twisted, landing on one hand and then remaining like that as the fire surrounded him.

"I've got you," Deathmask said, grinning.

Haern suddenly vanished and reappeared several feet to his right, still standing on his hand.

Neat trick, he thought as the assassin dove underneath his barrage of shadow bolts. He jumped and rolled in a circle, constantly seeking his back. Deathmask kept spinning, flinging shadow and conjuring fire in a desperate offense. The second he relented, and Haern closed the gap, he knew he was dead. He kept a ring of fire about him, ready to erupt in a moment's notice. Once he thought Haern ready to stab, but it was just a feint, and he wasted yet another bit of his concentration ripping the fire into a wall to protect himself.

In the light of the flame, he lost sight of Haern. Knowing he had erred, and badly, he crouched down and activated one last spell. Bat wings stretched from his back, and he lifted into the air, hoping to put as much distance between them as he could. A blade slashed his leg as Haern lunged, and he screamed as the blood ran down. He flapped the ethereal wings harder. Haern twisted as he fell, hit the roof, and then leaped as if gravity were a nuisance he could ignore at will. Stunned, Deathmask flung several orbs of fire, all missing. Haern slammed into him, cutting and slicing. They fell, a jumbled collection of wings, cloaks, and swords.

Deathmask landed atop of Haern, and he dismissed the wings. Pain flared up and down his chest, and he knew he had a dozen cuts. One of Haern's sabers lay far to the side, a wonderful blessing if he'd ever seen one. Deathmask clutched the wrist that held the other, and it took all his strength to keep it pressed against the rooftop. With his free hand he reached for Haern's face, fire swarming about his skin. Haern grabbed his wrist and held on, keeping back the deadly flame.

"Just a little fire," Deathmask said, gritting his teeth and flinging all the force of his weight down on his arm. Still Haern held back. The burning hand inched closer, closer. Haern's eyes locked on his, and they stared, watching, struggling. The hand lowered once more. And then it rose. His strength was not enough. Deathmask felt horror rise in his throat as the assassin began lifting him off.

"Don't you do this," Deathmask shouted. "Goddamn it, remember who you are! Remember who you serve!"

The muscles in his neck stretched, and he pushed down with all his might. If he could just touch Haern with his hand, just once, for only a moment…

"Delysia…" Haern suddenly whispered. The hand wavered. As they stared, Deathmask watched recognition slowly bloom in his eyes. The hand lowered. And lowered. And then, with one sudden tug, Haern flung Deathmask's hand against his cold dead face. As the fire burned, he smiled.

"Rest well," Deathmask said as the decaying body burst into flame, the gray robes and cloaks billowing smoke as they were consumed. He stepped back, tightened the cloth about his face, and looked to the wall. The archers atop fired volley after volley, and still he heard Rakkar roar. He might not be able to open the gates, but perhaps he could still help. He scooped a bit of the ash of Haern's corpse, flung it, and set it into motion about his face. With the mask complete, he climbed down to the street.

It was time the Ghost ignited the fires of rebellion.

⚔

Bernard knelt in prayer, hidden in a small alcove between two homes. If he'd looked up and opened his eyes, he would have seen the row of guards standing at the top of the steps guarding the castle doors. But he didn't, not for several minutes more. At last, when he felt any more delay would be cowardice only, he stood and approached. The guards drew their swords, but they were only four.

"Let me pass, and no harm will come to you," he said.

"Get lost," said one.

"Wait, I recognize those robes," said another. "He's a priest. Arrest him!"

"That wouldn't be wise," said Bernard.

When the first reached for his arm, Bernard turned his palm toward the soldier's face and spoke a word of power. Blinding light burst outward, and the man screamed and stumbled back. His foot slipped on the stairs, and then he rolled down them, landing hard on the street below. The second guard swung his sword, but the priest stepped back and clapped his hands. Two orbs of light flared into existence as his hands opened, then shot directly into his attacker's chest. The guard collapsed, his limbs shaking wildly.

The other two rushed at once, trying to close the distance. Bernard wore no armor, and wielded no blade to defend himself. It didn't matter. He blinded one, then made a slashing motion with his hand. A golden blade shimmered in the air, appearing just long enough to cut him down before fading away. Another slash with his hand, and the final guard toppled, blind and bleeding from a gash across his throat.

"A bad idea," the priest muttered, pulling open the castle doors and stepping inside.

He gasped at the sight within. Men and women hung from hooks along the walls, like slabs of meat at a butcher's hall. They stared with naked eyes, their lids sliced off. At his entrance they writhed against the hooks and reached out, moaning in warning. A shiver of fear ran through him, quickly replaced by anger.

"Such disrespect toward life," he said, taking a step toward the nearest. "You sad, wretched thing. Rest now. Death comes for you with its sweet respite."

His hand glowed a soft white, and then the corpse turned to dust, the dark magic within it unable to withstand such power. He looked to the others, spreading his arms toward each side of the hall.

"Be gone!" he cried, washing the grand entrance with his faith. The undead shook as if in great pain, and then went still. One by one they fell to the floor, their flesh now dust and their bones broken clay. A foreboding silence replaced their wails, and through the dust Bernard strode down the hall toward the throne room.

Even through the stone walls, he heard Rakkar's roar signaling its departure for the battlefield. Bernard offered a quick prayer for those who would face its wrath, then continued on. It was Rakkar that he had come to stop. Melorak was its ruler, its link to the world. It was time to end the priest-king and save Mordeina from his madness.

The throne room was equally defiled by the dead, and he spent a moment to give them the peace they'd been denied. He'd expected Melorak to be there, but was not. Closing his eyes, he let his magical senses wander. He was less attuned than any wizard or necromancer, but in matters of faith, his sense was strong, though it didn't matter. Melorak pulsed like a giant heart of darkness. It was like searching for a mountain with the eyes of a hawk.

He passed down the stone hallways, turning every now and then should he wander too far. He kept his hands at his sides, glowing with the light of Ashhur. His fingertips brushed the undead along the walls, turning them to dust and silencing their groans. At last he stepped into what had once been a garden, before Karak had had his way with it. Ugly runes covered the dead grass, carved with blood. The few trees were barren, their branches shriveled into themselves. In the center, amid torn earth, stood Melorak.

"I've wondered when I would meet you again," he said, slowly opening his eyes. They had a distant look to them, as if he were half-asleep. He smiled, his lone good eye smoldering red. "Perhaps you don't remember me, but I remember you. For twenty years you resisted the inevitable, protecting your pathetic temple to Ashhur while my faithful conquered the hearts and minds of the people."

"What was your name?" Bernard asked. The hairs on his neck stood on end, and he felt a wave of anxiety sweep over him. There, in that blasted clearing, he seemed so far away from Ashhur.

"It doesn't matter," said Melorak. "For I have a new name, one given to me by the true god of this world. I am the heir to Velixar, the right fang of the Lion. Can you hear its roar? Even now, my beautiful creation slaughters the last remnants that still swear their faith to Ashhur."

Bernard forced himself to calm. Ashhur hadn't gone anywhere. His faith was strong. It was only the foul sensation, the total culmination of a thousand prayers to Karak, gathered there in that clearing to take physical form in the beast, Rakkar. He still felt its echo, its taint. Light swirled around his hands as Melorak laughed.

"You cannot challenge me," he said. "You are nothing. Did you see the demons give chase to your angels? Even Avlimar is not safe. Karak will soon walk free. If you leave now, I will let you live to see his glorious return. Perhaps when you look upon his beautiful face you will throw yourself down and beg forgiveness for a lifetime of transgressions."

"You have not yet won," said Bernard.

Again Melorak laughed.

"Not yet, perhaps, but the time is coming. This is the end. Can you not feel it?"

The white light grew in his palms.

"Yes, I can. You are right about that. It is indeed the end."

Bernard pressed his wrists together and opened his palms. A beam of pure white light shot forth, releasing with a great crack that blew away the dead grass and rattled the gnarled branches. Melorak crossed his arms and summoned a shield of shadows. The light met the darkness. The ground shook from the impact. The shield held, but Bernard gave him no reprieve. He made slashing motions with his fingers, and golden swords shimmered into existence, hovering in the air directly before Melorak. They broke against the shield, unable to penetrate.

Melorak grabbed a chunk of dirt and flung it. Shadows swarmed about the projectile, and Bernard summoned his own shield. When the projectile struck, it exploded into a hundred lances of shadow, which splashed across the white dome protecting the priest.

"There is no chance for you," Melorak said, hurling bolt after bolt of darkness. He didn't seem to care that they splashed harmlessly against the shield, for he surely knew every impact drained a bit more of Bernard's energy. Bernard felt a moment of doubt but shrugged it away. He'd come to die. He'd made peace with that. The only thing that mattered was that he took Melorak with him, or at the very least, weakened his control over the dragon long enough for the others to stand a chance.

"Such certainty," Bernard said, dismissing his shield and slamming his palms to the ground.

A shockwave traveled across the dirt, throwing chunks to either side. In its very center swirled an orb of silver. Melorak leapt aside, knowing he could not protect against it. The orb struck the stone wall and then continued on, blasting a hole in the castle before continuing through. Bernard stood before the great trench it'd created and unleashed a second.

This time Melorak spun, his body rapidly cocooned with shadows. Just before the orb reached him, he vanished. Bernard summoned another shield, expecting an attack. He was right, for atop the tree Melorak reappeared, a beam of darkness already screaming from his palms. Bernard braced his legs and gasped as it hit. His head throbbed, and he felt his body slide several feet back along the grass. He was old, while Melorak was young and blessed with an unnatural life. His features shifted and changed, masking the death and rot behind. For some reason, Bernard felt anger at such an illusion. How dare he assume supremacy while hiding from what he was?

"Enough!" he cried, flinging aside the beam and then slamming his hands together. A wave of magic rolled over Melorak, dispelling the illusion. The red light left his eye, becoming a dull brown. The shifting of his features ended, revealing gray flesh pockmarked and in full rot. When he snarled, his lips drew back to reveal rotting teeth crawling with maggots.

"How dare you?" Melorak spat. He stood to his full height, two dark voids growing across his hands. "What is it you hope to prove? I have conquered death! I live when all others would have died! I am Karak's chosen. I am his beloved! Look upon me with fear, you pathetic mortal priest. I am the hand of the true god, and I do not fear your faith."

He flung the orbs, hollow, empty things that seemed to tear all light into them and snuff it out. Bernard summoned his shield, but then screamed at their contact. He felt his strength pouring away, the light swirling into them before becoming mixed with the nothingness. His mind blanked, and then he collapsed. The ground spun beneath him, and his breath came in wheezes. When he looked up, he saw Melorak glaring down, his face still a visage of death and decay.

"Tell Ashhur the walls of the Eternity grow ever thinner," Melorak said. "Tell him I come for him next, marching at the right hand of Karak himself."

He grinned, then suddenly staggered back as three daggers lodged deep into his face and throat. Despite such horrible wounds, he glared at the intruder. Bernard reached up, fighting off a swirling sense of vertigo to grab Melorak's wrist. Light shone about his fingertips.

"Only dead," he whispered. The spell flared out of him, powered by his faith. Melorak shrieked, first out of surprise, then agony. His rotted flesh turned to dust. His bones snapped and fell. Dark, ethereal strands of magic, like trapped spirits, soared out of his robe. And then Bernard held only a thin piece of bone.

"You stupid old bastard," Veliana said, standing over him with her hand offered. Her grin was ear to ear. "Deathmask thought you might need some help."

He accepted her hand. She pulled him to his feet, and he grabbed her shoulders to steady himself.

"Thank you," he said, leaning his weight against her. "Forgive me for not asking for your aid earlier. I guess I still succumb to the sin of pride."

"Enough of sins," she said, wrapping an arm around his waist. "Let's get to the streets. Our part in this is not over."

Bernard chuckled. "May an old man catch his breath first?"

There in the ruined garden, they heard a vicious roar, from deep within the throat of Rakkar.

"No," Veliana said, stepping toward the entrance. She stopped, drew her dagger, and looked back to Melorak's corpse. "Actually, yes. There's one thing I need first before we can go…"

29

He'd been told to trust the priests to open a way through the walls, but Antonil found himself doubting. They walked ahead of the soldiers, the one called Keziel leading the rest. They were but a handful, while the wall towered before them, white stone immensely thick. They seemed so diminutive in comparison.

"We've got no siege weaponry," said Sergan, riding beside him. "We entrust the success of our entire attack to those priests. No rope, no catapults, no ladders, no siege towers. We're doomed, completely doomed."

"Such optimism," Antonil said, though he felt similar sentiments. He glanced once more to the priests, then angled his horse over to speak with them.

"How much closer?" he asked as he trotted along.

"Just outside the range of their archers, if possible," Keziel said.

Antonil looked behind, to where the thousand stood to defend their rear. High above, the angels had begun their battle.

"No time," he said. "Begin now, if you can."

"Continue to the wall," the priest said. "Trust us, and we will fulfill our obligation."

He rode back to Sergan and relayed the information.

"Ride on?" he asked. "They're mad, right? They don't even want us to wait and see if they can make it through? This is suicide, Antonil. We can't. Turn back. Let's aid in the fight behind, and then conquer the city at our leisure."

Antonil looked to the priests, and then to the far end of the line, where Bram rode with his knights.

"No," he said. "No, we trust them. I won't doubt them, not now."

Sergan followed his gaze, saw Bram, and then lifted an eyebrow.

"What's this got to do with him?" he asked.

"Consider it opposing views of how to be a king. Send the men on."

The priests stopped, gathered together for a moment of prayer, and then turned to the wall.

"Keep our sight clear!" Keziel shouted, and the men shifted to either side, giving them a gap in the lines. Antonil thought about staying beside them, then rode on. He would not remain behind and appear the coward. His thousands continued their rush to the walls of Mordeina, though he felt a moment of despair when Bram's knights remained back.

"He keeps himself and his most trusted safe," Sergan said. "The cowardly sot."

"They'll charge when the walls fall," Antonil said. "I hope."

The priests' prayers echoed louder, and they knelt with their palms facing the wall. A great beam shot forth, collected together from their power, and then pressed against the city gate. The wood and stone buckled, and even from that distance they could hear it cracking.

"I'll be damned," Sergan said. "Hey, keep those men away from that...that...whatever the Abyss that thing is!"

The soldiers spread further away from the beam, and they charged with renewed hope.

And then the roar swept over them from the city. A great beast soared over the walls, looped about, and then dived for the charging men, its reptilian wings folded against its sides. Smoke trailed after it, as if billowing from its obsidian scales. Again it roared, and the wave of sound was like a fear curse placed upon every member of Antonil's army. They stopped and trembled, with many turning to flee.

"What is *that?*" Sergan asked, his jaw hanging open.

"It can't be," Antonil said, watching as it circled high above them. "Only stories, nighttime tales...a dragon. They don't exist. They can't."

The creature swooped low, belching dark fire in a wide arc. Antonil veered his horse to the side to avoid the last of it. Those caught in the blast rolled and screamed, their bodies covered with a clear liquid that burned black. The dragon circled again, then dived, and this time Antonil had the wits to issue a command.

"Attack!" he screamed at the top of his lungs. "Attack now, or we all die!"

He led the rush, bolting his horse directly into the dragon's path. The creature slammed into the ground, barreling through soldiers like they were twigs. It snapped and lunged, biting men in half. Those who tried to face it stopped before its great claws, as if confused how to attack. Its tail whipped left and right, breaking legs with each snap. Their archers fired arrows, but they plinked off without a dent. All thought to attack the walls halted in the face of that monster.

Antonil rode through his men, spurring his horse on. When he reached the dragon his mount leapt, and he swung his sword in a desperate arc. Men gave chase after, those brave enough to die at the side of their king. All Antonil saw was dark scales and burning eyes, and enormous teeth opened to engulf him. He slashed the scales across the dragon's snout, but his sword bounced off. Its warm breath blew against him. He felt more than saw the bite. He flew against the dragon's side as his horse screeched in pain, its body torn in two. Antonil dug his sword between the scales and held on for dear life while his men clamored toward it, slashing at its claws and stabbing at its face.

Seeing his men die, Antonil twisted the blade and rammed it deeper in until blood poured across his hands, black as ink. The dragon twisted once, then belched fire across the field, burning hundreds alive. Again he twisted the blade, but it didn't seem to matter. His army was lost. They would die without ever reaching the walls. So much for his throne. So much for his plans. They'd crumbled before the teeth and scales of Karak's pet.

"Not yet," he growled. He was just beneath the wing, and as it flapped he reached up and grabbed another scale, careful to lay flat against the body to avoid the spikes along the bone. When his grip was secure, he pulled his sword free and stabbed it higher. As if scaling a mountain, his sword his pick, he ascended amid the screams of the dying. At last he reached the dragon's back, its spine protruding through the flesh. He tried stabbing it, but the bone was too hard. His sword only slid aside.

Suddenly the dragon howled and leapt back, shaking from side to side. Antonil held on to the bone and looked to see what was the matter. Bram's knights had come riding in, hurling spears toward the dragon's face. The horses still circled, just outside the reach of its tail. When it turned to belch fire, those at its sides lunged in and thrust their swords through the grooves of its scales. As it turned, Antonil saw the priests' spell had ended, they too having given up on the wall. Instead he saw golden chains lash around the dragon's claws and face. It scratched and tore at them, but the distraction was enough for the footmen to assault. They died by the hundreds, but inky blood covered their corpses, stab after stab wounding the great beast.

"Its neck!" he heard someone shout, and the rest took up the cry. "Go for its neck!"

The men swarmed its front, and Bram's knights threw the last of their spears for its throat. As the blood continued to pour, the dragon beat its wings and tried to flee, but then came more glittering shackles. Kept landlocked by the priests' will, it started flailing and biting, slaughtering more and more in a horrific display of blood.

Forcing himself to look away, Antonil climbed along the spine toward the dragon's head, stopping only when its flailing was too much for him to move. At one point it reared back, and the ridge of its spine slammed into his chin. Blood filled his mouth, and he swore he'd bit his tongue in two. He turned, spat, and then continued on, his sword still clutched tight in hand. When he reached the neck, he lay flat and found a groove where the vertebrae connected. Before he could strike, the beast shuddered and screamed. Its flesh turned a sickly color, as if it had suddenly lost much of its strength. Not willing to waste such an opportunity, Antonil stabbed the sword with all his strength deep into the spine. This time the dragon's shriek was a lengthy wail. Its wings crumpled, and it collapsed to the field, whole body shaking. Antonil clutched the hilt and endured the violent throes. The remaining footmen swarmed over it like ants, stabbing and hacking it to pieces. Blood spilled across the battlefield like a black pool.

When at last it lay still, Antonil withdrew his sword and stood atop the corpse. He raised the blade high and hollered a mindless cry of victory to his troops. Bram's knights did not stay, for they were already riding south, to where their flank had weakened to the point of crumbling.

"Antonil the Dragon Slayer!" someone shouted as he climbed down, and others quickly took up the cry. A soldier brought him a horse, and he mounted it on shaking legs.

"Gather up," he said. "Back to formations! We still have a city to take!"

They cheered despite the thousands that lay dead around them, nearly a third of their force. He rode to the priests, who had gathered to resume their spell.

"Can you get us through?" he asked.

"We shall see," Keziel said. A grin tugged at his lips. "I'd hate to disappoint the Dragon Slayer."

Antonil laughed and slapped the priest on the back, leaving an inky handprint atop the white cloth. Trusting Bram to protect their flank, and the priests to open the way to the city, he rode back to the front and urged his army on. The white beam shot forth, slamming into the city gates. Already weakened, they crumbled and broke, gaining them access to the ground between the two walls. The beam continued, striking the thick stone. Though it seemed almost unaffected, Antonil urged them on.

⚔

"Keep them off of me!" Tarlak cried as he dropped to one knee, avoiding a swing that would have cut off his head. He flicked his hand, and a thin bolt of electricity arced into the soldier. As his muscles broke into spasms, Lathaar spun about and cut him down.

"Trying!" Jerico shouted back. He slammed his shield forward, its light flaring over the many attackers. They winced and stepped back, and then he shoved and swung with his mace, trying to clear a space for the wizard to cast. To the other side, Lathaar steadily weaved his sword back and forth, his blade of light shattering swords and ignoring what little armor the conscripts possessed. Compared to the battle-hardened men who fought beside him, having faced demons, undead, and the best soldiers of Mordan, these foes were unskilled and clumsy. But they also outnumbered them by a horrific amount.

Tarlak staggered to his feet, his vision swimming. He'd used nearly every spell in his repertoire, plus a few more he made up on the spot. He'd layered the battlefield with fire and ice, flung boulders, and lost count of how many bolts of lightning he'd thrown. Still they came. All around, they were hard pressed, cutting men down nearly three to one, but it didn't matter. They were dwindling, might have already crumbled if not for the stalwart paladins.

And every time the dragon roared, he felt their men weaken a little bit more. But this time, that roar seemed different…pained instead of victorious. He chucked a fireball over the heads of the paladins, not caring what it hit or how dramatic the explosion, and glanced back to the city. The dragon lay on the ground, its body swarming with soldiers.

"Not possible," he muttered, stunned.

"Get back!" Lathaar shouted, grabbing his arm and pulling him along. "It's a rout!"

The rest were fleeing toward the city, hoping for safety with the greater army gathered there. With no other choice, Tarlak ran along. As he gasped for air, he wondered just how closely they were followed. A conscript could be a mere pace away, his sword ready to thrust deep into his back, all because he was unprepared and couldn't…

He looked behind to settle his fears. He was wrong. The conscripts were five paces back, not one. This didn't make him feel much better.

"Faster," Lathaar urged, tugging on his arm. Tarlak's breathing quickened. His lungs felt on fire. He wondered how in the world Lathaar could run so long in his plate mail after flinging his sword around like a madman. If he lived, he vowed to drink less wine and try to exercise with Harruq occasionally. Sweat dripped down his neck.

"Can't," he said between puffs.

"Keep going," Lathaar said, glancing back.

Tarlak followed suit. Karak's army was maintaining pace, and one by one soldiers fell and were trampled underfoot. Jerico was only a step behind them, his shield slung across his back. His look to Lathaar was dire.

"I can't," Tarlak said again. He felt a stabbing pain in his side, as if one of his lungs had just rebelled and called it quits. He felt his legs stumbling, his vision swimming, and then he was lifted into the air. After the vertigo passed, he realized he was atop Lathaar's back, carried like a sack of grain. He opened his mouth to speak, but then dry heaved instead. A bit of spittle ran down his chin. He glanced at their pursuers, who seemed even closer. A spell...surely he knew a spell that might help?

But he didn't have the chance to think of one. The conscripts suddenly slowed, then stopped completely. Some turned to flee, but most flung down their weapons and fell to their knees. Before Tarlak could wonder why, hundreds of knights rode past them, their hoofbeats thunderous across the grass. They circled those who had surrendered, then gave chase after the rest. Tarlak felt his perspective change again, and then suddenly he was on his feet, held up by Lathaar's arms.

"You going to make it?" he heard the paladin ask.

Tarlak nodded, hoping for his heart to stop pounding at a million beats a second. Jerico ran up beside them, doubled over to catch his breath, then gestured to the knights.

"Good timing," he said, then laughed.

Tarlak looked past them to where the remaining forces of Karak gathered. Unlike the conscripts, they appeared better armed and trained. Very few were mounted, though, and when the knights came charging, their leaders came out to meet them.

"What's going on?" Lathaar asked, squinting to see.

"It's too far," Tarlak said.

"Don't you have a spell or something to help with that?"

The wizard rubbed his eyes. Surely he did...that was right. What were the words? It took a moment more, but his pounding head remembered them. He cast the spell, and his eyes zoomed further and further in, until he could just barely see the leaders as they stepped out on their mounts.

"They're carrying something," Tarlak muttered, still out of breath. "It's...hah. It's some demon's head. Oh, and there's his body."

The leaders dumped the body before them and then tossed the head as if it were a gift. The rest knelt and offered their swords.

"Looks like with the dragon dead and our forces coming to bear, they've switched sides," Tarlak said. "Can't blame them. Doubt they had much choice to serve Thulos in the first place."

"Let's go, then," Lathaar said, tugging Tarlak along. The wizard fought off a wave of vomit as his vision jostled every which way, far too sensitive for the sudden movement. He looked back to the wall, where Antonil was making his charge.

"Well, would hate to miss the rest of the fun," he said before limping along, wishing just for a moment where the stitch in his side might leave him alone.

Damn, he needed a glass of wine. If only...

"Uh, Tar?" he heard Lathaar ask, disturbing his thoughts.

"Yeah?"

Lathaar pointed to the sky far to the south.

"Who the Abyss are they?"

⊰⊱

Deathmask hurried from street to street, proclaiming the same message.

"The king returns!" he cried. "Bring forth your rage! Rebel against those who have raped, murdered, and stolen from you! The king is here, the king is here!"

At first his call went unanswered. The fear of the priest-king had been driven in deep over the past months, but he did not despair. The few guards he encountered he slaughtered with ease, and it seemed with each one he killed, the bloodlust grew among the crowd that watched him. It seemed forever that he cried in vain, but he gained his handful of stalkers, not many, and they did little but watch and listen. It was his seed, he knew, and it was time to help it germinate.

"Take back what is yours!" he shouted when he reached the main market running through the center of the city. "Remember your beloved queen. Did she die for nothing? Are your loyalties so thin?"

Angry murmurs echoed through the crowd. He knew they felt fear because of the war waging outside the wall. Should it be a foreign conqueror, the rape and murder would be massive. He had to counter that fear, and he knew how. He climbed atop a market stand with a wooden roof, lifted his arms, and set them aflame for effect.

"That is no enemy outside!" he screamed. "That is no conqueror! That is your king, bound by blood and marriage to queen Annabelle. A queen the priest-king murdered! Do you serve a murderer? Do you serve Karak? Throw off the chains. Drink in the blood of your oppressor! Strangle him with his whip. Drown him in your anger!"

Of the hundreds listening, he knew he had maybe thirty. It didn't matter. He felt the tension growing, and when a troop of Lionsguard arrived, they found the crowd none too willing to let them pass. They had to shove their way through, at last coming to where Deathmask stood atop his stall.

"You're under arrest!" one of them shouted.

Deathmask laughed.

"Why do you wait?" he asked the crowd. "Must I do all the killing for you? Now is the time! Now is the place!"

A guard with a bow drew an arrow, but before he could fire it, someone bumped him from behind, ruining his aim. The arrow sailed wide, and Deathmask snagged it in his mind with magic. It took only a little persuasion for it to hook sharply downward, piercing the leg of a man close by. His cry of pain was music to Deathmask's ears. Anger rippled through the crowd, and safe in its numbers, the people let out their anger and frustration. The Lionsguard drew their swords, but they had to face both Deathmask and the crowd, and they were far too few to face either.

"People of Mordeina!" a woman cried, and Deathmask smiled when he recognized her voice. Veliana stood atop a nearby building, looking beautiful and deadly as ever. "Behold the fate of your priest-king!"

She hurled a head to the street. It cracked in half upon the stone, and at that crack, it seemed the entire crowd exploded. They raged against the guards, tearing them from limb to limb. They tore at the stalls, broke windows, and gave in to the anger sweeping over them. They only needed directing, and though they might have headed for the castle, Deathmask knew a far better use.

"To the walls!" he shouted. "Throw open the gates to your saviors! Those loyal to Melorak are there. Kill them, people of Mordeina, kill them all!"

"To the walls!" Veliana shouted, echoing his cry. "Melorak is dead! To the walls!"

She leapt like an acrobat to the street and rushed ahead, still calling, still urging.

"To the walls!"

"Beautiful," Deathmask said, basking in the anger of his own making. He'd always wanted to start a riot, and it'd been more enjoyable than he'd hoped. Not wishing to miss the show, he followed after, pushing his way through so he might help lead. The Lionsguard that tried to stop them, those few who did not flee, died crushed and beaten. The mob surged toward the main gates, where the several thousand loyal to Melorak waited.

"Well done," Deathmask said as he slid beside Veliana toward the front. "Was that really his head?"

"What was left of it," she said. "Bernard did his part. Melorak's dead."

The mob gathered in numbers, growing like a parasite sucking in the violent, the frustrated, and the scared. By the time they reached the soldiers, they numbered in the thousands. Without armor or true weaponry, they still faced a tough test. Deathmask had no intentions of letting that stop them.

"Take out their leaders," he told Veliana.

Shadows leapt from his fingers, a barrage that slammed into the first of the many soldiers. They formed a line, but against such great numbers, he could see the fear in their eyes. Too many were upon the walls, unable to help. Just as the mob was to hit, the front wall shook, and a sound like a hundred trees snapping in half cracked through the tension. The sudden surprise was enough to make the Lionsguard turn and wonder, and that was all it took. The mob swarmed over them, grabbing their swords and slaughtering the rest. Many of the soldiers threw down their arms and fled. Deathmask let them go, focusing his spells to soften anywhere the soldiers tried to hold. Veliana flittered through them all, twisting and stabbing. Soon they were climbing up the ladders and stairs leading up the wall.

"Fall, fall, fall!" Deathmask laughed as the archers and soldiers found themselves accosted from all sides. One by one they plummeted to their deaths, those that did not surrender to avoid their wrath.

The inner wall shook. Cracks spread just left of the second gate. Deathmask raised an eyebrow as he watched. Veliana soon joined him, for the bloody work was beyond needing their help.

"What is that?" she asked.

"Not sure. I wonder if…"

And then a white beam of magic broke through, crumbling stone and knocking an enormous hole in the wall. Chunks flew through the city, crushing homes and men alike. Cracks spread in all directions, and more debris fell, but the wall held firm, a pathway made. With the rest of the soldiers surrendered, the mob flooded the opening. Soldiers entered, with what appeared to be Antonil leading the way. They clearly expected a fight, but instead hordes of men and women cheered and celebrated their arrival.

"The city's taken once more," Veliana said. "Looks like we're finally safe."

"This city, anyway," Deathmask said, looking up to Avlimar. "But there's still the matter of the demons…"

30

Side by side, Harruq and Aurelia fought and killed. When the demons first landed, they'd retreated inward, into the golden arches and pearl walls. It seemed they attacked from every opening, through windows and enormous doorways. Harruq blocked their way, and Aurelia cast her magic around him. Every time he ducked, a lance of ice would fly over his head. Every time he sidestepped, a shard of rock and fire went screaming by. But there were too many, and the angels with them were few. So further and further in they retreated.

"Where's the rest of them?" Harruq asked as they rushed through a series of bedrooms. "Would love to have...watch out!"

He shoved Aurelia atop one of the beds. A spear sliced through where she'd been, then embedded into the wall. Two demons crashed through the windows, their wings folded in. One landed on a second bed, the other rolling across the floor between them. Harruq stabbed the one on the ground before he could rise, twisting the blade just before tearing it out his side. Aurelia flung a pillow at the other demon, then ignited it with a word. When the demon tried to fling it aside, it instead exploded, bathing him with fire. As he writhed, Harruq slammed into him, stabbing with his twin blades.

"We need a room without windows," Harruq said, yanking his swords free.

"Or doors," she said, sliding off the bed. She brushed her hair away from her face, worry flashing in her eyes. Harruq sheathed one of his swords, squeezed her hand, and then pulled her along.

Outside the bedroom was a slender walkway across beautiful green grass. A series of thin pillars and an arched covering made of golden silk enclosed the walkway. Through the gaps in the pillars they saw a mad chaos of battle, angels and demons swarming across the city, killing one another. At the end of the walkway was a large tower, for what purpose, he didn't know.

"Run fast," he said, squeezing her hand again. "And try not to draw any attention."

She gave him a wink, then sprinted along the pathway, Harruq in fast pursuit. In the open air, they heard death screams, friend and foe alike. Halfway there, Aurelia dived to the ground as a battling pair crashed through a pillar. The demon landed atop, and he stabbed repeatedly with a vicious spike attached to his gauntlet. Before he could notice her there, Aurelia clamored to her feet and slammed a palm against his back. Lightning arced through the demon, and he let out a single cry before dying.

Harruq didn't slow, instead grabbing her waist and pulling her along. Three more demons crashed through the top, hurling their spears. Two struck the stone wide of the mark, and Aurelia shoved the third off course with a sudden gale.

"Faster," Harruq said as the demons left the walkway to take flight. He glanced to either side, catching only glimpses of them through the gaps in the pillars. Just before the door to the tower, one tore through the silk and landed, his serrated sword already stained with blood. Another landed behind them, also tearing through the silk. As for the third...

"Take the one at the door," Harruq whispered. He shoved her forward and spun as the third demon crashed through the pillars, his glaive leading. The half-orc parried it high, then stepped into the demon's charge. Harruq's elbow slammed into neck, and he roared when the two continued on, bouncing off into another pillar and to the grass outside. In the mad mess of wings and armor, Harruq twisted and stabbed on pure instinct. He felt warm blood splash across his face. The hairs on his neck stood up, and he twisted free. The other demon's attack missed, and Harruq gave him no chance to recover. He head-butted him, and when he staggered back, Condemnation sliced through his stomach and spilled his innards.

"Harruq!" Aurelia shouted from the door to the tower, a smoldering corpse slumped against a pillar beside her. He looked back to see a formation of demons diving toward him, and with a curse began sprinting. But they raced to the side, not going for him, but instead Aurelia.

"No!" he screamed, knowing he would never make it in time. Aurelia looked to him, terror marring her beautiful face. And then she slammed shut the door and set it aflame. The demons forced through, four rushing inside, a fifth standing guard, his glaive raised and pointed at the half-orc.

"You can't stop me," Harruq said, picking up speed. "Nothing can! Aurelia!"

He saw the doubt creep into the demon's eyes just before he hit, and that alone told him the exchange was already won. Salvation slapped aside the glaive like it were made of straw. Condemnation tore through the demon's throat. Harruq's weight slammed into him, burying the sword further. Snarling, he tore the blade free and kicked the body aside. When he turned to enter the tower, he stopped, for a wall of ice had formed across it, blocking the way.

"I have waited a long time to meet with you again, my dear apprentice," said a voice from a nightmare, deep and full of promises and lies.

Harruq turned to see Velixar grinning at him, his red eyes glowing with amusement. Beside him stood Tessanna, her head bowed and her eyes downcast. And not far behind them stood...

Stood...

"Qurrah?" he said, his swords going limp in his hand. "Qurrah, what has he done?"

Tessanna moved through the battle as if in a dream. All around she heard cries of death, and she knew at one time this would have exhilarated her, but no more. She knew who Velixar hunted for, what he desired. He wanted his victory, his great achievement to be complete. She would be a part of it, but only a small part. She was powerless. Helpless. A prisoner waiting to die at the hand of her lover.

"Can you sense him?" Velixar asked Qurrah after he struck down an angel using a long tendril of bone. For a moment Qurrah did nothing, then nodded. He shook as if he had fought against that nod with every muscle in his body.

"Then lead the way."

They weaved through the city, staying outside the buildings and remaining near the outer ring, even when the bulk of the combat moved deeper into the city. Only a few angels spotted them, for the demons were swarming, great in number and on the offensive. Those that fled, died. Those that dove to attack, died faster. Each time their bodies collapsed, bleeding from gashes torn in their bodies or gasping for air with crushed lungs, Velixar laughed.

At last they reached a large tower on the northern end of Avlimar. Tessanna felt her heart leap. There he was. Qurrah's brother.

"No," she whispered.

Velixar saw him trying to rush inside the tower after Aurelia, so he summoned a wall of ice to block his way. Tessanna clutched her hands behind her back, feeling a lump swell in her throat. This was it. She heard the half-orc cry out Aurelia's name, then turn to face them. She couldn't meet his eyes. What would he think of her? Nothing good. Nothing redeemable. She'd helped murder his daughter, then taken his brother away from him. She was the path to Karak, she knew that now. May all three gods damn her, she thought. It was the least she deserved. Velixar mocked him, and her heart flared with anger.

"Qurrah?" she heard Harruq ask. "Qurrah, what has he done?"

The lump grew.

What have I done, you mean. Oh gods, Qurrah, is this how we all end?

"Don't speak," Velixar said to her lover. "Don't answer. You know what you are, and what you must do. Kill him, Qurrah. Break the last chain that holds you to this mortal delusion of morality and sin."

"Don't!" Tessanna shouted. She couldn't control herself. "Don't do this!"

Velixar struck her, so hard she thought her jaw might be broken. As she crumpled to the ground, she sobbed in helpless fury. Qurrah approached Harruq, and the burning whip uncoiled from about his arm.

"You don't deserve this," Harruq said. "Fight him, brother. This isn't what you are!"

Through her tears, Tessanna watched Qurrah lash out with his whip. Harruq smacked it aside with his swords, and still he did not attack. He pleaded with his brother, and each word was a knife to her heart. Her fault. All her fault.

Please, she prayed to the goddess. *Please, this can't be. Let me stop it. Tell me how to stop it!*

Qurrah flung a bolt of shadow, and this time Harruq had no choice. He lunged to the side, pivoted, and then slammed into her lover. Qurrah rolled with the slam, his hands glowing darkness. When he landed on his back, he hurled seven orbs of shadow, each one pulverizing his brother's flesh. Harruq screamed at the tremendous pain. Silver electricity arced about his body. When he fell to one knee, Qurrah lashed his arms with the whip, burning through his armor and charring flesh.

Please! Goddess...mother...don't make me watch this. Don't leave me like this.

Harruq parried the third lash, then hurled himself at Qurrah. They toppled again, and this time he stabbed deep with his ancient blades. She felt a scream building inside her, but Qurrah showed no sign of pain. He dropped the whip and clutched Harruq's face with both hands. Red mist swirled about the two of them, and then Harruq flew back, his head striking the tower with a sickening crunch. His swords fell limp from his hands, yet still he looked up. Still breathing. Still pleading.

"This can't be you," he said, struggling against the spell so he might lift his arms. "That's not you, Qurrah. That's not you."

She felt the goddess's eyes upon her. She felt her presence beside her. The power taken from her seemed almost in reach, but something was wrong. Still, despite her pleadings, it wasn't enough.

What do you want from me? she begged. *What is it, mother?*

"Kill him, Qurrah," Velixar said as he stood beside his most beloved disciple. "He has turned against us both, and against the god he swore his life to. Such promises are not to be made in vain. Take back his life. Embrace it. Feel the thrill of the kill. There is no right. There is no wrong. There is order, and he is chaos. End it. End him."

"No," Tessanna whispered. She felt magic swirling around her, and her anger grew as she raged against the goddess. Her words went unheard by Velixar and her lover, and she wondered if they went unheard by the goddess, too.

"No, you can't do this. I won't allow it. I can stop it, mother. I can stop it! I won't let this happen. Give it to me. Return my strength! I am your daughter...your daughter...and I demand my birthright. Give me my power, mother! *Give me my wings!*"

The demand made, the demand answered. She shrieked as the last power of Celestia poured into her mortal vessel. Ethereal wings spread out her back, scattering black feathers. The pain was immense, as if every part of her body were burning away with cleansing fire. Her hands shook. Her hair swirled in a chaotic wind. And at last Velixar turned to face her.

"No," she said, and it seemed her words shook the very foundations of the city. "He is yours no longer."

Velixar was a master at controlling death, honed over centuries and given strength by Karak himself. But she could see the great tendril he held over Qurrah, the control, the denying of his will. And she took it back. Qurrah was hers, and she took him.

She gave him only one command.

"Be free," she said, every bit of her power given to protect Qurrah from Velixar's furious control.

And to her joy, he turned from his brother and glared at the man in black.

"I won't," he said. "I'm not yours anymore."

He struck the ice with a fist, shattering it. As Velixar shook with rage, Qurrah helped his brother to his feet and dismissed the curse upon him.

"Go to your wife," he said, glancing over his shoulder. "Velixar is mine."

"Good luck," Harruq said, retrieving his swords. "And thank you."

He rushed into the tower. Tessanna watched her lover turn toward his former master, and a shiver ran through her at the look he gave.

"You lack faith," Velixar said. "You are a fool and a failure. You cannot challenge me."

"Wrong."

He unleashed a stream of fire from his palms. Velixar brought up a shield, and as the fire spread to either side, he let his power flare. The fire died, and then he tore a chunk of the ground free and hurled it. Qurrah met it with an invisible force that cracked it in two and shoved the chunks to either side of the tower. The air swirled about his feet, tinged red with power. Lightning tore from his hands, arcing through Velixar. Karak's prophet screamed in pain, then let that pain feed his magic.

"We've done this before!" Velixar cried, hurling an orb of darkness that glimmered with stars and planets and many things Tessanna had no names for. Qurrah summoned his shield, and it did not break. Arms crossed, he shoved the orb back. Velixar stepped aside. The orb continued on, its detonation destroying several homes. As the gold and pearl rained down, Qurrah approached his former master. Velixar flung bolts of shadow, but they would not stop him. He flung meteors swirling with ice, but they did not stop him. Qurrah's eyes shimmered, and then he cast a spell neither Velixar nor Tessanna knew he could cast.

A single shaft of light shone from his hands, its essence clean and pure. When it flashed over Velixar's skin, he shrieked in pain, his flesh shriveling like cloth within a fire. His ever-changing visage halted, becoming nothing but dead skin clinging to an ancient skull. He lifted his arms to cast a spell, but Qurrah was there, grabbing his wrists. They wrestled, each incredibly strong. Tessanna felt Velixar's will fighting against her, desperate to give orders to Qurrah and reassert control. She denied him, even as it made her crumple against the ground and weep from the pain.

"Everything you've said," Qurrah said, his eyes shimmering gold. "Everything was a lie."

He crushed Velixar's wrists, broke the bone, and tore the hands free. Dropping them, he clutched Velixar's throat and let loose all his anger, all his frustration, all the despair and betrayal suffered at his hands.

"This is for Aullienna," he said as flames burst from every inch of Velixar's skin. "This is for making us your playthings. Go to your beloved Karak, you wretch, and see how free of the fire you'll truly be."

Tessanna felt the prophet's will no longer press against her. He thrashed and howled, but the fire consumed him, consumed his robes, his bones. When only ash remained, she stood, her wings breaking away in a thousand feathers floating on a strong wind. She ran to Qurrah, flung her arms around him, and buried her face in his chest.

"Oh Qurrah," she cried. "You're free! You're free!"

He clutched her tight, and his body quivered.

"Thank you," he whispered, and even in his dead state she could hear the emotion threatening to overtake him. "Thank you, Tess. Thank you."

Her tears spilled across the blood on his white robes, but she felt such relief, she could not bear to pull away.

The first thing Harruq saw within the tower was two dead demons, and his heart was beyond grateful. Still feeling sluggish, he looked about, trying to get his bearings as well as push Qurrah's struggle out of his mind. There was too much there he didn't understand. The tower was thin, and it looked like it contained little more than stairs winding upward. He staggered up them, his swords clacking against the walls. When he reached the top, a demon toppled down, smoke pouring from his mouth. He shoved it aside and climbed into a large chamber with windows on all sides. In the center was a bell, and leaning against the bell was Aurelia. Blood dripped down the bronze surface.

"Aurry!" he cried, sheathing his swords and taking her into his arms.

"I'm fine," she said, gently pushing him away. "Just a cut on the arm. Lucky he had little room to swing."

Harruq looked out the windows toward the inner parts of the city. The bulk of the demons were flocking toward a single building. It was the angels' temple, he remembered from his little time spent in Avlimar. It made perfect sense for Ahaesarus to make his last stand there.

"We've got to get to the temple," he said, pointing. "Can you walk?"

She rolled her eyes. "I'm cut, not dead. And I can do you one better."

The elf peered out the window, focusing on the temple. After a moment, she closed her eyes and cast a spell, summoning a swirling blue portal before her.

"Let's go," she said, taking his hand and pulling him through.

He felt a rapid moment of vertigo, then took in his new surroundings. They were inside the temple, its vaulted ceiling hundreds of feet above them. The windows were filled with painted glass, many broken and cracked from the fighting. They'd entered beside a wall not far from the doors, where the angels formed ranks to fight off the swarming demons.

"Watch the windows," he heard Ahaesarus shout, and Harruq glanced back at one behind him depicting a single tree growing alone in a field. A shadow passed over it, and then a war demon came crashing through.

"Down!" Harruq shouted, pulling Aurelia with him. They hit the ground as the demon rolled over them, still struggling to draw his weapon. As his wings unfolded, Harruq leapt atop him, slamming his head with his fists.

"Harruq!" Aurelia shouted, tossing him one of his dropped swords. He snatched it out of the air and thrust it between the wings, the blade scraping against spine. Twisting it free, he glanced back up to view the combat. More demons were crashing through windows, their wings folded against their sides to prevent injury. Ahaesarus's angels rushed to meet them, while at the far back, Azariah and his angel priests cast waves of blessings, healing wounds and bolstering the morale of the defenders.

"Join them at the back," Harruq said, grabbing his other sword. "Do what you can to protect them with your spells."

"And you?" Aurelia asked.

He gestured to the main conflict at the doors.

"Where else?" he asked.

Before he could go she grabbed his armor, pulled him close, and kissed him.

"Don't die," she said before hurrying to the angels at the altar, stopping twice to hurl bolts of fire through the windows at attacking demons.

Harruq forced himself to look away to the task at hand. He didn't know how many were left throughout the city, but less than fifty angels held the temple, with Ahaesarus leading them. Twirling his swords, he barreled through their ranks to the center, joining the leader's side.

"I'm glad to see you safe," Ahaesarus said, disemboweling his foe with his enormous sword. "I feared the worst."

Harruq parried a glaive, stepped forward, and tore out the demon's throat with Condemnation. When another thrust his sword, Harruq shoved it upward, his blades crossed. With his right weapon he shoved the attack aside, and his left, stabbed. Blood spilled from the demon's neck as he gasped for air. When he fell back, a third came flying in, hurling a spear. Harruq tensed, realizing he had no time to dodge, but then Judarius was there, slapping the projectile to splinters with his mace.

"On your toes, half-orc," the angel said, his face wrapped in bandages. "I will not be denied more duels because of your sloppiness."

Harruq chuckled but held back his retort. The sight outside the temple was too horrific for even him to joke about. War demons by the hundreds were funneling toward them.

They came in great waves, putting all of his skill to the test. He slashed and spun, giving every movement over to his deeper instincts, honed to perfection by thousands of hours practicing with Haern. Whenever one scored a cut, he never felt it, though he knew the blood ran freely down his armor. One after another he cut them down, matching even Judarius in kills.

"Fall back!" Ahaesarus cried. "Too many come through the windows!"

Harruq yanked his sword free of a punctured armor piece and stole a glance back. Even with Aurelia's magic, the few angels could not hold back so many pouring through.

"Go!" he screamed, shoving Judarius back. "I'll hold the doors!"

Half the angels retreated further into the temple, coming to the aid of their hard-pressed companions. Ahaesarus remained, along with two others. Side by side, they filled the great entryway to the temple.

"You do your mortal brethren proud," Ahaesarus said in the brief lull as twenty demons circled in the air, preparing for another rush.

"Not done yet," Harruq said, his chest heaving up and down with each breath. "And don't think you are, either."

He heard spells explode behind him, screams of death, and blades tearing flesh. He prayed Aurelia was safe among them, but he couldn't dare look. Down came the demons, their glaives leading. They had to bank upward just before hitting due to the way the stairs led to the door, and that brief slowdown was enough to keep Harruq and his allies from being slaughtered. They twisted and parried the sharp tips of the glaives, though one of the angels gasped as it pierced through the bone of his left wing, pinning him to the wall.

"Hold on!" Harruq shouted, stabbing a demon through the eye, spinning, and cutting another down in midair. He tried to protect the angel, but his sword swung too late. The angel fell, his throat cut. Though Harruq killed the attacker, he felt no satisfaction, only growing rage. Ahaesarus kept his sword swinging in wide arcs, steady and skillful. The bodies built up before them, and at last the demons pulled back, half of them dead, and several more injured.

The three spaced out to fill the void and waited.

"Harruq," said Ahaesarus. "He is almost here. I want you to stay back. Thulos is beyond your skill. Only with Ashhur's blessing do I stand a chance."

Harruq snorted. "Not leaving. We fight him together."

An honor guard of thirty flew before them, just outside of reach. They saluted in reverence, then landed. As they spread out, their wings folding in, Thulos stepped forward from their center. His armor shone in the light, his breastplate splattered with blood. He pulled his greatsword from his back and held it aloft with one hand. He smiled at Ahaesarus, as if all were right with the world.

"You may surrender," Thulos said. "Though I would be saddened. Otherwise, you may die honorably in battle. Choose, warrior of Ashhur."

Ahaesarus lifted his sword and made a single slashing motion. Thulos's smile grew.

"Excellent," he said.

His lunge was faster than Harruq would have thought possible, had he not seen it before in Veldaren. Before it gutted Ahaesarus where he stood, Harruq slammed both his blades in the way, snarling to ignore the pain in his arms.

"No!" he heard the angel scream. Before Harruq could pull his swords back, Thulos's fist smashed the side of his head, flinging him back. The other side of his face smacked the wall, and stars exploded across his vision. The sound of combat met his ears, steel ringing against steel at a horrific speed. He tried to clear his thoughts, but all he could think of was getting to Aurelia. At first he crawled on his knees, then found the strength to stand. The temple swam about him, and he swore the ground shook unsteady beneath him.

"Harruq," he heard his wife cry, and he felt such relief as her hands wrapped about him.

"Hold him steady," said another, a voice he vaguely recognized. One of the angels...

Light shone across him, soothing and pure. His disorientation faded, and he looked up to see Azariah standing over him. He wasn't looking back, though, instead staring at the door.

"Even here, the war god cannot be stopped," said the angel.

"No," Harruq growled. He clutched his swords tight. "How can you say that?"

"Because Ahaesarus cannot stop him," Azariah said. "And now Judarius joins his side, and still they cannot."

Harruq watched from his knees as the two angels battled Thulos. Their attacks were perfectly synchronized, the sword and mace striking high and low, protecting one's retreat or feinting to open up the other's attack. It didn't matter. Thulos's sword was a blur as he parried and blocked, just a deadly blur until it drew blood. Judarius fell back, a wicked gash in his chest. Ahaesarus leapt before him, blocking the killing blow. Their swords connected, and Thulos pressed the attack, challenging the angels' strength to stand against him.

"No," Harruq said again, feeling his rage grow. He stood, the rest of the battle fading away until all he saw was the war god. "Give me your blessing, Azariah. I can stop him."

"Harruq," Aurelia said, sounding worried. "Your eyes…"

"Azariah!" he cried, ignoring her.

The priest placed his hands on Harruq's forehead and whispered a single prayer. The half-orc prayed along, for the words came natural, the desire shared.

"Give him your strength."

As Thulos cut Ahaesarus down, Harruq charged. Salvation and Condemnation crashed in, their blades shining white, yet leaving an afterimage of red with the swing. Thulos blocked, and this time it was his turn to be surprised.

"Who are you?" Thulos asked.

Harruq chuckled.

The war god pulled back and swung, again putting every bit of his strength behind it. Harruq flung his sister swords into position, and again they met. The sound was thunder in the temple, showering sparks. Harruq did not falter. He pressed back, stepped close, and then swung. Thulos twisted to the side, shooting out an elbow. Harruq spun to avoid it, his blades twirling above his head. When he exited the spin he was already set to block the next attack. Instead of being cut in half, he shoved Thulos's sword aside and retreated a half step to reset his favorite stance Haern had taught him.

"Ashhur is with you," Thulos said, sounding winded. "At last, my brother dares make his presence known."

Harruq could also feel the presence, a soothing strength flowing through his limbs. His concentration narrowed, and it seemed all others moved slowly through time, all but Thulos. Their swords clashed, parried, and clashed again. Every counter met with block, every riposte met with a dodge. Harruq felt himself slipping into a dance, Thulos a well-familiar partner. The sparks grew, the swords shook, and the dance grew vicious. The elder magic in his swords held them together against the onslaught, blades forged by Karak, cursed by Celestia, and now made holy by Ashhur.

On went the dance. Harruq lost all sense of fear. Every movement came natural. He blocked an overhead chop, stepped closer, and then slashed with Salvation. Thulos was already twisting, as if he'd known the maneuver before he ever started it. His sword cut air, and then it was his turn to prepare the block. Thulos's sword feinted, turned, and clashed against his prepared block. They were twins, brothers, mirrors...but Harruq could feel it slipping. Despite everything, he was mere flesh and bone, and he fought a furious god. It was minor now, he knew, as he weaved his swords in a wicked series. He was yet to score a single cut, but his blocks were coming later and later.

He could not win.

Yet he continued, pouring every bit of his strength into each swing. What more could he do? He fell deeper and deeper into the dance, fighting with a skill he'd never before possessed. His swords were a red line racing through the air, the white shimmer flaring with each strike against Thulos's sword. His muscles were tiring. His mortal body would soon fail. He clutched his swords tighter, swung faster, but it never mattered. Every move was countered, every thought planned against ahead of time. He was dueling a mirror, and trying to out-react his own reflection.

He thought of all his friends who'd die should he fail. He thought of Ahaesarus and Judarius, bleeding out on the floor beside him. He thought of the child in Aurelia's womb, his child, waiting to be born. It would find no future, not while the war god reigned supreme. He couldn't fail. He couldn't! But he couldn't win, not locked in this dance. Thulos twisted his sword around, then thrust it straight for Harruq's chest. He felt his arms go to block.

But this time, he ended the dance. Deep in a battle of such skill, Thulos never expected it, never even thought it possible.

Harruq leapt into the stab, let it pierce his armor and deep into his chest. And in that half-second, with his weapon held still, Harruq's swords blazed with the might of Ashhur and cut off the war god's head.

"Harruq!" he heard someone shout. His wife, he realized. Blood poured down his chest. He tried to breathe, but his lungs refused to cooperate. He was falling to his knees, and he could not stop. The temple turned to a blur, and those shouting grew distant. He closed his eyes, not wanting to feel the pain anymore. A voice calling his name forced them open. That sound…it was familiar, so familiar.

The land was green, the sky gold. Aullienna was rushing toward him, her hair flowing behind her in long braids.

"Daddy!" she cried, flinging her arms around him. He held her as his tears fell.

"You're taller," he whispered, so confused, so happy.

She pulled back and kissed his nose. She looked beautiful, her smile the most precious thing in the world.

"I'll be waiting," she said, hugging him once more. The golden light faded. Her arms left him. He felt himself falling again, and as he cried he felt his pain return.

He was on his back. People stood above him.

"A gift," Azariah said, his glowing hands still pressed against his chest, healing the wound.

"Oh, Harruq!" Aurelia said, kneeling beside him. She looked ready to scold him, then flung herself into his arms. As her tears wet his neck, he clutched her with desperate strength.

"I saw her," he whispered. "Aurry, I saw her..."

The angels at the doors gave way as Qurrah entered, Tessanna at his side. As two angels helped him stand, Azariah approached the other half-orc, a stern look across his face. The silence was thick in the temple, for the demons had fled with the death of their leader.

"Such a form is a blasphemy," he said, the words causing Tessanna to clutch his hand tight. "But Ashhur goes now to slumber with Celestia, and I have one last gift for you as well, brother of Harruq Tun."

Qurrah closed his eyes and bowed, accepting whatever fate he might deserve. Azariah's hands shone brilliant, and that light passed into Qurrah's skin. It swarmed over him, peeling away the rot, banishing the death in his flesh. It fell off like scales, revealing healthy, living skin beneath. As the last of the light vanished, Tessanna touched his face with a trembling hand.

"You're...you're...you," she said, then flung her arms around him. Qurrah looked at a loss for words. Taking a careful step, and wincing against the pain, Harruq reached for his brother.

"Do I have you back again?" he asked.

"Apparently, yes," Qurrah said, accepting his embrace.

"Look," said Aurelia, gesturing out the door. "Dieredon's come!"

Elves rode through the city atop winged horses, flitting through the scattered demon army and shooting them down with their bows.

"He's late," Harruq said, laughing despite his pain. He hugged his brother once more, holding him as the last of the demons fled Avlimar, their war god defeated, their army broken.

Epilogue

A urelia and Harruq watched the last armies of Ker march
south, back toward their homes.

"Shame how much he mistrusts Antonil," Aurelia said.

"They'll get over it," Harruq said, holding her hand. They
stood outside the walls of the city, waiting. The rest of the
Eschaton waited with them, thick packs in hand.

"We'll march with them for a while," Lathaar said,
embracing Harruq and Aurelia. "But it is time we returned to
the Citadel's rubble and see to rebuilding it anew."

"Not going to be cheap," Jerico said, shooting Tarlak a
wink.

"We'll see about money once Antonil pays me back," the
wizard said, smacking both across the shoulder. "Stay safe
now. I'll make sure to visit, especially once you get a class full
of snot-nosed brats to try and brainwash."

Together the paladins trudged south, their armor shining
in the light. They weren't gone long before Dieredon landed,
Sonowin's wings blasting them with wind.

"About time," Tarlak said, joining Dieredon atop her
back. "I thought you'd left without me."

"The Ekreissar will find it odd I ride with a human," said
the elf.

"Then they'll really find it odd when we share the same
bedroll."

Dieredon gave him a mixed look of humor and horror.
Aurelia curtseyed to them both while Harruq waved.

"Don't be gone too long," Harruq said.

"I just want to see what shape Veldaren's in," Tarlak said.
"And I'll be back. Someone's got to raise your new baby
properly, and I doubt it'll be the big lug. Keep Antonil in line
while I'm gone."

"I'll do my best," Harruq said, laughing.

With a great flap of wings they soared into the air. Harruq and Aurelia held hands and watched until they were just a speck of white across the blue sky, one of many as the elves flew toward their homeland.

Not long after, Qurrah approached from the city exit, Tessanna with him, clutching his arm.

"Are you sure you have to go as well?" Harruq asked. "I swear, no one seems content to just sit back and relax."

"We need a chance to start anew," Qurrah said. "In Ker, we might be free to find a place of our own. We've hurt too many here, and in Neldar as well. But none begrudge my name there, and Bram has promised me a small parcel of land of my own."

"If you must," Harruq said, giving him a hug. "But make sure you visit."

Qurrah shifted his pack across his shoulders and stepped to leave, but Tessanna lingered. She lowered her head and looked bashfully at Aurelia.

"I don't know if you'll ever forgive me," she said. "But...but you know I loved Aullienna. I always will. Please, when your new baby is born...may I visit her? I promise to be good."

Harruq squeezed her hand, and that seemed enough comfort for her.

"You may," she said.

Tessanna's face lit up, and she wrapped her arms around Qurrah's. As they left, Aurelia called out.

"What do you mean, 'her'?"

Tessanna only smiled.

A note from the author:

Well, we made it. Hasn't been a smooth ride, but we're here. I started writing of these characters so long ago, part of me honestly felt I would never finish. This series would always linger in my mind, never complete. But here it is. I hope you've enjoyed it, reader, because it was often dark, bloody, and mean. But now this…this is an ending I can smile about. This is the happiness many of you have wanted. Velixar got his ass kicked.

Obvious question first: will there be more? Well, yeah. As you can see, I left plenty for me to do in this world of Dezrel. The angels linger, and already tensions are brewing between them and some of the normal men. Neldar is a wasteland overrun with orcs. Mordan and Ker view each other with suspicion. And Aurelia's pregnant with a little girl. How can I not continue? However, this Gods' War is finished, and I'll turn my eye to other matters. New villains, new focuses, and maybe a new hero or two. But Harruq and Qurrah…they'll be there. I promise. First off, I need to get a sequel out for Dance of Cloaks, but I have no intention to stop writing. The Tun brothers are close to me, and we've kind of bonded over the hell I've put them through.

Thanks to Derek for the edits, my Dad for the input, my Monday night gaming crew for the inspirations, a certain fan for the idea of a dragon, my little indie author mafia for the amusement and support, and last but not least, you, dear reader. You've stuck with me all the way to the end. I'm living a dream right now, and it is because of you. So to all of you who purchased my books, sent me fanmail, left reviews, and told others about my books: thank you from the bottom of my heart. I couldn't have done this without you.

David Dalglish
January 20th, 2011